P9-EMH-512

R.A. SALVATORE

GAUNTLGRYM

THE **NEVERWINTER** SAGA
BOOK
I

COVER ART
TODD LOCKWOOD

The Neverwinter™ Saga, Book I

GAUNTLGRYM

©2011 Wizards of the Coast LLC

This book is protected under the copyright laws of the United States of America. Any reproduction or unauthorized use of the material or artwork contained herein is prohibited without the express written permission of Wizards of the Coast LLC.

Published by Wizards of the Coast LLC. Manufactured by: Hasbro SA, Rue Emile-Boéchat 31, 2800 Delémont, CH. Represented by Hasbro Europe, 2 Roundwood Ave, Stockley Park, Uxbridge, Middlesex, UB11 1AZ, UK.

FORGOTTEN REALMS, NEVERWINTER, DUNGEONS & DRAGONS, D&D, WIZARDS OF THE COAST, and their respective logos are trademarks of Wizards of the Coast LLC in the U.S.A. and other countries.

All characters in this book are fictitious. Any resemblance to actual persons, living or dead, is purely coincidental. All Wizards of the Coast characters and their distinctive likenesses are property of Wizards of the Coast LLC.

PRINTED IN THE USA

The sale of this book without its cover has not been authorized by the publisher. If you purchased this book without a cover, you should be aware that neither the author nor the publisher has received payment for this "stripped book."

Cover art by Todd Lockwood
Cartography by Robert Lazaretti

Hardcover Edition First Printing: October 2010

This Edition First Printing: July 2011

9 8 7 6 5 4

ISBN: 978-0-7869-5802-3
ISBN: 978-0-7869-5804-7 (e-book)
62025395000001 EN

The Library of Congress has catalogued the hardcover edition as follows.

Library of Congress Cataloging-in-Publication Data

Salvatore, R. A., 1959-
  Gauntlgrym / R.A. Salvatore.
    p. cm. -- (The neverwinter trilogy ; bk. 1)
  ISBN 978-0-7869-5500-8
  I. Title.
  PS3569.A462345G38 2010
  813'.54--dc22
                                                    2010028403

Contact Us at Wizards.com/CustomerService
Wizards of the Coast LLC, PO Box 707, Renton, WA 98057-0707, USA
USA & Canada: (800) 324-6496 or (425) 204-8069
Europe: +32(0) 70 233 277

Visit our websites at www.wizards.com
www.DungeonsandDragons.com

Welcome to Faerûn, a land of magic and intrigue, brutal violence and divine compassion, where gods have ascended and died, and mighty heroes have risen to fight terrifying monsters. Here, millennia of warfare and conquest have shaped dozens of unique cultures, raised and leveled shining kingdoms and tyrannical empires alike, and left long forgotten, horror-infested ruins in their wake.

A LAND OF MAGIC

When the goddess of magic was murdered, a magical plague of blue fire—the Spellplague—swept across the face of Faerûn, killing some, mutilating many, and imbuing a rare few with amazing supernatural abilities. The Spellplague forever changed the nature of magic itself, and seeded the land with hidden wonders and bloodcurdling monstrosities.

A LAND OF DARKNESS

The threats Faerûn faces are legion. Armies of undead mass in Thay under the brilliant but mad lich king Szass Tam. Treacherous dark elves plot in the Underdark in the service of their cruel and fickle goddess, Lolth. The Abolethic Sovereignty, a terrifying hive of inhuman slave masters, floats above the Sea of Fallen Stars, spreading chaos and destruction. And the Empire of Netheril, armed with magic of unimaginable power, prowls Faerûn in flying fortresses, sowing discord to their own incalculable ends.

A LAND OF HEROES

But Faerûn is not without hope. Heroes have emerged to fight the growing tide of darkness. Battle-scarred rangers bring their notched blades to bear against marauding hordes of orcs. Lowly street rats match wits with demons for the fate of cities. Inscrutable tiefling warlocks unite with fierce elf warriors to rain fire and steel upon monstrous enemies. And valiant servants of merciful gods forever struggle against the darkness.

A LAND OF
UNTOLD ADVENTURE

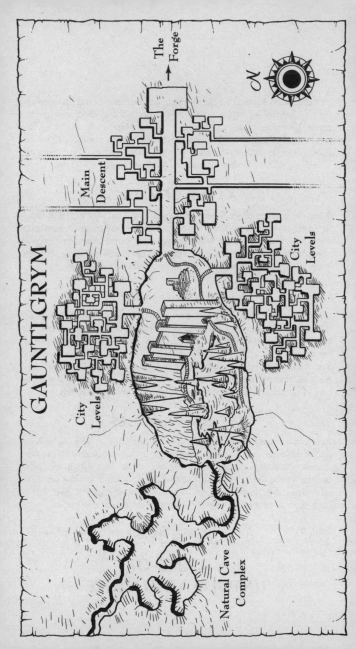

PROLOGUE

The Year of True Omens
(1409 DR)

A LOT COULD BE SAID OF KING BRUENOR BATTLEHAMMER OF Mithral Hall, and many titles could be rightfully bestowed upon him: warrior, diplomat, adventurer, and leader among dwarves, men, and even elves. Bruenor had been instrumental in reshaping the Silver Marches into one of the most peaceful and prosperous regions in all Faerûn. Add "visionary" to his title, fittingly, for what other dwarf might have forged a truce with King Obould of the orc kingdom of Many-Arrows? And that truce had held through the death of Obould and the succession to his son, Urlgen, Obould II.

It was truly a remarkable feat, and one that had secured Bruenor's place in dwarven legend, though many of the dwarves in Mithral Hall still grumbled about dealing with orcs in any way other than war. In truth, Bruenor was often heard second-guessing himself on the matter, year in and year out. However, in the end, the simple fact remained that not only had King Bruenor reclaimed Mithral Hall for his stout clan, but through his wisdom, he had changed the face of the North.

But of all the titles Bruenor Battlehammer could claim as earned, the ones that had always sat most comfortably on his strong shoulders were those of father and friend. Of the latter, Bruenor knew no peer, and all who called him friend knew without doubt that the dwarf king would gladly throw himself in front of a volley of arrows or a charging umber hulk, without hesitation, without regret, in the service of friendship. But of the former. . . .

Bruenor had never wed, never sired children of his own, but had come to claim two humans as his adoptive children.

Two children since lost to him.

"I tried me best," the dwarf said to Drizzt Do'Urden, the unlikely drow advisor to the throne of Mithral Hall—on those increasingly rare occasions when Drizzt was actually present in Mithral Hall. "I teached them as me father teached me."

"No one could ever say different," Drizzt assured him.

The drow rested back in a comfortable chair near the hearth in a small side room of Bruenor's chambers, and took a long look at his oldest friend. Bruenor's great beard was less red, even less orange, as more gray wound among the fiery locks, and his shaggy scalp had receded just a bit. On most days, though, the fire in his gray eyes sparkled as intensely as it had those decades before on the slopes of Kelvin's Cairn in Icewind Dale.

But not that day, and understandably so.

The melancholy so plain in his eyes was not reflected in the dwarf's movements, though. He moved swiftly and surely, rocking in his chair and hopping to his feet to grab another log, which he pitched perfectly onto the fire. It crackled and smoldered in protest and failed to erupt in flames.

"Damn wet wood," the dwarf grumbled. He stomped on the foot-bellows he had built into the hearth, sending a long, steady stream of air rushing across the coals and low-burning logs. He worked diligently at the fire for a long while, adjusting the logs, pumping the bellows, and Drizzt thought the display fitting for Bruenor. For that was how the dwarf did everything, from holding strong the tentative peace with Many-Arrows to keeping his clan operating in efficient harmony. Everything just right, and so too was the fire, at last, and Bruenor settled back in his chair and picked up his great mug of mead.

The king shook his head, his face a mask of regret. "Should o' killed that smelly orc."

Drizzt was all too familiar with the lament that had plagued Bruenor since the day he'd signed the Treaty of Garumn's Gorge.

"No," the drow replied, less than convincing.

Bruenor scoffed at him, somewhat viciously. "Yerself vowed to kill 'im, elf, and ye let him die o' old age, didn't ye?"

"Take care, Bruenor."

"Ah, but he cleaved yer elf friend in half, now, didn't he? And his spearmen bringed down yer dear elf lass, and the winged horse she rode."

Drizzt's stare reflected both pain and simmering anger, a warning to Bruenor that he was crossing the line here.

"But ye let him live!" Bruenor shouted, and he slammed his fist down on the arm of his chair.

"Aye, and you signed the treaty," Drizzt said, his face and voice calm. He knew he didn't need to shout those words for them to have a devastating effect.

Bruenor sighed and dropped his face into his palm.

Drizzt let him stew there for a few moments, but finally could take it no longer. "You're hardly the only one angered by the fact that Obould lived out his years in comfort," he said. "No one wanted to kill him more than I."

"But we didn't."

"And we did the right thing."

"Did we, elf?" Bruenor asked in all seriousness. "Now he's gone and they're wantin' to keep on, but are they really? When's it goin' to break? When're the orcs goin' to be orcs and start another war?"

Drizzt shrugged, for what answer could he give?

"And there ye go, elf!" Bruenor replied to that shrug. "Ye can't be knowing and I can't be knowing, and ye told me to sign the damned treaty, and I signed the damned treaty . . . and we can't be knowin'!"

"But we are 'knowing' that many humans and elves and yes, Bruenor, dwarves, got to live out their lives in peace and prosperity because you had the courage to sign that damned treaty. Because you chose not to fight that next war."

"Bah!" the dwarf snorted, throwing up his hands. "Been stickin' in me craw since that day. Damned smell o' orc. And now they're tradin' with Silverymoon and Sundabar, and them damned cowards o' Nesmé! Should o' killed them all to death in battle, by Clangeddin."

Drizzt nodded. He didn't disagree. How much easier his life would be if life in the North became a never-ending fight! In his heart, Drizzt surely agreed.

But in his head, he knew better. With Obould offering peace, Mithral Hall's intransigence would have pitted Bruenor's clan alone against Obould's tens of thousands, a fight they could never have won. But if Obould's successor decided to break the treaty, the resulting war would pit all the goodly kingdoms of the Silver Marches against Many-Arrows alone.

A cruel grin widened on the drow's face, but it fast became a grimace as he considered the many orcs who had become, at least somewhat, friends of his over the last . . . had it been nearly four decades?

"You did the right thing, Bruenor," he said. "Because you dared to sign that parchment, ten, twenty, fifty thousand lived out their lives that would have been shortened in a bloody war."

"I cannot do it again," Bruenor replied, shaking his head. "I got no more, elf. Done all I could be doin' here, and not to be doin' it again."

He dipped his mug in the open cask between the chairs and took a great swallow.

"Ye think he's still out there?" Bruenor asked through a foamy beard. "In the cold and snows?"

"If he is," Drizzt replied, "then know that Wulfgar is where he wants to be."

"Aye, but I'm bettin' his old bones're arguing that stubborn head o' his every step!" Bruenor replied, adding a bit of levity that both needed this day.

Drizzt smiled as the dwarf chortled, but one word of Bruenor's quip played a different note: old. He considered the year, and while he, being a long-lived drow, had barely aged, physically, if Wulfgar was indeed alive out there on the tundra of Icewind Dale, the barbarian would be greeting his seventieth year.

The reality of that struck Drizzt profoundly.

"Would ye still love her, elf?" Bruenor asked, referring to his other lost child.

Drizzt looked at him as if he'd been slapped, an all-too-familiar flash of anger crossing his once serene features. "I do still love her."

"If me girl was still with us, I mean," said Bruenor. "She'd be old now, same as Wulfgar, and many'd say she'd be ugly."

"Many say that about you, and said it even when you were young," the drow quipped, deflecting the absurd conversation. It was true enough that Catti-brie would be turning seventy as well, had she not been taken in the Spellplague those twenty-four years before. She would be old for a human, old like Wulfgar, but ugly? Drizzt could never think such a thing of his beloved Catti-brie, for never in his hundred and twelve years of life had the drow seen anyone or anything more beautiful than his wife. The reflection of her in Drizzt's lavender eyes could hold no imperfection, no matter the ravages of time on her human face, no matter the scars of battle, no matter the color of her hair. Catti-brie would forever look to Drizzt as she had when he first came to know he loved her, on a long-ago journey to the far southern city of Calimport when they had gone to rescue Regis.

Regis. Drizzt winced at the memory of the halfling, another dear friend lost in that time of chaos, when the Ghost King had come to Spirit Soaring, laying low one of the most wondrous structures in the world, the portend of a great darkness that had spread across the breadth of Toril.

The drow had once been advised to live his long life in a series of shorter time spans, to dwell in the immediacy of the humans that surrounded him, then to move on, to find that life, that lust, that love, again. It was good advice, he knew in his heart, but in the quarter of a century since he'd lost Catti-brie, he had come to understand that sometimes advice was easier to hear than it was to embrace.

"She's still with us," Bruenor corrected himself a short while later. He drained his mug and threw it into the hearth, where it shattered into a thousand shards. "Just that damn Jarlaxle thinking like a drow and taking his time, as if the years mean nothing to him."

Drizzt started to answer, reflexively moving to calm his friend, but he bit back the response and just stared into the flames. Both he and Bruenor had taxed, had begged Jarlaxle, that most worldly of dark elves, to find Catti-brie and Regis—to find their spirits, at least, for they had watched the spirits of their lost loved ones ride a ghostly unicorn through the stone walls of Mithral Hall on that fateful morning. The goddess Mielikki had taken the pair, Drizzt believed, but surely she could not be so cruel as to keep them. But perhaps even Mielikki could not rob Kelemvor, Lord of the Dead, of his hard-won prize.

Drizzt thought back to that terrible morning, as if it had been only the day before. He had awakened to Bruenor's shouts, after a sweet night of lovemaking with his wife, who had seemed returned to him from the depths of her confusing affliction.

And there, that terrible morning, she lay beside him, cold to his touch.

"Break the truce," Drizzt muttered, thinking of the new king of Many-Arrows, an orc not nearly as intelligent and far-seeing as his father.

Drizzt's hand reflexively went to his hip, though he wasn't wearing his scimitars. He wanted to feel the weight of those deadly blades in his grip once more. The thought of battle, of the stench of death, even of his own death, didn't trouble him. Not that morning. Not with images of Catti-brie and Regis floating all around him, taunting him in his helplessness.

"I don't like coming here," the orc woman remarked as she handed over the herb bag. She wasn't tall for an orc, but still she towered over her diminutive counterpart.

"We are at peace, Jessa," Nanfoodle the gnome replied. He pulled open the bag and produced one of the roots, bringing it up under his long nose and taking a deep inhale of it. "Ah, the sweet mandragora," he said. "Just enough can take your pain."

"And your painful thoughts," the orc said. "And make of you a fool . . . like a dwarf swimming in a pool of mead, thinking to drink himself to dry ground."

"Only five?" Nanfoodle asked, sifting through the large pouch.

"The other plants are full in bloom," Jessa replied. "Only five, you say! I expected to find none, or one . . . *hoped* to find two, and said a prayer to Gruumsh for a third."

Nanfoodle looked up from the pouch, but not at the orc, his absent gaze drifted off into the distance, and his mind whirled behind it. "Five?" he mused and glanced at his beakers and coils. He tapped a bony finger to his small, pointy white beard, and after a few moments of screwing up his tiny round face this way and that, he decided, "Five will finish the task."

"Finish?" Jessa echoed. "Then you will dare to do it?"

Nanfoodle looked at her as if she were being ridiculous. "Well along the way," he assured her.

A wicked little grin curled Jessa's lips up so high they seemed to catch the twisting strands of yellow hair, a single bouncing curl to either side, that framed her flat, round face and piggish nose. Her light brown eyes twinkled with mischief.

"Do you have to enjoy it so?" the gnome scolded.

But Jessa twirled aside with a laugh, immune to his words. "I enjoy excitement," the young priestess explained. "Life is so boring, after all." She spun to a stop and pointed to the herb pouch, still held by Nanfoodle. "And so do you, obviously."

The gnome looked down at the potentially poisonous roots. "I have no choice in the matter."

"Are you afraid?"

"Should I be?"

"I am," Jessa said, though her blunt tone made it seem more a welcomed declaration than an admission. She nodded somberly in deference to the gnome. "Long live the king," she said as she curtsied. Then she departed, taking care to pick her way back to the embassy of the Kingdom of Many-Arrows without drawing any more than the usual attention afforded an orc walking the corridors of Mithral Hall.

Nanfoodle took up the roots and moved to his jars and coils, set on a wide bench at the side of his laboratory. He took note of himself in the mirror that hung on the wall behind the bench, and even struck a pose, thinking that he looked quite distinguished in his middle age—which of course meant that he was well past middle age! Most of his hair was gone, except for thick white clumps above his large ears, but he took care to keep those neatly trimmed, like his pointy beard and thin mustache, and to keep the rest of his large noggin cleanly shaved. Well, except for his eyebrows, he thought with a chuckle as he noted that some of the hairs there had grown so long that their curl could be clearly noted.

Nanfoodle took up a pair of spectacles and pinched them onto his nose as he finally pulled himself from the mirror. He tilted his head back to get a better viewing angle through the small round magnifiers as he carefully adjusted the height of the oiled wick.

The heat had to be just right, he reminded himself, for him to extract the right amount of crystal poison.

He had to be precise, but in looking at the hourglass at the end of the bench, he realized that he had to be quick, as well.

King Bruenor's mug awaited.

Thibbledorf Pwent wasn't wearing his ridged, creased, and spiked armor, one of the few occasions that anyone had ever seen the dwarf without it. But he wasn't wearing it for exactly that reason: He didn't want anyone to recognize him, or more specifically, to hear him.

He skulked in the shadows at the far end of a rough corridor, behind a pile of kegs, with Nanfoodle's door in sight.

The battlerager gnashed his teeth to hold back the stream of curses he wanted to mutter when Jessa Dribble-Obould entered that chamber, first glancing up and down the corridor to make sure no one was watching her.

"Orcs in Mithral Hall," Pwent mouthed quietly, and he shook his dirty, hairy head and spat on the floor. How Pwent had screeched in protest when the decision had been made to grant the Kingdom of Many-Arrows an embassy in the dwarven halls! Oh, it was a limited embassy, of course—no more than four orcs were allowed into Mithral Hall at any given time, and those four were not allowed unfettered access. A host of dwarf guards, often Pwent's own battleragers, were always available to escort their "guests."

But this slippery little priestess had gotten around that rule, so it seemed, and Pwent had expected as much.

He thought about going over and kicking in the door, catching the rat orc openly that he might have her expelled from Mithral Hall once and for all, but even as he started to rise up, some rare insight told him to exercise patience. Despite himself and his bubbling outrage, Thibbledorf Pwent remained silent, and within a few moments Jessa reappeared in the corridor, looked both ways, and scampered off the way she had come.

"What's that about, gnome?" Pwent whispered, for none of it made any sense.

Nanfoodle was no enemy of Mithral Hall, of course, and had proven himself a steadfast ally since the earliest days of his arrival some forty years before. Battlehammer dwarves still talked about Nanfoodle's "Moment of Elminster," when the gnome had used some ingenious piping to fill caverns with explosive gas that had then blown a mountain ridge, and the enemy giants atop it, to rubble.

But then why was this friend of the hall cavorting with an orc priestess in such secrecy? Nanfoodle could have called for Jessa through the proper channels, through Pwent himself, and had her escorted to his door in short order.

Pwent spent a long while mulling that over, so long, in fact, that Nanfoodle eventually appeared in the corridor and hustled away. Only then did the startled battlerager realize that it was time for the memorial celebration.

"By Moradin's stony arse," Pwent muttered, pulling himself up from behind the kegs.

He meant to go straightaway to Bruenor's hall, but he paused at Nanfoodle's door and glanced around, much as Jessa had done, then pushed his way in.

Nothing seemed amiss. Some white liquid in the beakers on one workbench bubbled from the residual heat of recently doused braziers, but everything else seemed perfectly out of place—exactly the way the scatter-brained Nanfoodle always kept it.

"Hmm," Pwent mumbled and wandered about the chamber, trying to find some clues—maybe a cleared area where Nanfoodle and Jessa might have—

No, Pwent couldn't even let his mind take that tack.

"Bah, ye're a fool, Thibbledorf Pwent, and so's yer brother, if ye had a brother!" the dwarf scolded himself.

He started to leave, suddenly feeling like quite the terrible friend for even spying on Nanfoodle in such a way, when he noted something under the gnome's desk: a bedroll. Pwent's mind went back to that dark place, conjuring a tryst between the gnome and the orc, but he shook that thought away as soon as he realized that the bedroll was tightly tied, and had been for some time. And behind it was a backpack with all manner of gear, from bandages to a climbing pick, tied around it.

"Plannin' a trip to Many-Arrows, little one?" Pwent asked aloud.

He stood up and shrugged, considering the likely options. Pwent hoped that Nanfoodle would be smart enough to take along some guards if that was the case. King Bruenor had handled the transition of power from Obould to his son with great tact and had kept the tensions low enough, but orcs were orcs, after all, and no one really knew how trustworthy this son of Obould might turn out to be, or even if he had the charisma and sheer power to keep his wild minions in line, as had his mighty father.

Pwent decided he would talk with Nanfoodle next time he had the gnome alone, friend to friend, but he had put all of it out of his mind by the time he slipped back out into the hallway. He was running late for a most important celebration, and knew that King Bruenor wouldn't be quick to forgive such tardiness.

". . . twenty-five years," Bruenor was saying when Thibbledorf Pwent joined the gathering in the small audience chamber. Only a few select guests were in there: Drizzt, of course; Cordio, the First Priest of the Hall; Nanfoodle; and old Banak Brawnanvil in his wheeled chair, along with his son Connerad, who was growing into a fine young dwarf. Connerad had even been training with Pwent's Gutbusters, and had more than held his own against much more seasoned warriors. Several other dwarves gathered about the king.

"I miss ye, me girl, and me friend, Regis, and know that if I live another hunnerd years, I'll spend not a day not thinking of ye," the dwarf king said. He lifted his mug and drained it, and the others did the same. As he lowered the mug, Bruenor fixed his gaze on Pwent.

"Apologies, me king," the battlerager said. "Did I miss all the drink, then?"

"Just the first toast," Nanfoodle assured him, and the gnome hustled about, gathering up all the mugs before moving to the keg at the side of the room. "Help me," he bade Pwent.

Nanfoodle filled the mugs and Thibbledorf Pwent delivered them. Pwent thought it curious that the gnome didn't fill and hand over Bruenor's personal mug with the first group. Certainly no one could miss that mug among the others. It was a large flagon with the foaming-mug shield of Clan Battlehammer stamped on its side and a handle that sported horns at its top, into which the holder could settle his thumb. One of those horns, like Bruenor's own helmet, had been broken short. In a show of solidarity and promise of unending friendship to Mithral Hall, the mug had been a gift years before from the dwarves of Citadel Adbar to commemorate the tenth anniversary of the signing of the Treaty of Garumn's Gorge. No one would dare drink from that mug except for Bruenor himself, Pwent knew, and so he understood that Nanfoodle meant to deliver Bruenor's mead personally, and last. He didn't give it much thought, honestly, but it just struck him as curious that the gnome had pointedly not given that mug to Pwent to deliver.

Had he been paying close attention to the gnome, Pwent might have noted something else that would have surely raised his bushy eyebrows. The gnome filled his own mug first then turned his back more squarely to the gathered group, who were talking about old times with Catti-brie and Regis and paying him no heed anyway.

From a secret pouch on his belt, the gnome produced a tiny vial. He eased the cork off so it wouldn't make a popping sound, glanced back to the group, and poured the crystal contents of the vial into Bruenor's decorated grail.

He gave it just a moment to settle, then nodded his approval and rejoined the celebration.

"May I offer a toast to my lady Shoudra?" the gnome asked, referring to the emissary of Mirabar whom he had accompanied to Mithral Hall those decades ago, and who had been killed by Obould himself in that terrible war. "Old wounds healed," the gnome said, lifting his mug in toast.

"Aye, to Shoudra and to all them what fell defending the halls of Clan Battlehammer," Bruenor agreed, and he took a deep draw on his honey mead.

Nanfoodle nodded and smiled, and hoped that Bruenor wouldn't taste the somewhat bitter poison.

"O woe to Mithral Hall, and let the calls go forth to all the lords, kings, and queens of the Silver Marches, that King Bruenor has fallen ill this night!" the criers yelled throughout the dwarven compound just a few hours after the memorial celebration.

Filled were the chapels of the hall, and of all the towns of the North when word arrived, for King Bruenor was much beloved, and his strong voice had supported so much of the good changes that had come to the Silver Marches. Worries of war with the Kingdom of Many-Arrows filled every conversation, of course, at the prospect of the loss of both the signatories of the Treaty of Garumn's Gorge.

The vigil in Mithral Hall was solemn, but not morbid. Bruenor had lived a good, long life, after all, and had surrounded himself by dwarves of tremendous character. The clan was the thing, and the clan would survive, and thrive, long beyond the days of great King Bruenor.

But there were indeed many tears whenever one of Cordio's priests announced that the king lay gravely ill, and Moradin had not answered their prayers.

"We cannot help him," Cordio announced to Drizzt and a few others on the third night of Bruenor's fretful sleep. "He has fallen beyond us."

He flashed a quiet, disapproving smirk Drizzt's way, but the drow remained steadfast and solid.

"Ah, me king," Pwent moaned.

"Woe to Mithral Hall," said Banak Brawnanvil.

"Not so," Drizzt replied. "Bruenor has not been derelict in his responsibilities to the hall. His throne will be well filled."

"Ye talk like he's dead already, ye durned elf!" Pwent scolded.

Drizzt had no answer against that, so he merely nodded an apology to the battlerager.

They went in and sat by Bruenor's bed. Drizzt held his friend's hand, and just before dawn, King Bruenor breathed his last.

"The king is dead, long live the king," Drizzt said, turning to Banak.

"So begins the reign of Banak Brawnanvil, Eleventh King of Mithral Hall," said Cordio.

"I be humbled, priest," old Banak replied, his gaze low, his heart heavy. Behind his chair, his son patted him on the shoulder. "If half the king as Bruenor I be, then all the world'll know me reign as a goodly one—nay, a great one."

Thibbledorf Pwent stumbled over and fell to one knee before Banak. "Me . . . me life for ye, me . . . me king," he stammered and stuttered, hardly getting the words out.

"Blessed be me court," Banak replied, patting Thibbledorf's hairy head.

The tough battlerager threw his forearm across his eyes, turned back, and fell over Bruenor to hug him tightly, then he tumbled back with a great wail and stumbled from the room.

Bruenor's tomb was built right beside those of Catti-brie and Regis, and it was the grandest mausoleum ever constructed in the ancient dwarven clanhold. One after another, the elders of the Clan Battlehammer came forth to give a long and rousing recounting of the many exploits of the long-lived and mighty King Bruenor, who had taken his people from the darkness of the ruined halls to a new home in Icewind Dale, and who had personally rediscovered their ancient home, and had then reclaimed it for the clan. In more tentative voices, they spoke of the diplomat Bruenor, who had so dramatically altered the landscape of the Silver Marches.

On and on it went, through the day and night, for three full days, one tribute after another, all of them ending with a sincere toast to a most worthy successor, the great Banak Brawnanvil, who now formally added Battlehammer to his name: King Banak Brawnanvil Battlehammer.

Emissaries came from every surrounding kingdom, and even the orcs of Many-Arrows had their say, the Priestess Jessa Dribble-Obould offering a lengthy eulogy that was nothing but complimentary to that most remarkable king, and expressing the hopes of her people that King Banak would be equally wise and well-tempered, and that Mithral Hall would prosper under his leadership. Truly there was nothing controversial, or anything but correct, in the young orc's words, but still, more than a few of the thousands of dwarves listening to her grumbled and spat, a poignant reminder to Banak and all the other leaders that Bruenor's work healing the orc-dwarf divide was far from completed.

Exhausted, worn out, drained emotionally and physically, Drizzt, Nanfoodle, Cordio, Pwent, and Connerad fell into chairs around the hearth that had been Bruenor's favorite spot. They offered a few more toasts to their friend and launched into private discussions of the many good and heroic memories they had shared with the remarkable dwarf.

Pwent had the most stories to tell, all exaggerated, of course, but surprisingly, Drizzt Do'Urden said little.

"I must apologize to your father," Nanfoodle said to Connerad.

"Apologize? Nay, gnome, he values your counsel as much as any other dwarf," the young Prince of Mithral Hall replied.

"And so I must apologize to him," said Nanfoodle, and all in the room were listening. "I came here with Lady Shoudra, never meaning to stay, and yet I find that decades have passed. I'm not a young one anymore—in a month I'll be celebrating my sixty-fifth year."

"Hear hear," Cordio interrupted, never missing a chance to toast, and they all drank to Nanfoodle's continuing health.

"Thank you all," Nanfoodle said after the drink. "You've been as a family to me, to be sure, and my half-life here's been no less a half than the years before. Or the years after, I am sure."

"What are ye saying, little one?" asked Cordio.

"I've another family," the gnome replied. "One I've seen only in short visits, lo these last thirty-some years. It's time for me to go, I fear. I wish to spend my last years in my old home in Mirabar."

Those words seemed to suck all the noise from the room, as all sat in stunned silence.

"Ye'll owe me dad no apology, Nanfoodle of Mirabar," Connerad eventually assured the gnome, and he lifted his mug in another toast. "Mithral Hall'll ne'er forget the help of great Nanfoodle!"

They all shared in that toast, heartily so, but something struck Thibbledorf Pwent as curious then, though, in his exhausted and overwhelmed state, he couldn't sort it out.

Not quite yet.

Huffing and puffing, the gnome wriggled and squirmed his way through a tumble of boulders, great smooth gray stones lying about as if piled by a catapult crew of titans. Nanfoodle knew the area well, though—indeed, he had set the place for the rendezvous—and so he was not surprised when he pushed through a tightly twisting path between a trio of stones to find Jessa sitting on a smaller stone in a clearing, her midday meal spread on a blanket before her.

"You need longer legs," the orc greeted.

"I need to be thirty years younger," Nanfoodle replied. He let his heavy pack slide off his shoulders and took a seat on a stone opposite Jessa, reaching for a bowl of stew she'd set out for him.

"It's done? You're certain?" Jessa asked.

"Three days of mourning for the dead king . . . three and no more—they haven't the time. So Banak is king at long last, a title he's long deserved."

"He steps into the boots of a giant."

Nanfoodle waved the thought away. "The best work of King Bruenor was to ensure the orderliness of Mithral Hall. Banak will not falter, and even if he did, there are many wise voices around him." He paused and looked at the orc priestess more closely. Her gaze had drifted to the north, toward the still-young kingdom of her people. "King Banak will continue the work, as Obould II will honor the desires and vision of his predecessor," Nanfoodle assured her.

Jessa looked at him curiously, even incredulously. "You're so calm," she said. "You spend too much of your life in your books and scrolls, and not nearly enough time looking into the faces of those around you."

Nanfoodle looked at her with a curious expression.

"How can you be so calm?" Jessa asked. "Don't you realize what you've just done?"

"I did only as I was ordered to do," Nanfoodle protested, not catching on to the gravity in her voice.

Jessa started to scold him again, meaning to school him on the weight of feelings, to remind him that not all the world could be described by logical theorems, that other factors had to be considered, but a commotion to the side, the scraping of metal on stone, stole her words.

"What?" Nanfoodle, slurping his stew, asked as she rose to her feet.

"What was ye ordered to do?" came the gruff voice of Thibbledorf Pwent, and Nanfoodle spun around just as the battlerager, arrayed in full armor, squeezed out from between the boulders, metal ridges screeching against the stone. "Aye, and be sure that meself's wonderin' who it was what's orderin' ye!" He ended by punching one metal-gloved fist into the other. "And don't be doubtin' that I'm meanin' to find out, ye little rat."

He advanced and Nanfoodle retreated, dropping the bowl of stew to the ground.

"Ye got nowhere to run, neither of ye," Pwent assured them as he continued his advance. "Me legs're long enough to chase ye, and me anger's more'n enough to catch ye!"

"What is this?" Jessa demanded, but Pwent fixed her with a hateful glare.

"Ye're still alive only because ye might have something I need to hear," the vicious dwarf explained. "And if ye're not yapping words that make me smile, know that ye'll be finding a seat." As he finished, he pointed at the large spike protruding from the top of his helm. And Jessa knew full well that more than one orc had shuddered through its death throes impaled on that spike.

"Pwent, no!" Nanfoodle yelped, holding his hands up before him, motioning the dwarf to stop his steady approach. "You don't understand."

"Oh, I'm knowin' more than ye think I'm knowin'," the battlerager promised. "Been in yer workshop, gnome."

Nanfoodle held up his hands. "I told King Banak that I would be leaving."

"Ye was leaving afore King Bruenor died," Pwent accused. "Ye had yer bag all packed for the road."

"Well, yes, I have been considering it for a—"

"All packed up and tucked right under the bench of *poison* ye brewed for me king!" Pwent yelled, and he leaped forward at Nanfoodle, who was nimble enough to skitter around the side of another stone, just out of Pwent's murderous grasp.

"Pwent, no!" Nanfoodle yelled.

Jessa moved to intervene, but Pwent turned on her, balling his fists, which brought forth the retractable hand spikes from their sheaths on the backs of his gloves. "How much did ye pay the rat, ye dog's arse-end?" he demanded.

Jessa kept retreating, but when her back came against a stone, when she ran out of room, the orc's demeanor changed immediately, and she snarled right back at Pwent as she drew forth a slender iron wand. "One more step. . . ." she warned, taking aim.

"Pwent, no! Jessa, no!" Nanfoodle yelped.

"Got a big burst o' magic in that puny wand, do ye?" Pwent asked, unconcerned. "Good for ye, then. It'll just make me angrier, which'll make me hit ye all the harder!"

On he came, or started to. Jessa began her incantation, aiming her explosive wand at the dwarf's dirty face, but then both paused and Nanfoodle's next shout caught in his throat as the sound of sweet bells filled the air, joyously tinkling and ringing.

"Oh, but now ye're goin' to get yers," Pwent said with a sly grin, for he knew those bells. Everyone in Mithral Hall knew the bells of Drizzt Do'Urden's magical unicorn.

Slender and graceful, but with lines of powerful muscles rippling along his shimmering white coat, ivory horn tipped with a golden point, blue eyes piercing the daylight as if mocking the sun itself, bell-covered barding announcing the arrival in joyous notes, Andahar trotted up to the edge of the boulder tumble and stomped the ground with his mighty hoof.

"Good ye come, elf!" Pwent yelled to Drizzt, who sat staring at him with his jaw hanging open. "Was just about to put me fist into—"

How Thibbledorf Pwent jumped back when he turned to regard Jessa and found himself confronted by six hundred pounds of snarling black panther!

And how he jumped again when he caught his balance, just in time to see Bruenor Battlehammer hop down from his seat on the unicorn just behind Drizzt.

"What in the Nine Hells?" Bruenor demanded, looking to Nanfoodle.

The little gnome could only shrug helplessly in reply.

"Me . . . king?" Pwent stammered. "Me king! Can it be me king? Me *king!*"

"Oh, by the pinch o' Moradin's bum," Bruenor lamented. "What're ye doing out here, ye durned fool? Ye're supposed to be by King Banak's side."

"Not to be *King* Banak," Pwent protested. "Not with King *Bruenor* alive and breathin'!"

Bruenor stormed up to the battlerager and put his nose right against Pwent's. "Now ye hear me good, dwarf, and don't ye never make that mistake again. King Bruenor ain't no more. King Bruenor's for the ages, and King Banak's got Mithral Hall!"

"But . . . but . . . but me king," Pwent replied. "But ye're not dead!"

Bruenor sighed.

Behind him, Drizzt lifted his leg over the saddle and gracefully slid down to the ground. He patted Andahar's strong neck, then lifted a unicorn-fashioned charm hanging on a silver chain around his neck and gently blew into the hollow horn, releasing the steed from his call.

Andahar rose up on his hind legs, front hoofs slashing the air, and whinnied loudly then thundered away. With each stride, the horse somehow seemed as if he had covered a tremendous amount of ground, for he became half his size with a single stride, and half again with the next, and so on, until he was seen no more, though the air in his wake rippled with waves of magical energy.

By that time, Pwent had composed himself somewhat, and he stood strong before Bruenor, hands on hips. "Ye was dead, me king," he declared. "I *seen* ye dead, I *smelled* ye dead. Ye *was* dead."

"I had to be dead," Bruenor replied, and he, too, squared up and put his hands on his hips. Once more pressing his nose against Pwent's, he added very slowly and deliberately, "So I could get meself gone."

"Gone?" Pwent echoed, and he looked to Drizzt, who offered no hint, just a grin that showed he was enjoying the spectacle more than he should. Then Pwent looked to Nanfoodle, who merely shrugged. And he looked past the panther, Guenhwyvar, to Jessa, who laughed at him teasingly and waved her wand.

"Oh, but yer thick skull's making Dumathoin's task a bit easier, ain't it?" Bruenor scolded, referring to the dwarf god known more commonly as the Keeper of Secrets under the Mountain.

Pwent scoffed, for the oft-heard remark was a rather impolite way of one dwarf calling another dwarf dumb.

"Ye was dead," the battlerager said.

"Aye, and 'twas the little one there what killed me."

"The poison," Nanfoodle explained. "Deadly, yes, but not in correct doses. As I used it, it just made Bruenor look dead, quite dead, to all but the cleverest priests—and those priests knew what we were doing."

"So ye could run away?" Pwent asked Bruenor as it started to come clear.

"So I could give Banak the throne proper, and not have him stand as just a steward, with all the clan waiting for me return. Because there won't be a return. Been done many the time before, Pwent. Suren 'tis a secret among the dwarf kings, a way to find the road to finish yer days when ye've done all the ruling ye might do. Me great-great-great-grandfather did the same, and it's been done in Adbar, too, by two kings I know tell of. And there're more, don't ye doubt, or I'm a bearded gnome."

"Ye've run from the hall?"

"Just said as much."

"Forevermore?"

"Ain't so long a time for an old dwarf like meself."

"Ye runned away. Ye runned away and ye didn't tell me?" Pwent asked. He was trembling.

Bruenor glanced back at Drizzt. When he heard the crash of Pwent's breastplate hitting the ground, he turned back.

"Ye telled a stinkin' orc, but ye didn't tell yer Gutbuster?" Pwent demanded. He pulled off one gauntlet and dropped it to the ground, then the other, then reached down and began unfastening his spiked greaves.

"Ye'd do that to them what loved ye? Ye'd make us all cry for ye? Ye'd break our hearts? Me king!"

Bruenor's face grew tight, but he had no answer.

"All me life for me king," Pwent muttered.

"I ain't yer king no more," said Bruenor.

"Aye, that's what I be thinkin'," said Pwent, and he put his fist into Bruenor's eye. The orange-bearded dwarf staggered backward, his one-horned helm falling from his head, his many-notched axe dropping to the ground under the severe weight of the blow.

Pwent unbuckled his helmet and pulled it from his head. He had just started throwing it aside when Bruenor hit him with a flying tackle, driving him backward and to the ground, and over and over they rolled, flailing and punching.

"Been wanting to do this for a hunnerd years!" Pwent cried, his voice muffled at the end as Bruenor shoved his hand into his mouth.

"Aye, and I been wantin' to give ye the chance!" Bruenor shouted back, his voice rising several octaves at the end of his claim, when Pwent bit down hard.

"Drizzt!" Nanfoodle yelled. "Stop them!"

"No, don't!" Jessa cried, clapping in glee.

Drizzt's expression told the gnome in no uncertain terms that he had no intention of jumping in between that pile of dwarven fury. He crossed his arms over his chest, leaned back against a tall stone, and truly seemed more amused than concerned.

Around and around went the flailing duo, a stream of curses coming from each, interrupted only by the occasional grunt as one or the other landed a heavy blow.

"Bah, but ye're the son of an orc!" Bruenor yelled.

"Bah, but I ain't yer smelly son, ye damned orc!" Pwent yelled back.

As it happened, they rolled around just then, coming apart just enough to look straight at Jessa, her arms crossed, glaring at them from on high.

"Err . . . goblin," both corrected together as they came to their feet side by side. Both shrugged a half-hearted apology Jessa's way, and they went right back into it, wrestling and punching with abandon. They stumbled out of the boulder tumble and across a small patch of grass to the top of a small bluff, and there Bruenor gained a slight advantage, managing to pull Pwent's arm behind his back. The battlerager let out a shriek as he looked down the other side of the bluff.

"And I been wanting ye to take a bath all them hunnerd years!" Bruenor declared.

He bulled Pwent down the hill into a short run, then threw the dwarf and flew after him right into the midst of a cold, clear mountain stream.

Pwent hopped up, and anyone watching would have thought the poor frantic dwarf had landed face down in acid. He stood in the stream shaking wildly, trying to get the water off. But the ploy had worked at least. He had no more fight left in him.

"Why'd ye do that, me king?" a heartbroken Pwent all but whispered.

"Because ye smell, and I ain't yer king," Bruenor replied, splashing his way to the bank.

"Why?" Pwent asked, his voice so full of confusion and pain that Bruenor stopped short, even though he was still in the cold water, and turned back to regard his loyal battlerager.

"Why?" Thibbledorf Pwent asked again.

Bruenor looked up at the other three—four, counting Guenhwyvar—who had come to the top of the bluff to watch. With a great sigh, the dead King of Mithral Hall turned back to his loyal battlerager and held out his hand.

"Was the only way," Bruenor explained as he and Pwent started up the bluff. "Only fair way to Banak."

"Banak didn't need to be king," said Pwent.

"Aye, but I couldn't be king anymore. I'm done with it, me friend."

That last word gave them both pause, and as the implications of it truly settled on both their shoulders, they each draped an arm across the other's strong shoulders and walked together up the hill.

"Been too long with me bum in a throne," Bruenor explained as they made their way past the others and back toward the boulder tumble. "Not for knowing how many years I got left, but there's things I'm wanting to find, and I won't be finding 'em in Mithral Hall."

"Yer girl and the halfling runt?" Pwent reasoned.

"Ah, but don't ye make me cry," said Bruenor. "And Moradin willing, I'll be doing that one day, if not in this life, then in his great halls. But no, there's more."

"What more?"

Bruenor put his hands on his hips again and looked out across the wide lands to the west, bordered by the towering mountains in the north and the still-impressive foothills in the south.

"Gauntlgrym's me hope," said Bruenor. "But know that just the open road and the wind in me face'll do."

"So ye're going? Ye're going forever, not to return to the hall?"

"I am," Bruenor declared. "Know that I am, and not to return. Ever. The hall's Banak's now, and I can't be twisting that. As far as me kin—our kin—are forever to know, as far as all the kings o' the Silver Marches are forever to know, King Bruenor Battlehammer died on the fifth day of the sixth month of the Year of True Omens. So it be."

"And ye didn't tell me," said Pwent. "Ye telled th'elf, ye telled the gnome, ye telled a stinkin' orc, but ye didn't tell me."

"I telled them that's going with me," Bruenor explained. "And none in the hall're knowing, except Cordio, and I needed him so them priests didn't figure it out. And he's known to keep his trap shut, don't ye doubt."

"But ye didn't trust yer Pwent."

"Ye didn't need to know. Better for yerself!"

"To see me king, me friend, put under the stones?"

Bruenor sighed and had no answer. "Well I'm trusting ye now, as ye gived me no choice. Ye serve Banak now, but know that telling him is doing no favor to any in the hall."

Pwent resolutely shook his head through the last half of Bruenor's words. "I served King Bruenor, me *friend* Bruenor," he said. "All me life for me king and me friend."

That caught Bruenor off his guard. He looked to Drizzt, who shrugged and smiled; then to Nanfoodle, who nodded eagerly; then to Jessa, who answered, "Only if ye promise to brawl with each other now and again. I do so love the sight of dwarves beating the beer-sweat out of each other!"

"Bah!" Bruenor snorted.

"Now where, me ki—me friend?" Pwent asked.

"To the west," said Bruenor. "Far to the west. Forever to the west."

PART I

POKING A MAD GOD

It is time to let the waters of the past flow away to distant shores. Though never to be forgotten, those friends long gone must not haunt my thoughts all the day and night. They will be there, I take comfort in knowing, ready to smile whenever my mind's eye seeks that comforting sight, ready to shout a chant to a war god when battle draws near, ready to remind me of my folly when I cannot see that which is right before me, and ready, ever ready, to make me smile, to warm my heart.

But they will ever be there, too, I fear, to remind me of the pain, of the injustice, of the callous gods who took from me my love in just that time when I had at last found peace. I'll not forgive them.

"Live your life in segments," a wise elf once told me, for to be a long-lived creature who might see the dawn and dusk of centuries would be a curse indeed if the immediacy and intensity of anticipated age and inevitable death is allowed to be forgotten.

And so now, after more than forty years, I lift my glass in toast to those who have gone before: to Deudermont; to Cadderly; to Regis; perhaps to Wulfgar, for I know not of his fate; and most of all, to Catti-brie, my love, my life—nay, the love of that one segment of my life.

By circumstance, by fate, by the gods . . .

I'll never forgive them.

So certain and confident these words of freedom read, yet my hand shakes as I pen them. It has been two-thirds of a century since the catastrophe of the Ghost King, the fall of Spirit Soaring, and the dea—the loss of Catti-brie. But that awful morning seems as if it was only this very morning, and while so many memories of my life with Catti seem so far away now, almost as if I am looking back at the life of another drow, one whose boots I inherited, that morning when the spirits of my love and Regis rode from Mithral Hall on a ghostly unicorn, rode through the stone walls and were lost to me, that morning of the deepest pain I have ever known, remains to me an open, bleeding, and burning wound.

But no more.

That memory I now place on the flowing waters, and look not behind me as it recedes.

I go forward, on the open road with friends old and new. Too long have my blades been still, too clean are my boots and cape. Too restless is Guenhwyvar. Too restless is the heart of Drizzt Do'Urden.

We are off to Gauntlgrym, Bruenor insists, though I think that unlikely. But it matters not, for in truth, he is off to close his life and I am away to seek new shores—clean shores, free of the bonds of the past, a new segment of my life.

It is what it is to be an elf.

It is what it is to be alive, for though this exercise is most poignant and necessary in those races living long, even the short-lived humans divide their lives into segments, though they rarely recognize the transient truth as they move through one or another stage of their existence. Every person I have known tricks himself into thinking that this current way of things will continue on, year after year. It is so easy to speak of expectations, of what will be in a decade, perhaps, and to be convinced that the important aspects of one's life will remain as they are, or will improve as desired.

"This will be my life in a year!"

"This will be my life in five years!"

"This will be my life in ten years!"

We all tell ourselves these hopes and dreams and expectations, and with conviction, for the goal is needed to facilitate the journey. But in the end of that span, be it one or five or ten or fifty years hence, it is the journey and not the goal, achieved or lost, that defines who we are. The journey is the story of our life, not the achievement or failure at its end, and so the more important declaration by far, I have come to know, is, "This is my life now."

I am Drizzt Do'Urden, once of Mithral Hall, once the battered son of a drow matron mother, once the protégé of a wondrous weapons master, once loved in marriage, once friend to a king and to other companions no less wonderful and important. Those are the rivers of my memory, flowing now to distant shores, for I reclaim my course and my heart.

But not my purpose, I am surprised to learn, for the world has moved beyond that which I once knew to be true, for this realm has found a new sense of darkness and dread that mocks he who would deign to set things aright.

Once I would have brought with me light to pierce that darkness. Now I bring my blades, too long unused, and I welcome that darkness.

No more! I am rid of the open wound of profound loss!
I lie.

—Drizzt Do'Urden

CHAPTER 1

THE DAMNED

The Year of Knowledge Unearthed
(1451 DR)

IT WAS A CLEVER DEVICE SHE HAD FASHIONED, A THIMBLELIKE, conical piece of smooth cedar with a point like a spear and an opening that allowed her to fit it onto her finger. She slipped it on and gently rotated a knot in the wood, and the mundane became magical as the finger spear diminished and took the form of a beautiful sapphire ring.

The glittering adornment fit the majestic image of Dahlia Sin'felle. Her tall, lithe elf form was topped by a head shaved clean but for a single thin clutch of raven black and cardinal red locks, woven to run down the right side of her shapely head and nestle in the hollow of her deceptively delicate neck. Her long fingers, wrapped with more than that one jeweled ring, were tipped with perfect nails, painted white and set with tiny diamonds. Her icy blue eyes could freeze a man's heart or melt it with a simple look. Dahlia appeared the artist's epitome of Thayan aristocracy, a lady great even among the greatest, a young woman who could enter a room and turn all heads in lust, in awe, or in murderous jealousy.

She wore seven diamonds in her left ear, one for each of the lovers she had murdered, and two more small, sparkling studs in her right ear for the lovers she had yet to kill. Like some of the men of the day, but few if any other Thayan women, Dahlia had tattooed her head with the blue dye of the woad plant. Dots blue and purple decorated the right side of her nearly hairless skull and face, a delicate and mesmerizing pattern enchanted by the master artist to impart various shapes to the viewer. As the woman gracefully turned her head to the left, one might see a gazelle in stride among the reeds of blue. When she snapped back angrily to the right, perhaps a great cat would rear up to strike. When her blue eyes flashed with lust, her target, be it man or woman, might fall helplessly into the dizzying patterns of Dahlia's woad, entrapped and mesmerized, perhaps never to emerge.

She wore a crimson gown, sleeveless and backless, and cut low in the front, the soft round curves of her breasts contrasting starkly with the sharp seam of rich fabric. The gown reached nearly to the floor, but was slit very high up the right side, drawing the eyes of lusting onlookers, man and woman alike, from her glittering red-painted toenails, past the delicate straps of her ruby sandals, and up the porcelain skin of her shapely leg, nearly to her hip. From there, one's eyes could not help but be drawn to the base of the **V**, and up to the shining tip of the singular black and red braid, the image there framed by a wide, high open collar that presented her slender neck and her perfectly shaped head like a colored glass vase holding a fresh bouquet.

Dahlia Sin'felle knew the power of her form.

The look on Korvin Dor'crae's face when he entered her private room only confirmed that. He came at her eagerly, wrapping his arms around her. He was not a tall man, not thick with muscle, but his grip was strengthened by his affliction and he pulled her to him roughly, raining kisses along her jaw.

"You will not be long in pleasing yourself, no doubt, but what of me?" she asked, the innocence in her voice only adding to the sarcasm.

Dor'crae moved back enough to look up into her eyes, and smiled widely, revealing his vampire fangs. "I thought you enjoyed my feast, milady," he said, and he went right back at her, biting her softly on the neck.

"Be easy, my lover," she whispered, but she moved in a teasing way as she spoke to ensure that Dor'crae could do no such thing.

Her fingers played along his ear and swirled amidst his long, thick black hair. She had been teasing him all night long, after all, and with sunrise nearing he hadn't much time—not up in the many-windowed tower. He tried to walk her back to the bed, but she held her ground, and so he pressed in more tightly and bit down more forcefully.

"Be easy," she whispered with a giggle that coaxed him on all the more. "You'll not make me one of your kind."

"Play with me through eternity," Dor'crae replied, and he dared bite harder, his fangs finally puncturing Dahlia's beautiful skin.

Dahlia lowered her right hand to her side and reached her thumb over the illusionary ring on her index finger, tapping the gem. She slid both of her hands onto Dor'crae's chest, undoing the leather ties of his shirt and pulling the fabric wide, her fingers fluttering over his skin. He groaned, pressed in closer, and bit down harder.

Dahlia's right hand felt his breast and slipped delicately to the hollow of his chest, and there she cocked back her index finger as if it were a viper readying to strike.

"Retract your fangs," she warned, though her voice was still throaty, still a tease.

He groaned, and the viper struck.

Dor'crae sucked in a breath he didn't need, let go of Dahlia's neck, and eased back, grimacing every inch as the pointed wooden tip invaded his flesh and prodded at his heart. He tried to back away, but Dahlia expertly paced him, keeping the pressure just right to exact excruciating, crippling pain without killing the creature outright.

"Why do you make me torment you so, lover?" she asked. "What have I done to so deserve such pleasure from you?" She turned her hand just a bit as she spoke, and the vampire seemed to shrink before her, his legs buckling.

"Dahlia!" he managed to plead.

"A tenday has passed since I gave you your task," she replied.

Dor'crae's eyes went wide with horror. "A Dread Ring," he blurted. "Szass Tam would expand them."

"I know that, of course!"

"To new areas!"

Dahlia growled and twisted the tiny spike, driving Dor'crae down to one knee.

"The Shadovar are strong in Neverwinter Wood, south of the city of Neverwinter!" the vampire grunted. "They have chased the paladins from Helm's Hold and patrol the forest unhindered."

"Imagine that!" Dahlia exclaimed sarcastically at yet another bit of common knowledge.

"There are rumblings . . . the Hosttower . . . magical wards and unleashed energy . . ."

Wicked Dahlia cocked her shapely head despite herself, and eased up her prodding finger just a bit.

"I know not the full tale as of yet," the vampire said, his words coming more easily. "It is shrouded in mystery older than the oldest elf, in a time long ago when the Hosttower of the Arcane in Luskan was first built. There are—" He stopped with a grunt as Dahlia's wood-covered finger burrowed in.

"To the point, vampire. I haven't an eternity." She looked at him slyly. "And if you offer me eternity one more time, I'll show you an abrupt end to your own."

"There is magical instability there, due to the fall of the Hosttower," Dor'crae blurted. "It is possible that we could create carnage on a scale sufficient—"

Again the woman twisted the words from his mouth, silencing him. Luskan, Neverwinter, the Sword Coast . . . the significance of that region was no mystery to Dahlia. The mere mention of the area rekindled memories of her childhood, memories she clutched close to her heart as constant reminders of the wretchedness of the world.

She shook the haunting images away—it was not the time, not with a dangerous vampire held at arm's length.

"What more?" she demanded.

A panicked look came over the vampire, who obviously had nothing substantial to add and expected a sudden end to his existence at the hands of the merciless elf.

But Dahlia was more intrigued than she showed. She retracted her hand so suddenly Dor'crae fell to hands and knees and closed his eyes in silent thanks.

"There is no time you are near me when I cannot kill you," the woman said. "The next time you forget that and try to afflict me, I will utterly, happily, joyously destroy you."

Dor'crae looked up at her, his expression conveying that he didn't doubt her for a heartbeat.

"Now make love to me, and do it well, for your own sake," the elf said.

It had been a fine trip to the stream for water. The pollywogs had just hatched and the twelve-year-old elf lass had found hours of enjoyment observing their play. Her mother had told her not to rush, since her father was out on the hunt that day anyway, and the water would not be needed until supper.

Dahlia came over the rise and saw the smoke, heard the cries, and knew the dark ones had come.

She should have fled. She should have turned around and run back to the stream, and across it. She should have abandoned her doomed village and saved herself, hoping to rejoin her father later on.

But she found herself running home, screaming for her mother. The Netherese barbarians were there, waiting.

Dahlia pushed away the memories, channeling them, as she always channeled them, into her need for dominance. She slapped the vampire aside and rolled atop him, taking full control. Dor'crae was a most excellent lover—which was why Dahlia had kept him alive for so long—and the woman's distraction had given him the upper hand. But only for a short while. She went at him angrily, turning their lovemaking into something violent, punching him and clawing at him, showing him the wooden finger prod at just the right moment to deny him his pleasure while she experienced her own.

Then she pulled away from him and ordered him gone, and warned him that her patience neared its end and that he should not return to her, should not come into her sight, until he had more to reveal about the Hosttower and the potential for catastrophe in the west.

The vampire slunk away like a beaten dog, leaving Dahlia alone with her memories.

———

They murdered the men. They murdered the youngest and the oldest of the females, who were not of child-bearing age, and for the two poor villagers with child, the barbarians were most cruel of all, cutting the children from their wombs and leaving both to die in the dirt.

And for the rest, the Netherese shared their seed, violently, repeatedly. In their demented fascination with mortality, they sought the elves' wombs as if partaking of an elixir of eternal youth.

———

Her dress was much like the one Dahlia had been wearing that same day, high collar, open neck and low cut, and none could deny that Sylora Salm wore it in an enticing manner. Like her rival, her head was cleanly shaven, with not a hair on her pretty head. She was older than Dahlia by several years, and though Sylora was human, her beauty had surely not dimmed.

She stood on the edge of a dead forest, where the diseased remnants of once proud trees reached to the very edge of the newest Dread Ring, a widening black circle of utter devastation. Nothing lived within that dark perversion, where ashes could be naught but ashes and dust could be naught but dust. Though she was dressed as if to attend a royal ball, Sylora did not seem out of place there, for there was a coldness about her that complemented death quite well.

"The vampire inquired," explained her lone companion, Themerelis, a hulking young man barely into his twenties. He wore only a short kilt, mid-calf boots, and an open leather vest, showing off his extraordinary musculature, his wide shoulders exaggerated by the greatsword he wore strapped diagonally across his back.

"What is the witch's fascination with the Hosttower of the Arcane?" Sylora asked, talking more to herself as she turned away from Themerelis. "It has been nearly a century since that monstrosity tumbled, and the remnants of the Arcane Brotherhood have shown no indication that they intend to rebuild it."

"Nor could they," Themerelis said. "The dweomers of its bindings were far beyond them even before the Spellplague. Alas for magic lost to the world."

Sylora looked at him with open mockery. "Something you heard in the library while spying on Dahlia?" She held up her hand as her consort started to reply. The man was too dim to understand the insult. "Why else would you be in a library?" she asked, and she rolled her eyes in disgust when he looked at her with obvious puzzlement.

"Do not mock me, Lady," the warrior warned.

Sylora turned on him sharply. "Pray tell me why?" she asked. "Will you take out your greatsword and cleave me in two?"

Themerelis glared at her, but that only evoked a burst of laughter from the Thayan sorceress.

"I prefer other weapons," Sylora said, teasing him, and she let her hand come up to stroke Themerelis's powerful arm. The man started toward her, but she moved her palm before him to halt his advance.

"If you earn the fight," she explained.

"They are leaving this day," Themerelis replied.

"Then be quick to your work." She gave him a little push backward then waved at him to be gone.

Themerelis offered a frustrated snort and spun away, stomping back through the trees and up the distant hill toward the castle gate.

Sylora watched him go. She knew how he was so easily getting near to the wary and dangerous Dahlia, and she wanted to hate him for that, to murder him even, but she found she couldn't blame the young man. She narrowed her eyes into hateful slits. How she wanted to be rid of Dahlia Sin'felle!

"Those thoughts do not serve you well, my pretty," came a familiar voice from within the Dread Ring—and even if she hadn't recognized the voice, only one creature would dare enter so new a ring.

"Why do you tolerate her?" Sylora said, turning back to stare into the fluttering wall of blowing ash that marked the circumference of the necromantic place of power. She couldn't actually see Szass Tam through that opaque veil, but she could feel his presence, like a blast of a winter wind carrying sheets of stinging sleet.

"She is just a child," Szass Tam replied. "She has not yet learned the etiquette of the Thayan court."

"She has been here for six years," the woman protested.

Szass Tam's cackling laughter mocked her anger. "She controls Kozah's Needle, and that is no minor thing."

"The break-staff," Sylora said with disgust. "A weapon. A mere weapon."

"Not so 'mere' to those who feel its bite."

"It is just a weapon, absent the beauty of pure spellcasting, absent the power of the mind."

"More than that," Szass Tam whispered, but Sylora ignored him and continued.

"Swashbuckling trickery," she said. "All flash and dazzle, and strikes a child should dodge."

"I count her victims at seven," the lich reminded her, "including three of considerable renown and reputation. Could I not bring them back to my side in a preferable form,"—the manner in which he so casually referred to his reanimation of the dead sent a freezing shiver along Sylora's already cold spine—"I would fear that the Lady Dahlia might be thinning my ranks too quickly."

"Count it not as her skill," Sylora warned. "She coaxed them, every one, into vulnerable positions. Her youth and beauty fooled them, but now I know, now we all know."

"Even Lady Cahdamine?" said Szass Tam, and Sylora winced. Cahdamine had been her peer, if never really her friend, and they had shared many adventures, including clearing the peasants from the land for the very Dread Ring she stood before—clearing the peasants' souls, at least, for their rotting flesh had fed the ring. During that pleasurable time, three years before, Cahdamine had spoken often of Lady Dahlia, and of how she had taken the young elf under her wing to properly instruct her in the arts carnal and martial.

Had Cahdamine underestimated Dahlia? Had she been blinded by her arrogance to the dangers of the heartless elf?

Cahdamine had become the middle diamond on Dahlia's left ear, the fourth of seven, Sylora knew, for Sylora had caught on to the elf's little symbolism. And Dahlia wore two studs on her right ear. Dor'crae was one of her lovers, of course, and—Sylora glanced toward the distant castle, along the path Themerelis had taken.

"You will not have to suffer her here for some months—years, more likely," Szass Tam remarked as if reading her mind. "She is off to Luskan and the Sword Coast."

"May the pirates cut her to pieces."

"Dahlia serves me well," the disembodied voice of Szass Tam warned.

"You speak so to keep me from destroying her."

"You serve me well," the lich replied. "I have told Dahlia as much."

Outraged, Sylora spun away and departed. How dare Szass Tam elevate the wayward waif to her level with such an insinuation!

❖

An important night, she knew, and so she had to look the part. It wasn't vanity that drew Dahlia to the mirror but technique. Her art was a matter of perfection, and anything less would be a death sentence.

Her black leather boots rose up above her knees, touching her matching black leather skirt on the outside of her left thigh. Nowhere else did leather meet leather, though, for the skirt was cut at a sharp angle, climbing up well above the mid-point on the thigh of her other shapely leg. Her belt, a red cord, carried leather pouches on each hip, both black with red stitching. She wore a puff-sleeved white blouse of the finest silk, cinched with diamond cuffs to allow her free movement. A small black leather vest provided some padding, but her real armor came from a magic ring, an enchanted cloak, and small magic bracers hidden under the cuffs of her blouse.

As with all of her outfits, Dahlia left the top of the low-cut vest unbuttoned, and the stiff collar turned up to frame her delicate head. It would not do to be along the road under the sun with no hair to protect her pate, though, so she wore a wide-brimmed black leather hat, pinned up on the right, revealing her black and red braid, banded in red silk and stylishly plumed with a red feather.

When she bent her right leg and turned it out just so, striking an alluring pose, what man could resist her?

But what she saw in the mirror did not quite match the reality of her beauty.

⸻

They caught her easily and threw her down, but didn't pile one after another atop her as they had with the others. Dahlia caught the gaze of one burly barbarian, the Shadovar of huge size and strength who had led the raid. While most of the raiders appeared as dusky-skinned humans, the leader was obviously a convert, a horned half-demon—a tiefling.

The young and delicate captive, barely a woman, was his, he decreed.

They stripped her down and held her for the sacrifice, and for the first time, Dahlia truly understood her foolishness in running back to the village, understood what she, and not just what her People, had to lose.

She heard her mother screaming for her, and from the corner of her eyes, saw the woman running at her, only to be tackled and sat upon.

Then he stood over her, the huge tiefling, leering at her. "Loosen and ease, girl, and your mother will live," he promised.

He had her. She managed to turn her head to look at her mother as he lay down atop her, and managed to bite back her screams as he tore into her, though she felt as if she was ripping in half. The act itself was over quickly, but her humiliation had only just begun.

Two barbarians grabbed her by the ankles and lifted her up into the air, upside down.

"You will keep the seed of Herzgo Alegni," they mocked as they pawed and slapped at her.

Eventually they lowered her so that her head twisted painfully on the ground. She turned it enough to keep an inverted, distorted view of her mother—enough to see the tiefling, Herzgo Alegni, cross into her field of vision.

He looked back at her and smiled—could she ever forget that smile?—then he so very casually stomped on the back of her mother's neck, fine elf bones shattering under the blow.

Dahlia took a deep breath and closed her eyes, fighting to hold her balance. But only briefly did she swoon, for she was not that child of a decade before. That young elf girl was dead, killed by Dahlia, murdered internally and replaced by the exquisite, deadly creature she saw in the mirror.

Her hand went across her hard abdomen, and she recalled, just briefly, when she had been with child—with his child, with the smiling one's child.

With another deep breath, she adjusted her hat then swung away from the mirror to grab up Kozah's Needle. The slender metal staff stood fully eight feet, and though it appeared glassy smooth from even a short distance, its grip was solid and sure. Its four joints were all but invisible, but Dahlia knew them as well as she knew her own wrist or elbow.

With the flick of a hand, she cracked the staff at its midpoint, letting it swing down to fold onto itself into a comfortable four-foot walking stick. She noted the slight discharge of energy as it swung, feeding her, and the muscles in her forearm twitched under the soft folds of her sleeve.

She took a last glance around her bedchamber. Dor'crae had taken her larger packs to the wagon already, but she let her eyes linger a few heartbeats, wanting to ensure that she had forgotten nothing.

When she left, she didn't look back, though she expected that several years, perhaps many years, would pass before she again looked upon that place, which had been her home for more than half a decade.

The roots tasted bitter—she couldn't help but gag as she stuffed one after another into her mouth. But the Netherese would return, the elders assured her. They knew where she was and knew she carried the child of their leader.

One old elf woman had tried to talk her into killing herself to be done with it.

But that girl who had foolishly run back to her village instead of away was already dead.

She felt the pangs in her abdomen soon after, the terrible convulsions, the tearing agony of childbirth through a body too young to accept it.

But Dahlia didn't make a sound, other than her heavy breathing as she worked her muscles and pushed with all her strength to get the beast child out of her. Covered in sweat, exhausted, she at last felt the rush of relief, and heard the first cries of her baby, of Herzgo Alegni's son. The midwife placed the babe upon her chest and a mixture of revulsion and unexpected warmth tore at the woman as surely as the Shadovar had torn at her loins, as surely as his son had ripped her in birth.

She didn't know what to think, and took a tiny measure of comfort in hearing the women discussing their success, for she had beaten the return of the father and his brutes by several tendays.

Dahlia rested back her head and closed her eyes. She couldn't let them return. She couldn't let them determine her life's path.

"You are not gone yet?" Sylora Salm surprised Dahlia almost as soon as she had exited her room. "I would have thought you halfway to the Sword Coast by now."

"Seeking to claim what fineries I've left behind, Sylora?" Dahlia replied. She paused to strike a pensive pose for just a moment before adding, "Take the mirror, and let it serve you well."

Sylora laughed at her. "It will prefer my reflection, I am sure."

"Perhaps true, though I doubt many would agree. But no matter, human, for soon enough, you will be old, gray, and haggard, while I am still young and fresh."

Sylora's eyes flashed dangerously, and Dahlia clutched Kozah's Needle a bit more tightly, though she knew the wizard wouldn't risk the wrath of Szass Tam.

"Peasant," Sylora replied. "There are ways around that."

"Ah, yes, the way of Szass Tam," Dahlia mumbled, and she moved suddenly right up to Sylora, face to face so that the woman could feel her breath hot on her face. "When you entwine with Themerelis and inhale deeply of him, does it feel as if I am in the room beside you?" she whispered.

Sylora sucked in her breath hard and fell back just a bit, moving as if to slap Dahlia, but the young elf was quicker and had anticipated the reaction. "And you will be pallid and unbreathing," she said as she cupped her free hand and grabbed Sylora's crotch. "Cold and dry, while I remain warm and. . . ."

Sylora wailed, and a laughing Dahlia spun away and skipped down the hall.

The wizard growled at her in rage, but Dahlia spun back on her, all merriment flown. "Strike fast and true, witch," she warned as she put Kozah's Needle up in front of her. "For you get but one spell before I send you to a realm so dark even Szass Tam couldn't drag you back from it."

Sylora's hands trembled before her in nearly uncontrollable rage. She didn't speak, of course, but Dahlia surely heard every word: *This child! This impertinent elf girl!* Her small breasts heaving with gasps as she tried to regain her composure, Sylora only gradually calmed and let her hands fall to her sides.

Dahlia laughed at her. "I didn't think so," she said, then skipped down the hall.

As she neared the keep's exit, two corridors presented themselves. To the left lay the courtyard, where Dor'crae waited with the wagons, and to the right, the garden and her other lover.

She had picked the spot well, and knew it as soon as she came to the edge of the cliff overlooking the encampment of Herzgo Alegni's Shadovar barbarians. They couldn't get to her without running for nearly a mile to the south, and could reach up the hundred-foot cliff with neither weapon nor spell.

"Herzgo Alegni!" she cried.

She presented the baby in the air before her. Her voice boomed off the stones, echoing throughout the ravine and reaching beyond to the encampment.

"Herzgo Alegni!" she shouted again. "This is your son!" And she kept shouting that over and over as the camp began to stir.

Dahlia noted a couple of Shadovar running out to the south, but they were of no concern to her. She shouted again and again. A gathering approached, far below, staring up at her, and she could only imagine their surprise that the foolish girl would come to them.

"Herzgo Alegni, this is your son!" she screamed, presenting the child higher. They heard her, though they were a hundred feet down and more than that away.

She scoured the crowd for a tiefling's form as she yelled again to the father of her baby. She wanted him to hear her. She wanted him to see.

She couldn't quite read the look on Themerelis's square-jawed face as she came out into the garden. The night was dark, with few stars finding their way out from behind the heavy clouds that had settled in that evening. Several torches burned in the stiff wind, bathing the area in wildly dancing shadows.

"I didn't know if you would come," the man said. "I feared—"

"That I would leave without a proper farewell?"

The man started to answer, found no words, and simply shrugged.

"You would make love one last time?" Dahlia asked.

"I would go with you to Luskan, if you would have me."

"But since you cannot. . . ."

He started toward her, arms outstretched, begging a hug. But Dahlia stepped back and to the side, easily keeping her distance.

"Please, my love," he said. "One moment to remember until again we meet."

"One last barb I might stab into the side of Sylora Salm?" Dahlia asked, and Themerelis's face screwed up with puzzlement for just a moment until the notion fully registered, replacing curiosity with a stare of disbelief.

Dahlia laughed at him.

"Oh, I will stab her this night," she promised, "but you'll not stab me."

She brought her right arm forward in a sweeping motion, then flicked her wrist, uncurling her staff to its full length.

Themerelis stumbled backward, eyes wide with shock.

"Come, lover," Dahlia teased, bringing the staff horizontally in front of her chest. With a slight move, unseen by her opponent, she cracked two joints, leaving a four-foot center section in her hands, with twin two-foot-long sections dropping to the ends of short chains at either side. Again barely moving, Dahlia set those two side-sticks spinning, both forward at first, then one forward and one backward. She began rolling the center bar in the air in front of her, dipping its ends alternately, heightening the spins of the respective sides.

"It need not be—"

"Oh, but it does!" the woman assured him.

"But our love—"

"Our *lust,*" she corrected him. "I am already bored, and I'll be gone from here for years. Come then, coward. You profess to be a grand warrior—surely you're not afraid of a tiny creature like Dahlia." She worked the tri-staff more furiously then, rotating the central bar in front of her and all the while keeping the two side sticks spinning.

Themerelis put his hands on his hips and stared at her hard.

Dahlia grabbed the center of the long bar in one hand and broke the rotation. As the side sticks swung back to slap against the central bar they created lightninglike bolts that Dahlia expertly directed at her opponent.

Themerelis was lifted backward by the stinging bolts, once, then again. Neither did any real damage, but Dahlia's laughter seemed to sting him quite profoundly. He drew his greatsword and hoisted it in both hands, taking a deep breath and setting his feet widely—just as Dahlia charged.

She leaped in, slapping Kozah's Needle's center bar forward and back while the side sticks extended and rotated yet again. She dropped her left foot back suddenly, pulled in her left hand, extended her right, and turned so that the spinning side stick whipped at Themerelis's head.

No novice to battle, the fine warrior blocked it with his sword then brought the blade back the other way in time to pick off the other spinning extension as Dahlia reversed her pose and thrust.

But she rolled the leading edge back and over high, reversing her grip on the center bar as the weapon turned under. She stabbed straight ahead with the leading butt of the center bar, jabbing Themerelis in the chest.

Again he staggered backward.

"Pathetic," she teased, backing a step to allow him to regain his battle posture.

The warrior came on with sudden fury, slashing his claymore in great swings that hummed powerfully through the air.

And he hit nothing but air.

Dahlia leaped sidelong, a full somersault that set her again to her feet, with her back to Themerelis. When the warrior pursued, thrusting his weapon at her, she whirled around and slapped his sword with the left side stick then turned the blade with the angled center bar and struck it again with the spinning, trailing right side stick, and all three sent jolts of electricity into the sword and into Themerelis.

The man fell back, clamping his jaw against the shocking sensation.

Dahlia put the staff into a dazzling spin before her again, the side sticks moving too quickly to follow. She feigned a charge but fell back instead, extending her arms fully to leave the center bar horizontal in front of her. She came forward, retracting her arms so that the bar slammed her own chest, and as it did it broke in half.

Themerelis could hardly follow the movements then as Dahlia put her two smaller weapons, each a pair of two-foot-long metal poles bound end to end by a foot-long length of chain, into a wild dance. She rolled the flails sidelong at her sides, brought one or another, or both or neither, under and around her shoulder—or one around her back to be taken up by the other hand while the other moved across in front to similarly and simultaneously hand off.

And never with a break, never slowing, she began smacking the twirling sticks together with every pass. Each strike crackled with the power of lightning.

Above them, the clouds thickened and thunder began to rumble, as if the sky itself answered the hail of Kozah's Needle.

Finally, her fury unabated, Dahlia reached out at Themerelis with a wide swing.

She missed badly.

She missed on purpose.

Themerelis came in right behind the strike with a burst and a stab.

Dahlia never stopped her turn and continued right around, stepping back as she went to stay out of reach of the deadly blade. She came around with a double parry, her weapons smacking the greatsword one after another.

Neither, though, released a charge into the sword, something Themerelis didn't register. The effective double block had him slowed anyway, retracting the blade, but as Dahlia broke her momentum and reversed the swing of her left hand, he came right back in.

Her parries came simultaneously, one metal rod smacking the greatsword on either side, the right lower down the blade than the left, and Dahlia released the building charge of Kozah's Needle.

The powerful jolt weakened Themerelis's grip even as the woman drove through the swings, and the greatsword was lost to him, spinning end over end and falling away.

He reached for it, but Dahlia and her spinning weapon blocked his way, smacking at him in rapid succession. She hit one arm then the other, again and again, and that was only when he managed to block them. When he didn't, the stick cracked him about the chest and midsection, and once in the face, fattening his lips.

She quickly got ahead of his blocks, the weapons coming at him from any and every angle, battering him, cutting him, raising welt after welt. One strike hit his left forearm so forcefully they both heard the crack of bone before he even knew he'd been hit.

Stunned, off balance, and nearing the end of his strength, the warrior desperately punched out at Dahlia.

She dropped, turned, and swung her right arm up, looping her weapon under and around his extended shoulder. She continued her turn, throwing the back of her hip into his, bending him over her, and with a sudden yank on the entangling weapon, she flipped Themerelis right over her shoulder.

He fell flat on his back, his breath blasted from his lungs, his eyes and thoughts unfocused.

Dahlia didn't slow, spinning circles, finally squaring up to the fallen man as she brought her hands clapping together in front of her, rejoining the central four-foot length of Kozah's Needle. She waved the break-staff up one way then reversed, expertly aligning the side sticks and calling upon the weapon to rejoin. The instant she was holding a singular eight-foot staff again she drove one end to the ground and pole-vaulted off it high into the air, turning the weapon as she went and screaming, *"Yee-Kozah!"* to the dark clouds above.

She landed right beside Themerelis, driving the break-staff's forward tip down like a spear into the man's chest.

Fingers of lightning crackled out from the impact and the weapon slid through the man, clipping his backbone and pressing down into the ground.

Dahlia screamed out to the ancient, long-forgotten god of lightning again as she stood victorious, one hand holding the impaled weapon at midpoint, the other arm straight out to the other side, her head thrown back so she was looking up to the sky.

A blast of lightning coupled with a tremendous thunderstroke hit the upper tip of the staff and channeled down. Some of its burning force entered Dahlia, bathing her in crawling lines of blue-white energy, but most of it jolted into Themerelis with devastating effect. His arms and legs extended out wide, to their limits and beyond, kneecaps and elbows popping in protest. His eyes bulged as if they would fly from their sockets, and his hair, all of his hair, stood out straight, dancing wildly. A great hole was blown right through the man along the length of the metal staff that impaled him.

And Dahlia held on, basking in the power as it flowed through her lithe form.

She looked down at the gathered barbarians.

Finally she spotted Herzgo Alegni among them, moving forward through their ranks.

"Herzgo Alegni, this is your son!" she cried.

She threw the baby from the cliff.

CHAPTER 2

AN OLD DWARF'S LAST ROAD

H E WAS JUST A BOY . . . MANY YEARS AGO," THE WOMAN protested. She rubbed her elderly father's shoulders, and the man was clearly uncomfortable with the obvious contradictions between his tale and the reality before them.

Drizzt Do'Urden held up his dark hands to reassure the two, to show the older man that he didn't disbelieve him.

"It was here," the man, Lathan Obridock, said. "As wondrous a wood as I've e'er seen or heard tell of. Full o' springtime and warmth, and singing, and bells ringing. We all seen it, me and Spragan, and Addadearber and . . . what was that captain's name now?"

"Ashelia," Drizzt answered.

"Aye!" the old man said. "Ashelia Larson, who knew the lake better than any. Great captain, that lady. Just out fishing, you know. And we come across the lake . . ." He pointed back at the dark waters of Lac Dinneshere, tracing a line from a distance out to the rotted old remnants of what had once been a wharf, the ruins of an old shack just up the shore from it. "We were bringing that ranger . . . Roundie. Aye, Roundie. He paid Ashelia to get him across the lake, I guess. You should be speaking with him."

"I did," Drizzt replied, trying to keep the exasperation out of his voice, for he had told Lathan that bit of information a dozen times at least that day, and twice that number the day before, and even before that. The previous year, Drizzt had met with the ranger, commonly known as Roundabout, or Roundie, to the south of Icewind Dale, at the urging of Jarlaxle.

Roundabout's description of the wood was exactly the same as Lathan's: a magical place, inhabited by a beautiful witch with auburn hair, and a halfling caretaker who lived in a hillside cave-home by a small pond. According to Roundabout, though, only the wizard Addadearber had actually seen the halfling, and only Roundabout himself and a man named Spragan had seen the woman, and they had come away with very different impressions. To the ranger, she had seemed as a goddess dancing on a ladder of stars, but Spragan, according to Roundabout and confirmed by Lathan, had never truly recovered from the horror of that encounter.

Drizzt sighed as he looked around at the sparse trees and stony ground of the sheltered nook at the end of a small cove, cleverly hidden by rocky outcroppings. Up above on the hillside stood scattered small pine trees typical of Icewind Dale.

"Perhaps it was north of here," Drizzt offered. "There are many sheltered vales along the high ground at the northeastern stretches of Lac Dinneshere."

The old man shook his head with every word. He pointed to the cabin. "Right behind the lodge," he insisted. "No other lodge near here. That's the place. This is the place. The forest was here."

"But there is no forest," said Drizzt. "And no sign that any forest ever was here, beyond these few trees."

"Telled you that, too," said Lathan.

"They came back after their encounter," his daughter, Tulula, said. "They looked for it. Of course they did, and so did many others. Roundie'd been here many the time before that day, and came back many the time after, and never did he see the same forest again, or the witch or halfling."

Drizzt put his hand on his hip, his expression doubtful as he continued his scan, seeking something, anything, he could bring back to Bruenor, who, along with Pwent, was visiting with some clan dwarves in the tunnels under the lone mountain of Kelvin's Cairn, the complex that had housed Clan Battlehammer in the decades before Bruenor had reclaimed Mithral Hall.

Mithral Hall. Four decades had passed since they'd left that wondrous dwarven kingdom, since Bruenor had abdicated his throne in a most extreme and irreversible manner. How many adventures the three of them had shared, along with Nanfoodle the gnome and Jessa the orc. Drizzt couldn't help but smile as he considered those last two, gone from the band for more than twenty years now.

And once more he'd found himself in Icewind Dale, the land of Drizzt's first real home, the land of the Companions of the Hall, the land of Catti-brie and Regis and Wulfgar, of a displaced dwarf king and a wayward dark elf searching, forever searching, it seemed, to find a place he could rightly call his home. What a troupe they had been! What adventures they had known!

Drizzt and Bruenor had put those three lost friends far behind them, of course, and had long ago given up any notion of finding the wayward spirits of Catti-brie and Regis, or of rejoining Wulfgar, for a human's lifetime had passed, more than two-thirds of a century, and none of the three had been young on those fateful days so long ago. With Pwent, Nanfoodle, and Jessa, they had searched the hilly crags east of Luskan and the foothills of the Spine of the World for Gauntlgrym, the elusive ancient homeland of the Delzoun dwarves. A thousand maps had led them down a thousand trails, through a hundred deep caves, their thoughts only of Gauntlgrym, or, on those occasions when Bruenor and Drizzt quietly reminisced about Bruenor's adopted children and their halfling friend, it was just to share their memories, so dear.

An unexpected meeting with Jarlaxle in Luskan a few years previous had rekindled great hopes and great pains. Immediately after the loss of Catti-brie and Regis, both Drizzt and Bruenor had enlisted the worldly Jarlaxle to find them, at any cost. The passage of seven decades and more hadn't deterred the clever dark elf, apparently, or perhaps it had just been dumb luck, but Jarlaxle had stumbled upon a legend that was growing in the northwestern corner of Faerûn, the legend of a magical forest inhabited by a beautiful witch who apparently quite strikingly resembled the human daughter of King Bruenor Battlehammer.

The hunt had led Drizzt, Bruenor, and Pwent to Roundabout the ranger, in the small mountain village of Auckney, and he had directed them to Lac Dinneshere, one of the three lakes about which were scattered the communities that gave Ten-Towns its name.

Drizzt looked at Lathan, whose story verified what the old ranger in Auckney had said, but where was the forest? Icewind Dale had changed little in the last century. Ten-Towns had not grown—in fact, it seemed to Drizzt that there were less people in each of the towns than had been there when he'd called the place home.

"Are ye even listening to me, then?" Tulula scolded, her tone telling the daydreaming Drizzt that she had asked that question several times already.

"Just thinking," he apologized. "So they and others searched for the forest, but nothing was ever found? Not a trace, nor a hint?"

Tulula shrugged. "Rumors," she said. "And when I was a young girl, one boat came in with the crew all atwitter. Do ye remember that, Da?"

"Barley Farhook's boat," Lathan said, nodding. "Aye, and Spragan wanted to put right out, he did, after all them years where folk snickered at our own tale. Aye, and we did go out, a few boats, but there was nothing to be found here, and they laughed at us again."

"Where are your crewmates now?" Drizzt asked.

"Bah, all dead," Lathan replied. "Addadearber taken in the Spellplague, Ashelia's boat taken by the lake with Spragan aboard her, too. All gone, many years ago."

Drizzt scanned the ruined cottage and the vale behind it, trying to figure out if there was anything left to do. He hadn't expected to find anything, of course—the world was full of wild tales of the most unusual sort, especially in the sixty-six years since the Spellplague had descended upon Faerûn, since the death of Mystra and the great turmoil and tribulations that had shaken the foundation of civilization itself.

Then again, the world was full of actual surprises, as well.

"You got enough?" Tulula asked, glancing back across the lake. "We've a long ride home and you promised we'd be back in Caer-Dineval tomorrow."

Drizzt hesitated a bit, helplessly scanning the horizon, then he nodded. "Help your father back into the wagon," he told her. "We'll be away soon."

The drow trotted off to the cottage and poked about it for a bit, then moved up into the scraggly wood, hardly a forest, crunching through the dried pine needles of seasons past. He looked for clues, any clue: the hint of a door on a hillside, a patch of ground that once might have been a pond, the hint of music in the windy air. . . .

From the side of one hillock, he looked back to see Tulula in the open wagon, her father beside her. She waved to Drizzt, ready to depart.

He moved about a bit more, hoping against all reason that he would find something, anything, to give him hope that this place—Iruladoon, Roundie had called it—had once been the forest as described to him, that the caretaker had been Regis and the marvelous witch, Catti-brie. He thought of his return to Kelvin's Cairn, and dreaded telling Bruenor that their journey to Icewind Dale had been for naught.

Where might they go now? Did old Bruenor have any more roads left in him?

"Come along then!" Tulula called from the wagon, and reluctantly the drow started down, his keen eyes still scanning the ground and trees for some sign, any sign.

Drizzt's eyes were keen, but not sharp enough to see all. In his passing, he brushed by some trees and old branches, and dislodged something that fell behind him. He didn't notice, and went on his way to the wagon. The trio started off on the long road that would take them around the lake and back to Caer-Dineval.

As the sun dipped lower over the lake, the light flashed white on bone—a fish bone, a piece of scrimshaw carved into the likeness of a woman holding a magical bow.

The same bow Drizzt Do'Urden carried on his back.

The air was unseasonably chilly, and storm clouds had gathered off in the northwest on the morning Drizzt walked back out of Caer-Dineval, a reminder that the season was soon to turn. He looked to the distant peak of Kelvin's Cairn and thought that perhaps he should spend another day in town and let the storm pass.

Drizzt laughed at himself, at his cowardice, and not for anything to do with the weather. He didn't want to tell Bruenor that he'd found not a sign, not a tease. He knew he shouldn't tarry, of course. Autumn was falling, and in a matter of tendays, the first snows would come sweeping down upon Icewind Dale, sealing the one pass through the mountains to the south.

On the rocky cliff between the town's welcoming inn and the old castle of the Dinev family, the drow lifted his unicorn pendant to his lips and blew into the horn. He spotted Andahar, a tiny flash of white before him, approaching fast.

The steed seemed no bigger than his closed hand at first, but each stride along the rift between dimensions doubled its size, and in moments, the powerful equine beast trotted to a stop in front of Drizzt. Andahar pawed the ground and shook his thick neck, white mane flying wildly.

Drizzt heard the excited chatter of the guards at the caer's gate, but he didn't even look back to acknowledge them, nor was he surprised by their reaction. Who would not be awe-stricken at the first glimpse of Andahar, tacked and with barding that glittered in the daylight with rows of bells and jewels?

Drizzt grabbed the steed's mane and agilely leaped into the saddle. Then he did salute the gawking folk at the gate before turning the magnificent unicorn to the north and thundering off toward Kelvin's Cairn.

What a wonderful gift Andahar had been, the drow thought, and certainly not for the first time. The ruling council of Silverymoon had commissioned the mount for Drizzt, in gratitude for his work, both with the blade and diplomacy, in the Third Orc War.

The wind whistled past his ears as Andahar galloped across the miles. The drow wasn't cold, though, not with the warmth generated by the unicorn's great muscles. His hair and cloak flew wide behind him. He called forth the bells to sing with the ride, and they answered to his will. Trusting in Andahar, Drizzt let his thoughts slip back to pleasant memories of his old friends. He was disappointed, of course, in not finding any sign of the mysterious witch of the wood, or the curious halfling

caretaker, disappointed at the reaffirmation of tha~
already knew to be true.

He still had his memories, though, and on occasions like this, alone
and on the trail, he looked for them and found them, and couldn't
help but smile as he thought of that previous life he had known.

That previous life he knew he should forget.

That previous life he could not forget.

The sun was still high in the sky when he dismissed Andahar
and entered the dwarven tunnels. Once the complex had been the
home of Clan Battlehammer, and those few dozen dwarves who had
remained there still considered themselves part of the clan. They
knew of Drizzt, though only a couple had ever met the drow. They
also knew of Pwent and the legendary Gutbuster Brigade, and glad
they were to welcome travelers from Mithral Hall, including one
who named himself as a distant cousin to the late King Bruenor
Battlehammer himself.

"To King Connerad Brawnanvil Battlehammer!" the leader of the
Kelvin's Cairn Battlehammers, Stokely Silverstream, greeted Drizzt
when he entered the main forge area. Stokely lifted a mug in toast
and waved to a younger dwarf, who hustled to get Drizzt a drink.

"He fares well, I would hope," Drizzt replied, not surprised
that, four decades on, Connerad had succeeded his father, Banak.
"Good blood."

"Ye fought with his father."

"Many the time," Drizzt replied, accepting the mug and taking
a welcomed swallow.

"And yer own salute?" Stokely asked.

"There can be only one," Drizzt replied, and he lifted his
mug high and waited until all the dwarves in the room turned
to regard him.

"To King Bruenor Battlehammer!" Drizzt and Stokely said
together, and a rousing cheer went up in the chamber. Every dwarf
drank deep then scrambled to get their mugs refilled.

"I was but a dwarfling when me dad brought us back to Icewind Dale," Stokely explained. "But I'd've known him, and well, had I not been a fool and stayed so close to me home up here."

"You served your own clan," Drizzt replied. "Short are the times of respite in Icewind Dale. Could your father have fared as well, had you, and others with the wanderlust, traveled all the way to Mithral Hall?"

"Bah, but true enough! I'm guessin' me and me boys'll have to settle for yer tales, elf, and we're holdin' ye to that promise! Yerself and old Pwent and Bonnego Battle-axe, of the Adbar Battle-axes."

"This very night," Drizzt promised. He set his mug down and patted Stokely on the shoulder as he moved past him, heading for the lower tunnels, where he knew his friends to be.

"Well met, Bonnego," he said to Bruenor when he entered the small side room, to find Bruenor, as always, spreading maps across the floor and taking notes.

"What do ye know, elf?" Bruenor replied a bit too hopefully.

Drizzt winced at the optimism, and let his expression convey the truth of the rumor.

"Just a few pines and a bit of scrag," Bruenor said with a sigh and a shake of his head, for that was what they had heard of this supposedly enchanted forest from practically everyone in Icewind Dale they had asked.

"Ah, me king," said Thibbledorf Pwent, limping into the room behind Drizzt.

"Shoosh, ye dolt!" Bruenor scolded.

"Perhaps there was once a forest there," said Drizzt. "Perhaps enchanted in some way, and with a beautiful witch and halfling caretaker. The tale of Lathan mirrored that of Roundabout, and both I find credible."

"Credible and wrong," said Bruenor, "as I was knowin' they'd be."

"Ah, me king," said Pwent.

"Ye quit calling me that!"

"Their words are no longer accurate," Drizzt replied. "But that does not mean their memories are wrong. You saw the eyes of both men when they remembered that time, that encounter. Few could wear such expressions falsely, and fewer still could tell tales so aligned, separated by miles and decades."

"Ye think they saw her?"

"I think they saw something. Something interesting."

Bruenor growled and shoved a table over onto its side. "I should've come here, elf! Those years ago, when first we lost me girl. We sent that rat Jarlaxle on the hunt, but it was me own road to be walkin'."

"And even Jarlaxle, with resources beyond any we could imagine, found no trail at all," Drizzt reminded him. "We know not the truth or fancy of this forest called Iruladoon, my friend, and could not have found it in time in any case. You did as your station demanded, through two wars that would have grown to engulf the whole of the Silver Marches had wise King Bruenor not been there to end them. The whole of the North owes you its gratitude. We have seen the world beyond that land we once called home, and it's a dark place indeed."

Bruenor considered the words for a few heartbeats then nodded. "Bah!" he snorted, just because. "And I'm for seeing Gauntlgrym afore me old bones surrender to the years." He indicated some maps on the far side of the floor. "One o' them, I'm thinking, elf. One o' them."

"When're ye thinking to be on the road?" Thibbledorf Pwent asked, and there was something in his voice that caught Drizzt off guard.

"It has to be soon, very soon," the drow replied, studying Pwent through every word.

Always before, the battlerager had shown eagerness, a fanatical need, even, to march beside his King Bruenor. On many occasions, particularly their infrequent visits to Luskan, Bruenor had looked for ways to avoid taking Pwent along. The dirty dwarf was always a sight, of course, and always drew attention, and in the pirate-run City of Sails, such notice was not always a welcomed thing.

But there was something else in Pwent's eye, in his posture, and in the timbre of his voice when he asked the question.

"We'll be going right this day, then," said Bruenor and he began rolling a parchment to stuff it back into his oversized pack.

Drizzt nodded and moved to help, but again he watched the hesitating battlerager.

"What do ye know?" Bruenor finally asked Pwent, noticing that the dwarf didn't move to help with the packing.

"Ah, me king . . ." Pwent replied, voice full of regret.

"I told ye not to call me—" Bruenor started to scold him, but Drizzt put his hand on Bruenor's shoulder.

The drow locked stares with Pwent for a long while, then silently nodded his understanding. "He's not coming," Drizzt explained.

"Eh? What're ye saying?" Bruenor looked at Drizzt with puzzlement, but the drow deflected his gaze to Pwent.

"Ah, me king," the battlerager said again. "I'm fearin' that I can'no go. Me old knees. . . ." He sighed, his face long, like a dog that couldn't head out on the hunt.

Thibbledorf Pwent wasn't as old as ancient Bruenor Battlehammer, but the years, and thousands of particularly violent fights, had not been kind to the battlerager. The journey to Icewind Dale had taken a lot out of him, though of course Pwent had never complained. Pwent never complained at all, unless he was being excluded from a fight or an adventure, or told to take a bath.

Bruenor turned his stunned expression back to Drizzt, but the drow just nodded his agreement, for both knew that Thibbledorf Pwent would never have made such a claim unless he knew in his old heart that he simply couldn't make the journey, that he had reached the end of his adventuring days.

"Bah, but ye're just a child!" Bruenor said, more to boost the spirits of his friend than to try to change his mind.

"Ah, me king, forgive me," Pwent said.

Bruenor considered him for a moment, then walked over and crushed Pwent in a great hug. "Ye been the best guard, the best friend an old dwarf could e'er know," Bruenor said. "Ye been with me through it all, ye been, and how could ye even be thinking that ye're needin' me forgiving? I'm the one what's should be asking! For all yer life—"

"No!" Pwent interrupted. "No! It's been me joy, me king. It's been me joy. And this isn't how it's supposed to end. Been waiting for that one great fight, that last fight. To die for me king . . ."

"Better in me own heart that ye *live* for me, ye dolt," said Bruenor.

"So you mean to live out your days here in the dale?" Drizzt asked. "With Stokely and his clan?"

"Aye, if they'll have me."

"But they'd be fools not to, and Stokely ain't no fool," Bruenor assured him. He looked to Drizzt. "We go tomorrow, not today."

The drow nodded.

"Today, tonight, we drink and talk o' all the old times," Bruenor said, looking back to Pwent. "Today, tonight, we toast every sip to Thibbledorf Pwent, the greatest warrior Mithral Hall's e'er known!"

It may have been a bit of an exaggeration, for Mithral Hall had known many heroes of legend, not the least of whom was King Bruenor himself. But none who had ever battled Pwent would argue that claim, to be sure, what few who'd faced the rage of Thibbledorf Pwent were still around to argue anyway.

They spent all the day and night together, the three old friends, drinking and reminiscing. They talked of reclaiming Mithral Hall, of the coming of the drow, of their adventures on the road, to the dark days of Cadderly's library, of the coming of Obould and three wars they had suffered and survived. They toasted to Wulfgar and Catti-brie and Regis, old friends lost, and to Nanfoodle and Jessa, new friends lost, and to a life well-lived and battles well-fought.

And most of all, Bruenor lifted his mug in toast to Thibbledorf Pwent, who, alongside Drizzt, had to be counted as his oldest and dearest friend. The old king was almost ashamed as he spoke words of gratitude and friendship, silently berating himself for all the times he had been embarrassed by the Gutbuster's gruff demeanor and outrageous antics.

Under it all, Bruenor realized, none of that mattered. What mattered was the heart of Thibbledorf Pwent, a heart true and brave. Here was a dwarf who wouldn't hesitate to leap in front of a ballista spear flying for a friend—*any* friend, not just his king. Here was a dwarf, Bruenor realized at long last, who truly understood what it was to be a dwarf, what it was to be of Clan Battlehammer.

He hugged his friend again the next morning, long and hard, and there was moisture in the eyes of King Bruenor as he and Drizzt walked out of Stokely Silverstream's halls. And Pwent stood there at the exit, watching them go and quietly muttering, "Me king," until they were long out of sight.

"A great dwarf is King Bruenor, eh?" Stokely Silverstream said, coming up to Pwent's side.

The battlerager looked at him curiously, then widened his eyes in near panic as he feared that he'd just surrendered Bruenor's identity with his foolish mumbling.

"I knowed from the moment ye arrived," Stokely assured him. "What with Drizzt beside ye—could it be any but Bruenor himself?"

"Bruenor died many years ago," Pwent said.

"Aye, and long live King Connerad!" Stokely replied, and he nodded and smiled. "And none need know otherwise, but don't ye doubt, me new friend, that it does me heart good to know that he's out there still, fightin' the Battlehammer fight. Me only hope's that we'll see him again, that he'll come back to Icewind Dale in his last days."

Stokely put a hand on Pwent's shoulder then, a shoulder bobbing with sobs.

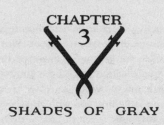

CHAPTER 3

SHADES OF GRAY

As HE WALKED PAST THE GLASS, HERZGO ALEGNI couldn't help but utter a soft growl. His skin had once been so beautifully red, a shining tribute to his devilish bloodline, but the gray pall of the Shadovar had dulled it. His eyes had escaped that change, though, he noted with some satisfaction. The red irises remained in all their hellish splendor.

Alegni accepted the trade-off, though. The dulling of his skin was a minor price to pay for the extended lifespan, and numerous other benefits his life among the Shadovar offered. And though they shared a xenophobic bias with so many of the other closed-minded races of Faerûn, he had found his own path within the ranks of his adopted people. In less than a decade, Herzgo Alegni had become a battle group leader, and barely a decade after that, he had been given the awesome responsibility of leading the Netherese expedition to Neverwinter Wood, in search of fallen Xinlenal Enclave.

He lingered in front of the mirror, admiring his new black weathercloak, its fabric satiny and shimmering, the interior of its stiff collar the most wondrous hue of bright red, matching the blade of his large sword and so beautifully complementing the long purple hair that flowed around his ramlike horns. The high collar diverted most of his hair so it wouldn't hang down his back, but rather flow out around his neck and over his muscular chest. He kept his leather vest partially untied, of course, to emphasize the rippling muscles of his massive torso.

Appearance was important, the warrior knew, and Herzgo Alegni had never been one to shy from a mirror, in any case. He was the leader—intimidation worked in his favor, particularly when he planned to rendezvous with Barrabus the Gray. That one, Alegni did not trust. That one, above all others in his charge, he knew would one day try to kill him, and with good reason.

And Barrabus was quite accomplished at the art of murder.

The hard heels of his high black leather boots clicking loudly on the cobblestones, Herzgo Alegni strode from his house full of purpose and full of power that morning. He didn't even attempt to hide his obvious Netherese affiliation. There was no need to do so in Neverwinter any longer, for Alegni's expedition had been so successful already that none would dare move against the shades.

The Lucky Drake was the newest building in Neverwinter, set up high on a hill overlooking the city and the thundering surf of the Sword Coast. Surveying the city from the porch of the inn, Alegni was reminded yet again of the vast expansion of Neverwinter in the past few decades, since the fall of Luskan to the pirate captains and the floundering of Port Llast. How many lived within the walls of Neverwinter, and just outside the city proper? Thirty thousand, perhaps?

Despite their numbers, they were an unorganized bunch to be sure, with a feeble militia and a lord more concerned with his evenfeast than with protecting his city. For so long, Lord Hugo Babris had been secure in his position. With wild Luskan to the north, her rival pirates uniformly glad for the expanding buffer city, and mighty Waterdeep to the south, Neverwinter had enjoyed great security of late. No ships bent on attack would dodge the armada of Waterdeep, only to be raided by the many privateers running free along the coast north of that greatest of cities.

All of that had left Neverwinter ill-prepared for the arrival of the Netherese—but then again, could anyone truly be prepared for the fall of darkness?—a weakness Herzgo Alegni had been quick to exploit. And since Neverwinter had not been the target of his mission, that being the forest to the southeast, the tiefling had allowed Hugo Babris the illusion that he was still in control of his city.

Alegni's gaze drifted down to the wharf, the precinct that had changed the least in the last tumultuous decades. The Sunken Flagon was there—Barrabus had no doubt spent the night at that very inn. Alegni couldn't help but smile at long-ago memories of that place, back before the Spellplague, when he was a young warrior come to find his treasure and his legacy like so many other confident adventurers. Back then, tieflings had to lurk in the shadows, to hide their proud lineage and heritage. How fortunate, Alegni thought, for in those very shadows he had found something more, something greater, something darker.

The warlord shook himself from his wistful contemplation and moved his gaze to the Neverwinter River and the three ornate bridges crossing it. All were beautiful—the tradesmen of Neverwinter took great pride in their work—but one in particular, built with ornamental wings spread wide to either side, caught and held Alegni's attention. Truly, of the three bridges connecting the halves of the city, north and south, it was the most impressive, for it was carved into the likeness of a wyvern taking wing, great and graceful. For many decades, the bridge had held strong and solid, its substructure supported by a metal grid forged by dwarves and continually reinforced. From a distance, it was beautiful to behold, and that feeling only grew on closer inspection. The bridge had been crafted to perfection in every facet—except for its name: the Winged Wyvern Bridge.

The fools had allowed the simple physical depiction, and not the artistry, to give the magnificent structure its mundane name.

Alegni started down the cobblestone road, determined to arrive on that bridge, the appointed rendezvous, before Barrabus. He hadn't seen his assassin in months, after all, and wanted that first image he presented to be one that reminded Barrabus the Gray of why he hadn't dared to move against the great Alegni.

He arrived at the bridge in short order, climbing the easy slope along the wyvern's "spine" and taking pleasure in the way the mostly human folk of Neverwinter parted before him, scurrying to get far out of his way, every eye turning warily to his magnificent red-bladed sword, hung in a loop on his hip. He walked out to the bridge's mid point, its high point, just behind the wing joints, and put his hands on the western stone railing, staring out to the other two bridges, the Dolphin and the Sleeping Dragon, while silently noting, with considerable enjoyment, how traffic on the Winged Wyvern had slowed.

It wasn't just one of the many Netherese shades skulking about Neverwinter who had come out onto the bridge after all, but Herzgo Alegni himself.

Yes, he was quite pleased as he stood there, surveying the river and the coast, noting the disrepair showing on the lesser bridges, right up until the moment he heard the quiet voice behind him— somehow behind him, somehow *unnoticed* behind him. "You wished to see me?"

Alegni resisted the urge to draw his weapon and whirl on the man. Instead, he continued to stare straight ahead and answered, "You're late."

"Memnon is far to the south," Barrabus the Gray replied. "Would you have me blow in the sails to speed the ship?"

"And if I said yes?"

"Then I would remind you that such a task is more fitting for those who fancy themselves royalty."

The clever riposte had Alegni turning to regard the small man, and the warlord's eyes widened at the sight. Dressed in black leather and cloth as always, with little ornamentation other than his diamond-shaped metal belt buckle that conveniently opened into a most vicious dagger, and a slight tilt to his stance, as if all the world bored him, Barrabus surely appeared as the assassin Herzgo had grown to know so well. But the man's black hair had grown long and unkempt, and he wore a beard, of all things.

"Your discipline falters?" the tiefling asked. "After all these years?"

"What do you want?"

The warlord paused and leaned back, scrutinizing the killer more thoroughly. "Ah, Barrabus. . . . You grow sloppy, slovenly, in the hope that your skills will fail and someone will kill you and release you from your torment."

"If that were the case, I would kill you first."

Herzgo Alegni laughed, but instinctively put a hand on his devastating sword. "But you cannot, can you?" he taunted. "As you cannot allow your considerable skills to lapse, as you have with your appearance. It is simply not in your character. Nay, perfection is your defense. You fool no one, Barrabus the Gray. Your slovenly appearance is naught but a ruse."

The small man shifted from one foot to the other, the only confirmation—and more than he would ever typically offer—that Alegni's words had struck close to the man's heart.

"You summoned me from Memnon, where I was not idle," Barrabus said. "What do you want?"

Alegni wore a clever little smirk as he turned to watch the flow of the Neverwinter River once more, draining into the great sea just north of the bustling docks. "This is a fine structure, both beautiful and functional, don't you think?" he asked, not turning to regard the killer at all.

"It gets me across the river."

"Beyond its utility," the tiefling retorted.

Barrabus didn't bother to answer.

"The beauty," Alegni explained. "No simple abutments or pillars! Nay! Every one covered in small designs destined to complete the whole of the image. Yes, the true signature of the craftsmen. I do so love when craft becomes art. Do you not agree?"

Barrabus didn't answer, and Alegni turned to look at him, and laughed.

"As with my sword," the tiefling said. "Would you not agree that it is a most marvelous artwork?"

"Were its wielder as much the artist as he pretends, he would not need my services."

Alegni's shoulders sagged at the relentless sarcasm, but only momentarily. He turned again on the small man, his red eyes glowing with threat. "Consider yourself fortunate that I am bound by my superiors not to eviscerate you."

"My good fortune knows no bounds. Now, I ask you again, why did you bring me here? To admire a bridge?"

"Yes," Alegni answered. "This bridge. The Winged Wyvern Bridge. Its name does not suit it, and so I wish it changed."

Barrabus looked at him, his expression unreadable.

"The lord of this fine city is a curious little creature," Alegni explained. "Surrounded by guards and behind his stone walls, he does not understand how narrow is the ledge upon which he stands so high."

"He won't change the name?" Barrabus's tone showed little interest.

"Such a traditionalist," Alegni replied with a mock sigh. "He does not appreciate the simple suitability and beauty of the Alegni Bridge."

"The Alegni Bridge?"

"Wonderful, do you not agree?"

"You summoned me from Memnon to convince a petty lord to rename a bridge in your honor?"

"I cannot go against him openly, of course," said Alegni. "Our business in the forest progresses, and I'd not divert the resources."

"And if you went against him openly, you would risk a war with the lords of Waterdeep. Your superiors would hardly be pleased with that."

"You see, Barrabus, even the simple-minded can follow simple logic. Now, pay our esteemed Lord Hugo Babris a visit this night and explain to him that it would be in his interest to rename the bridge in my honor."

"Then I can depart this swine kennel?"

"Oh, no, Gray, I have many more duties for you before I release you to your games back in the desert south. We have encountered some elves in the forest who need persuasion, and there are deep holes we've uncovered. I'd not send a true Shadovar into them until I am certain of their integrity and their occupants. You are here for years, my slave, unless I can persuade the princes that your trouble is not worth your value and thus be rid of you once and for all."

Barrabus the Gray stared at the tiefling hatefully for a few heartbeats, his posture easy, his thumbs looped under his thin belt.

With a disgusted shake of his head, he turned and started away.

As soon as the small man took his first steps, Herzgo Alegni reached under the edge of his open leather vest to a hidden sheath and drew forth a peculiar two-pronged implement. He reached back and tapped it against the side of his powerful, sentient sword, and it began to hum with residual vibrations and offered magic. Grinning wickedly, he waved it beside the hilt of his sword, as if awakening the beast within the blade.

Barrabus the Gray cringed and lurched to the side. His hands went out wide, folding into tight, white-knuckled fists. His jaw clenched so hard he was fortunate not to have bitten off part of his tongue.

The hum continued, the song of Claw, rolling through him like little waves of lava, boiling his blood.

Grimacing, trembling, he sank down to one knee.

Presenting the humming fork in front of him, Alegni walked around the man. He locked eyes with the dangerous killer for a short while then grasped the fork's tines with his free hand, ceasing the hum, the conduit of the sword's call, and the agony.

"Ah, Gray, why do you force me to keep reminding you of your place here?" the tiefling asked, his voice thick with regret, though thin with sincerity. "Can you not just accept your lot in life, and show gratitude for the gifts the Netherese have given you?"

Barrabus hung his hairy head low, trying to regain his sensibilities. When Alegni brought his hand under the man's lowered face, Barrabus took it, and allowed the tiefling to help him back to his feet.

"There," Alegni said. "I am not your enemy, I am your companion. And I am your superior. If you would commit that truth to memory, I would not have to continually remind you."

Barrabus the Gray glanced at the tiefling only briefly then started away at a determined stride.

"Shave your beard and trim your hair!" Herzgo Alegni called behind him, a clear command, and a clear threat. "You look the part of a vagabond, and that will not do for one who serves the great Herzgo Alegni!"

"Elf, I got something!" Bruenor yelled, his voice echoing off the uneven stones of the cave complex's walls. So that by the time it reached Drizzt's ears, it sounded only as "Elf elf elf elf elf elf elf . . ."

The drow ranger lowered his torch and looked to the main corridor just outside the small side chamber in which he was working. He stepped out into the corridor as the dwarf called to him again. Drizzt smiled, recognizing from the tone that his friend wasn't in any trouble. But looking at the catacombs in front of him, he realized he had no idea how to even begin looking for Bruenor.

He smiled again, thinking that maybe he did have a way. He pulled an onyx figurine from his belt pouch and called out, "Guenhwyvar."

There was no insistence nor urgency, and barely any volume to his call, but he knew it had been heard even before gray mist began to swirl around him and take the shape of a great feline. It coagulated even more distinctly and darkened in hue, then Guenhwyvar stood beside him, as she had for more than a century.

"Bruenor's in the caves, Guen," the drow explained. "Go and find him."

The black panther looked back at him, gave a little growl, and padded away.

"And sit on him when you do," Drizzt called after her as he followed. "Make sure he doesn't wander away before I arrive."

Guenhwyvar's next growl came a bit louder, and she picked up her pace, apparently more eager in her hunt because of the added instructions.

Down the main tunnel, Guenhwyvar froze in place, ears twitching as Bruenor's next shout echoed. The panther moved to one side passage, sniffed the air, and darted to a different one. After only a brief pause, she leaped away.

Drizzt tried to keep up, but Guenhwyvar moved swiftly and sure-footedly, darting under overhangs the drow had to crouch to pass through and springing down side passages with confidence. The lagging Drizzt was left to guess at her choices.

They moved deeper into the narrow, crisscrossing tunnels, and when Drizzt next heard Bruenor's yell, so full of outrage, he knew that Guenhwyvar had caught her prey.

"Ye durned elf!" Bruenor griped when Drizzt entered a sizable though low-ceilinged chamber, roughly square in shape and showing signs of some workmanship, as opposed to the natural cave tunnels that dominated the complex.

In the far corner, beside a dropped, low-burning torch, lay Guenhwyvar, calmly licking her paw, and Drizzt could just make out a pair of dwarven boots protruding from under her.

"A hunnerd years and ye still think it's funny," Bruenor said from the other side of the cat, and Drizzt could only guess that the dwarf's head was wedged into a corner somewhere over there.

"I haven't been able to keep up with you since the Tribe of Fifty Spears directed us to this place," Drizzt replied.

"Ye think ye might send the cat away?"

"I welcome her company."

"Then ye think ye might get the damn thing off o' me?"

Drizzt motioned to Guenhwyvar, who stood up at once and headed his way, growling with every stride.

"Ye pointy-eared devil," Bruenor grumbled, pulling himself to his knees.

He gathered up his one-horned helm and hopped to his feet, his horn nearly scraping the ceiling. Hands on hips, he turned and glared at the drow then muttered some more curses as he retrieved his torch.

"You moved more deeply in than we had agreed," Drizzt remarked, dropping to sit cross-legged on the floor, rather than crouching low under the ceiling. "Deeper than we'd previously—"

"Bah, nothing's in here," said the dwarf. "Nothing big, anyway."

"These tunnels are very old, and long unused," Drizzt agreed and scolded all at once. "An old trap or a weak floor might have dropped you to the Middledark. I have warned you many times, my friend, do not underestimate the dangers of the Underdark."

"Ye thinking there might be more tunnels below, are ye?"

"The possibility has entered my mind," said Drizzt.

"Good!" said Bruenor, his face brightening. "Keep it there, and know it's more than a possibility." As he finished, he stepped aside and pointed to a crease in the apparently worked stone of the corner where he'd been working.

"More levels," Bruenor said, pride clear in his tone. He reached over and pressed on the stone just to the side of the crease, and a sharp *click* came back in reply. As the dwarf moved his hand back, that portion of the wall popped out a bit, enough for Bruenor to grasp its edge and slide it farther out.

Drizzt crawled over, lifting his torch in front of him as he peered into the secret chamber. It wasn't a large room, less than half the size of the outer one, and its floor was dominated by a small circle of rectangular stones—bricks?—forming a lip around a dark hole.

"Ye know what I be thinking," Bruenor said.

"It's not proof of anything more than . . . a well?" Drizzt replied.

"Something made that wall, made this room, and made that well," said the dwarf.

"Something indeed, and there are many possibilities."

"It's dwarf work," Bruenor insisted.

"And still that leaves many possibilities."

"Bah!" Bruenor snorted and waved his hand dismissively at Drizzt.

Guenhwyvar jumped to her feet again and issued a long and low growl.

"Oh, shut yer maw!" Bruenor replied. "And don't ye be threatenin' me! Tell yer cat to shu—"

"Be silent!" Drizzt interrupted, waving his free hand, his eyes locked on Guenhwyvar, who continued to growl.

Bruenor glanced from drow to panther. "What d'ye know, elf?"

It arrived suddenly, a sharp roll of the floor, walls shaking, dust falling all around them.

"Quake!" Bruenor yelled, his voice tiny within the earthy rumble of grinding stones and falling blocks, and worse.

A second roll of the floor threw all of them into the air, Drizzt smacking hard against the doorjamb and Bruenor falling over backward.

"Come on, elf!" Bruenor yelled.

Drizzt was face down in the dirt and dust, his torch fallen aside. He started to pull himself to his hands and knees, but the blocks above him broke apart and tumbled down across his shoulders, laying him low.

～～～

Barrabus the Gray fished through the bag, tossing aside the various implements Herzgo Alegni had given him to "aid" in his craft. The assassin had to admit that the tiefling had some powerful friends and did indeed manage to gather many useful items—like the cloak Barrabus even then wore. Fine elven handiwork and enchantment were woven into every thread, and its dweomer aided in keeping the already stealthy Barrabus hidden from view. The same was true of the elven boots he wore and his ability to step silently in them, even through a field of dry leaves.

And of course, the belt-buckle dagger showed the very finest craftsmanship and enchantment. Never once had it failed to spring open to Barrabus's command. Its poison delivery system, real human veins etched along the five-inch blade that pumped poison to the edges and the point, was one of the more remarkable weapons the assassin had ever carried. All Barrabus had to do was fill the "heart" of the knife, set in the hilt, and with the slightest of pressure, he could make that poison flow to its deadly blade.

Still, to Barrabus's thinking, there was a danger to so many enhancements. His art, assassination, remained a test of skill, wisdom, and discipline. Reliance on too many magical aids could bring sloppiness, and sloppiness, he knew, would mean failure. Thus he had never worn the spider-climbing slippers Alegni had once offered him, nor the hat that allowed him to disguise himself nearly at will. And of course he had pushed aside the gender-altering girdle with a derisive snort.

He brought forth from the trunk a small coffer. The poisons inside it he had purchased himself; Barrabus would never allow a third party to deliver his most critical tools. He used only one poison merchant, an alchemist in Memnon he had known for many years, and who personally extracted the various toxins from desert snakes, spiders, lizards, and scorpions.

He lifted a small green phial before the candle and a wicked smile creased his face. It was a new one, and not of the desert. The toxin had come from the bay beyond Memnon's docks, from a cleverly disguised, spiny fish. Woe to the fisherman who stepped on such a creature. Any who walked the beaches of the southern coastal regions had heard tales of the most exquisite screaming.

Barrabus held his knife hilt up. He flipped back the retractable bottom half of the ball counterweight at the base of the knife, revealing a hollow needle. Onto this he jabbed the rubber stopper of the phial. Barrabus's eyes sparkled as he watched the translucent heart of the knife fill with the yellow liquid.

He thought of the fisherman's screams, and almost felt guilty. Almost.

When all was ready, Barrabus gathered up his cloak. He passed a small mirror on his way to the door and was reminded of Alegni's order that he trim his beard and hair.

He walked out of the room, just another visitor to Neverwinter on a fine night with a warm sunset over the water, a simple, small man, walking openly and apparently unarmed. He had just one belt pouch, on his right hip, which lay flat against the side of his leg, seeming empty, though of course it was not.

He stopped at a nearby tavern—he didn't know its name and didn't care—to get a single drink of harsh BG rum, the Baldurian concoction that had become the favorite of sailors all along the Sword Coast since it was quite inexpensive, and tasted so wretched few would bother stealing it.

For Barrabus, who downed it in one gulp, the rum served as his transition, the moment when he moved himself into a higher state of being and consciousness, when all those years of training and expert work crystallized in his thoughts. He closed his eyes a few moments later and felt the inevitable cloudiness of downing so potent a drink, and refocused his attention many times over in tearing through that dullness, in coming to the very edge of preparedness.

"Ye want another?" the barkeep said to him.

"He'll be on his back if he does!" one smelly brute insisted, to rowdy laughter from his three companions, all of whom outweighed Barrabus by a hefty amount.

Barrabus looked at the man with curiosity. The fool obviously didn't understand that Barrabus was wondering if he might kill all four of the ruffians and still complete his task as planned.

"What're ye thinking?" the man demanded.

Barrabus didn't blink and didn't let a hint of a smile, of any expression, come forth. He placed the glass down on the bar and started to walk away.

"Ah, but go ahead and have another," one of the man's friends said, stepping up beside Barrabus. "Let's see if ye can swig it and still stand, eh?"

Barrabus did stop, for a heartbeat, but never bothered to look at the man.

And for that insult, the drunk shoved against Barrabus's shoulder, or tried to. The moment his hand touched the assassin, Barrabus knifed his own hand up behind it, over it, and hooked the man's thumb with his own then jerked down with such force that the ruffian lurched to the side and down, his hand twisted right over backward.

"Do you need two hands to pull fish into your boat?" Barrabus calmly asked him.

When the man tried to wriggle free instead of answering, Barrabus expertly added another quarter twist and re-angled his pressure just enough to keep his opponent from gaining any balance.

"I suppose you do, so for the sake of your family, I will forgive you this once." With that, he let the man go. As the fool stumbled, Barrabus started for the door.

"I got no family!" the man shouted at him, as if that was some kind of insulting retort, and Barrabus heard the charge.

He turned at the last moment, his hands coming up to deflect the awkward grabs of the drunken fool, his knee coming up to abruptly halt the man's bull rush. The many tavern patrons watching the incident weren't sure what happened, just that the ruffian had stopped suddenly and was clenched with the much smaller man.

"And likely now you'll never have one," Barrabus whispered to the man. "And the world will be a better place."

He gently moved the man back and even helped him regain his balance, though the man's stare was blank and his thoughts surely spinning as his hands moved center and down as he bent, trembling fingers trying to help secure his crushed testicles.

Barrabus paid him no heed and just walked out of the tavern. He heard a crash as he exited, and knew that the fool had tumbled. Then he heard, predictably, the outrage of the man's three companions as the shock of his bold move wore thin.

They burst out onto the street, all spit and curses, leaping up and down, looking this way and that and shouting into the empty night. They shook their fists and promised revenge, but went back inside.

Sitting atop the tavern, legs dangling over the edge of the rooftop, Barrabus just watched and sighed at their utterly predictable idiocy.

He was at the lord's grand four-story home soon after, in the shadows and trees behind the back of the house. Hugo Babris was a careful man, it seemed, and Barrabus was surprised to see so many guards patrolling the grounds and moving along the balconies. Barrabus had seen that sort of thing before, where a leader perceived as weak had surrounded himself with substantial protection. What that usually meant, the assassin knew, was that the leader served as a mouthpiece, a puppet, for the true powers behind him, though what those powers might be in the strange and fast-growing city of Neverwinter, Barrabus could not be certain. Pirates, likely, or a merchants' guild getting fat off the policies of Lord Hugo Babris. Certainly someone was paying a hefty sum to provide that level of protection.

Barrabus glanced around, thinking that perhaps he should be on his way. He understood why Herzgo Alegni had gone out of his way to send for him, but it occurred to him that perhaps the tiefling had set him up to fail.

With that thought in mind, Barrabus moved, but not away. He wouldn't give Alegni the satisfaction.

The assassin slithered up the wall and peered into the courtyard, noting one patrol in particular, a pair of guards each with a very large, angry-looking dog.

"Wonderful," he silently mouthed.

Back down the wall, he walked a perimeter outside of the compound several times. He saw only one possible approach. A tree hung its branches into Hugo Babris's compound, though getting from the branch to the house would require a great leap, and that to the edge of a patrolled balcony.

Again, Barrabus thought it might be time to go speak with Herzgo Alegni.

And again, the thought of admitting any limitations to the tiefling had him moving up the wall onto the tree, and up to the higher branches. He paused and noted movement in the courtyard and on the balconies, marking the moment of greatest opportunity. It seemed desperate, ridiculous even, but that was ever the way of it.

He ran out on the branch and leaped out, coming to the edge of the second story balcony at the corner of the house. He ducked back behind the corner when the sentry came around the opposite corner. Barrabus was tucked tightly underneath the balcony as the man paced past, then he was over the rail and up the wall, over the next balcony, and continuing until he sat on a narrow window sill on the highest floor.

He reached into his "empty" pouch, which was actually an extra-dimensional space, and brought forth a pair of suction cups set on narrow poles and joined end to end by a small cord. Once he had them in place on the window glass, he tapped open a catch on one of his rings that released a line of wire, attached on one end to the ring and capped on the other end with a diamond tip.

Barrabus began to draw a circle on the window with the diamond tip, etching the glass a tiny bit more with each rotation. He worked furiously, hid himself as the guards crossed below, then went right back. It took him many, many heartbeats to weaken the glass enough so that he could hold the suction cups and tap lightly, three times, to break the circle of glass free. He pushed the cut circle into the room and gently lowered it to the floor so that it leaned against the wall. With a glance around to make sure the room was clear, Barrabus hooked his fingers on the top of the window frame, gracefully and powerfully lifted his legs, and slid them through.

He rocked back, his feet almost exiting the hole, then went forward with such speed and grace that his momentum carried him fully through without so much as a brush of the remaining glass, and not so much as a whisper of sound.

He knew that the fun had only begun, of course—Hugo Babris kept many guards inside as well—but he was committed. His focus grew narrow and pure, and it was as though he were a ghost; ethereal, silent, and invisible. He had to be perfect, and that was why Herzgo Alegni had summoned only him.

It was said of Barrabus the Gray that he could stand in the middle of a room unnoticed, but of course the man's trick was that he didn't stand in the middle of the room. He knew where alert sentries would look, and so he knew where not to be. Whether the optimum hiding place was behind the open door or above it, behind a canopy or in front of one, in the right place to appear as no more than another figure in a mural, Barrabus knew it and found it. How many times over the decades had a sentry simply looked right past him?

Hugo Babris had guards—so many guards that Barrabus changed his mind about how he might influence the man's thinking—but not enough guards to do more than slow the inexorable progress of Barrabus the Gray.

Soon enough, he sat atop the back of an unconscious sentry who was sprawled across Lord Hugo Babris's desk. Barrabus stared at the nervous, trapped, helpless lord.

"Take the gold and go, I-I beg of you," Hugo Babris pleaded. The lord was a bald, round, thoroughly unimpressive little man, and that only reinforced Barrabus's belief that he was no more than a front for far more dangerous men.

"I don't want your gold."

"Please . . . I have a child."

"I don't care."

"She needs her father."

"I don't care."

The lord brought a trembling hand to his lips, as though he was going to be sick.

"What I want of you is simple, simply done, and at no cost—nay, but at great gain—to you," Barrabus explained. "It's a simple matter of changing the name of a bridge."

"Herzgo Alegni sent you!" Hugo Babris exclaimed and started out of his chair. He reversed direction immediately, falling back and throwing his hands up in front of him when a knife appeared in Barrabus's hands, seemingly out of nowhere.

"I cannot!" Hugo Babris whined. "I told him I couldn't. The Lords of Waterdeep would never—"

"You have no choice," Barrabus said.

"But the lords, and the pirate captains to the n—"

"Are not here, while Herzgo Alegni and his shades are—while *I* am," said Barrabus. "You need to recognize the gain, and understand the potential loss resulting from inaction."

Hugo Babris shook his head and started to protest further, but Barrabus cut him short. "You have no choice. I can come here anytime I wish. Your sentries are of no concern to me. Are you afraid to die?"

"No!" Lord Hugo Babris said with more resolve than the assassin would have imagined him capable of mustering.

Barrabus rolled his dagger in his hand, letting Hugo Babris see the veins. "Have you ever heard of the rockstinger?" he asked. "It is an ugly fish possessed of a beautiful and perfect defense." He hopped from the desk. "You will announce the Herzgo Alegni Bridge tomorrow."

"I cannot," Hugo Babris wailed.

"Oh, you can," said Barrabus.

He flashed the knife near to Hugo Babris, who shrank back pitifully. But Barrabus didn't stick him. Long experience had taught the assassin that the anticipation of pain provided more incentive than the pain itself.

He turned and lightly poked the unconscious sentry, just a gentle stick, but one that delivered the rockstinger venom.

He offered a nod to Lord Hugo Babris and said again, "I can return to you anytime I wish. Your sentries are of no concern to me."

He strode from the room, disappearing into the hall, and was halfway out the hole in the window when the poison jolted the sentry from his semi-conscious daze. The man's agonized screams brought a resigned sigh to Barrabus.

The assassin countered a wave of self-loathing with a silent promise that one day, Herzgo Alegni would feel the bite of the rockstinger.

Guenhwyvar clamped her teeth around Drizzt's cloak and leather vest and pulled hard, her great claws screeching on the stone.

"Tug," Bruenor instructed as he pushed another block of stone away. "Come on, elf!"

The dwarf managed to wriggle a hand under the heaviest stone, one too great to be hoisted aside. He set his strong legs under him, straddling Drizzt, hooked both his hands under the block, and lifted with all his strength.

"Tug," he implored Guenhwyvar, "afore another roll o' the stone!"

As soon as the pressure eased, Guenhwyvar dragged Drizzt free, and the drow came to his knees.

"Go on!" Bruenor yelled at him. "Get yerself away!"

"Drop the stone!" Drizzt shouted back at him.

"Whole ceiling'll fall!" the dwarf protested. "Go on!"

Drizzt knew Bruenor meant it, that his oldest friend would gladly give his life to save Drizzt's.

"Go! Go!" the dwarf implored, grunting under the strain.

Unfortunately for Bruenor, Drizzt felt the same way toward his friend, and the dwarf yelped in surprise when he felt the dark elf's hand grab the back of his hair.

"Wha—?" he started to protest.

The drow yanked Bruenor hard, pulling him back from the rubble and right around, then shoving him down the corridor behind the retreating Guenhwyvar.

"Go! Go!" Drizzt yelled, scrambling after him as the stones tumbled and the ceiling groaned in protest, then cracked apart.

The trio ran one step ahead of catastrophe all along that corridor, stones and dust pouring down right behind them all the way. Guenhwyvar led them true, down a side passage to a chute, where the panther leaped straight up the dozen feet to the next level. Bruenor skidded to a stop right below the shaft, turned, and set his hands. Drizzt never broke stride, stepping in and lifting away as Bruenor heaved him upward. Drizzt caught the floor of the next level and secured his grip even as Bruenor grabbed onto his legs. Guenhwyvar bit Drizzt's ruffled cloak and vest again, tugging with all of her considerable strength.

On they went, with a century of knowledge, coordination, and most of all friendship showing them the way. They spilled out of the cave mouth as another aftershock rolled through the area. Clouds of dust rushed out behind them, and the roar of the catastrophe deep within echoed around them.

Just a few strides from the cave mouth, they collapsed side by side on a patch of grass, sitting and panting, and staring back at the cave that had almost been their tomb.

"Lot o' digging to do," Bruenor lamented.

Drizzt just started to laugh—what else could he say or do?—and Bruenor looked at him curiously for just a moment before joining in. The drow rolled onto his back, staring up at the sky, laughing still at the ridiculous idea that an earthquake had almost done what thousands of enemies had failed to do. What a ridiculous ending for Drizzt Do'Urden and King Bruenor Battlehammer, he thought.

After a while, he lifted his head to regard Bruenor, who had walked to the cave opening and stood staring into the darkness, hands on his hips.

"That's it, elf," the dwarf decided. "I'm knowin' it, and we got a lot o' digging to do."

"Roll on, Bruenor Battlehammer," Drizzt whispered, a litany he had recited for a hundred years and more. "And know to your pleasure that every monster along our trail will mark well your passing and keep its head safely hidden."

From the corner of a building farther down the avenue, Barrabus the Gray watched a bloodied man stumble out of the tavern, followed closely by four familiar ruffians. The poor victim fell face down on the cobblestones and the group waded past him, alternately kicking him and spitting on him. Two of them hit him with their clubs, newly extracted from the legs of a table. One even reached down with a small knife and stuck the man repeatedly in the buttocks and the backs of his legs. But another stood off to the side, cursing, limping, one hand waving a table-leg club, the other held between his own legs.

Barrabus paid little attention to the details, and heard not the man's pitiful cries. In his mind, Barrabus still heard the screams of the sentry at Lord Hugo Babris's house, rockstinger poison coursing through him like sharp-edged fire. He would be well into the second phase of the poison by then, his muscles contracting painfully, his stomach knotted, vomiting still though he had nothing left to discharge. The morning would bring to him a tremendous weariness and a dull ache, both of which would last for days. Whether the sentry deserved such a trial, Barrabus could not know. The man's only "crime" had been to arrive at Hugo Babris's door soon after Barrabus had entered the chamber. That, and a bit too much curiosity. . . .

The assassin sneered and shook the unwelcome notions from his thoughts. He turned back to the foursome, coming his way, though they couldn't see him in the shadow of the building.

Good sense told Barrabus to fade back into the alleyway, to be gone from that place. Prudence demanded that he attract no unwanted attention in Neverwinter. But he felt dirty at that dark hour, and so he felt the need to be cleansed.

"Well met, again," he said as the gang of four came up even with him out in the middle of the road. They turned as one to regard him, and he pulled back the cowl of his elven cloak to give them a clear view.

"You!" exclaimed the one he'd earlier pained.

Barrabus smiled and faded back into the alleyway.

The four, three brandishing crude clubs, the fourth with a knife, rushed in after him, roaring in outrage and promising retribution, though one staggered more than rushed. Three of them entered the alley at full speed, not even realizing that Barrabus had only faded in a couple of steps and was in no way trying to get away from them. How the timbre of their obscenities changed when he appeared in their midst, all elbows and fists and flying feet.

Just a few moments later, Barrabus the Gray walked out of the alley onto the dimly lit Neverwinter street, and not a groan followed him forth.

He felt better. He felt cleaner. Those four had deserved it.

CHAPTER 4

THE HOSTTOWER'S SECRET

"DARK ELVES," DAHLIA SAID, SEEMING QUITE AMUSED BY THE prospect. "So it is true."

"Truer in the past," Dor'crae replied. "They're more rare in the city these days, since Luskan has lost its luster as a trading port. But still they remain, or visit at least, advising the High Captains and offering their wares."

"Interesting," Dahlia replied, but she was, in fact, losing interest in her lover's dissertation of the politics of the City of Sails.

Dor'crae had led her to a most unusual place, a cordoned-off area of ancient ruins overgrown with roots and the hulking remains of dead trees, like a long untended and decrepit garden.

"What is this place?" she asked.

"Illusk," Dor'crae replied. "The most ancient part of an ancient city. And more than that, Illusk is Luskan's barrier between the present and the past, between the living and the dead."

Dahlia took a deep breath, inhaling the heavy aroma of the air around her.

"Do you not feel it?" Dor'crae asked. "You, who have lived at the edge of the Dread Ring of Szass Tam, must sense the transition."

Dahlia nodded. She did indeed feel the damp chill, the smell of death, the sense of emptiness. Death, after all, was about all that she had known for the past decade of her life—continuously, personally, pervasively.

"It's a sweet thing," Dor'crae whispered to her, his voice going husky as he moved near to her exposed neck, "to walk in both realms."

Dahlia's eyelids felt heavy and for a few heartbeats she was hardly aware of the vampire's approach. It was as if she smelled the invitation to the other realm, permeating her very being.

She popped open her eyes and they flashed dangerously at the nearby vampire. "If you bite me, I will utterly destroy you," she whispered, mimicking Dor'crae's teasing tones.

The vampire grinned and stepped back, remembering to bow once as he did.

She shifted just a bit to show Dor'crae the brooch she wore, the gift from Szass Tam that granted her heightened powers against the undead. A vampire would prove a formidable opponent to any living warrior, but with that brooch, and her own amazing physical discipline, Dahlia was quite capable of following through on her threat.

"Why did you bring me here?" she asked.

"Behold the gateway to the undercity," Dor'crae explained, moving to a nearby ruin, a pile of broken stones scattered in a roughly circular pattern as if they had once formed the rim of a well.

Dahlia hesitated and glanced across to the island that had once held the Hosttower of the Arcane, its rubble still clearly visible, and her expression remained doubtful.

"There are tunnels," Dor'crae explained. "Beneath the waves."

"You have been down there?"

The vampire smiled and nodded. "It is where I seek my respite from the sunlight. A most remarkable place, and with a most remarkable hostess."

That last remark had Dahlia looking at the vampire with intrigue. "Host*ess?*" she asked.

"Yes, an exquisite creature."

"Do not mock me."

"You will like Valindra Shadowmantle," the vampire promised.

With a flourish of his arms, Dor'crae flipped his cloak up over his shoulders. He seemed to blur, and Dahlia had to momentarily look away as the vampire transformed into a large bat, which dived into the well, disappearing from sight. With a sigh, knowing Dor'crae knew she couldn't easily follow, Dahlia slipped into the hole. She had her staff doubled into a four-foot walking stick, and she spoke a quiet command and tapped it against the stone. Its folded end reacted to her command with flickering bursts of blue-white light.

Down Dahlia went, staff in one hand, her free hand and two feet working fast to bring her down the well. After about thirty feet, the narrow shaft opened up below her, so she crouched as low as she could and poked her staff below, illuminating the chamber. The floor was barely a dozen feet below her, so she didn't even bother to squirm lower and hook her fingers to hang, but just folded up and dropped.

She landed in a crouch and glanced all around to find Dor'crae back in human form and waiting for her near another hole. Down they went again, to a crossing corridor and through a door into a side chamber. Several staircases, ladders, and narrow chutes later, they came into a labyrinth of tunnels and corridors, ancient structures, walls and doors and broken stairs, the oldest incarnation of the city that had come to be known as Luskan.

"That corridor," Dor'crae indicated, pointing west, "will take us out to the islands."

Dahlia walked over, leading with her illuminated walking stick, studying the walls and floor.

"Along its ceiling, you'll find a mystery of the Hosttower," Dor'crae explained.

Dahlia opened her staff to its full length and allowed the crackling light to wander to the tip once more. Then she thrust it above her, nearly touching the remarkably high ceiling of the tunnel.

"What is it?" she asked, running the staff tip along what seemed like veins in the ceiling.

"Roots?" Dor'crae asked as much as answered.

Dahlia looked at him curiously, but recalled the tree-shaped appearance of the now destroyed Hosttower of the Arcane.

Then a hissing sound from the tunnel spun her around, staff at the ready as some undead beast rushed at her, its long tongue darting between pointy yellow teeth.

Dahlia put her staff into a spin, but Dor'crae intervened, stepping forward and lifting his hand toward the ghoul and staring at it intently.

The ghoul slowed and stopped, staring back at the vampire, a greater being among the enigmatic pecking order of the undead. With a howl of protest, the stinking creature skulked back into the shadows the way it had come.

"The catacombs are full of the ravenous things," Dor'crae explained. "Ghouls and lacedons, half-eaten zombies. . . ."

"Lovely," Dahlia remarked, and she lamented that the undead seemed to follow her wherever she went.

"Most are small, but there are at least two large ones," the vampire explained, turning his attention and the conversation back to the curious roots. "Hollow tubes, one running out from the foundation of the ruined Hosttower to the open sea, the other running back inland to the east, southeast."

"How far?"

The vampire shrugged. "Well beyond the city walls."

"What magic is this?" Dahlia asked, lifting the light and peering again at the nearly translucent greenish tube and the streaks of red.

"Ancient."

Dahlia shot the vampire an unappreciative look.

"If I had to guess, I'd say dwarven," Dor'crae elaborated.

"Dwarven? It's too delicate."

"But the stonework around it is impeccable, all the way to the Hosttower's foundation stones, which certainly showed the mark of dwarf craftsmen."

"You're asserting that the Hosttower of the Arcane, one of the most magnificent and magical structures in all of Faerûn, a wizards' guildhouse from beyond the memory of the oldest elves, was made by dwarves?"

"I think it likely that dwarves worked with the ancient architects of the Hosttower," Dor'crae replied, "who were likely not dwarves but elves, I would guess, given the history of the region, and the treelike shape of the place before its fall."

Dahlia didn't argue, though she suspected that more than a few humans would have needed to be involved to bring the elves and dwarves together.

"Roots?" Dahlia asked. "And you think these are import—" She stopped as she noticed some movement above, then screwed up her face curiously when she saw some kind of liquid sloshing through the tube above her.

"The tide," Dor'crae explained. "When it rises, some water is forced along the tunnels—the roots, the veins, whatever you wish to call them. It's not much, though, and goes back out with the tide."

Dahlia had no idea what any of this surprising information might mean. She and Dor'crae had come to Luskan to learn if the destruction of the Hosttower had anything to do with the earthquakes that had been wracking the Sword Coast North since its fall. Magical wards had burst in the fall of the tower, it was said, and somehow, given the timing of the quakes, those wards affected not only Luskan but the forested hills known as the Crags.

She turned to follow the line of the strange "root" back to the southeast.

"What else have you learned?" the warrior elf asked.

"Come, I will take you to the lich Valindra, and an older and more powerful being—or one who was more powerful, before he was driven insane in the Spellplague."

He started away, but Dahlia didn't immediately follow, silently recounting what she knew of the recent history of Luskan, something she had studied intently before leaving Thay.

"Arklem Greeth?" she asked, referring to the lich who had once commanded the Hosttower in the name of the Arcane Brotherhood, and who had been defeated in its fall. Defeated, but not likely destroyed, she knew, for that was the manner of liches, after all.

Dor'crae grinned, showing his approval.

"A formidable foe," Dahlia warned. "Even with Szass Tam's brooch protecting me."

Dor'crae shook his head. "Once, perhaps, but no more. The drow have taken care of that matter for us."

A short while and a dozen chambers and corridors later, the pair came into a strange room.

"What is this place?" Dahlia asked, for it seemed more the drawing room of a fancy inn than a subterranean chamber amidst a network of damp caves. Colorful tapestries hung around the chamber, which was set with lavishly-decorated and well-crafted furniture, including a marble-topped vanity with a large, gold-gilded mirror set atop it.

"It is my home," said a woman seated on a delicate chair in front of that vanity. When she turned in her seat and smiled at the couple, Dahlia tried hard not to wince. She might have been beautiful, with long, lustrous black hair and delicate features, though what color her eyes might once have been was long lost to the red dots of a lich's unnatural inner fires. Her smile was a ghastly thing, for her gums had rotted back, making her teeth seem far too large, and her pallid skin seemed almost to crack as she smiled.

"Do you not like it?" she asked sweetly—too sweetly, as if she was a young girl at play, perhaps.

"Oh, we do, Valindra! Oh, we do!" Dor'crae said with exaggerated enthusiasm before Dahlia could even begin to reply. The warrior looked to her vampire companion then back at the lich.

"You are Valindra Shadowmantle?" she asked.

"Why, yes, I am," Valindra replied.

"I have heard stories of your greatness," Dahlia lied, and Dor'crae squeezed her hand in approval. "But even those flattering tales greatly understated your beauty."

With that, Dahlia bowed low, while Valindra tittered and laughed.

"Where is your husband, good lady?" Dor'crae asked, and when Valindra spun as if looking for someone, Dor'crae nodded his chin up toward a shelf on a glass-fronted hutch, where sat a most curious, skull-shaped gem the size of Valindra's fist.

As they all considered that phylactery, the eyes of the skull flared red, brightly for a moment before going soft once more.

"Greeth is in there?" Dahlia quietly asked her companion.

"What's left of him," the vampire replied. He directed Dahlia's gaze the other way, to a second skull-shaped gem, which showed no life within its smoky white crystal.

"Valindra's phylactery," Dor'crae explained.

Dahlia felt at the brooch on her vest as she considered the gems. She dared walk over to the hutch, and noting that Valindra still smiled stupidly, she dared to open the door. Dahlia glanced back at Dor'crae, who held up his hands, having no answer.

"A most beautiful gemstone," Dahlia said to Valindra.

"It's my husband's," the lich replied.

"May I hold it?"

"Oh, please do!" said Valindra.

Dahlia wasn't sure if that sweetness was from her apparent simple-mindedness, or if it was an enthusiastic prodding for more nefarious reasons. Holding the phylactery of a disembodied lich, after all, was reputedly the easiest way to get oneself possessed.

But Dahlia wore Szass Tam's brooch, which offered great protection from such necromancy, and so she took the gemstone in her hand.

Almost immediately, she felt the rush of confusion, anger, and terror contained within that gemstone. She knew it was Arklem Greeth, and would have even if Dor'crae hadn't told her so, for the lich screamed at her to release him, and to kill someone named Robillard.

She saw flashes of the glory that had been Hosttower of the Arcane, for Arklem Greeth had been its final master. So many images assaulted her, so many discordant thoughts flickered in her consciousness. She felt herself being drawn into the inviting depths of the gemstone.

She began to wonder where Dahlia ended and Arklem Greeth began.

In a flicker of recognition, Dahlia dropped the skull gem back onto the shelf and quickly stepped back, gasping for breath and trying hard to hold her composure.

"Your husband has a magnificent gemstone, Valindra," she said.

"Oh, but he does, and mine is no less wondrous," the lich answered, and her voice sounded different then, husky, threatening, sober.

Dahlia turned on her.

"Why are you here?" Valindra asked. "Did Kimmuriel send you?"

"Kimmuriel?" Dahlia asked, looking more at Dor'crae than the lich.

"One of the leaders of the dark elves in Luskan," the vampire explained.

"Where is he?" Dahlia asked.

"He went home," Valindra unexpectedly answered, her voice full of regret. "Far, far away. I miss him. He helps me."

The warrior and the vampire exchanged curious glances.

"He helps me remember," Valindra went on. "He helps my husband."

"Did he give you the gemstones?" Dahlia asked.

"No, that was Jarlaxle," Valindra answered, "and the stupid dwarf."

Dahlia looked to Dor'crae, who shook his head, then back at Valindra.

"Bwahaha!" Valindra erupted, ending with a sour expression and an even more sour sigh. "Stupid dwarf."

"So, Jarlaxle is a dwarf?"

"No!" said Valindra, seeming quite amused by that notion. "He is drow. Handsome and clever."

"And he is in Luskan?"

"Sometimes."

"Now?"

"I . . . I . . ." The lich's eyes darted around, seeming at a loss.

Dahlia looked to Dor'crae, who had no answers. "What do you know of the Hosttower?" she asked the lich.

"I lived there once, for a long time."

"Yes, then it was destroyed. . . ."

The lich turned away, throwing her arm up across her eyes. "It fell! Oh, it fell!"

"And its magic was broken?" Dahlia pressed, moving near to the distraught woman. She asked again, and when Valindra looked at her blankly, she rephrased the question several different ways.

But it was soon obvious that the lich had no idea what she might be talking about, so Dahlia wisely shifted the conversation to other, more mundane things, then to the topic of Valindra's beauty once more, something that seemed to calm the undead woman.

After some time, she asked, "May I visit you again, Valindra?"

"I do so enjoy company," the lich replied. "But tell me before, that I might prepare . . ." She paused and looked around, and appeared increasingly distressed.

"I . . . where is my food?" Valindra asked, and she looked at Dahlia curiously. Then she threw her hands up over her face and fell back with a great wail.

Dahlia moved toward her, but the lich thrust one hand forward to keep the elf warrior away. "My food!" she said, then she began to laugh.

"I will bring you some food," Dahlia promised, and Valindra laughed all the louder.

"I need no such sustenance," the lich replied. "Not for so many years now. Not since the Hosttower fell." She looked at Dahlia with a sad grin. "Not since I died."

She seemed to calm then and Dahlia retreated to stand by Dor'crae.

"I forget sometimes," Valindra explained, her voice sober once more. "It is so lonely." She cast her longing gaze at the skull gem phylactery of her husband.

"Then you would welcome us back?" Dahlia asked.

Valindra nodded.

Dahlia motioned for Dor'crae to follow and started out of the room.

"But no food," Valindra called after her.

"There are still answers to be found down here," Dor'crae said when they were away. "In the roots of the Hosttower, if not in Valindra's home."

"There are answers to be found in there, as well."

"I doubt she knows much of the Hosttower's origins, or wards."

"But Arklem Greeth may well know," Dahlia assured him. "I would speak with him again."

"You spoke with him? When you held the gem? It is not wise—"

"Short conversations," Dahlia promised with a grin. "It's near dawn now. I'm going back to the city—I have an audience with Borlann the Crow, one of the High Captains. Perhaps he will tell me more of these drow, this Kimmuriel and Jarlaxle."

"And I?"

"Follow the inland root of the Hosttower," Dahlia ordered. "I would know where it goes."

Dor'crae nodded.

"I will return to Valindra tomorrow night, and every night thereafter. Join us as soon as you can."

"Should I escort you up?" asked the vampire.

Dahlia just looked at him.

"Ghouls, ghasts, and other beasts . . ." Dor'crae started to explain.

He stopped when Dahlia stared at him as though he'd lost his mind at long last, and she took up her fighting staff.

Before the next dawn, Dahlia hung by one arm from the bottom lip of the uppermost well, peering into the chamber below. She slowly turned, scanning the room for the undead she knew were there, but knew she wouldn't see.

They could see her, hanging up high, her walking stick sparking with blue light, but it didn't matter. Even if she'd come down in complete darkness and as silent as a shadow, they would know. They would smell her. The aroma of her sweet, living flesh would almost overwhelm them.

Dahlia dropped to the floor below, springing open her staff as she descended. She landed in a crouch and hopped in circles.

There were too many.

Out they came in a swarm, from every exit and every shadow: ravenous ghouls, hunched low, running on all fours, their long nails scratching against the stone. They appeared as emaciated human corpses, gray skin stretched over skull and bones, but there was more to them than that: claws and teeth and a hatred for all things living, and a hunger for all flesh, alive or dead. There was a score of them at least, and Dahlia had nowhere to run to gain a more defensible position.

But neither did they.

She sprang straight up, inverting with her hands set firmly at the top of her planted staff. She straightened upside down, thrusting her legs back inside the well. She snapped her legs out wide to the sides, locking them against the sides of the well, and bent up, hand-walking her staff before her until she turned upright back in the well, with the swarm of ghouls below her.

"Enjoy this," she whispered to the ghouls and she tugged a ruby gemstone free from her necklace and dropped it. It exploded the moment it hit the floor, flames rolling out in every direction, nearly reaching back up into the well with Dahlia.

With her legs still locking her firmly in place, the warrior clapped her hands over her ears to diminish the awful keening below.

The fireball lasted only a heartbeat, a single, devastating gout of flames, but the sting remained, fires clinging to the ghouls' skin, eating hungrily. They shrieked and screamed in high-pitched, other-worldly voices, hellish calls befitting the Abyss itself. They ran about madly, arms flailing to chase the biting flames away, claws slashing to keep their insane companions at bay, for indeed some jumped upon others and began chewing and tearing at undead flesh, at any flesh, at anything that might make the pain stop.

In the midst of that insanity, Dahlia dropped back to the floor, releasing two-foot lengths at the ends of her four-foot center pole. She had those outer poles spinning even as she landed, and she came right out of her crouch and pivoted left, launching a strike that caved in the skull of the nearest undead beast.

They were too agonized, too agitated and insane, to coordinate their movements against her, and Dahlia waded through them. Every reaching arm shattered under the weight of her spinning staff. Any ghoul's face that got too near to her felt the butt end of Kozah's Needle's center pole.

She sprinted clear, down a tunnel, and when she heard pursuit, she broke the center pole apart and set her two weapons into coordinated motion, building momentum.

The ghouls neared—a pair of them, she believed.

Dahlia rounded a corner, her free poles spinning furiously at her sides, back to front. Then on one turn, she flipped her wrists under, bringing that spin even tighter so that the poles came up into her armpits, where she locked them tight. And she never eased the pull from those front poles in her hands right before her, up and angled away, straining to pull their ends free. Dahlia growled and tightened every muscle in her body, it seemed, straining greatly to hold the back poles in place while at the same time straining to yank them free.

She leaped out at the last moment to face the pursuing ghouls, and at that instant lifted her elbows. The poles shot forward with tremendous force, each flying like a spear into the ugly face of a surprised ghoul. The sickening splat of their butt ends cracking through skulls, one sounding wetter as it drove right through a ghoul's eye, came as sweet music to the elf.

Everything seemed to freeze in place at that moment, Dahlia and the ghouls holding that macabre pose for what seemed like many heartbeats. The elf woman exploded into action again, tugging the ends free of the ghouls' already rotten brains. They snapped straight back behind her own head where she shifted her hands ever so slightly to use that momentum to put them into reverse spins at her sides, then overhead with her right hand and down and across to smash the side of the skull of the ghoul on her left. At the same time, her left hand went up over her head and followed the same path as the first, only left to right, and that other ghoul's head snapped to the side as it flew against the wall and crumbled into a dead heap.

Dahlia casually set the poles into motion again and stared back the way she'd come, though even with her keen elf vision, she couldn't see much.

But there was no pursuit. She reformed her staff and buckled it once more into a single walking stick, then tapped it on the stone to bring forth the flickering blue light.

"Ah, Valindra Shadowmantle," she whispered as she started away, "I do hope you're worth all this trouble."

Dor'crae was a vampire, and a vampire couldn't sweat, of course, but still he felt the moisture all over his body, his clothes clinging uncomfortably to him. Normally, Dor'crae wouldn't have needed a light to navigate subterranean chambers, but his complete inability to see anything piqued his curiosity.

He brought forth a candle and some flint and steel, and when the wick finally caught, the vampire peered around even more curiously. He was in a wide, high chamber, as he had suspected, but he still couldn't see very much at all, just an opaque wall of steam brightened by his pitiful candle.

"What is this place?" he whispered to himself.

He had passed into a chamber full of steam that smelled like piles of rotten eggs, and that hissed as if he'd entered a pit of vipers. He'd traveled many miles from Luskan after several days following the inland "root" of the fallen Hosttower. The tunnels were of dwarven craftsmanship, surely, though it was obvious to Dor'crae that no dwarves had been there in a long, long time.

He kept the candle burning, though it was all but useless, and slowly navigated the chamber. He moved toward one hissing sound, and found it to be a vent in the floor, a crack in the stone through which poured more hot steam, and the awful smell only worsened.

He found no other easy exit from the chamber, but his eyes widened with surprise when he noted that the root of the Hosttower did not continue through it but snaked down one wall and disappeared through the floor. The vampire smiled, thinking his journey at its end. He blew out the candle and became as insubstantial as the steam around him. The vampire flowed through a crack in the floor, descending beside the root.

Several days later, somewhat shaken but thoroughly intrigued, Dor'crae arrived once more in the chambers of Valindra Shadowmantle.

The queen of Luskan's underworld had many candles burning, and seemed more animated than usual, more lucid. She greeted Dor'crae pleasantly, even expressing her regret at not having seen him for a tenday.

"I followed the root of the Hosttower," he explained. "You remember the Hosttower . . . ?"

"Of course."

"Do you know the place, the grand hall where it disappears under the ground?"

"She has no answers for you," came another voice.

Dahlia stepped into sight from around one of the many decorative screens set about the chamber. She gave a little grin and nodded toward the skull gem on the shelf, the one inhabited by the spirit of Arklem Greeth. "But he does."

"You've been . . . ?"

"Tell me of this 'grand hall'."

"It's a most remarkable place, as big as some cities in the Under—"

"Gauntlgrym," Dahlia interrupted, and Dor'crae looked at her, obviously not understanding.

"The ancient homeland of the Delzoun dwarves," Dahlia explained. "Long lost—some consider it a myth."

"It is real," said Dor'crae.

"You explored it?"

"I was turned away before I could get too far."

Dahlia looked at him with one eyebrow raised.

"Ghosts," the vampire explained. "Dwarf ghosts, and darker things. I thought it prudent to return to you with what I had unearthed. What did you call it? Gauntlgrym? How can you know?"

"Greeth told me. The Hosttower was tied to that most ancient of dwarven cities, and was built by dwarves, elves, and humans in a long-ago age, and for the benefit of all, though few dwarves ever lived in the Hosttower itself."

"But its power benefitted this city, this 'Gauntlgrym'?"

Dahlia crossed the room, shrugging as she went. "I would expect as much. Arklem Greeth knows little more, or at least I could discern little more, though I will try again soon enough. He is old—not that old, of course, but he seems confident of the work, masonry and magical, that built the Hosttower of the Arcane, and that it was indeed somehow tied to . . ." Her words trailed off as she noticed the puzzled look upon Dor'crae's face.

"You wear two diamonds again in your right ear," the vampire explained. "Eight in your left, and two, again, in your right."

"Surely you cannot be jealous," Dahlia replied.

"Borlann the Crow needed incentive, I expect?"

Dahlia merely smiled.

"Jealous?" Dor'crae replied then, with a laugh. " 'Relieved' would be a better word. Better another in your right ear than you come to believe your left might look better with nine."

Dahlia stared at him for a very long time, and the vampire feared that perhaps he hadn't been wise to tip her off to the fact that he understood the significance of her jewelry.

"We know where to look now," Dahlia said after a very long and uncomfortable silence. "I will continue my work with Arklem Greeth, gaining whatever insight he has to offer, and you must gather as much information as can be found about Gauntlgrym, or of how we might navigate its wards, like these ghosts you speak of."

"It's a dangerous road," the vampire replied. "Were I trapped in this physical body, I would have had to fight my way in, and fight my way out, against formidable foes."

"Then we will find even more formidable allies," Dahlia promised.

CHAPTER 5

A DROW AND HIS DWARF

WERE IT NOT FOR THE MORNINGSTARS SET DIAGONALLY across his back, their glassteel heads bobbing with every stride, Athrogate might have struck passersby as a diplomat rather than a warrior. His thick black hair was well kept, and his long beard was neatly tied into three thick braids set with shining onyx gems. He wore another onyx—a magical one—set into a circlet on his head, and his broad belt, dyed black, imbued him with great strength. Black boots showed the scuffs of a thousand mountains and a thousand trails. The rest of his clothing was of the finest cut and style: breeches of deep gray velvet, a shirt the color of the darkest of amethysts, and a black leather vest that served as a harness for the mighty weapons strapped to his back.

He was a common sight in Luskan, and his shadowy relationship with the dark elves was the worst kept secret in the City of Sails. But Athrogate walked the streets openly and often, in appearance, at least, alone. It was almost as if he was inviting some opportunist to take a try at killing him. And the dwarf liked nothing more than a good row, though that pleasure had been hard to find of late. His partner frowned upon it.

He walked to the corner of a building across the street from his favorite pub, Bite o' the Shark—an apt name for anyone who had ever sampled the establishment's private stock of Gutbuster. At the corner of an alley, Athrogate put his back against the wall and took out a huge and curvy pipe and began tapping down his pipeweed.

He was well into his smoke, blowing rings that drifted lazily over the street, when a striking elf woman exited Bite o' the Shark and paused near a gathering of drunks, who began throwing suggestive, lewd comments her way.

"Ye see her, then?" the dwarf said out of the corner of his mouth, pipe still firmly in place.

"Hard to miss that one," a voice answered from the shadows beside him. With the suggestive cut of her skirt, the high black boots on her shapely legs, the low cut of her blouse and a striking black and red braid, his words seemed a great understatement.

"Aye, and I'm bettin', sure as the sun's settin', that one o' them fools'll go for her jewels. And oh, then they'll know in the heartbeats to come, that her sticks'll play skulls with the sound of a drum."

The voice in the shadows sighed.

"Never gets old, does it?" Athrogate asked, quite pleased with himself.

"Never was young, dwarf," came the reply, and Athrogate bellowed, "Bwahaha!"

"Someday, perhaps, I'll come to understand how your thoughts flow, and on that day, I fear, I'll have to kill myself."

"What's to know?" Athrogate asked. "One o' them'll go too far with her, and she'll put the lot of 'em on the ground." As he posited that very thing, one of the drunks stepped toward the elf and reached for her buttocks. She neatly dodged and smiled at him, wagging her finger and warding him away.

But he came on.

"Here it comes," Athrogate predicted.

The man seemed to fall over her in a hug, from the vantage point of the dwarf and his companion, at least, but when the dwarf started congratulating himself on being right, the voice in the shadows pointed out that the drunk was up on his tiptoes. He started to turn slowly, the woman coming around to put her back to the open street. The elf had spun her walking stick and poked it up as he came at her, locking its tip under his chin and driving him up to his toes.

She was still smiling sweetly and whispering to the man in tones so low his companions apparently couldn't hear, and she had angled the ruffian so they couldn't see her walking stick, either. She released him and stepped away, and the man staggered and nearly tumbled then reached up and grabbed his chin, coughing to accompany his friends' laughter.

"Bah, thought she'd deck 'em all," Athrogate grumbled.

"She's too smart for that," said the voice in the darkness, "though if they pursue her now, she'd be more than justified in putting that weapon of hers to good use."

There was no pursuit, however, and the elf made her way up the road, toward Athrogate.

"She's seen you," the voice commented.

The dwarf blew another smoke ring, and walked across the alley and continued on his way, his work done.

The elf moved up to where the dwarf had been standing, and with a quick and subtle glance both ways, slipped into the alley.

"Jarlaxle, I presume," she said when she saw the drow standing before her, with his great, wide-brimmed, feathered hat and purple jodhpurs, his flamboyant white shirt opened low on his black-skinned chest, and his assortment of rings and other glittering accessories.

"I like your hat, Lady Dahlia," Jarlaxle replied with a bow.

"Not as ostentatious as your own, perhaps," Dahlia replied. "But it gets the attention of those I wish attentive."

"Osten—" Jarlaxle stammered as if wounded. "Perhaps I use mine to *distract* the attention of those I wish to *harm.*"

"I have other ways of doing that," Dahlia was quick to answer, and Jarlaxle found himself smiling.

"That is quite an unusual companion you keep," Dahlia went on. "A drow and a dwarf, side by side."

"We are anything but common," Jarlaxle assured her. He grinned again, thinking of another pair he knew, drow and dwarf, who had forged an amazing friendship over many decades. "But yes, Athrogate is an unusual creature, to be sure. Perhaps that is why I find him interesting, even endearing."

"His words do not match the cut of his clothing."

"If one can call *'bwahaha'* words," Jarlaxle replied. "Trust me when I tell you that I have civilized him beyond my wildest expectations. Less spit and more polish."

"But have you tamed him?"

"Impossible," Jarlaxle assured her. "That one could fight a titan."

"We'll need that."

"So Athrogate has told me, as he told me that you've found a place of great dwarven treasures, an ancient homeland."

"You sound skeptical."

"Why would you come to me? Why would an elf seek the alliance of a drow?"

"Because I need allies in this endeavor. It's a dangerous road, and underground at that. As I've considered the powers that be in Luskan, it seems that the dark elves are more reliable than the High Captains, or the pirates, and that leaves me with . . . you."

Jarlaxle's expression remained unconvinced.

"Because the place is thick with dwarf ghosts," Dahlia admitted.

"Ah," said the drow. "You need a dwarf most of all. One who can speak to his ancestors and keep the hordes at bay."

The elf shrugged, not denying it.

"I'm offering you fifty percent of the take," she said, "and I expect that take to be considerable."

"Which fifty?"

It was Dahlia's turn to wear a puzzled expression.

"You take the mithral and I get a mound of copper coins?" Jarlaxle explained. "I'll take fifty, but my preferred fifty."

"One to one," Dahlia argued, meaning alternating picks on the booty.

"And I pick first."

"And I, second and third."

"Second and fourth."

"Second and third!" Dahlia demanded.

"Have a fine journey," Jarlaxle replied, and he tipped his hat and started away.

"Second and fourth, then," the elf agreed before he'd gone three steps.

"Yes, I need you," she admitted as the drow turned back to regard her. "I've spent months uncovering this place, and tendays more narrowing down my first choice as guide."

"First choice?" Jarlaxle said.

"First choice," Dahlia replied, and again the drow wore that doubting expression.

"Not Borlann the Crow?" Jarlaxle asked with a derisive snort. "Do you truly believe that one as striking as you can move about the city unseen?"

"Borlann served in the search, but was never the goal of it," Dahlia replied. "I'd sooner take the drunks down the street with me." She returned the drow's sly grin. "He doesn't think much of you, by the way, or of your many black-skinned comrades. He takes great pride in having driven you from the City of Sails."

"Is that what you believe?"

The elf didn't answer.

"That I am driven from the very city I now stand within?" Jarlaxle elaborated. "Or that my . . . associates would fear the wrath of Borlann the Crow, or any of the High Captains—or *all* of the High Captains should they band together against us? Which they would never do, of course. It would not take much of a bribe to turn two of them against the other three, or three of them against the other two, or four of them against Borlann, if that was the course we wished. Do you, who claim to have learned the secrets of power in Luskan, doubt that?"

Dahlia considered his claims for a moment then replied, "And yet, by all accounts, drow are more scarce in the city of late."

"Because we've used it up. We've long ago emptied Luskan of all the treasures that interested us. We remain in the shadows, for the city remains a marginally useful source of information. Some ships still dock here, and from every port on the Sword Coast."

"And so Borlann the Crow and the other High Captains are the true power after all."

"If it serves us for them to believe so, then let it be so."

That reply had Dahlia shifting uncomfortably for the first time, Jarlaxle noted, though she did well to hide it. He would have to play his hand carefully with her. She had ulterior motives, and he didn't want to scare her off by making her fear that she would be getting herself in too far over her head with him. Still, the elf intrigued him, and the mere fact that she had so beautifully and thoughtfully engaged Athrogate to get to him showed him that she was not ill-prepared—in anything she did, he presumed.

"My associates' interests in Luskan are minor in these times," Jarlaxle clarified. "Their network is vast, and this but a minor endeavor."

"Their network?"

"Our network, when it serves me," Jarlaxle replied.

"And my proposition?"

The drow pulled off his great hat and swept a low bow before her. "Jarlaxle, at your service, dear lady," he said.

"Jarlaxle and Athrogate," Dahlia corrected. "I need him more than I need you."

Jarlaxle straightened and met her stern gaze with a wicked little grin. "I doubt that."

"Don't," she said, and she walked out of the alley.

Carefully scrutinizing her every alluring movement as she walked away, Jarlaxle's grin only widened.

"The power in the west mounts," Sylora said to Szass Tam. "The tremors grow stronger. There is great danger and great potential to be found there."

"You have spoken with our agent?"

Sylora propped the mirror she carried up before her and closed her eyes, bringing forth its scrying magic once more. The shiny glass dulled, as if with a mist within and only a small circle in the middle of the looking glass cleared. It no longer showed the reflection of the Dread Ring, but a clear image of a single object, a skull-shaped crystal.

"There is much more to the skull gem than to serve as a phylactery for a lich," Sylora explained. "It serves me as conduit to our agent, and when the time comes, as a guide on my journey."

"You wish to leave at once."

"It would have been better had I gone instead of Dahlia," the Thayan sorceress replied.

"You question me?"

"Neverwinter is thick with Netherese."

"A cult of the upstart Asmodeus is there, at my bidding, to . . . trouble them."

"But not to defeat them. There is a Dread Ring to be created, to be forged from the secrets that Dahlia seeks to uncover, a power of uncontrollable catastrophe, and exquisite beauty."

"More credit to Dahlia, then," Szass Tam reminded. "It was she who identified the signs of approaching peril, and sought to exploit them."

"They are beyond her," Sylora insisted. She could hardly see Szass Tam through the haze of ash in the Dread Ring—and that was a good thing, given the archlich's horrid features—but it seemed to her as though his posture showed indifference to her excitement.

"Dahlia is not alone," Szass Tam assured her. "She thinks she is, and that is to our benefit. It is my hope that she will need us not at all to accomplish what she has set out to do. But you will watch her, and you will know, and we will . . . support her as we deem necessary."

"Am I to travel to Neverwinter Wood, as we discussed?" Sylora asked, not willing to push any further. She knew when Szass Tam had heard enough, and knew, too, that arguing with him was a sure way to be invited into his dark realm—as a slave.

"Not yet," Szass Tam instructed. "The cult—the Ashmadai—will keep our Netherese friends occupied. The greater prize will come from Dahlia's work, so I would have you learn as much as you can, both through your work here in our libraries and through your regular contact with our agent. This is of utmost importance. Should we succeed, we will have another Dread Ring, and better, it will come in no small part through the suffering of those ancient relics, the Netherese."

"This is my charge?"

"It is."

"And my credit?" the wizard pressed.

"In your rivalry with Dahlia?" Szass Tam responded with a sly cackle, one that ended abruptly as he continued, his tone much more severe. "Dahlia suspected the link between the rising catastrophe and the fall of the Hosttower of the Arcane, not you. She has performed wonderfully, though it pains you to admit that. My suggestion to you is that you perform equally as wonderfully, for our greater purpose and for your own well-being. I have granted you this opening for redemption and excellence because of your history with Dahlia—if anyone in Faerûn will watch over that one's every movement, it is you.

"But you serve me, Sylora," Szass Tam reminded. "You serve my ends and not your own, or your own will come quickly, I assure you. My desire is that Dahlia succeeds, and you will work toward that end. Our enemies are the Shadovar."

His tone left no room for debate.

"Yes, Your Omnipotence," Sylora replied, dipping her head in a scant bow.

Sylora's only comfort then was her deep-rooted belief that Dahlia was far too young and inexperienced, and far too dedicated, to succeed in the facilitation of the needed catastrophe. The wizard horded the very real possibility, indeed the probability, that she would have to rescue Szass Tam's victory in the west. Then, she hoped, the archlich would come to see the true limitations of that wretched elf.

"Borboy, really?" Athrogate asked with a snicker for the tenth time since he and Jarlaxle had watched Dahlia enter High Captain Borlann's keep. The slim stone tower, known as Crow's Nest, had been only recently erected on Luskan's Closeguard Island where the River Mirar spilled out into the Trackless Sea.

Jarlaxle continued his amusement at the dwarf's use of the derogatory nickname so many in Luskan had tagged on High Captain Borlann. He possessed his father's title, and the magical

Cloak of the Raven, handed down to him from his grandfather Kensidan. But there, at least according to the old seadogs haunting Luskan's allies, the resemblance ended.

"Skinny little runt," Athrogate remarked.

"As was Kensidan," Jarlaxle replied. "But possessed of a presence that could fill a room."

"Yeah, I'm remembering that one. Tough old bird. Bwahaha! *Bird,* eh?"

"I understood you."

"Then why ain't ye laughing?"

"Figure it out."

The dwarf shook his head and muttered something about finding a companion with a sense of humor.

"Ye think she's layin' down for him?" Athrogate asked after a while.

"Dahlia uses every weapon to her advantage, of that I am certain."

"But for that one? Borboy?"

"Surely you're not jealous over an elf," Jarlaxle remarked with eyebrows raised.

"Bah!" the dwarf snorted. "Ain't nothing like that, ye fool." He paused and put his hands on his hips as he looked at a candlelit window high up the moss-covered walls of Crow's Nest. Athrogate gave a little sigh. "Though I'd have to be a dead dwarf not to see the fight'n'fun in that one."

Jarlaxle gave a wry little grin but let it go at that. Like the dwarf, he stood staring at the keep. Nothing seemed amiss for a long while, but then from the window came a shriek that sounded like the excited screech of a giant crow. Both dwarf and drow came forward a step, peering more intently at that lone window—and the candlelight was snuffed all at once. Men began rushing around the compound, and another pair of shrieks sounded along with a blue-white flicker from behind the window, like the sudden flash of a lightning bolt.

Then came a still louder screech, a brighter flash, and a report of thunder that shook the ground beneath their feet. The window exploded outward, glass shattering and flying, and along with it . . . black feathers.

Athrogate emitted a strange, gulping sound then blew it out with a "Bwahaha!" Across the way, a giant black bird dived out the window, opened wide its wings, and floated across the compound, over the water, and dived to the ground right in front of Jarlaxle and Athrogate.

Before either dwarf or drow could say a word, the crow disguise flipped back into a fine, glossy cloak, to reveal its new owner.

"Let us be quick," Dahlia said to the pair, walking past and fiddling with one of the two earrings in her right ear as she did. "Borlann was a minor nuisance, but the murderous arms of his House are long."

"Be quick for . . . where?" Athrogate asked, but Dahlia didn't slow.

"Illusk," Jarlaxle answered before she could, and with one glance back at the compound, the drow started away, sweeping the dwarf along beside him. "And the undercity."

The stunned Athrogate mumbled and muttered, chortled and giggled, before finally remarking, "Bet Borboy wishes ye'd left last night!"

Korvin Dor'crae paced about Valindra Shadowmantle's decorated chamber. He stopped and stared into a large mirror and imagined the reflection he once saw in such a glass, trying to use those memories of his past life as a distraction.

It didn't work.

He thought of Dahlia again soon enough, waiting for her to return with Jarlaxle and the dwarf. She had gone to see Borlann the Crow—her newest diamond, her newest lover. Surely Dor'crae wasn't jealous of that. He cared not at all for such petty issues as sex, but there remained implications for him in the elf's promiscuity.

The vampire ran his hand through his black hair, and could clearly picture the movement in the mirror, though of course the glass showed no image. Borlann was Dahlia's tenth lover—ten he knew about, anyway—and all ten were accounted for, two on her right ear, Borlann and Dor'crae, and eight on her left. Among the Thayans, Dahlia had been given many nicknames, most alluding to a certain species of spider known for mating then eating the males, though not all of those diamonds on Dahlia's left ear represented males.

Dahlia didn't murder her lovers, however. No, she challenged them to a fair fight then utterly destroyed them. When Dor'crae had entered his tryst with the elf, he'd known that, and was confident in his power to defeat her, should it come to that. In fact, he'd entertained the notion of not only defeating her, but had fantasized about converting her into a servile vampire.

But he had come to know better. Dor'crae had mentally played a fight with Dahlia in his mind a thousand times. He had seen her training with Kozah's Needle, and had witnessed two of the fights with her former lovers. And more than that, he had come to appreciate the elf warrior's cunning.

He couldn't beat her, and he knew it. When Dahlia had had her fill of him, when she decided to move along, for expediency, to make a point to Szass Tam, or for simple boredom or whim, he would face oblivion.

"Your friend is here again," Valindra said, drawing Dor'crae from his thoughts.

He turned and looked at the doorway, expecting the lich referred to Dahlia. But seeing nothing there, he glanced back at Valindra, who redirected his attention to the empty skull gem, her own phylactery, which had come to serve Dor'crae in an entirely different manner.

The eyes of the gem flared red.

Nervous, Dor'crae glanced back at the door, and if he had any breath, he would have held it.

"She comes," he whispered to the spirit in the skull gem, "with our allies for the journey to the source of power."

The skull gem's eyes flared. "Szass Tam watches," a woman's voice replied, and it sounded tinny and thin through the magical conduit. "He would not have this opportunity pass us by."

"I understand," Dor'crae assured her.

"He will blame one, I will blame the other," the voice of Sylora assured him.

"I understand," Dor'crae dutifully replied, and the flaming eyes went quiet.

Dahlia entered the chamber, and as soon as Dor'crae saw her, he noted the new ratio of her earrings, nine to one.

Valindra, too, noted the entrance of Dahlia, but more because of the drow and dwarf that followed not far behind her. The lich gave a little hiss as Athrogate showed himself, but managed enough of her composure to wish Jarlaxle well.

"It has been too long, Jarlaxle," she said. "I am lonely."

"Too long indeed, dear lady, but my business has kept me away from your fair city."

"Always it is business."

"Just lie down and die, ye rotten thing," Athrogate muttered, the dwarf obviously having little regard for Valindra.

"Is this a problem?" Dahlia asked Jarlaxle. "You knew that Valindra would be accompanying us."

"My little friend has a particular distaste for the walking dead," Jarlaxle replied.

"It ain't right," muttered the dwarf.

Jarlaxle looked to Dor'crae and asked Dahlia, "This is your associate?"

"Korvin Dor'crae," she replied.

Jarlaxle studied the vampire for just a moment before grinning in understanding. "And this is my associate, Athrogate," he said to Dor'crae. "I expect you two will get along wonderfully."

"Yeah, well met and all," Athrogate added with a slight nod, though he glanced again Valindra's way, his expression sour, revealing that he was, in all likelihood, oblivious to Dor'crae's true nature.

"Let us be on our way," Dahlia instructed. She moved to usher Valindra toward the other exit, waving for Jarlaxle and Athrogate to lead the way.

As soon as the four had moved out the door, the vampire began to follow, taking a roundabout course to pass the skull gem. He quietly dropped it into his pocket. The eyes flared as he did, showing that his unseen ally was still there, in the extra-dimensional pocket of the phylactery, and the vampire could have sworn the inanimate gem smiled at him as it disappeared into the folds of his clothing.

CHAPTER 6

ANOTHER DROW AND HIS DWARF

BRUENOR STOOD THERE, STARING AT THE WELL, A STONE TAKEN from its base in his hand.

Drizzt didn't know what to expect. Would Bruenor throw the stone in rage? Or would he insist that it didn't matter and that they press on anyway, deeper into the unstable—and not as ancient as they'd first believed—underground complex.

The dwarf heaved a sigh and tossed the stone to the ground, its lettering—a *human* alphabet—clear to see. The well bore the signature of its all-too-human builder, and the mark of his barbarian clan. Bruenor had found the well before the earthquake had driven them out, and cost them days of digging to get back to the spot.

"Well, elf," the dwarf remarked, "got us a hunnerd more maps to follow."

He turned to face Drizzt and Guenhwyvar, hands on his hips, but there was no anger and little disappointment showing on his hairy face.

"What?" Bruenor added, seeing Drizzt's obvious surprise at his measured reaction.

"You show great patience."

Bruenor hunched his shoulders and snorted. "Ye remember when we was looking for Mithral Hall? Them months on the road, through Longsaddle, the Trollmoors, Silverymoon, and all?"

"Of course."

"Ever knowing better months, elf?"

It was Drizzt's turn to smile, and he conceded his friend's point with a nod.

"Ye telled me a million times, it's the journey and not the ending," said Bruenor. "Might be that I've come to believe ye. Come on, then," the dwarf added, and he walked between the pair, throwing a suspicious glance at the ever-troublesome panther. "I got more journeyin' in me old legs yet."

They came out of the cave under a perfect blue sky, with the rolling hillocks of the Crags tightening the horizon around them. It was late summer, almost fall, and the cool winds had been fairly comfortable of late. They figured they had about three more months of easy exploring before them until they had to retreat to a town for the winter—perhaps Port Llast, but Drizzt had suggested a journey out to Longsaddle to visit the Harpells. The strange clan of wizards had been decimated by the Spellplague, but after more than six decades they were finally rebuilding their ranks, their mansion on the hill, and the town beneath it.

That was a decision for another day, though, and the trio went back to their small encampment and Bruenor opened his pack and produced a pile of scroll tubes, parchment, and a mound of skins and tablets, all maps to the many known caves in the Sword Coast North. He also produced several ancient coins minted in the days of Delzoun, a very old smith hammer's head, and some other suspicious and obviously ancient artifacts tumbled out as well. All had been procured across the North, from barbarian tribesmen or small villages, and the coins had come from Luskan. They were proof of nothing, of course. Luskan could trace her history as a trading port as far back as most dwarf scholars put the time of Gauntlgrym, and if that was the case, then one would expect a few Delzoun coins in the various coffers of the City of Sails.

To Bruenor, though, those artifacts represented confirmation, and a heartening lift to his tired old shoulders, so Drizzt didn't dissuade him from that.

Not if it would make the journey more interesting, after all.

Bruenor sorted through the scroll tubes, one after another, reading the notes he had scribbled on their sides. He selected two and tossed them aside before stuffing the rest back into his pack. A similar pile of the parchment produced yet another promising map, before the rest of those, too, went into the pack.

"Them three're closest to us," the dwarf explained.

To Drizzt's surprise and amusement, Bruenor finished filling his bag then slung it over his shoulder and started collecting the rest of his items, and breaking their camp.

"What?" the dwarf asked when Drizzt made no move to do likewise. "We got a few more good hours o' sunlight, elf. No time for wastin'!"

Laughing, Herzgo Alegni walked out from behind the tree and onto the forest path before a pair of surprised tieflings. One had horns similar to Alegni's, rounded back and down, while the other sported only a pair of nubs on her forehead. Both wore leather vests left open to reveal jagged brands, layered lines combining the symbols of their god and some other devilish patron. Alegni had come to know the symbol well in his time in Neverwinter Wood.

Both carried red scepters, fashioned with clever facets to look like crystal, though they were in fact made of solid metal. Around three feet in length, they could serve as club, short staff, or spear, with one end tapered to a nasty tip.

"Brother. . . ." the male said, startled by the sudden appearance of the larger tiefling.

"Nay—Shadovar!" the female quickly corrected, even as she leaped back into a defensive posture.

She set her weight back on her right leg, and her left arm extended, palm toward Alegni, her weapon drawn in tight against her right breast, pointing the Shadovar's way as a sword or spear might.

The male reacted in much the same way, crouching with his legs wide and his scepter up over his right shoulder, as if to swing it as a club.

Herzgo Alegni smiled at them both and didn't yet draw his magnificent sword, the red blade hanging easily along the side of his left leg.

"Ashmadai, I presume," he said, referring to the cultists of Asmodeus, a group he had never heard of until recently, when they had begun to trickle into Neverwinter Wood.

"As you should be, devil brother," said the female. Her eyes, solid silver orbs, widened with lustful excitement.

"Devil brother who has embraced the shade," the male added, "and the Sharran Empire of Netheril."

"Who sent you?" Alegni asked. "Whose hand guides this cult of misbegotten zealots?"

"One who is no friend of Netheril!" the female retorted, and she came forward suddenly, thrusting her spear at Alegni's massive chest.

But Alegni moved first, drawing his sword and lifting the blade up and left to right as it came free of its belt loop—and more, something neither of his opponents could have expected—as the blade rent the air it left an opaque trail of ash.

Through that veil prodded the female's spear, but behind the wall of ash, Alegni had already dodged off to his right, letting the momentum of the sword carry him.

As the female retracted, he said from just off the path, "Here." And just before the male leaped forward to swing his club, and both turned their horned heads to regard him, and even started to re-orient their feet, the ash wall exploded. A slender figure leaped through, flipping in mid-air as he passed between the Ashmadai couple, easily avoiding their attempts to align their weapons to the new threat. He landed behind them, though facing them, having twisted around in the air.

"Blow the horn!" the male cried, spinning to meet the challenge, but even as he spoke, the female stumbled a step or two to the side, her free hand slapping against her throat—against a puncture wound inflicted by the newcomer's dagger. Her silver eyes went wider still, in shock at his precision, perhaps, or in fear that she was mortally wounded.

"Makarielle!" her companion cried, and he leaped at the knife-wielder, leading with a great swing of his club.

The pallid human leaned away from the first cut and ducked the backhand. On the third attempt, he leaped at the weapon, accepting the shortened hit against the side of his chest as he landed. The club hooked under his armpit, and he spun out to the side with such force, confidence, and balance that he took the weapon from his opponent's hand.

The disarmed tiefling hissed and rushed to follow, more than capable of doing battle with his fists and teeth.

But even as he moved out to the side, Barrabus the Gray drove his right elbow, the arm trapping the scepter, up and out in front of him, flipping the weapon into the air. He caught it mid-shaft with his right hand then stopped and reversed, throwing his right hip back and around. Cupping the back end of the scepter with his left hand for balance and power, he thrust it out behind him.

He felt the heavy impact with his pursuer's chest and didn't continue around to his right, but rather stopped and brought the scepter back in front of him, flipping it easily and catching both hands low on one end as he turned to his left, stepping toward the retreating tiefling as he brought the club to bear.

To his credit, the tiefling managed to get his arm up to block the blow—and break his forearm in the process—but before he could even shriek out from the explosion of pain, Barrabus went back around the other way and reversed his hands as if to launch a tremendous blow, up-angled for the tiefling's head. Even as the tiefling began to react accordingly, Barrabus revealed the feint, dropping and kicking out with his foot instead. He connected solidly with the tiefling's knee, driving the leg out wide, and again his hands moved quickly along the scepter, so his right hand gripped the middle, his left low on the back end. Barrabus drove the weapon forward and upward from his crouch, and the off-balance tiefling had no defense as the tip slammed hard into his groin.

"Well done," Alegni congratulated Barrabus, walking up beside the female, who was on one knee then, both hands tight against her punctured throat, her weapon on the ground beside her. "Will she live?" he asked.

"No poison," the man confirmed. "Not a mortal wound."

"Good news!" Alegni said, stepping past her toward the stunned but stubborn male, who stood, his face locked in a tight grimace. "Well, not for you," the Shadovar corrected, and his sword came across suddenly, brutally, nearly cleaving the poor fellow in two.

"I need only one prisoner," Alegni explained to the already dead Ashmadai cultist. He stepped back and grabbed the kneeling female by her thick black hair and jerked her to her feet with such force that she came right up off the ground.

"Do you believe yourself the fortunate one?" he asked, putting his face right up to hers and staring coldly into her tear-filled eyes. "Take their weapons and anything else worth salvaging," he instructed his lackey, and he started away, yanking the female from her feet and dragging her off by the hair.

Barrabus the Gray watched him go, but mostly he was looking at the expression of sheer anguish on the female's face. He didn't mind the fighting, certainly, and had few pangs of conscience in killing the strange fanatics of a devil god. Any of them would have gladly disemboweled him in one of their sacrificial rituals, after all, as Herzgo Alegni's soldiers had discovered when three of their own had gone missing in the wood only to be found strapped and gutted on a slab of stone.

Despite that, Barrabus couldn't help but wince at the sight of the female, knowing that she would soon experience the unbridled cruelty of Herzgo Alegni.

Indomitable.

It was the word that most came to mind when Drizzt considered Bruenor Battlehammer, along with the drow's own oft-repeated, "Roll on."

Drizzt stood in the shade of a wide-spreading oak, leaning on the trunk, inadvertently spying on his friend. Below the higher patch of ground with the oak, in a small clearing, sat Bruenor, with a dozen of his maps opened and spread out on a blanket.

Bruenor had kept Drizzt going for years, and the dark elf knew it. When hope of raising Catti-brie and Regis had faded to nothing, when even the best memories of those two, and of Wulfgar—and the barbarian had to be dead, dead or a hundred and twelve years old—had faded, too, only Bruenor's insistence that the road ahead was worth walking, that there was something grand to be found, had somewhat cooled the anger simmering within the drow.

The anger, and so much more, none of it good.

He watched the dwarf for a long while, shifting from map to map, making little notations on one or another, or in the small book he kept at all times, a journal of his road to Gauntlgrym. That book symbolized Bruenor's admission that he might never get to the ancient Delzoun homeland, the dwarf had admitted to Drizzt. But if he failed, he meant to leave behind a record, so that the next dwarf taking up the quest would be well on his way before he ever took his first step.

In that action, in the admission that, for Bruenor at least, it might well be all for naught, and the determination that such a possibility, indeed even a probability, was still all right, resonated within Drizzt as a statement of cause, of continuity and of . . . decency.

It wasn't until he'd brought his clenched fist out before him that Drizzt even realized he'd broken off a piece of the tree trunk. He opened his black fingers to see the chip, and stared at it for a long while then threw it to the ground, his hands going reflexively to the hilts of his belted scimitars. Drizzt turned away from Bruenor, scanning the rolling hills and forests, looking for smoke, for some sign that others were near—likely goblins, orcs, or gnolls.

It seemed ironic to him that as the world had grown undeniably darker, his battles had come fewer, and farther between. Drizzt found that ironic—and unacceptable.

"Tonight, Guen," he whispered, though the panther was at home on the Astral Plane and he didn't take out the onyx figurine to summon her to his side. "Tonight, we hunt."

With hardly a thought, he drew out Twinkle and Icingdeath, the blades he'd carried for so many decades, and put them into an easy series of practiced movements, simulating parries, counters, and clever ripostes. His pace increased, his movements shifting from defensive and reactive routines to more aggressive, more radical attacks.

He had done those exercises for almost all of his life, learned while training with his father Zaknafein in the Underdark city of Menzoberranzan, then in the drow academy of Melee-Magthere. They had followed him along the entirety of his life's journey. The movements were a part of him, a measure of his discipline, a sharpening of his skills, an affirmation of his purpose.

So attuned was Drizzt to his practice that he hadn't even noticed the subtle internal shifts he'd undergone when executing the routines. The exercises were mostly about muscle memory and balance, of course, and in the routine, blocks and turns, stabs and spins were designed to counter the attacks of imaginary opponents.

But in the last several years, those imagined opponents had become far more vivid to Drizzt. He didn't even remember that when he'd first begun those routines, and for all his life to the time of the Spellplague, he'd visualized his opponents only as weapons. He would turn and lift Twinkle vertically to block an imagined sword, and whip Icingdeath across down low the other way to deflect a thrusting spear.

Since that dark time, though, and particularly since he, Bruenor, Jessa, Pwent, and Nanfoodle had taken to the road, his imagined opponents became much more than simple weapons. Drizzt saw the face of an orc or the grin of an ogre, or the eyes of a human, drow, elf, dwarf, or halfling—it didn't matter! As long as some bandit was there, or some monster, ready to scream in pain as Twinkle drove hard for its heart, or gurgle in its own blood as Icingdeath swept across its throat. . . .

Furiously, the drow attacked his demons. He sprinted ahead and leaped, spinning over and coming back to his feet in such a tilt as to propel him farther ahead with sudden fury, legs speeded by magical anklets, scimitars reaching ahead to skewer. Another dart, another leaping somersault, landing unbalanced to the right then throwing himself that way with a devastating spin, a whirlwind of slashing blades.

Ahead again, up and over, and out to the left, whirling fury, abruptly halted in a sudden and brutal reverse-grip, behind-the-back stab.

Drizzt could feel the added weight on his blade as it impaled a pursuing orc. He could imagine the warmth of blood spilling down on his hand.

So deeply was he into the moment, the fantasy, that he actually turned, thinking to wipe the blood from Icingdeath on the fallen opponent's jerkin.

He stared at Icingdeath, clean and shining, and noted the sweat glistening on his forearm. He looked back toward the oak, scores and scores of running strides away.

Somewhere deep inside, Drizzt Do'Urden knew he used the daily regimen—and actual battles when he could find them—to deny the truth of his loss and pain. He hid in his fighting, and forgot the pain only in those moments of brutal battle, real or imagined. But he did well to keep it inside, to keep it hidden from his conscious thoughts, to bury it under the other truth, after all, that he needed to practice.

And he did well to pretend that all of the many fights he had found on the road those last decades had been unavoidable, after all.

***

"Two Ashmadai tieflings taken in a matter of a few heart-beats," Herzgo Alegni congratulated Barrabus that night on the outskirts of Neverwinter, at the edge of the forest with the city in clear sight.

"They were surprised, and focused on you," Barrabus replied. "They had no idea I was there."

"Can you not simply accept the compliment?" Herzgo scolded with a little laugh.

From you? Barrabus thought but didn't say, particularly in the dismissive and sarcastic manner in which it no doubt would have come forth. Still, his sour expression spoke volumes.

"Oh, be not so surprised," Alegni scolded. "If I saw no value in your skills, do you think I would keep you alive?"

Barrabus didn't bother to answer, other than to smirk and glance at Alegni's hip and the red-bladed sword.

"Of course, you believe I would do so simply to torment you," Alegni reasoned. "No, my small friend. While I'll not deny that I do take great pleasure in your frustration, it alone would not be worth the trouble. You're alive because you are of value. The Herzgo Alegni Bridge in Neverwinter is a testament to that, as is your work here in the forest—a complete and competent minion. And such competence is hard to find these dark days, and harder to control when it is found." He smiled as he said that and gripped the sword hilt as he added, "Though, fortunately, such is not the case with you."

"It pleasures me greatly to be of such use," Barrabus said with unrelenting sarcasm.

"Indeed, you serve as diplomat with Hugo Babris, as warrior against the Ashmadai, as assassin against the agents of our enemies, and as spy when called upon."

Barrabus put his hands on his hips and waited, knowing then that some new mission was about to be presented.

"The arrival of these Ashmadai fanatics is not coincidence, I am sure," Alegni said on cue. "There is word of Thayan agents in the North, likely in Luskan."

Barrabus winced at the mention of the City of Sails, having no desire to go anywhere near it.

"I wish to know who they are, why they've come, and what further trouble they will attempt against our work here," Alegni finished.

"Luskan . . ." the assassin said, as if repeating the name might remind Alegni that sending Barrabus the Gray to Luskan might not be such a good idea.

"You are a master of stealth, are you not?"

"And Luskan is thick with those who mock the supposed stealth of humans, even Shadovar. Is it not?"

"Few drow have been seen in the city of late."

"Few?" Barrabus echoed, as if that fact should hardly matter.

"I'm willing to risk it."

"How big of you."

"Indeed. I am willing to risk the loss of one of my . . . of *you*," the tiefling remarked. "It would be a pity, but my options are few, for you are one of the few of my band who can still pass for human. I trust you will take care to garner little notice, and that there are few enough dark elves in the City of Sails to trouble you."

"You have secured my passage?"

"Not by sea. You will accompany a caravan to Port Llast. Begin your investigation there. Then, when you have learned what you may, you're on your own to Luskan."

"That will take longer."

"The road, too, is worth study."

"And the road will close behind me, perhaps not to open again until next spring."

Herzgo Alegni laughed at that. "I know Barrabus the Gray better than to think a bit of snow could stop his travels. Your time in Port Llast will be short, I'm sure. There are few people there of interest to us, so you'll be in Luskan before the autumn equinox. Be quick about your duties and return to me before the snows block the passes."

"I haven't been in Luskan in . . . forty years," Barrabus protested. "I have no contacts there, no network."

"Most of the city has remained intact since the fall of the Hosttower. Five High Captains rule from their various—"

"And *they* are ruled by the mercenary dark elves," Barrabus finished. "And if the talk is of fewer of them seen in the city now, you can bet those accounts were sent forth by the dark elves themselves, so that people like you, and the lords of Waterdeep, can nod and turn their eyes elsewhere."

"Well, you will find out the truth for me, then."

"If the reports you claim are *not* true, I won't likely be coming back. Do not underestimate the memory of a dark elf."

"Why, dear Barrabus, I don't think I've ever seen you scared before."

Barrabus straightened at that and glowered at the tiefling.

"Before winter," Herzgo Alegni told him. He glanced toward Neverwinter and motioned with his chin. "The caravan leaves in the morning."

His thoughts spinning in a hundred different directions, and none of them leading to a pleasant conclusion, Barrabus the Gray walked toward the city. He'd made a point of staying far afield of Luskan for years—one did not double-cross a character like Jarlaxle Baenre without consequences, after all.

He thought back to that fight in Memnon those decades before, when agents of Bregan D'aerthe had paraded his lover before him, taunting him and warning him of the consequences should he reject their offer to rejoin with them. He saw again the three dead drow, but he dismissed the image, focusing instead on the few tendays he had subsequently known with his lover.

Those had been among the best days of his life, but alas, she had run off, or disappeared—had the dark elves taken her again? Had they killed her as payback for his violence?

Or was it that infernal sword? He almost glanced back at Herzgo Alegni as that unsettling thought bubbled up. Very soon after his loss, the Shadovar had come into his life, had taken his freedom.

Had taken everything.

That last thought brought a self-deprecating smile to the lips of Barrabus the Gray. "Had taken everything?" he whispered aloud. "And what was there to take?"

By the time he reached Neverwinter's gate, Barrabus had let all those memories fly away. He had to look ahead, his focus tight and complete. If any drow remained in Luskan, the slightest error would likely cost him his life.

CHAPTER
7

GAUNTLGRYM

JARLAXLE KEPT HIMSELF IN THE REAR OF THE GROUP OF FIVE. THE tunnels underneath Luskan were long natural corridors that reached out to the southeast and the Crags. Korvin Dor'crae led the group and served as its scout, often moving off ahead of the others. Next came Athrogate, eager to see the place Dahlia had described, and always ready to serve as point-dwarf of any patrol—he always wanted to be the first into any fight. Dahlia and Valindra formed the third rank. The elf walked with a measure of calm and patience Jarlaxle would have expected in a much older and more seasoned warrior, and Valindra glided along as if in a daze, with hardly the presence—of mind or body—one would expect of a creature as powerful as a lich.

Not that Jarlaxle was complaining. Valindra Shadowmantle had been no minor spellcaster in life, commanding an entire wing of the powerful Hosttower of the Arcane. Should she ever regain her acuity and confidence, she would only prove more formidable in undeath—and thinking straight, honestly reflecting on the events of the last days of her living existence, she wouldn't likely be too pleased with the meddling drow.

They moved easily for more than a day, and though they heard the shuffling and scratching of ghouls and other lesser undead echo all around them, they never actually encountered any. Jarlaxle found that confusing. After all, ghouls feared nothing, their hunger for living flesh insatiable, and their ability to smell and track living flesh quite keen. Why didn't they approach? But soon he came to recognize the true nature of one of his companions.

"We been lucky," Athrogate said to him during a break the next day. "Lots o' side tunnels, and full o' ghouls and such."

"No luck," Jarlaxle replied. He nodded ahead, drawing Athrogate's attention to Dahlia and Dor'crae, who were discussing their next move. The tunnel forked, and Dor'crae reported that each of those tunnels split again, not much far away. Both Dahlia and Dor'crae kept pointing to the ceiling and tunnel walls, where the glistening tendrils reflected a wet, shiny green in the torchlight.

"What're ye meaning?" Athrogate asked. "A magic tunnel?"

"Come along," Jarlaxle instructed, and he rose and moved toward Dahlia as Dor'crae started off along the left-hand divide.

"We will solve it quickly," Dahlia promised as the pair neared.

Jarlaxle motioned for Athrogate to keep walking, along the same path Dor'crae had taken. "I have no doubt of that, dear lady," he said, drawing out a wand and pointing it down the tunnel.

Dahlia's expression changed to one of shock and trepidation, but Jarlaxle spoke the command word before she could react, and the tunnel brightened with magical light.

"What the—?" Athrogate yelped in surprise, for the light stung his eyes. As his temporary blindness subsided, though, the dwarf caught a glimpse of Dor'crae—or at least it should have been Dor'crae. Instead, a large bat fluttered away, out of the light and down the tunnel.

"Why did you do that?" Dahlia scolded.

"To mark Dor'crae's return," Jarlaxle replied, moving toward the conjured light. "And to better view these strange veins along the tunnel walls. I had thought it a vein of gemstone—perhaps some variant of bloodstone—at first." He kept walking, Dahlia hustling to catch up. "But now I see them differently," Jarlaxle said as he came into the light and peered closer at a nearby vein. "They appear almost as hollow tubes, and full of some liquid." He drew out another wand, of which he seemed to have an inexhaustible supply, and pointed it at the tendril.

Dahlia grabbed the wand. "Take great care!" she warned in no uncertain terms. "Do not break the tendril."

"The what?" asked Athrogate.

Jarlaxle pulled the wand away and executed its dweomer, which detected the presence of magic. He appeared quite impressed as he turned back to Dahlia and said, "Powerful magic."

"Residual magic," she replied.

"Well, obviously you know more of this than I do," Jarlaxle said.

Dahlia started to answer, but then caught on to the ruse and put her hands on her hips, glaring at the drow. "You knew the undercity of Luskan well," she said.

"Not so well."

"Enough to know that these are not gemstone veins."

"What's she babbling about?" Athrogate demanded.

"They are the roots of the fallen Hosttower," Jarlaxle explained, "sapping the strength of the sea and the earth, so we thought, though never did we imagine they spread so far from the city."

Dahlia offered up a wry grin.

"And they follow the left fork here, but not the right," Jarlaxle went on.

Dahlia shrugged.

"We're following them," the drow said, and he let a bit of suspicion creep into his voice.

"Ah, but what's yer game, then?" Athrogate demanded of the elf. "What of the dwarven city ye told me to get me to come along? What o' the treasures, elf, and ye best be telling me true!"

"The tendrils lead to the place I described," Dahlia said. "Following them was how Dor'crae found the mines and the great forge and structures that will steal your breath, dwarf. Perhaps in an age long lost, the dwarves crafted more than weapons, perhaps they forged a pact with the great wizards of the Hosttower. Even dwarven-forged weapons needed a wizard's enchantments, yes? And armor blessed by the magic of great mages can withstand much stronger blows."

"Are ye sayin' my own ancestors used these . . . these roots, so the wizards could send a bit o' magic their way?"

"It is possible," said Dahlia. "That is one—and one likely—explanation."

"And what are the others, I wonder?" Jarlaxle asked with unmasked suspicion.

Dahlia offered no answer.

"We'll know soon enough, then," said Athrogate. "What, right?"

Dahlia replied with a disarming smile and a nod. "Dor'crae thinks there may be a shortcut. Perhaps you'll find your treasures sooner than we expected, good dwarf."

She smiled again and walked back the other way, to where Valindra stood, eyes closed and singing some strange song. Every so often, the lich stopped singing and scolded herself, "No, that's not right, oh, I've forgotten. That's not right. It's not right, you know. No, that's not right," and all without ever opening her eyes, before launching back into a voice-lifting refrain of, "Ara . . . Arabeth . . ."

"You saw Dor'crae?" Jarlaxle asked the dwarf when they were alone.

"Was him, eh? Good cloak he's got there."

"It wasn't his cloak."

Athrogate eyed him. "What do ye know?"

"It's his nature, not a magic item," Jarlaxle explained.

Athrogate mulled on that for just a moment, before his eyes went wide and he slapped his hands onto his hips. "Ye ain't sayin' . . ."

"I just did."

"Elf . . . ?"

"Fear not, my friend. Some of my best friends were vampires." Jarlaxle patted Athrogate on the shoulder and moved back toward Dahlia and Valindra.

" 'Were?' " Athrogate remarked, trying to sort out that bit of information. He realized then that he was standing alone, and with a vampire out there somewhere with him. He glanced over his shoulder and hurried to catch up to Jarlaxle.

"He knows the way," Jarlaxle explained to Athrogate a couple of days later. "And he's valuable in keeping the undead in check."

"Bah, but there ain't no more, and them what was would've kissed me morningstar balls," the dwarf grumbled back.

Jarlaxle cringed and replied, "He moves swiftly, and silently, and again, he knows the way."

"Yeah, yeah, I'm knowin'," Athrogate grumbled and waved the drow away.

Up ahead in the line, Valindra began to sing again, still questioning every line, scolding herself for getting it wrong before launching once more into "Ara . . . Arabeth . . . Arararar . . . Arabeth!"

"So I'm gettin' why she bringed the bat-boy," Athrogate said. "But why that idiot?"

"That idiot is not without power . . . great power."

"I'm hardly waitin' for her to blow us all up with a fireball."

"Great power," Jarlaxle said again. "And Dahlia can control it."

"What? How're ye knowing that?"

Jarlaxle just held up his hand and stared ahead at the two women. For years, Kimmuriel Oblodra, Jarlaxle's lieutenant and the current leader of Bregan D'aerthe, had used his psionic abilities to scout Valindra's mind. Only Kimmuriel had kept Valindra from utter insanity in those first days after Arklem Greeth had converted her to her undead state. And in those sessions, Kimmuriel had assured Jarlaxle that within the trappings of apparent dementia, there remained the quite powerful, quite sinister, and quite cogent being who had once been Valindra Shadowmantle, Mistress of the North Tower of the Hosttower of the Arcane . . . not just a wizard, but an overwizard. That Valindra had begun to emerge again soon after.

And Dahlia was too careful to not know that. She would never have brought such an unpredictable and potent creature along if she wasn't sure she could control her.

Jarlaxle considered the consequences if Dahlia somehow managed to return Valindra her full consciousness. Valindra Shadowmantle had been formidable in life, by all accounts. The drow could only imagine the trouble she might affect as a lich.

"If the vampire knows the way, and the lich is such a 'great power,' then what in all Nine Hells're we doin' here, elf?" Athrogate asked.

Jarlaxle scrutinized his friend, a formidable sight indeed in his heavy coat of chainmail links, his iron helmet, and those devastating morningstars criss-crossed on his back. He thought back to his original conversation with Dahlia, when she had explained why she needed them. Had he allowed his own hubris to take her at face value on that?

No, he reminded himself. Dahlia needed him, needed his connections so that she could dispense with the promised trove of artifacts and coins.

He looked again at Athrogate. Dahlia had specifically explained her need for the dwarf, of course, and perhaps gaining the services of Athrogate meant also bringing along Jarlaxle, as the two were inseparable.

Was Jarlaxle, then, just add-on baggage?

Jarlaxle never answered Athrogate's question. A few moments later they caught up to Dahlia and the others, who stood at the edge of a deep pit, staring down.

"We've arrived," Dahlia announced when they joined her at the edge.

"Not much of a city," Athrogate grumbled.

"The shaft drops fifty feet," Dahlia explained. "Then curves at a steep but traversable decline off to the left a bit. It winds in various directions for a few hundred feet beyond that, and ends at a . . . well, you'll see soon enough."

She turned to Valindra, and Jarlaxle noticed that Dahlia reached under the edge of her tunic to a strange brooch, touching her fingers to its onyx stone.

"Valindra," she whispered. "Is there something you can do to help our friends go down this hole?"

"Throw them in!" the lich keened. With Ara . . . oh, yes, with that one!"

"Valindra!" Dahlia barked, and the lich shook her head and sputtered as if Dahlia had thrown a bucket of water in her face. "*Safely* down," Dahlia clarified.

With an exaggerated sigh and hardly any effort at all, Valindra waved one hand and a blue-glowing disc appeared in the air, suspended over the hole.

"You, too," Dahlia explained to the lich, taking her by the hand and guiding her to stand on the disc. "We'll need more, I think, for the drow and the dwarf."

With another exhale and a wave of her left hand, then one more and a wave of her right, Valindra created floating discs in front of Jarlaxle and Athrogate.

Dahlia let go of Valindra's hand and bade her to proceed. Valindra's disc floated down into the pit. A nod from Dahlia to Dor'crae had him lifting his cape up behind him. It fluttered over his head, and as it descended, obscuring his form, he became a large bat and dived off after Valindra.

Dahlia motioned to the two remaining discs then grabbed the edges of her own magical cloak—the cloak she'd taken from Borlann.

"What do you know?" Jarlaxle asked before she'd gone. "About Valindra, I mean?"

"I expect that, in a strange way, her insanity protected her from the Spellplague," the elf replied. "She's a unique combination of what was and what is. Or perhaps she's simply a wizard gone mad, undead and gone beyond any hope. But whatever she is, I know she's useful."

"So to you she's just a tool . . . a magic item," Jarlaxle accused.

"Pray tell me what use you and your drow have had for her these many years."

Jarlaxle grinned at the astute comeback and tipped his wide-brimmed hat. He started to step on his disc and bade Athrogate to do the same, but as soon as the dwarf hopped up, Jarlaxle hopped back down. "After you, good lady."

"I ain't likin' this," the dwarf said, in a crouch with his hands out to the sides, as if he expected the disc to vanish and leave him scrambling to find something to hold onto.

"You will be soon, I promise," Dahlia said, and she pulled the magical cloak around her and in the blink of an eye had transformed herself into a crow. She dived into the pit.

Next went Athrogate, with Jarlaxle bringing up the rear. Before he stepped back onto Valindra's conjured disc, the drow put his hand near the insignia he wore, of House Baenre of Menzoberranzan. He had his own levitation magic, just in case.

But he needn't have feared any mischief from the lich, he soon discovered. The discs floated steadily and easily, moving to the mental commands of their riders. Fifty feet down, the tunnel changed from a sheer drop to a steep decline, as Dahlia had said, but they didn't dismiss the discs or step off them. It was easier to float above the broken, uneven floor than to walk.

The corridor grew tighter around them, forcing a crouch or a lean here and there, and at one point, they actually had to lie down on their discs to pass under a low overhang. Still, they wound their way left and right, and ever downward.

Because of one last obstacle, Athrogate pulled a bit ahead of Jarlaxle over the final expanse of broken tunnel, and just as the drow came to see that the narrow passage widened up ahead, he heard Athrogate mutter in tones reverent and awe-filled, "By Dumathoin."

The reference to Dumathoin, in dwarven lore the Keeper of Secrets Under the Mountain, somewhat prepared the drow for what might be beyond, but still he found it hard to breathe when he came out onto the ledge beside his four companions.

They were on a natural balcony overlooking a huge chamber, perhaps a third the size of Menzoberranzan. Whether from natural lichen or residual magic, there was enough light for him to make out the general contours of the cavern. A pond lay before them, its still, dark waters interrupted by a series of large stalagmites, some ringed by stairwells and balconies that must once have served as guard posts or trade kiosks. Stalactites hung from the ceiling on their end of the cavern as well, and Jarlaxle noted similar construction on several of them. The dwarves who had worked the cavern had adopted the fashion of the drow, he realized, and had used the natural formations as dwellings. Jarlaxle had never heard of such a thing before, but he had little doubt in his guess. The work on the stalagmites and stalactites was surely not drow in nature, not delicate and curving, nor limned with glowing faerie fire.

"There are ballistae up there," Dor'crae, who had returned to his human form, explained, pointing to the stalactites. "Guard stations overlooking the entrance."

"No . . . no it canno' be," Athrogate whispered, and he slouched on his disc as if the strength simply fled his body.

But Jarlaxle heard hope in the dwarf's voice more than anything else, a recognition beyond anything Athrogate had, perhaps, dared to hope, and so Jarlaxle paid the dwarf no concern at that moment and continued instead his study of the cavern.

On the far side of the dark pond, a couple hundred feet or more from their balcony, stood half a dozen clusters of small structures, each grouping set at the end of a mine rail, and more than one of those lines held an ancient mine cart, battered and rusted. The rail lines converged straight away from the balcony, running toward the back of the expansive cavern beyond even his superior darkvision.

"Come," Dahlia bade them, her voice whistling like a giant bird. She slipped over the balcony's low natural rail and glided on black feathered wings down to the water and across. Dor'crae became a bat once more and quickly followed, as did Valindra on her disc.

"Are you joining us?" Jarlaxle asked Athrogate when he saw that the dwarf made no move to follow.

Athrogate looked at him as if he'd just awakened from a deep, though tumultuous slumber. "It canno' be," he whispered, barely able to get the words out.

"Well, let us see what it be, my friend," Jarlaxle replied, and started away.

He'd barely descended to skim above the pond on his disc when Athrogate passed him by, the dwarf apparently shaking off his stupor and willing his own disc on with all speed.

On the far side of the pond, Dahlia, an elf once more, was helping Valindra off her disc, and Athrogate simply leaped down from his, which was still half a dozen feet above the ground. The fall didn't hinder the dwarf at all, though—in fact, he didn't even seem to notice it as he bounced right back to his feet and stumbled and scrambled forward, following the central rail line.

"This place knew much battle," Dor'crae remarked after shedding his bat form and bending low to pick up a whitened bone. "Goblin, or a small orc."

Jarlaxle glanced around to confirm the vampire's observations. The soft ground was scarred and many bits of bone showed clearly. More interesting, though, were the sights that lay ahead, the image that had Athrogate on his knees, and though his back was to the drow, Jarlaxle could well imagine the tears streaming down his hairy face.

And who could blame him? For even Jarlaxle, only partially acquainted with the legends of the Delzoun dwarves, could guess easily enough that they had stumbled upon Gauntlgrym, the legendary homeland of the Delzoun dwarves, the most sacred legend of their history, the place Bruenor Battlehammer himself had sought for more than half a century.

A great wall faced them, sealing off the end of the cavern. It was built much like one would expect of a surface castle, with gate towers on either side of a massive set of mithral doors, and a crenellated battlement lining the top of the wall that spanned the cavern and seemed as if it had been built deep into the stone at either end. The strangest part, aside from the huge silvery doors, was the tightness of it all. Looking up the wall, Jarlaxle almost expected to see it give way to open sky, but instead there was only a very short space to the natural ceiling of the cavern. A tall human would have a hard time even standing straight up there, and even Jarlaxle would have to crouch in many places.

"It canno' be," Athrogate was saying as Jarlaxle came up beside him, and confirmed that the dwarf was indeed crying.

"I can think of no other place it could be, my friend," Jarlaxle replied, patting Athrogate's strong shoulder.

"You know it, then?" asked Dahlia, moving up behind them with Dor'crae and Valindra in tow.

"Behold Gauntlgrym," Jarlaxle explained. "Ancient homeland of the Delzoun dwarves, a place thought to be but a legend—"

"Never did a dwarf doubt it!" Athrogate bellowed.

". . . by many nondwarves," Jarlaxle finished, flashing a smile at his friend. "It's been a mystery even among the elves, with memories long, and among the drow, who know the Underdark better than any. And doubt not that we have searched for it all these centuries. If one-tenth of the claims of the treasures of Gauntlgrym are true, then there is unimaginable wealth behind that wall, behind those doors." He paused and considered the sight before him, and their location and depth in a region that was far from remote, by Underdark standards.

"Great magic must have masked this place all these years," he said. "Such a place as this cavern alone could not have gone unnoticed in the Northdark through so many centuries."

"How do you know this is Gauntlgrym?" Dor'crae asked. "The dwarves have built, and abandoned, many kingdoms."

Before Jarlaxle could respond, Athrogate broke out into verse:

> Silver halls and mithral doors
> Stone walls to seal the cavern
> Grander sights than e'er before
> In smithy, mine, and tavern
>
> Toil hard in endless night
> In toast, oh lift yer flagon!
> Ye'll need the drink to keep ye right
> At forge that bakes the dragon.
>
> Come, Delzoun, come one and all!
> Rush to grab yer kin
> And tell 'em that their home awaits
> In grandest Gauntlgrym!

"Old song," Athrogate explained. "And known to every dwarfling."

"The stone walls and mithral doors, I see, but that alone is all the evidence—"

"All the evidence I'm needin'," Athrogate replied. "None other place's built with such doors as that. No dwarf'd do it, out o' respect. None'd try to imitate that which can't be copied. It'd be an insult, I tell ye!"

"We'll know more once we get inside," Jarlaxle conceded.

"I've been inside," Dor'crae explained, "and can't confirm the silver halls, nor did I discover any great hoards of treasure, but I understand the verse about the forge."

"Ye seen the forge?"

"You can feel its warmth levels away."

"It's still fired? How is that possible?" Jarlaxle asked.

The vampire had no answer.

"Are ye saying someone's *living* in there?" Athrogate demanded.

Dor'crae sent a nervous glance Dahlia's way and said, "I found nothing . . . *living* in there," he explained, "but the complex is not deserted. And yes, there is a great forge several levels below us that is indeed still fired. Heat like I've never felt before. Heat that could melt an inferior sword to a puddle."

"Heat that could bake a dragon?" Jarlaxle asked with a wry grin.

"There are crawl tunnels down from the parapet," the vampire explained. "But they're all blocked."

"Ye said ye been inside."

"I have my ways, dwarf," Dor'crae replied. "But I expect we'll need to do some tunneling of our own if you are to gain entrance."

"Bah!" Athrogate snorted. He turned and walked up to the gates. "By Moradin's arm and Clangeddin's horn, by Dumathoin's tricks and Delzoun true born, open I tell ye, open yer gates! Me name's Athrogate, me blood's Delzoun, and I'm told me home awaits!"

Illuminations of shining silver appeared on the door, runes and images of ancient dwarven crests, and like a great exhale from some sleeping mountain giant, the doors cracked open. Then, without a whisper of sound, they drifted apart, sweeping wide to reveal a narrow, low tunnel beyond, lined with murder holes.

"By the bearded gods," Athrogate muttered. He looked back at the others in amazement.

"A rhyme told to every dwarfling?" Jarlaxle asked with a grin.

"Telled ye it was Gauntlgrym!" he snapped his stubby fingers at them and started in.

Dor'crae rushed to him and grabbed him by the shoulder. "Likely trapped!" he warned. "Heavily guarded by ancient wards and mechanical springs that I assure you still operate."

"Bah!" Athrogate snorted, tearing away. "Ain't no Delzoun trap or ward to hit a Delzoun dwarf, ye dolt!"

Without hesitation, Athrogate started into the complex and the others were quick to follow—and quicker still when Jarlaxle warned them that perhaps it would be a good idea for them to stay very close to the dwarf.

Halfway in, Dahlia brought up the sparking blue light on her walking stick. Not to be outdone, Jarlaxle flicked his wrist, producing a dagger from a magical bracer, then flicked it again to elongate that dagger into a fine sword. He whispered something into the hilt and the sword glowed white, illuminating the area as well as a bright lantern.

Only then did they see the forms ahead, shuffling to escape the light.

"Me brothers?" Athrogate asked, clearly at a loss.

"Ghosts," Dor'crae whispered. "The place is thick with them."

They soon came into a huge chamber, circular and crossed by rail tracks, one from each of the three other exits. Along the curving wall of the chamber were building facades, and many with shingles hanging to describe the place therein—an armor merchant, a weaponsmith, a barracks, a tavern (of course), another tavern (of course), and on and on.

"Like Mirabar's Undercity," Jarlaxle remarked, though on a grander scale by far.

As they moved out toward the middle of the chamber, Athrogate grabbed Jarlaxle's arm and pulled it lower so that the sword would illuminate the floor. It was a mosaic, a great mural, and they had to scurry about with the light for a while before they realized that it depicted the three dwarf gods of old: Moradin, Clangeddin, and Dumathoin.

In the very center of the floor was a raised circular dais, a singular throne atop it, and the sparkles as they approached marked it as no ordinary seat. Gem-studded and grand, with sweeping arms and a high, wide back of mithral, silver, and gold, it was the throne of a great king. Even the dais was no ordinary block of stone, but a composite design of those same precious metals, and set with lines of glittering jewels.

Jarlaxle waved his glowing sword near it, showing the rich purple fabric still intact. "Mighty magic," he remarked.

"Undo it, that we might pilfer the gems," Dor'crae insisted.

That brought him a hateful glare from Athrogate. "Ye pluck one stone from that chair and know that I'm filling the hole with yer black heart, vampire," the dwarf warned.

"Did we come here as mere visitors, then?" Dor'crae retorted. "To gasp and fawn over its beauties?"

"I'm bettin' ye'll find plenty o' treasures—more than we can carry—layin' about," Athrogate answered. "But some things ye're not defiling."

"Enough," said Dahlia. "Let us not presume, and not quarrel. We are merely at the entrance. There is so much more we need learn about this place."

Athrogate moved as if to do exactly that. He stepped tentatively toward the throne and turned to sit down. He paused there, not quite sitting, his hands not yet even touching the carved, jeweled arms of the great seat.

"Take care with that," Jarlaxle warned. He pulled forth a wand, pointed it at the chair, and spoke a command word. His eyes popped open wide when he sensed the strength of the magic in that throne—ancient magic, powerful magic, as mighty as anything Jarlaxle had ever encountered before.

"Athrogate, no," he said, his voice raspy and breathless.

"A dwarf seat!" Athrogate argued and before Jarlaxle could stop him, he sat down.

The dwarf's eyes opened wide, and his mouth opened wider in a silent scream as he glanced all around.

"Not a king," he gasped, but he didn't even know he was saying it.

Athrogate was thrown from the throne, sent flying a dozen feet to skid down on the mosaic floor. He lay there for a long while, trembling and covering his face, until Jarlaxle finally coxed him up to his knees.

"What did you see?" Dahlia asked, moving toward the throne.

"Ye ain't no dwarf!" Athrogate yelled at her.

"But you are, and still it rejected you," Dahlia shot back.

"It'll shrivel ye!"

"Dahlia, do not," Jarlaxle warned her.

The elf paused in front of the throne and reached out one hand, her fingers barely away from the seat. But she didn't touch it.

"You said 'not a king' right before you were thrown," Jarlaxle said.

Athrogate could only look at him, befuddled, and shake his hairy head. He looked past Jarlaxle to the throne then, and nodded in deep respect.

Jarlaxle helped him to his feet and left him to his own accord, and the dwarf immediately went back to admire the throne. He didn't touch it, though, and certainly entertained no thoughts of ever sitting in it again.

"Let us take our rest here," Jarlaxle suggested. He paused and tilted his head, as if listening to a sound far in the distance. "I suspect we'll need all our strength to pass these halls. You've been here, Dor'crae," he added. "What . . . residents might we find?"

The vampire shrugged and shook his head. "I saw only the dwarf ghosts, and hundreds of them," he replied. "I was here only briefly, following the Hosttower's tendrils, a narrow course in a huge complex, and one you cannot walk directly. But I saw only dwarf ghosts. I doubt not that they would swarm us were we not armed against them. But we are." He looked to Athrogate, then to Dahlia, to make his point. "They welcome those of Delzoun blood, as you saw with the doors."

"Because they're trustin' that I won't let ye defile the place," Athrogate replied. "And I'm telling ye that their trust is well placed. Ye scratch one altar, poke a jeweled eye out o' one king's image, and them ghosts'll be the least o' yer problems."

"Not ghosts," Jarlaxle assured Dor'crae. "Something with footfalls. Something . . . corporeal."

"Ghouls, perhaps," answered the vampire. "Or living dwarves?"

"By the bearded gods," Athrogate muttered, imagining what he might say to a dwarf of Gauntlgrym.

"They would have been on the walls to greet us, and none too kindly," Jarlaxle reasoned.

"What then?" asked Athrogate, obviously a bit peeved at the drow for stealing his moment of fantasy.

"Pick from a long list, friend," Jarlaxle answered. "Many are the choices, and it has been my long experience that rarely will you find a deserted cave in the Underdark."

"We'll know soon enough," Dahlia interjected. "Take your rest and let us be on our way." She looked to Dor'crae and nodded, and the vampire walked off to the far edge of the circular room and disappeared from sight.

"He will scout out our route," Dahlia explained. "To find those tunnels that most closely mirror his own journey to the forge of Gauntlgrym."

They sorted out areas around the central dais and set their bedrolls, but none found much rest, particularly Athrogate, who was so agitated, so overwhelmed. What dwarf in all Faerûn hadn't dreamed of that moment—of the discovery of Gauntlgrym?

Dor'crae returned some hours later, confident that he had discovered the tunnels that would bring them to the forge. He confirmed Jarlaxle's suspicions, as well, for though he hadn't seen any monsters—dwarves, ghouls, goblins, or whatever they might be—he had heard some shuffling in the dark.

That ominous report did nothing to daunt the eagerness of the group, though, for they were confident they could handle whatever might come their way.

Athrogate led the way, with Dor'crae close behind and calling out directions. They exited the circular room straight back from the gate that had brought them in, moving along wide corridors with still more shops, and a temple of Clangeddin, where Athrogate had to stop to offer a prayer.

Always at the corner of their vision, they caught the dreamy movements of gliding ghosts, inquisitive, perhaps, but never approaching.

They came to a great sweeping stairway, descending in a gentle arc, and only after they had gone down several dozen steps, down below the thick stone that supported the upper level, did they begin to realize the enormity of both the stairway and the complex. The view opened wide below them, a gigantic cavern with hundred-foot-tall buttresses climbing up from the far-distant floor like massive, stoic sentries. Two lines of giant pillars supported a lower section of the vast, multi-sectioned chamber, each decorated with thousands of reliefs and carved symbols.

Two hundred more steps down, nearing the floor, they saw that the stairway would continue through the floor to lower levels, which Dor'crae indicated they should follow.

"Ye canno' ask me to walk through this place without a look!" Athrogate argued, raising his voice a bit too loudly. It echoed all around them, over and over again.

"We can come back to it, good dwarf," Dahlia said.

"Bah!" Athrogate snorted.

"Athrogate . . . there," Jarlaxle said, and he pointed a wand back toward the nearest wall. As the others peered in the indicated direction, Jarlaxle activated the wand and its magic illuminated the area of interest. Even Valindra gave a little cry of surprise and awe at the sight.

The wall had been carved, and colored with various metals, jewels, and paint into the giant likeness of the god Moradin, ten times the size of a mortal dwarf. The Soulforger had his shoulder turned in behind a bejeweled shield, a great warhammer raised in his other hand up behind him. His bearded face seemed a mask of bloodlust, battle hungry, ready to meet and destroy any foe.

Jarlaxle glanced down at Athrogate, who was on his knees, his face in one palm, trying to control his gasping breath.

Eventually, they went on, level after level down, along corridors wide and narrow, through grand halls and modest chambers. For a long while, the only disturbance in the thick dust that had settled about the place was their own footprints, and it stayed that way until they came to a strong stone door, barred on their side with thick iron.

"This is the end of the city proper," Dor'crae explained, motioning for Athrogate to move the locking bars aside. "The areas beyond are less worked, open to the mines, and with one path leading to the forge."

"Ah, but I wish we might lock it behind us," Athrogate said as the last bar was pulled aside. "I'd not be the one to open Gauntlgrym to whatever walks the depths below."

"When we leave, we'll secure the door behind us," Dahlia assured him.

The change in the atmosphere was palpable the moment they passed through the door. Where before there had been ghostly silence, only their own scuffling accompanying their march—and even that muted by the thick dust and heavy air—on the other side of the stone door there was sound: creaking and groaning, the scraping of stone on stone. Before they'd walked in the normally comfortable temperatures of the Upperdark, but that had given away to a great increase in both heat and humidity. The stone stairs beyond were slick with moisture, and blacker somehow, unlike the muted, dusty gray of the city.

They pressed on, though the treacherous footing made them move slowly and carefully down the stairs. Dahlia and Valindra both commented on the sudden humidity—it felt almost as if they were walking through a misty spring rain—and the elf asked how that might be possible, but none of her charges offered an explanation.

At the next landing, two hundred steps or more below the door, the corridor broke off into three directions. One corridor was of worked stone, while the other two were either natural caves or rough-cut mines. Dor'crae hesitated at what seemed the obvious choice—the carefully-worked corridor.

"We're close," he assured his companions.

"Listen," Jarlaxle bade them, and he tilted his head.

"Don't hear nothing," Athrogate replied.

"I do," Dahlia said. "Furnaces. The forge, far below."

"Get us there," the dwarf demanded of Dor'crae. "The Forge of Gauntlgrym. . . ."

Despite his reservations about the direction, the vampire led them along the worked tunnel, which brought them to wider chambers and longer tunnels still. But more importantly, it brought them through a closed door and into a gray and impenetrable veil of steam.

"What in the Nine Hells?" Athrogate asked

Jarlaxle held his glowing sword up in front of him, and even tried shifting the hue of the light, but to no avail. All it did was reflect back in his eyes. He moved to the side of the room, found another door, and pushed through, but all the rooms seemed similarly filled with opaque mist, and worse, they discovered that the steam was beginning to sweep out into the corridors they'd left behind.

"This is not the way," Dor'crae decided, and led them back the way they'd come, closing the doors behind them as they went. After a long while they at last returned to the three-way intersection, and Dor'crae pointed to one of the more natural tunnels, which seemed to go in the right direction.

"I thought ye scouted it," Athrogate grumbled at him.

"I couldn't have gotten to the forge and back in so short a time if I walked," the vampire retorted.

"Oh, but that's a smart reply," said the dwarf. "I'm likin' ye less and less, and soon enough to be needin' ye less and less, if ye get me meanin'."

Jarlaxle noticed Dahlia looking at him as if asking him to intervene, but the drow found the whole affair quite amusing, and wouldn't much regret the destruction of a vampire, so he just smiled back at her.

The tunnel wound on but didn't seem to be descending. They passed many side corridors and the place soon became a maze.

"Perhaps we should camp again and let Dor'crae sort it out," Dahlia offered, but Athrogate just rambled along.

She was about to repeat that suggestion when the dwarf called out, and when the others caught up to him, they found him standing in front of another amazing mithral door, this one perfectly dwarf-sized, and with no apparent handle.

Athrogate repeated the Delzoun rhyme that had opened the great front gates of the complex, and again it worked, the ancient door gliding open with not a whisper of sound.

They heard the furnaces of Gauntlgrym then—angry, grumbling fires—though Jarlaxle had no idea how the furnaces could still be burning. Beyond the portal, a narrow stair wound downward. It wasn't as pitch dark as before, but flashed with the orange-red glow of some distant fire.

Athrogate didn't hesitate, hustling along the stair, moving down at such a pace that the others, except for Dor'crae, had to run to keep up.

"I will be with you presently," Dor'crae explained when Dahlia turned back to regard him. "There's one other corridor I wish to inspect."

She nodded and ran off to catch up with the other two, as the vampire turned back the other way.

vDor'crae turned back, but didn't leave. Instead, he produced the skull gem and placed it in a sheltered nook next to the door, where it wouldn't be obvious. He stared at it with great lament, wondering, and not for the first time, if he'd been wise to enlist such dangerous allies. But Dor'crae looked back to the stairwell and thought of Dahlia and the lone diamond stud she wore in her right ear, the stud to represent her only remaining lover.

What choice had she given him?

He glanced down at the skull gem. "Down the stair, Sylora," he whispered. He paused only a moment longer before moving off to catch up to the rest of the band.

The vampire was barely out of sight when the eyes of the skull gem began to glow red once more, the artifact coming alive with the spirit of Sylora. A short while later, it did more than that, blowing forth a magical mist that took the form of the great Thayan lady.

Once she was through, opening a gate for her minions proved no difficult task.

CHAPTER 8

PRIMORDIAL POWER

ATHROGATE KEPT UP HIS GREAT PACE FOR ONLY A SHORT WHILE, and soon enough he came to a spot where he stopped cold, staring hesitantly. The walls of the stairway to either side simply stopped, and the narrow circular stairway continued to loop treacherously below him, absent even a handrail, in a wide-open chamber of many crisscrossing bridges and rail lines. The chamber was deep, the walls black with shadow, and far, far below, the floor glowed with orange and red streaks of lava. The air shimmered and waved from the rising heat.

It was loud, too, with the clanking of chains, grinding of stones, and the rumbling of massive fires.

"The stairs ain't wet, at least," the dwarf said to himself.

He wiped the considerable sweat from his face and started down more slowly, knowing that any misstep would lead to a long, long fall.

It seemed to go on forever, stair after stair after a hundred more stairs. Athrogate, and the others who soon followed, felt vulnerable enough on the open stairway. Then, having gone hundreds of feet below the walled section, they discovered that they were not alone.

Humanoid creatures scrambled along the lower, parallel passageways, certainly aware of the intruders. It took a while for the group to realize that the creatures moved in a coordinated manner, as if a defense was being set against them. Many of the other walkways were near enough for an archer or a spearman to be brought to bear, and many were above them, too, which left them in a terrible fix.

"Keep moving," Jarlaxle implored the dwarf. It was rare to hear concern in the voice of Jarlaxle Baenre, but there it was.

The net around them was closing, and they all knew it—all except for Valindra, of course, who picked that moment to begin singing again.

The unknown creatures responded to that song with sharp calls of their own, birdlike but guttural, as if someone had bred a blue jay with a growling mastiff.

"Dire corbies," Jarlaxle muttered.

"Eh?" asked Athrogate.

"Bird-men," the drow explained. "Rare in the Underdark, but not unknown. Half-civilized, afraid of nothing, and incredibly territorial."

"At least it ain't orcs," said Athrogate.

"Better that it were," Jarlaxle replied. "Hustle, good dwarf."

Athrogate hadn't even touched his lead foot to the next stair when a sharp crack sounded just above them, as a stone thrown from high above clipped the metal stair.

Down they went, as more cracks of stones sounded. Valindra's song hit an unexpected note as one rock bounced off her shoulder, though she otherwise seemed not to notice

Athrogate stopped again. Just below their position, several stone walkways crowded near the central stair, and they were not empty. Man-sized, black-bodied, bird-footed and bird-headed, the dire corbies rushed along the narrow walkways with ease and speed, and obviously without fear of missteps and deadly falls. Some glanced up at the intruders and squawked, holding wide their arms, which showed webbing from forearm to ribs, as if the appendages were caught halfway between a human's arm and a bird's wing.

"So, we fight," said Jarlaxle. He snapped his wrists, his magic bracers bringing a throwing dagger into each hand. "Find the weak spots in their line, Dor'crae, and drive them from the ledges."

"Wait," Dahlia said before either could act. "They're not just animals?"

"No," the drow explained, "but close: tribal, barbaric."

"Superstitious?"

"I would expect."

"Keep your position here," Dahlia bade them, and with a wry grin, she fell off the side of the stair, throwing her cloak over her head as she went.

She came out of the fall as a great crow, and uttered a series of loud, echoing cries to announce her flight. Dahlia swooped down near the dire corbies below, and when they didn't throw their stones at her, she dared alight on the walkway in the midst of one group.

The bird-men fell to their knees and averted their eyes. Dahlia cawed again, more loudly, trying to sound angry, and succeeding, they all realized, when the dire corbies scampered away.

"Go," Jarlaxle implored Athrogate.

And the dwarf went, with all the speed he would dare on the dizzying open stair. Dahlia flew around them, darting toward any dire corbies who ventured too near. They crossed by the area of converging walkways and came to a lower landing, where Dor'crae instructed the dwarf to turn left along an open, flat stone walkway.

Finally they came out of the vast open chamber and into another complex of ancient shops and chambers. Barely in, though, and with Dahlia still flying around outside, they ran headlong into a group of the vicious birdmen.

A pair leaped at Athrogate, who took up a battle song and a hearty "Bwahaha!" and swatted them aside with his spinning morningstars. He charged on recklessly, shouldering through another doorway, the impact knocking still more of the dire corbies aside.

"Out! Out! Ye damned freaks!" the dwarf yelled, his devastating weapons swinging fast and hard to shatter bone and throw the bird-men aside. "This is not yer place!"

Jarlaxle ran off behind Athrogate, out to the dwarf's left, a stream of spinning daggers leading the way and driving back a group of dire corbies. He stopped throwing as he neared, double-snapping his wrists to elongate his latest pair into swords once more and leaping at the stung and dodging bird-men with a dramatic flourish. He stabbed and spun, swept one blade about in front of him then quick-stepped and thrust hard with his other blade behind the sidelong cut.

But more dire corbies rushed into the room, from a multitude of dark doorways.

"Ara . . . Arabeth!" Valindra cried. "Oh, watch me Arabeth, oh do. I am strong, you know."

The lich stamped her foot and a burst of fire rolled out in every direction across the floor, beneath the feet of the drow and the dwarf, to roll up in front of them in a circle of scalding flames. Jarlaxle and Athrogate fell back in surprise, and the dire corbies shrieked and fell away, but their cries were drowned by the magically heightened song of the lich. "Ara . . . Arabeth! Did you see? Are you afraid? Ara . . . Arabeth!"

Dahlia, still in the form of a huge crow, set down in front of the group of burned dire corbies and cawed her displeasure.

The bird-men ran away.

And the expedition pressed onward.

The second group to move down the circular stair had no such protection as Dahlia had against the agitated and ferocious bird-men.

Stones flew at the dozens of Ashmadai and the red-gowned Thayan wizard as they made their cautious way in pursuit of Dahlia.

The cult warriors replied in kind, with crossbows instead of stones, and while most were shooting at distant, fleeting shadows, more than a few dire corbies screamed out in pain as barbed bolts invaded their black flesh. Sylora held her magic until the situation grew more dangerous, where the many walkways converged below the stairs.

She dropped a fireball in the middle of the convergence, warding the dire corbies away, and when she came level with the walkways, she sent bolts of lightning flashing along each. She snapped her fingers and Ashmadai warriors leaped out from the stairway above, landing on the various walkways, firing off the last of their missiles and rushing eagerly to meet the bird-men in melee, red scepters in hand.

As the battle was joined, Ashmadai and dire corbie alike tumbled to their deaths. Sylora and her main group continued down, at last coming to the tunnels. A few broken bird-men and a room scarred by flames marked their path, and whenever a choice lay before them, Sylora held aloft the skull gem in her open palm and let it point the way toward Dor'crae.

She could even sense how far ahead the vampire might be, for the multi-magical gem had attuned to him well.

A finger to her pursed lips reminded the eager Ashmadai to be silent, and on they went.

Through several sets of broken doors and under a low arch, the five adventurers came upon the remains of varied creatures, most recently those of dire corbies, and when they glanced around the wide, long, pillared corridor before them, they saw the ghosts of Gauntlgrym, watching them.

At the other end of the hall, through another arch and a barred portcullis, came the glow of furnaces, and despite the ghosts, or perhaps in part because of them, Athrogate was compelled to move forward. The others huddled close behind him, warily watching the spirits that mirrored their every step.

But the ward of a Delzoun dwarf proved effective yet again.

No cranking mechanism could be found near the heavy gate, so Athrogate tried his poem a third time.

Nothing happened.

Before Jarlaxle or Dahlia could offer a suggestion, the dwarf growled and leaned against the grate, grabbing a crossbar in both hands. He could clearly see the ultimate goal of his expedition in front of him: a line of furnaces and forges, the great Forge of Gauntlgrym itself, and the heat on his face as he peered through that portcullis surely warmed an old dwarf's heart.

With a growl and a heave, Athrogate tugged hard at the portcullis. At first, nothing happened, but then the dwarf broke through an old lock, it seemed, and the gate inched upward.

"There must be a lever," Jarlaxle offered, but Athrogate wasn't listening, not with the Forge of Gauntlgrym so near at hand.

A fog rolled past him and Dor'crae rematerialized on the other side of the portcullis.

"No ghosts in here," the vampire reported. "Shall I look for a way to open the gate?"

The sight of the vampire within the Forge of Gauntlgrym only drove the dwarf on harder. He growled and groaned, and lifted with all his tremendous strength, his magical girdle lending the power of a giant to his thick limbs. Up inched the portcullis. He grabbed lower, the next bar down, and heaved again, lifting it to his waist. With a sudden jerk and a roll of his hands, he dropped down into a crouch under it, and straining and groaning with every inch, Athrogate stood up straight once more.

Jarlaxle went under, Dahlia right after him, and she coaxed the distracted Valindra in behind her.

"I'll try to help," Jarlaxle offered, moving up in front of Athrogate and grabbing at the bars, "but I haven't your strength."

Even as he finished talking, a clicking sound came from the stone surrounding the heavy portcullis, and both drow and dwarf backed off just enough to realize that the heavy grate had been set in place.

"A room to the side," Dahlia explained, tipping her chin toward a door through which Dor'crae passed.

Athrogate hustled into the forge, stumbling as he moved near the central furnace, the largest of the many within. It had a wide, thick tray in front of the grate of the furnace, and in looking at that, Athrogate felt as if he was peering through the faceplate of the helmet of some great fire god.

Little did he know how close to right he was.

"Ye ever seen such power, elf?" he asked Jarlaxle when the drow moved up beside him.

"How can it still be fueled, after all these centuries?" Jarlaxle asked. On a whim, the drow brought forth a throwing dagger and flipped it through the grate.

It never even seemed to land against anything, just turned to liquid and fell away, dispersing into the flames.

" 'To bake the dragon,' " Athrogate muttered.

"Incredible," the drow agreed.

They finally managed to move aside from the blinding image to study the decorated anvil on the other side of the tray, and to note a mithral door set against the wall at the side of the main forge.

"There is more to see back there," Dor'crae explained, "but I couldn't open that door when I was here before. I had to slip in around the hatch using other means."

Athrogate was already at the door. He started his rhyme once more, but paused and just pushed on the hatch, which swung in easily, revealing a short passageway to another gleaming door.

Doubting eyes fixed on the vampire, who merely shrugged.

Dahlia led the way to the next door, but found that it would not open no matter how hard she shoved against it. Until Athrogate came up, that is, and merely touched it, and like the one before, it swung open easily.

"It would seem that these old dwarves were possessed of great magic, if their doors recognize one of their blood," Jarlaxle remarked.

"And can tell a king from a peasant," Athrogate added, remembering the throne above.

Athrogate led the way through another doorway then a fourth, and as that one opened, the group heard the sounds of a tremendous rush of water, like a waterfall, and the air grew moist and thick. The tunnel wound for a fair distance before emptying onto a ledge that ringed a steamy oblong chamber, centered by a very wide, very deep, deep pit. And there the riddle of Gauntlgrym took away the breath of dwarf, drow, elf, vampire, and lich alike.

Looking down that great shaft, they could hardly see the pit's walls. A rushing swirl of water spun continuously, like the breaking wave of a hurricane's tide, or a perpetual sidelong waterfall. All the way down the water spun, giving way at the bottom to a bubbling lake of lava. Water hissed loudly in the heat, steam forming and rushing up into chimneys far above.

And somehow, that orange-red glow seemed more than just molten rock, more than inanimate magma. It appeared almost like a great eye staring back at them . . . with hate.

"We're below them steamy rooms," Athrogate noted. "A chimney must be plugged up there."

"Over there," Dor'crae remarked, pointing to a narrow metal walkway, thankfully with railings, that spanned the pit and ended at a ledge across the way, with a wide, decorated archway leading to a small room, barely visible, beyond. "There's more."

Sylora and the Ashmadai could feel the hatred of the dwarf ghosts all around them, but the Thayan wizard held aloft the skull gem, shining with power, and it was great enough to keep the ancient defenders of Gauntlgrym at bay.

They passed by the foolish and eager Ashmadai woman who had entered the room before consulting with Sylora. She had been quickly and horribly torn limb from limb by the ghosts right before their eyes.

But so be it. They were Ashmadai, and the tiefling female had died in the service of her god. Each uttered a prayer to Asmodeus for their lost sister as they stepped over various severed body parts.

"I can't touch it," Dor'crae explained, standing in front of a large lever set in the floor of the room, barely more than an alcove, beyond the archway from the water-encircled lava pit. "When I tried, it threw me back. Some great magic wards it."

"Only a dwarf could pull it, ye fool. Like them doors."

"And don't you dare," said Jarlaxle, who stood a few steps away, studying the old runes inscribed on the archway's curving top. He enacted one of the powers of his enchanted eyepatch, which could allow him to comprehend almost any known language, even many magical ones, but this writing was beyond even the eyepatch's power. "We know not what it would unleash."

He continued studying the runes—he understood that they were very ancient, some in an old Elvish tongue that had more than a little connection to Jarlaxle's own drow tongue, and some in ancient Dwarvish. He couldn't make out the exact wording, but thought it was a memoriam of sorts, a tribute, perhaps a celebratory accounting of something grand represented by this chamber.

As the moments passed by, Athrogate inevitably slid toward the lever, licking his lips in anticipation. He was right in front of the thing when Jarlaxle put a hand on his shoulder to stop him. Glancing up at the drow, the dwarf followed his gaze to the walls and ceiling of the chamber, which were heavily veined with the tendrils of the Hosttower.

"What is it?" Athrogate asked.

"I believe it's the lever to power all of Gauntlgrym," Dor'crae replied. "Magical lights and rail carts that move of their own power—magic to give the city life once more!"

Athrogate started forward eagerly, but again Jarlaxle held him back. The drow turned to Dahlia with a questioning expression.

"Dor'crae . . . knows the place better than I," the woman explained.

Jarlaxle let go of Athrogate, who leaned toward the lever, but the drow kept staring at Dahlia and made no move to stop him.

"What is it?" Jarlaxle asked her, for there was something in Dahlia's voice then, some great uncertainty, some hesitation, that Jarlaxle had never heard from her before.

"I . . . agree with Dor'crae that it will bring Gauntlgrym back to life," Dahlia remarked, aiming the words at Athrogate.

"Or set loose the power of the fallen Hosttower upon us all," the drow argued. He knew she was lying, and knew that she was struggling with those lies.

"So we should just leave it and seek out the treasury?" Dahlia asked, waving her hand as if the thought was absurd—waving her hand a bit too dismissively.

"A fine idea," Jarlaxle agreed. "I am ever in favor of baubles."

Behind the drow, though, Dor'crae whispered to Athrogate, "Pull the lever, dwarf."

Jarlaxle knew then that there was more to that request, that the vampire was trying to exert his undead willpower over the dwarf. That, of course, came as a clear warning to Jarlaxle. He stepped toward Athrogate, but stopped abruptly as Valindra materialized right in front of him, staring at the drow with hunger, her fingers waggling in the air between them.

"What do you know?" the drow demanded of Dahlia.

"I like you, Jarlaxle," Dahlia replied. "I might even allow you to live."

"Athrogate, *no!*" Jarlaxle cried, but Dor'crae kept whispering and the strong dwarf moved to grasp the lever.

In her thoughts, she was a girl again, barely a teenager, standing on the edge of a cliff, her baby in her hands.

Herzgo Alegni's child.

She threw it. She killed it.

Dahlia proudly wore nine diamond studs in her left ear, one for every lover she had defeated in mortal combat. She always counted her kills as nine.

But what of the baby?

Why didn't she wear ten studs in her left ear?

Because she was not proud of that kill. Because, among everything that she had done in her flawed life, that moment struck Dahlia as the most wrong, the most wicked. It was Alegni's child, but it had not deserved its fate. Alegni the Shadovar barbarian, the rapist, the murderer, had deserved its fate, had deserved to witness that long fall, but not the child, never the child.

She knew what the lever would do. She had enlisted the drow because of the dwarf. Only a Delzoun dwarf could close that lever. And that was the point after all, to close the lever, to initiate the cataclysm, to free the power that fueled Gauntlgrym, to create the Dread Ring.

The circle of devastation would not be built on the soul of Herzgo Alegni, or even on those of a few wicked lovers deserving their doom. It would be built on innocents, on children, like the one she had thrown from the cliff.

"Athrogate, stop!" Dahlia heard herself saying, though she could hardly believe the words as they came forth.

All eyes turned to her—the confused dwarf, the suspicious drow, the surprised vampire, and the obviously amused lich.

"Do not touch it," Dahlia said, with strength seeping back into her voice.

Athrogate turned to her and put his hands on his hips.

"What do you know?" Jarlaxle asked her.

The image in front of Athrogate blurred, replaced by visions of Delzoun ghosts. They gathered before him, and begged him to pull the lever.

Free us! they implored him in his mind.

Give to us, and to Gauntlgrym, life anew! one pleaded.

The elf fears it! said another. *She fears us, and the return of the greatest dwarf kingdom!*

Athrogate stared with hatred at Dahlia, and turned back to the lever.

"Dahlia?" Jarlaxle asked.

The elf was stricken as she stared into the eyes of the drow. "It frees . . . the beast," she whispered.

Jarlaxle glanced back at Athrogate and Dahlia followed his gaze. Both looked on in alarm as the dwarf grabbed the lever in both hands.

"Athrogate, no!" they yelled together, but the dwarf was listening to other voices then, voices he thought belonged to the ghosts of his ancestors.

"He cannot hear you," Sylora assured the pair from the anteroom. As one, they spun to regard her, and her contingent of fierce Ashmadai warriors, standing just outside the archway, crowded on that side of the pit room.

Behind them came a grinding sound as Athrogate pulled the heavy lever.

"Tell him, Dahlia," Sylora said, tilting her chin at Jarlaxle.

The ground beneath them rumbled. Out past the anteroom came the sound of a great rush of water, like a tremendous waterfall rushing over the stones, then a hiss that sounded like a million giant vipers.

Looking past Sylora, Dahlia witnessed the rise of billowing steam, and within it, she noted living, watery forms—elementals, she presumed.

"What have we done?" Jarlaxle asked.

Sylora laughed at him. "Come Dor'crae," she bade the vampire. "Leave them to their doom."

"You betrayed me!" Dahlia shouted at the vampire. She noted just a hint of regret on his face, then she took up her staff and leaped at him, determined to destroy him first.

But Dor'crae was a human one blink and a bat the next. He fluttered past her, and past Jarlaxle into the anteroom, where Sylora had opened a magical gate once more, through which she and most of her prized Ashmadai zealots took their leave.

Valindra laughed hysterically then and blinked away, appearing at Sylora's side.

"Yes, you, too, my sweet," Sylora said to her, and showed her the skull gem, her phylactery, and bade her to enter the portal. "Tell him," Sylora called to Dahlia right before she too stepped through the portal, which would take her to Neverwinter Wood, where she could witness the carnage and glory of her triumph. "Tell your dark elf stooge of the end of the world." She laughed and disappeared, but closed the portal behind her, leaving a dozen Ashmadai behind.

"Occupy them, so they cannot leave," Sylora's disembodied voice instructed her warriors.

"Elf?" Athrogate asked from near the lever. "The ghosts told me to!"

"Sylora Salm told you to pull that lever," Dahlia explained, her voice full of rage and of regret, full of guilt and venomous spit.

"Tell me," Jarlaxle insisted.

The floor bucked again beneath them. From the pit came more hissing, more billowing steam, and a guttural roar that sounded as if Faerûn itself had been uncomfortably awakened.

"We've not the time," Dahlia replied. She took up her staff, snapping it open to its eight-foot length.

The Ashmadai charged.

Jarlaxle drove them back with a sudden barrage of thrown daggers that appeared as if from nowhere, then Athrogate drove them back further, bursting between the elf and the drow, morningstars in hand, his heart full of absolute outrage. "Defiled it!" he wailed. "Ruined it!"

Tiefling and human warriors came at him front, left, and right, swinging and stabbing their crimson scepters. But Athrogate didn't even try to stop the weapons, his focus purely on the offense. A morningstar head crushed the skull of the human on the left, a second swatted the half-elf on the right, and he met the head-butt of the tiefling in the center with his own armored skull.

And he bulled forward, undaunted. The dazed tiefling fell in front of him and Athrogate ran right over the half-blood thing to get to the next in line, his morningstars spinning furiously.

A stream of daggers flew over the dwarf's right shoulder, clearing that flank, then over his left to similar effect.

Then came Dahlia, running, planting the end of her staff and using it to vault right past Athrogate. By the time she'd landed, she had pulled the staff in and broken it into the twin flails. Around and over they went, out to the side and straight head, clipping scepter and clipping arms and cracking skulls when any got too near.

Not to be outdone, Athrogate paced her, though her fury was truly no less than his own.

The ground bucked, the floor rolled and cracked. The wall split on one side of the anteroom, and dust and stones fell from the ceiling.

As they neared the edge of the pit, the Ashmadai broke ranks and fled across the walkway, Dahlia and Athrogate giving chase, for that was the only way to go.

Jarlaxle came last, and he stubbornly paused and waited for the hot, billowing steam to clear enough so that he could see down to the lava.

So that he could stare into the face of the fire primordial.

He understood then the source of the power for Gauntlgrym's famed forge. He understood then the magic of the Hosttower, bringing in great elementals of water from the ocean to serve as a harness for that godlike beast. That magic had been gradually dissipating since the tower's fall, obviously, given the earthquakes that had wracked the region for so many years.

And Athrogate had shut the magic down entirely.

The elementals were fleeing, and the beast would be free.

Jarlaxle glanced back toward the lever, though he couldn't see it through the steam. They could reverse it, perhaps, and put the beast back in its harness.

He yelled out to Athrogate, but his voice couldn't rise above the wind and hiss of the rushing steam.

Then flames mixed with steam, rising up all around the walkway and the drow, and Jarlaxle had to run away, pulling tight his *piwafwi* and cowl to shield his eyes and skin.

He caught up to Dahlia and Athrogate in the forge room, facing off against the half-dozen remaining Ashmadai, who had no choice but to stand their ground before the portcullis, which was closed again. Beyond that gate huddled the angry ghosts of Gauntlgrym.

"If you surrender, we can guide you out of here!" Jarlaxle yelled to them, putting a sword in one hand as he took his place flanking Athrogate.

"They're Ashmadai," Dahlia explained. "Zealots of Asmodeus. They do not fear death, they welcome it."

"Then let's oblige 'em," Athrogate growled, and charged.

It struck Jarlaxle profoundly that the dwarf made no rhyme there, with battle so clear before him. But indeed, the dwarf was trembling with outrage at that point, and channeling all of his power to those devastating morningstars.

The Ashmadai howled and met the dwarf's charge with glee. Dahlia flanked out to the left, her twin weapons spinning to match Athrogate's morningstars, and Jarlaxle rushed up from the right. One against two, and two to each, they engaged.

Jarlaxle's free left hand snapped out a line of spinning daggers, down low at first as he neared the closest opponent, a tiefling bearing a strange symbol branded into his dusky flesh. But then he switched them up high with the last throw, forcing the cultist to lift his forearm to deflect the missile. And in that evasive movement, the tiefling lost sight of the drow for just a heartbeat.

A heartbeat too long.

Jarlaxle slid past on one knee, using the tiefling to block his own companion.

A stab to the back of the leg left that Ashmadai stumbling and skidding down, hamstrung.

Across came the other, stabbing his spear-staff for the drow's head.

But a second sword appeared in Jarlaxle's grasp, and swept up and around, parrying perfectly. And when the first followed behind that parry, the cultist had no defense.

Athrogate waded in, disregarding again the stab of one cultist and the heavy swing of the other. He took hits to trade the hits, and his weapons were better by far. A human Ashmadai stabbed him deep in the front of his shoulder as he brought his arm around, but that didn't deter the blow, for the dwarf was beyond feeling pain at that terrible moment, at the realization that he had destroyed the most sacred and ancient of dwarven homelands.

He felt his muscles tearing, but didn't care, and completed the rotation. The morningstar crashed down upon the human's lowered, leading shoulder with such force that it threw the cultist face down to the floor.

Athrogate stomped on the back of the Ashmadai's neck as he turned to face the second, and accepted a crack on the hand holding his other morningstar, the price of a missed block. Normally such a hit would have taken the weapon from his grasp, but not with Gauntlgrym exploding around him.

He plowed on with fury, both weapons swinging, driving the cultist back toward the lowered portcullis.

The Ashmadai ran out of room to retreat, so he worked his staff furiously to deflect and block. But a blow got through, crunching him in the side, driving him into a lurch. A second blow from the other side straightened him again, only to be hit again on the first side, higher up.

Then from the second side again, battering him, crushing his bones to dust, tearing his skin and sending his blood and brains flying wide to one side, then the other.

He crumpled to his knees and Athrogate kept hitting him—the only thing holding the dead cultist up were the dwarf's blows.

Dahlia was far more cautious. She worked her weapons defensively, picking off every thrust and swing, still fighting two enemies—a human woman and a male half-orc—long after Athrogate began to bull his remaining opponent backward.

She played for her opponents' mistakes, and as good as they were, Dahlia was better.

The Ashmadai to her left, the half-orc, moved to flank her, and the woman to her right predictably used her turn to come ahead boldly with a stab for Dahlia's turning hip.

But Dahlia reversed, and her swing indicated that she would send her left weapon all the way across to try to hook the spear aside.

The half-orc braced for the ruse, and was caught by surprise as Dahlia's right-hand weapon came up and under instead, yanking the spear-staff nearly from his grasp—and indeed, it would have taken that weapon away had that been Dahlia's intent. She disengaged with a subtle twist instead, and allowed herself to overbalance and fall to her leading, right knee, where she reversed the spin of that weapon and swept it low, taking the human's legs out from under her.

Dahlia rotated fully to bring her second weapon to bear, though she had no angle for such a spinning flail to do any real damage.

Except it was no longer a flail in her left hand, but a four-foot length of spear, and a slight twist stabbed it down hard into the woman's face, driving right into her opened mouth as she tried to scream. A burst of lightning exploded with the impact, and it seemed to jolt Dahlia back to her feet, where she broke the staff once more into twin flails, and waded into her remaining opponent.

She had the half-orc cultist backing up, though the ugly brute was skilled and managed to hold his ground well as Dahlia played out her momentum.

A flicker of silver flashed over Dahlia's shoulder and she dodged away and glanced back at the same time. She turned right back to her opponent, though, when she realized the flash was from one of Jarlaxle's endless daggers, which he'd buried deep into the half-orc Ashmadai's left eye.

Dahlia spun back as her last opponent fell aside, to see Jarlaxle rushing for the portcullis. Athrogate had amazingly hoisted the gate up to his shoulders once more.

Under went Jarlaxle, and Dahlia was quick to follow, fearing that those two would drop the gate and leave her to die—and who could blame them?

Jarlaxle rushed to brace his shoulder under one end, Dahlia the other, and Athrogate managed to scramble through.

The floor rumbled, the walls shook. The ghosts of Gauntlgrym were all on their knees, eyes and hands lifted in prayer to Moradin.

The trio ran on.

By the time they reached the circular stair, the complex was shaking violently. As they climbed back into the vast open cavern, they saw dire corbies falling and flailing. Bridges of stone that had survived the millennia cracked apart and tumbled down into oblivion.

"What have I done?" Athrogate wailed. "Oh, but a cursed creature I am!"

"Fly away!" Jarlaxle yelled at Dahlia. "Become a crow and be gone, you fool."

Dahlia tugged at her cloak, but not to enact its magic. She pulled it off and threw it into Jarlaxle's face. "Go!" she yelled at him.

The drow could hardly believe it, but he didn't don the cloak and flee. He urged Athrogate on instead, and tugged at Dahlia to keep up.

They reached the top of the stair exhausted, but they couldn't rest. The quaking diminished in violence as they ascended, but arches cracked and tumbled, and jambs tilted, sealing doors, perhaps forever.

But still they ran on, and kept running until they again came to the circular chamber with the jeweled throne, and kept running through the tunnel and out the gates, and kept running to the edge of the underground pool.

Jarlaxle threw the cloak back at Dahlia. "Make your way," he told her. "And we'll make ours."

"How will you cross?" she asked.

Jarlaxle looked at her as if she was mad. "I am Jarlaxle," he said. "I will find my way."

Dahlia donned the cloak and became a great bird. She flew away, across the lake and down the tunnels.

A mere two days later, she emerged into the dirty streets of Luskan, surprised to see that the city was still standing, and that life there seemed normal. She looked to the southeast, to the sky above Gauntlgrym.

There was nothing.

Perhaps she had overestimated the power of the trapped primordial. Perhaps they had merely shut down the forge, and had not loosed a cataclysm.

"Say nothing of our adventure," Jarlaxle bade Athrogate when they, too, made it back to Luskan, later that same day, having ridden their summoned mounts—hell boar and nightmare—all the way from Gauntlgrym. They had crossed the underground pond on the back of a giant, flightless bird, created from the feather on Jarlaxle's hat, for thankfully, the pond was quite shallow.

"Ye should've left me to die there," the sorely wounded Athrogate replied.

"We'll find a way to fix it," Jarlaxle promised. "If it even needs fixing," he added, for he, too, was somewhat surprised to see the normalcy of life in Luskan.

Soon after, though, the very next dawn, he realized that it would indeed need to be fixed, for in the distant southwest, Athrogate spotted a plume of black smoke rising lazily into the air.

"Elf," he said, his voice somber.

"I see it."

"What is it?"

"Catastrophe," Jarlaxle answered.

"Ye said we'd fix it," Athrogate reminded him.

"At the very least, we'll repay those who did this."

"Was meself!" Athrogate said, but Jarlaxle shook his head, knowing better.

For surely the worldly drow had recognized the distinctive garb of the woman who had arrived in the anteroom to mock Dahlia and steal away with Valindra and Dor'crae. She was Thayan, a disciple of Szass Tam, no doubt.

As he considered that, Jarlaxle looked back at the plume of black smoke, so many miles distant, but still visible in the morning sky. He didn't know much about the archlich of Thay, but from what he did know, he thought, perhaps, that they might be better off facing the primordial.

From her room at the inn halfway across the city, Dahlia, too, plotted her revenge, and she, too, spotted the plume.

She had done her research well, though, and harbored no hope that the smoke would be the end of it. And no hope of averting the catastrophe.

The primordial would shake off the last remaining elementals—great creatures of water put in place by the ancient wizards of the Hosttower to harness the power of the fiery, godlike being for the benefit of the dwarven forge.

It would have broken free eventually, Dahlia knew, for the fall of the Hosttower had begun the erosion of that harnessing magic.

But not so soon. Not without some warning for the wizards and scribes of the Sword Coast.

Disaster, swift and complete, would come, and nothing she or anyone else could do could stop it, even slow it, now.

CHAPTER 9

WHEN THE WORLD BLEW UP

S HE KNEW SHE WAS BEING FOLLOWED. FOR A LONG WHILE, SHE had thought it her imagination, her very real fear that she had made some powerful enemies down there in Gauntlgrym, who would not so easily allow her to escape their wrath.

But how had they found her? Wouldn't they have presumed her killed in the ancient dwarven city?

Sylora would have assumed the deaths of the Ashmadai she'd left behind, but then Dahlia reached up and felt the brooch she still wore, the brooch that gave her some power over the undead, the brooch that tied her to Szass Tam. Horrified, she yanked it from her blouse and threw it into the next open sewer hole she passed.

She wound a zigzagging course through the city, taking every available alley, vaulting to a roof at one point, and running on with all speed. But still they followed her, she sensed when weariness slowed her some time later.

Dahlia turned down the next alleyway, determined to double back so that she could get a better look at her pursuers. A wooden fence blocked the far end, but Dahlia knew she could scale it easily enough. A few strides short of it, she picked up her pace to leap but skidded to a quick stop as two large men—tieflings—stepped out from behind some piled crates to block her way.

"Sister Dahlia," one said. "Why do you run?"

The elf glanced back, and was hardly surprised to see three more of the burly half-devils moving down the alleyway toward her. They were all dressed in the typical garb of a Luskar, but she knew the truth of who they were, confirmed by the speaker's referral to her as "sister."

Sylora had moved quickly to the chase.

Dahlia stood up straight and replaced her concerned expression with one of amusement. That was her way. When no option for flight presented itself, there remained the joy of battle.

She snapped her staff to its eight-foot length and presented it horizontally in front of her, dropping the two-foot length off either end to form her tri-staff.

"Would any challenge me directly, or must I kill all five of you at once?" she asked, starting the ends spinning in slow, end-over-end loops.

None of the Ashmadai moved toward her, fell into a defensive crouch, or even drew a weapon, and that unnerved the elf.

What did they know?

"You will continue this course?" a woman's voice said in front of her while Dahlia was glancing over her shoulder at the three Ashmadai behind her. She turned to see Sylora standing between the two tieflings, looking magnificent as always in her red, low-cut gown, with that stiff, high collar framing her hairless head. "You would turn your failure into betrayal? I had thought you wiser than that."

Dahlia took her time digesting those words, unsure how to respond.

"When the moment of glory came, Dahlia failed," Sylora explained. "Do you think we, who are truer servants of Szass Tam, were surprised that our brash young sister could not execute the initiation of the Dread Ring? Do you believe that we, that I, ever expected anything better of you? And so I intervened to ensure that Szass Tam would not be disappointed. You did so much fine work in locating the primordial, after all, even if you then—"

"Then you tried to kill me," Dahlia interrupted.

Sylora shrugged. "I couldn't trust you to come with us, not when you had such powerful allies, that dwarf and his dark elf patron. You left me little choice, and even tried to stop what had to be done."

"And now you've come to kill me," Dahlia stated instead of asked, and her pretty blue eyes flashed with excitement. "Will you hide behind your zealot lackeys again, or will you join in the fight this time?"

"Were it up to me, you would be dead already," Sylora replied, and she tossed something at Dahlia's feet. The elf warrior dodged and braced, expecting a fireball or some other disaster to erupt, but when nothing happened and she got a good look at the item Sylora had tossed, she recognized her recently discarded brooch and nothing more.

"Our master sees potential in you still," Sylora explained. "He bade me take you under my wing, as my servant."

"Never!"

Sylora held up a finger. "You have a chance to get through this alive, Dahlia, and again serve in the ranks of the lich-lord. Perhaps you might even redeem yourself in his eyes, perhaps even in mine. And it's that or die. Would you forfeit your life so easily?"

Dahlia mulled on the offer for a few heartbeats. She knew Sylora would make her life miserable, of course, but at least she might have a chance.

"Come," Sylora bade her. "Reconsider. There is heated battle joined in the south. With the Netherese, no less. You would enjoy killing Shadovar, would you not?"

Dahlia felt the defiance draining out of her so completely she wondered if Sylora had enacted an enchantment upon her. The worry was fleeting, though, for she knew the source of her melting resolve. Was there anything in the world Dahlia hated more than the Netherese?

She looked at Sylora, hardly trusting the Thayan.

"My dear, if I wanted you dead, you would be dead already," Sylora replied to that suspicious expression. "I could have filled this alley with killing magic, or with murderous Ashmadai." She held out her hand. "Our road is to the south, to battle the Netherese. I will count you among my lieutenants, and as long as you fight well, I will trouble you little."

"I am to trust Sylora Salm?"

"Hardly. But I serve Szass Tam, and he holds hope for you. When the beast comes forth, I claim the credit for the catastrophe, as it is mine to take. Your role will be seen as minor—an agent gathering information, and in the critical moment, failing. But you're young still, and will redeem yourself with every Netherese beast you slay."

Dahlia stopped her end-poles from spinning, clicked the staff back whole, and broke it into a four-foot walking stick once more. She bent and picked up the brooch, holding it in front of her eyes for just a few moments before fastening it once more to her blouse.

On the other side of the wooden fence, Barrabus the Gray listened to every word. Of particular concern, despite the obvious gravity of the conversation, was the reference to a drow and a dwarf, connected somehow to this elf warrior, Dahlia. He had learned little in his short time in Luskan, though he'd traveled to the undercity and had seen and spoken with the phylactery that held the spirit of Arklem Greeth.

He couldn't yet put all the pieces together, but he felt he had enough to satisfy that wretch Alegni.

He was on the road soon after, riding hard to the south on a summoned nightmare that didn't tire, and watching, every stride, the line of smoke rising into the clear late-summer sky far to the southeast.

Parallel to Barrabus, but many miles away, Drizzt Do'Urden, too, rode a magical mount and watched that same plume. He had left Bruenor at their latest camp, a small village where they had bartered work for food and shelter, the first afternoon of the smoke's appearance.

Andahar's great strides carried him swiftly, the unicorn charging across the woodland, hilly terrain with ease. Drizzt let the bells of the barding sing for the run, welcoming the diversion of the song.

It had been a difficult and frustrating summer for the drow and his dwarf friend. The continuing disappointments of one dead end after another had started to wear on Bruenor. Drizzt recognized that the former king missed his rugged, rough friend Pwent, though of course Bruenor would never admit any such thing.

There was a restlessness growing in Drizzt, too, but he did well to keep it from Bruenor. How many years could he spend hunting in holes for some sign of an ancient dwarven kingdom? He loved Bruenor as much as any friend he had ever known, but it had been just the two of them for a long time. Their parting a couple days before had been of mutual agreement.

The drow rode Andahar hard, and when he at last found a trade road, Drizzt didn't stay to the side of it, as prudence always demanded in those times of banditry in the wild Crags.

He didn't think of it openly, didn't admit it to himself, but Drizzt Do'Urden would have liked nothing more at that time than to be confronted by highwaymen, and hopefully a sizable band. Too long had his blades sat in their scabbards, too long had Taulmaril the Heartseeker sat quiet across his back.

He rode for the smoke, hoping that it signaled something amiss, some battle waiting to be joined or already joined.

As long as there remained enemies worth fighting. . . .

He continued on a southerly route, not going straight for the plume. He knew the ground fairly well, and noted that the smoke was coming from Mount Hotenow—one of the few hills in the Crags tall enough to rightfully be called a mountain. It had two peaks, the lower one to the north, the taller south-southeast of that, and of both of bald stone the result of some long-ago fire that had burned the trees away, and had allowed erosion to wash away most of the soil.

The best approach to the two-peaked mountain was from the southeast, Drizzt knew, where he could get a good look at the area before riding in. As he passed by the mountain, he veered even farther away, riding to the southeast and another tall hill from which he could gain a better vantage point. It seemed as if the smoke poured out of the top of the lower, northern peak.

Drizzt dismissed Andahar at the base of the steep, forested hill. Bow in hand, he scaled the mountainside, moving from tree to tree so he could brace himself before attempting to move any higher. At last he gained the top. Drizzt thought to climb a tree, but saw a better option in a rocky outcrop on the mound's western side, directly facing the distant, twin-peaked mountain.

He came out into the open and cupped a hand over his eyes to gain a better view of the distant, smoking peak. He could see no armies moving about, and no dragons in the blue sky.

A bonfire from a barbarian encampment, perhaps? A giant's forge?

None of it made sense to Drizzt. To sustain a fire of such magnitude for so long—the smoke plume had been visible for several days—would have taken a forest of lumber. Bruenor had, of course, claimed that it must be a dwarven forge, a dwarven fire, an ancient dwarven kingdom—but he always made that claim, at any sign.

Drizzt continued to stare into the distance for a long while, following the line as close to the mountain stones as he could make out. He noted, too, when a breeze temporarily cleared the opaque veil, some redness there, streaking the stones.

Then the world blew up.

Standing on the Herzgo Alegni Bridge in Neverwinter, Barrabus the Gray and Herzgo Alegni also noted the smoke plume, so clear in the sky from their nearer vantage point.

"A forest fire?" Barrabus guessed. "I never got too near to it, and the folk in Port Llast had no more insight into it than anyone here in Neverwinter, apparently."

"You didn't think it prudent to go and investigate?" Alegni scolded.

"I thought my information regarding the Thayans and this catastrophe they're planning was more urgent."

"And you haven't thought that these events might be connected? Is there, perhaps, a red dragon just northeast of here, waiting to fly to this Sylora creature's call?" As he spoke, the Netherese commander walked to the bridge's edge closest the distant spectacle and locked his hands on the rail, peering to the north.

"And if I went there and couldn't return to you in time, you would be even less prepared," Barrabus argued.

Alegni didn't look back at him.

"I grant you that," the tiefling said after a short pause. "Go there now and learn what you may." He glanced over his shoulder to see Barrabus scowling. "It's not so far."

"Difficult terrain, far from the road."

"You speak as if I—" Alegni started to say, but he stopped when Barrabus's eyes went wide with shock.

Herzgo Alegni spun back toward the plume, toward the low mountain—

—the low mountain that had leaped into the sky, it seemed, solid rock transforming into something more malleable, like a cloud of impossibly thick ash.

The Ashmadai in Neverwinter Wood fell to their knees in prayer and joy, overwhelmed at the sight of what they knew would be the beginning of a grand Dread Ring.

"Oh, but the gods are with us!" Sylora cried as the mountain flew high, and she noted the angle of the blast. "If I had aimed it myself . . ."

The fall of the mountain seemed perfectly aimed at the city of Neverwinter—and indeed it was. Mount Hotenow had not simply erupted. The angry primordial sought carnage as hungrily as did Szass Tam.

Sylora dropped her arm across Dahlia's shoulders and shook the elf with familiarity.

"We must take cover, quickly!" Sylora instructed her charges, and they were not unprepared. "The beast, *our* beast, has roared!"

All around Dahlia, Ashmadai rushed to and fro, gathering their belongings and running for the cave they had chosen as their shelter. Dor'crae and Valindra were already in there, shielded from the stinging daylight.

Dahlia didn't move. She couldn't move, frozen in awe, in horror, at the spectacle of the freed primordial, of the exploding volcano.

What had she done?

Drizzt watched the lower peak of the mountain as it seemed to simply come apart and leap skyward. He thought of a long-ago day on a beach outside of Waterdeep, a hot summer day. He and Catti-brie had been serving with Deudermont aboard *Sea Sprite,* and had put into port for supplies and respite. The couple had wandered down to the shore to spend a quiet afternoon.

He thought of that peaceful time in that most terrifying of moments, for he had played a game that day, burying Catti-brie's legs under the wet beach sand.

Watching the mountain break apart reminded him of when Catti-brie had lifted her sand-covered legs. The stones in the distance seemed to come apart like beach sand, but revealing lines of angry red lava instead of the smooth flesh of Catti-brie's calf.

Strangely silent for many heartbeats, the lifting mountain expanded and stretched, twisting and blending with the heavy cloud into a weird shape, like the neck and head of a bird.

Only then did Drizzt realize that the silence was only because the shockwave, the devastating wall of sound, hadn't yet reached him. He saw trees in the far distance falling over toward him, falling over away from the mountain.

Then the ground beneath his feet lurched and rolled, and the sound of a hundred roaring dragons had him falling aside and covering his ears. He caught one last glimpse of the volcano as the mountain stone tumbled down, a wall of stone and ash many times taller than the tallest tree, running madly for the ocean, burying and burning everything in its path.

"By the gods," Herzgo Alegni whispered.

The mountain leaped, tumbled, and had begun to roll at tremendous speed, devouring everything in its path.

And its path led directly for Neverwinter.

"The end of the world," Barrabus the Gray whispered, and those words from that man, so out of place, so hyperbolic and yet so . . . inadequate, spoke volumes to them both.

"I go," Alegni announced just moments later. He looked at Barrabus and shrugged. "Farewell."

And Herzgo Alegni stepped into the Shadow Fringe, leaving Barrabus alone on the bridge.

Alone, but not for long, for the folk of Neverwinter saw their doom then and took to the streets, running and screaming, crying and calling for loved ones.

Barrabus watched people rush into buildings, but one look at the coming avalanche of fiery rock and it was clear the waddle and daub buildings of Neverwinter would provide no shelter.

Where could he run? How could he possibly escape?

The assassin looked to the water, naturally, and thought for just a moment of leaping into the river to swim for the sea. But when he glanced back the other way, he saw that the mountain was almost upon him, and there, in the river, lay certain doom.

Huge, fiery stones began raining down around him, splashing into the river, shattering houses.

What could survive?

Barrabus the Gray went over the side of the bridge, but didn't jump or fall. He climbed right under it and tucked himself into the iron substructure.

Around him the screams of the Neverwintan increased in pitch and magnitude, until the roar of a hundred dragons drowned them out. Then came the crunching explosions of more buildings being shattered, the splash of water, and the hiss of protest as the hot flow swept over the river.

Barrabus shielded himself as much as he could, not even daring to look as the flow rushed beneath him, nearly reaching him. He felt the intense heat, as if he was sitting with his face inches from the hot fires of a blacksmith's oven. The bridge shook, and he thought it would surely crumble to pieces and drop him to his death.

On and on it went, the thunder and fire, the falling fireballs, the ultimate devastation of an entire city.

Then, as instantly as the first wave of sound had roared in his ears, there was silence.

A dead, muted silence.

Not a scream, not a groan, not a wail. A bit of wind, but nothing more.

After a long while, an hour or more, Barrabus the Gray dared crawl out from under the Herzgo Alegni Bridge. He had to put his cloak over his face as a filter against the burning ash that permeated the air.

Everything was gray and deep, and dead.

Neverwinter was dead.

PART II

II

THE KING'S MINIONS

The fights are increasing and it pleases me.

The world around me has grown darker, more dangerous . . . and it pleases me.

I have just passed a period of my life most adventurous and yet, strangely, most peaceful, where Bruenor and I have climbed through a hundred hundred tunnels and traveled as deep into the Underdark as I have been since my last return to Menzoberranzan. We found our battles of course, mostly with the oversized vermin that inhabit such places, a few skirmishes with goblins and orcs, a trio of trolls here, a clan of ogres there. Never was there any sustained battle, though, never anything to truly test my blades, and indeed, the most perilous day I have known since our departure from Mithral Hall those many years ago was when an earthquake threatened to bury us in some tunnels.

But no more is that the case, I find, and it pleases me. Since that day of cataclysm, a decade ago, when the volcano roared forth and painted a line of devastation from the mountain all the way to the sea, burying Neverwinter in its devastating run, the tone of the region has changed. It is almost as if that one event had sent forth a call for conflict, a clarion call for sinister beings.

In a sense, it did just that. The loss of Neverwinter in essence severed the North from the more civilized regions along the Sword Coast, where Waterdeep has now become the vanguard against the wilderness. Traders no longer travel through the region, except by sea, and the lure of Neverwinter's former treasures has pulled adventurers—often unsavory, often unprincipled—in great numbers to the devastated city.

Some are trying to rebuild, desperate to restore the busy port and the order it once imposed upon these inhospitable lands. But they battle as much as they build. They carry a carpenter's hammer in one hand, a warhammer in the other.

Enemies abound: Shadovar, those strange cultists sworn to a devil god, opportunistic highwaymen, goblinkin, giants, and monsters alive and undead. And other things, darker things from deeper holes.

In the years since the cataclysm, the northern Sword Coast has grown darker by far.

And it pleases me.

When I am in battle, I am free. When my blades cut low a scion of evil, only then do I feel as if there is purpose to my life. Many times have I wondered if this rage within is just a reflection of a heritage I have never truly shaken. The focus of battle, the intensity of the fight, the satisfaction of victory . . . are they all merely an admission that I am, after all, drow?

And if that is the truth, then what did I actually know about my homeland and my people, and what did I merely paste onto a caricature I had created of a society whose roots lay in passion and lust I had not yet begun to understand or experience?

Was there, I wonder—and I fear—some deeper wisdom to the Matron Mothers of Menzoberranzan, some understanding of drow joy and need that perpetuated the state of conflict in the drow city?

It seems a ridiculous thought, and yet only through battle have I endured the pain. Only through battle have I found again a sense of accomplishment, of forward movement, of bettering community.

This truth surprises me, angers me, and paradoxically, even as it offers me hope to continue, it hints at some notion that perhaps I should not, that this existence is only a futile thing, after all, a mirage, a self-delusion.

Like Bruenor's quest.

I doubt he'll find Gauntlgrym, I doubt it exists and I doubt that he believes he'll find it, either, or that he ever believed he would find it. And yet every day he pores over his collection of maps and clues, and leaves no hole unexplored. It is his purpose. The search gives meaning to the life of Bruenor Battlehammer. Indeed, it seems the nature of the dwarf, and of the dwarves in general, who are always talking of things gone by and reclaiming the glory that once was.

What is the nature of the drow, then?

Even before I lost her, my love Catti-brie, and my dear halfling friend, I knew that I was no creature of calm and respite. I knew my nature was that of the warrior. I knew I was happiest when adventure and battle summoned me forth, demanding of those skills I had spent my entire life perfecting.

I relish it more now—is that because of my pain and loss, or is it merely a truer reflection of my heritage?

And if that is the case, will the cause of battle widen, will the code that guides my scimitars weaken to accommodate more moments of joy? At what point, I wonder—and I fear—does my desire for battle, that which is in my heart, interfere with that which is in my conscience? Is it easier now to justify drawing my blades?

That is my true fear, that this rage within me will come forth in all its madness—explosively, randomly, murderously.

My fear?

Or my hope?

—Drizzt Do'Urden

CHAPTER 10

BATTLING THE DARKNESS

The Year of the Elves' Weeping
(1462 DR)

HERE THEY COME! OH, BE BRAVE BOYS AND HOLD THE TEAMS!"
the caravan boss cried out to the men and women crouched
in and around the wagons, weapons in hand. Off to the side of the
road, the thicket shook with the approaching storm of enemies.

"Scrabblers," one man said, his nickname for the agile and swift
undead humanoids that had infested the region.

"Dustwalkers," corrected another, and that name seemed equally
fitting, for those marauders, undead monsters, left rails of gray
powder in their wake, as if every step they took was their first out
of the ashes of a burned out hearth—and indeed, the rumors said
that the monsters were the animated corpses of those who had been
buried beneath the volcanic ash a decade before.

"Guard!" the boss called out after a few more tense moments
passed, without any clear sight of the enemy. "Go and scout the
tree line."

The hired guard, a stocky old dwarf with a beard of silver and
orange, a shield emblazoned with the crest of the foaming mug, a
many-notched axe, and a one-horned helmet, turned a wary eye
on the leader.

The man swallowed hard under that withering gaze, but to his
credit, managed to summon enough courage to once again motion
toward the trees.

"I told ye when ye hired me," the dwarf warned. "Ye might
be telling me what to fight, but ye ain't telling me how to fight."

"We cannot just sit here while they plot!"

"Plot?" the dwarf echoed with a belly laugh. "They're dumb dead, ye dolt. They ain't plottin'."

"Then where are they?" another man cried, who seemed on the verge of desperation.

"Maybe they aren't out there. Maybe it's just the wind," said a woman from a wagon near the back.

"Ye all ready for a fight?" the dwarf asked. "Ye got yer weapons in hand?" He looked at the boss, who stood tall, scanned the five wagons, and nodded.

Bruenor stood up, stuck his thumbs in this mouth, and blew a loud whistle.

Everyone but the dwarf reflexively ducked then as a shot of lightning creased the air to the side of the caravan, emanating from somewhere behind and streaking horizontally across the way to disappear into the trees. A horrid shriek came back, and a rustle of branches.

A second bolt knifed into the trees.

The branches began to rustle again.

"Here they come now," the dwarf said, loud enough for all to hear. "Ye fight well and die better!"

Across the way, the scrabblers, the dustwalkers, the ash zombies—whatever name anyone wanted to put on the small, shriveled gray humanoids—came forth in a sudden rush, leaping from branches or running out of the tree line, some upright and swaying back and forth as if they might tip over with every stride, others hunched and scrambling on all fours.

And the other way, behind the crouching drivers and caravanners, came the sound of bells singing sweetly, and the pounding of hooves.

Another streaking arrow shot past from a magical bow, blinding and devastating as it exploded into the head of the nearest monster, blasting it apart in a puff of gray ash.

The caravan's horses neighed as mighty Andahar approached, and one team reared when the magnificent unicorn cleared a wagon in one great leap, landing clean on the other side with Drizzt already readying another arrow.

He shot dead a pair of zombies, the bolt blasting through one and into the other, and in one fluid motion he shouldered the bow, drew out his scimitars, and rolled off the side of the galloping mount.

Andahar continued on, lowered his head, and plowed through the nearest monsters, impaling one on his spiral horn and blasting aside the other.

Drizzt hit the ground in a controlled roll, turning right back up to his feet and charging along as smoothly as if he'd been running the whole time. He rushed between a pair of zombies, scimitars slashing out to either side, cutting them down. He skidded to a stop before a third, bringing his blades up in a circling maneuver over his head, back to front, the blades sliding past each other above and in front of him as he brought them forward. He drove his left arm out straight, blade horizontal and at eye level to block the wild overhead swings of a charging zombie—and the creature showed no sign of pain at all as its forearms dived into a solid defensive block, as its ashen skin gashed on the fine edge of Twinkle.

In the same movement Drizzt executed the block with Twinkle, he cocked his right elbow back behind him, and as he turned his leading blade off to the side, further skinning the zombie's arms, he stepped forward and thrust Icingdeath hard into the monster's chest. The scimitar blasted through with such force that Drizzt noted a puff of ash behind the zombie.

That hole seemed barely to affect the monster, but it was hardly a surprise to the seasoned drow ranger. Even as he retracted Icingdeath, he brought Twinkle in with a downward slash, one that got tangled with the zombie's arms and kept it off-balance and defenseless as Icingdeath went down, under and around and back in from the other side, connecting solidly across the monster's neck and chopping it down.

All of it—the block, the stab, the two slashes—happened so quickly that Drizzt hardly slowed his forward progress, and he simply ran up and over the zombie as it tumbled backward. He managed to glance back, to see his mighty steed lift its hind quarters in a double kick and explode a zombie into a cloud of ash. Most of the other monsters chased after Andahar, with only a few continuing for the caravan.

Creatures turned in for Drizzt from left and right, moving with startling agility and speed for undead, and yet still not quickly enough to catch up to the blur that was Drizzt Do'Urden, his legs speeded by magical anklets, his balance always perfect, his strategy three steps ahead.

He veered left, blasting right into a group of zombies—so many that the caravan crew and Bruenor collectively gasped as he disappeared into a sea of gray ash. But so fast and perfect were his slashes, driving aside impediments, and so fast his stabs, to the side, in front of him, even a backhand to defeat pursuit, that he didn't slow, and the collective gasp became a collective cheer when he reappeared out the other side, seemingly in the clear, but with a horde of zombies still in pursuit.

And behind the zombies, Drizzt knew, came Bruenor, cutting down the distracted undead as they chased the dark elf.

But the drow had to skid to a stop, surprised, when out of the thicket to the side charged another enemy, another zombie. The newcomer was not one of the humans, elves, or dwarves shriveled in the hot flow of the volcano, though, but a gigantic and formidable beast, one which in life would have challenged Drizzt and in undeath, feeling no pain, knowing no fear, and all but immune to minor wounds, was all the more formidable. It stood nearly twice Drizzt's height and outweighed him at least four times over with giant pincers protruding from its face and long wiry arms ending in claws that could rend stone as easily as a man could dig in soft dirt. Drizzt had battled umber hulks before, as had so many of his kin, growing up in the Underdark, but in addition to the ashen gray look of those creatures killed by the hot volcanic flow, the hulk had about it a darker pall, a shadowy essence as though it had stepped out of the depths of the Shadowfell.

Drizzt managed to avert his eyes just in time to avoid the creature's magical gaze, known to debilitate the finest warriors. He didn't wait to look back before moving, guessing correctly that any delay would cost him dearly. He darted right at the monster, just within the sweeping reach of its powerful claws. The shadow hulk tried to stomp him as he skidded past, but Drizzt tucked into a roll and got out of the way in time, even managing to stab that stomping foot for good measure. He came up to his feet and darted straight behind the thing, keeping it turning, and landed several heavy slashes in the process.

But felling the monster would be like chopping down a thick oak, and an oak that savagely fought back.

"Keep it moving, elf!" he heard Bruenor yell from across the way, still back near the caravan wagons.

"Indeed," the drow whispered in reply, having no intention of facing up squarely against that beast.

He got in one last slash and darted away, drawing forth an onyx figurine as soon as he put some space between himself and the shadow hulk.

"Come to me, Guenhwyvar," Drizzt called softly. He hadn't wanted to summon the panther, for she had fought beside him the night before and needed her rest in her Astral home.

He saw the gray mist appearing and ran beyond it, the shadow hulk in swift pursuit.

"Keep him moving, elf!" he heard Bruenor cry from the side.

Drizzt glanced that way to watch the dwarf rush out to the side of the wagons toward a large boulder flanked by a few birch trees. With a knowing nod, Drizzt spun, surprising the shadow hulk just enough so that he could again rush inside the deadly sweep of its clawing hands. He snapped off several stabs and left with a heavy slash—or feigned leaving. Again he spun, just outside the creature's turn. He went past again with another flurry of stabs and slashes. He'd just started to run once more when he heard the growl then the impact as a leaping Guenhwyvar slammed against the shadow hulk's back. Drizzt darted off to the side as the monster staggered under the weight of six hundred pounds of muscled panther.

"The little ones, Guen!" Drizzt yelled in alarm, seeing that many ash zombies still surrounded Andahar and more moved to press the caravan crew.

With a puff of smoky ash, the panther leaped away, even as Drizzt again came in at the shadow hulk. The creature foolishly turned as if to follow Guenhwyvar, allowing the ranger several heavy strikes.

Then Drizzt was running again, the shadow hulk in close pursuit. He glanced in the direction of the caravan, nodding in satisfaction to see that Guenhwyvar was already rounding up the zombies and shredding them with her powerful claws.

Drizzt kept just ahead of the shadow hulk—dangerously close. He wanted the creature's focus on him alone as he ran in a loop, bringing it right in front of the boulder where Bruenor had disappeared. He rushed out only a few strides from the stone then spun back to squarely face the monster.

A clawed hand swung down from on high, too powerfully for Drizzt to even dare attempt a block. He dodged aside and the arm crashed down against the ground, the monster's three claws digging deep gashes in earth and stone alike.

Drizzt stabbed and dodged, whirled to one side then the other, striking where he could find an opening, but fighting defensively, just trying to keep the shadow hulk engaged and distracted.

Out of the corner of his eye, he caught sight of Bruenor again, running to the top of the boulder and beyond, descending from on high with a great leap, his many-notched axe up high over his head and held in both hands. The dwarf's whole body seemed to bend and snap forward, like the jaws of a giant wolf, his muscles only adding to his momentum as he drove the axe home.

A weird grunt came forth from the shadow hulk, sounding far more surprised, even curious, than pained. The creature took a step toward Drizzt, its expression somewhat pensive, as if it were only then grasping the reality of its sudden end.

Drizzt stared at that curious expression for many heartbeats—so many that he had to dive aside to avoid being buried by the falling monster.

Despite the many undead still left to be dealt with, Drizzt couldn't suppress a smile as he watched Bruenor ride the shadow hulk the last couple of feet to the ground. His shield hand still gripping his axe, his free hand up behind him, it looked as though the dwarf was breaking a wild horse.

"Elf, I'm thinking of a yeti on the tundra," the dwarf said, tearing his axe free. "Always seems as if ye're needin' saving!"

"So, as you did with the yeti, will you try to cook this one's brains?" Drizzt asked, spinning away and heading for the nearest monster.

"Bah!" the dwarf snorted. "Tastin' like dust or I'm a bearded gnome!"

For all the years and all the battles, for all the loss and all the strange roads, there was nothing Bruenor might have said to better comfort Drizzt just then, and to better launch him into the next fight, and the one after that.

With Andahar and Guenhwyvar, and some small assistance from the caravanners, the attack was beaten back in short order, leaving only minor wounds for a few of the merchants and guards, and no real damage to any of the wagons or horse teams. They were on their way in short order, with Drizzt riding flank.

By dawn, the road had turned directly west and they broke out of the woodland and onto an open plain. The sea flanked them on the left, and with so much open ground to their right, most of the crew settled in for some sleep.

Drizzt dismissed his magical mount and climbed aboard the jockey seat of the last wagon, Bruenor beside him. They would make Neverwinter by noon, so the boss informed them, and even though so many were weary, they wouldn't stop the caravan.

"A fine, well-paying journey," Drizzt remarked to Bruenor, speaking as much to keep himself alert as for any desire for conversation.

"Not that ye're caring," a sleepy Bruenor replied.

Drizzt cocked an eyebrow the dwarf's way.

"Bah, but ye only did this for the fightin'!" Bruenor accused.

"We need the coin," Drizzt replied.

"Ye'd do it for free. Anything to sing yer blades."

"Our funds are not inexhaustible, my friend. You paid good gold for that last map you acquired."

"An investment, I tell ye! Think o' the treasures Gauntlgrym'll give us!" Bruenor insisted.

"And that map will lead us there?"

"Not for knowing," Bruenor admitted. "But one o' them will."

"That map, scrawled by a Calishite sailor, a pirate no less, will lead us to our destination, which a thousand-thousand dwarves have not found in a thousand years of searching?"

"Ah, shut yer mouth."

Drizzt grinned at him.

"Ye hide in yer blades," Bruenor said more seriously.

Drizzt didn't answer, just looked straight ahead at the road and the wagons in front of them.

"Ye always did. I know," the dwarf continued, "I seen it in Icewind Dale when first we met. I remember me boy shaking his head and callin' ye crazy when ye took him into the lair o' that giant, Biggrin. But never like this, elf. I'm thinking that if ye had a choice o' two roads, one safe and one thick with monsters, ye'd take the thick one."

"I didn't pick this road, you did," Drizzt replied.

"Nah, yerself signed us on as guards, ready for the fight."

"We need the coin, O Great Cave Crawler."

"Bah," Bruenor grumbled, shaking his head.

They were indeed short of funds, but not destitute by any means, having taken a rather tidy sum along with them from Mithral Hall those many years ago, and really, other than Bruenor's quest for maps and trinkets, they had little on which they needed to spend the coin.

The dwarf let it go at that, and drifted off to sleep, where he found comfortable dreams of yesteryear, of Kelvin's Cairn in Icewind Dale, and the high perch upon it known as Bruenor's Climb. Of running with the Companions of the Hall, him and the elf, and his boy and his girl and the halfling he so often found fishing on the banks of Maer Dualdon.

It had been a good life, Bruenor decided. Good and long, and full of fine friends and fine adventures.

They came in sight of Neverwinter soon after, and no one spoke a word of protest when the boss stopped the lead wagon on a high ridge overlooking the place, so that all could take in the sight. Once it had been a sprawling city, a great port, then, with the eruption of Mount Hotenow, it had been no more than a desolate, barren ruin of black stone and deep gray ash.

But the wounds in the land were healing, plants growing thick in the rich volcanic soil, and while many of the ruins of old Neverwinter were still visible, new structures had been built. Few in number, none approaching the grandeur of old Neverwinter as of yet, the small settlement seemed truly discordant. The most impressive structure to be seen, by far, was the old Winged Wyvern Bridge, which had briefly been called something else no one remembered. It had escaped the devastation nearly unscathed, with only one abutment taking any noticeable damage, and it had come to serve as the centerpiece, the promise, of what Neverwinter might become anew.

So entranced were Bruenor and Drizzt at the sight of the distant town, neither noticed the approach of the caravan boss.

"She'll be rebuilt to all her glory," the man said, drawing them from their personal contemplations. "Not to doubt the resilience of the folk of the Sword Coast. They'll . . . *we'll* make Neverwinter what she once was, and more.

"What do you say, lads and lasses?" he called, turning so all could hear. "Do you think we might convince the leaders of Neverwinter to name a bridge or some other new structure in honor of Drizzt Do'Urden or Bonnego Battle-axe?"

"O' the Adbar Battle-axes, and don't ye never forget it," Bruenor shouted as cheers rose up.

"This caravan isn't leaving Neverwinter until the spring, at least," the boss informed the duo. "I'd be glad to have you along for that journey to Waterdeep."

"If we're about—" Drizzt started to reply.

"But we won't be," Bruenor cut in. "We got roads o' our own to walk."

"I understand," the boss said. "The offer stands—at twice the pay."

"It's possible," Drizzt said with a wry grin aimed at Bruenor. "My friend here has a fondness for maps . . . one that oft empties our purses."

Bruenor's responding look was not in jest, the dwarf upset with Drizzt for giving away so much information.

"Maps?" the boss asked. "We'll be re-drawing the map of Neverwinter soon, to be sure, with such fine craftsmen and brave warriors who have come to rebuild and defend her. We'll be battling the darkness, do not doubt, and in a way that will make all of Faerûn look to Neverwinter with hope."

Cheers again erupted all around them.

"The city is always recruiting new guards and scouts," the boss said, another offer.

Drizzt smiled, but wisely deferred to Bruenor, who repeated, "We got roads o' our own to walk."

"As you will," the boss replied with a bow. "Though every road in these parts seems filled with danger now." He shook his head and looked back in the general direction of their last fight. "What were those things?"

"What did they look like?" Drizzt replied.

"Like children buried under the ash of the rolling mountain."

"Not children," Bruenor explained. "Burned and shriveled by the hot ash, we're fighting them that once lived in Neverwinter, and ye might be wise to take care to keep yer new buildings off any old spots that would've been filled with folk, if ye catch me meaning."

"And they rise again from their natural tombs?" the boss said with a shake of his head. "Did the catastrophe carry such magic in its hot flow?"

Drizzt and Bruenor just shrugged, for no one had an answer yet about the recent turn of events, where undead monsters walked forth in such large numbers.

"Just zombies," said Bruenor against the dispirited look on the face of the boss.

"Quicker, more agile, more fierce," the drow added.

"They been seen all about Neverwinter Wood," a driver on the next wagon informed them.

Drizzt nodded. "So many killed in the cataclysm. . . ." he lamented. "A feast for necromancers and carrion birds alike."

"Consider my offer," the boss said, turning to leave. "Both of them."

When the caravan started moving again, Drizzt looked at Bruenor.

"Our own roads, elf," the dwarf remarked.

Drizzt just smiled and let it go at that.

They arrived in Neverwinter soon after, to cheers and greetings from all in the camp, and even Drizzt's dark skin and drow heritage did little to quell the enthusiasm toward the newcomers. The wagons were stripped in short order, craftsmen and merchants of all types rushing up to fill their orders then bustling back to work. The sound of hammers and saws filled the air, men and women rushing to and fro with purpose and good spirits.

It reminded Drizzt and Bruenor of Icewind Dale, of their earlier days. So full of hope. So full of purpose. So full of determination. Bruenor knew his current quest didn't quite live up to that, by the drow's estimation. He didn't doubt that Drizzt would recommend that they remain in Neverwinter through the winter, that they should scout and fight for those good folk who were indeed battling the darkness to rebuild a city.

But Drizzt let it go, and as the pair departed the town early the next morning, they both took care to not even look back.

They traveled north along the road, thinking to stop in at Port Llast and strike out into the Crags again from there. When they sat at their midday meal, the conversation was one-sided. Bruenor could hear himself babbling on about his newest acquisition and where they might meet up with some of the landmarks mentioned on the map. Hardly listening in the first place, Drizzt appeared distracted by his water bottle, which the dwarf could see shivering—so much so that it seemed to be crawling across the ground, as if something alive was trapped within it.

"A water sprite?" the dwarf asked after a moment, but even as he spoke the words, the ground beneath them began to shake.

Both dropped low to secure themselves as the momentum of the quake grew, the ground jostling violently.

It passed quickly.

"Might be that they're not so smart in putting Neverwinter back where it was," Bruenor remarked. "Them quakes're startin' again."

Indeed, after a decade of quiet, the last few months had brought several heavy tremors, as if some malevolent force was stirring once more.

Bruenor looked to the east, toward where the twin-peaked mountain had once stood, but only a single peak remained. It seemed to him that the mountain stood a bit larger than he remembered, as if it was some dwarf warrior puffing out his chest. He shook his head, thinking it to be his imagination, so soon after the recent tremor. Drizzt had traveled to that mountain soon after the destruction of Neverwinter, seeking some clue as to what had happened, but had found nothing beyond the cooling crater of Mount Hotenow. Bruenor's observation was undeniable, though. The quakes were beginning again, though the ground had been silent soon after the eruption for ten years.

The dwarf glanced back the way they'd come, back to the fledgling city of Neverwinter. Perhaps it would be better if distant Waterdeep remained as the vanguard of the North, he thought.

But only briefly, for as he considered the determined looks on the faces of those he'd seen rebuilding Neverwinter, the dwarf couldn't believe they were wasting their time.

Even if pursuing their purpose came at the price of their lives.

There was no real communication between them, no hierarchy, king, or government. The ghosts of Gauntlgrym had been trapped by the cataclysm that destroyed their ancient homeland in millennia past, events lost to the ages in Faerûn. But they did have purpose, to defend the halls against intruders. And they had regret. It had been a dwarf, a Delzoun dwarf and his companions, allowed passage by the defenders of the hall, who had released the primordial. Confused and saddened by the destruction the primordial had wrought, the ghosts had nevertheless continued their quiet vigil.

But the tremors had returned. The beast stirred once more.

There was no conversation, no directive, but even those pale spirits knew they couldn't stop the coming storm, could not fulfill their purpose. It began with one defection, not so much a conscious thought as a desperate flight. Then out of Gauntlgrym went the spirits, drifting along the reaches of the Underdark, seeking aid.

Others followed, and many left, walking forlornly from their ancestral home, seeking Delzoun blood—living allies who could entrap the beast once more. Following the tendrils of the Hosttower, some were drawn toward Luskan. Others found darker roads, descending to the deeper Underdark, endless corridors few living dwarves would dare to walk.

They carried with them their sorrow for what once had been, their pain for what had recently been marred, and their fears for what would yet come when the primordial awakened in all its mad rage.

CHAPTER
11

THE WAR OF DARK AND DARKER

BLACK SMOKE ROSE IN SERPENTINE SPIRALS ABOVE THE DEATH-scorched ground. Like a river of death, a line of decay and necromantic magic reached out from the main hub of disaster across a field and into the pyroclast, seeking spirits that had been trapped within the shriveled corporeal husks and calling them forth to serve.

Sylora Salm watched this newest outreach with her typically sparkling eyes and satisfied grin. Though nearing forty, the years had not yet dulled the Thayan sorceress's beauty—changed it, perhaps, making her a bit thicker about the waist, her skin a bit less smooth, and some small wrinkles had appeared around her eyes. But more than counterbalancing those unavoidable physical changes, there had come to the formidable woman even more inner substance and strength, more confidence and an increased air of power. It showed in her eyes, and in her grin.

Her Dread Ring was becoming a reality at long last, though the number of dead in the sparsely populated area of Neverwinter Wood, even before the cataclysm, had been deemed inadequate by several of Szass Tam's ambassadors, most of whom were Sylora's rivals. Szass Tam had trusted in Sylora's judgment, though, and she continued to have faith that she would deliver on that trust, that her Dread Ring would come to fruition, giving the lich lord the hold he had so long desired on the Sword Coast.

The pyroclast began to stir, a shaking of the black volcanic stone. Some loose ash and dirt fell into growing cracks. A small gray hand appeared, withered and shriveled, its fingers twisted in a pose of perpetual agony. Slowly at first, but with increasing frenzy, the hand clawed and shoved at the rock. A pair of Ashmadai attendants started toward the spot to help the newest child of Szass Tam break free from its decades-old tomb, but Sylora held them back with an upraised hand.

She smiled widely, even giggled as the zombie pushed aside enough of the debris to poke forth its other arm, then prying the two limbs apart, shoved its head from its pyroclastic womb. Its scrabbling movements grew increasingly frenetic, the creature demanding to come free, desperate to hunt the living—but only those living, of course, who were not attuned to His Omnipotence Szass Tam.

Standing beside Sylora, Dahlia was far less imposing than she had been a decade before, though she looked exactly the same, her elf heritage protecting her from the ravages of a mere decade. She wore her traveling garb: the high black boots, the red-banded black hat, the white blouse under the black leather vest, the black skirt that climbed diagonally nearly to her hip, and the nine diamond studs in her left ear and one in her right. She had been ordered not to remove them, or to change the pattern—a reminder to Korvin Dor'crae that Sylora's intervention had been to his benefit. And of course she still commanded Kozah's Needle. But as there seemed something more formidable about Sylora, more solid and confident, so Dahlia appeared diminished.

She didn't smile as she watched the birth of their newest minion—she hardly ever smiled anymore.

"Take heart, young one," Sylora said to her, more of a tease than a gesture of goodwill. "See what we have done."

The obedient Dahlia nodded, and wondered, not for the first time, how it had happened, how she'd fallen so far. Obviously her descent in the ranks of Szass Tam's hierarchy had been facilitated by those long-ago pangs of conscience, her failure to finish the deed and begin that which she had promised. It hadn't helped her, of course, that Sylora Salm had been the one to rescue her mission. That Dahlia had even been allowed to live after being captured in Luskan had surprised her, and still she wasn't sure if the mercy had been because of her work in locating the primordial, or simply so that Sylora could subjugate her, and keep her in thrall.

Many were the days when Dahlia wished they'd killed her.

Beyond her predictable descent in the hierarchy, though, it was the other fall that had troubled Dahlia even more, the loss of swagger, of lust, of the devil-may-care attitude that had guided her life for so very long.

"I have spoken with Szass Tam about you," Sylora remarked as she sent the zombie on its way, out into the forest to hunt Shadovar. She turned a wry grin on Dahlia. "He is pleased by your willingness to submit to my will."

Dahlia tried hard to keep the hatefulness out of her blue eyes, but not hard enough, she knew from Sylora's widening smile. Of course Sylora would bring it to that. She had taken such pleasure in putting Dahlia in her place, day by day and year by year. She had never once exacted any physical punishment on Dahlia, as Sylora often did with the Ashmadai. No, her abuse of Dahlia had been strictly emotional, one game of mental cat-and-mouse after another, and with every remark holding a double meaning.

"Our beast is awakening once more," Sylora went on. "It will rain greater death and destruction this time, feeding the Dread Ring, securing our hold here. Even without that, the agents of Shade Enclave are retreating."

"They're still about," Dahlia dared say.

"But not in Neverwinter Town in any numbers," said Sylora. "Their grip on that city was undisputed before I awakened the beast, was it not?" Her tone with that last question made it quite clear to Dahlia that she was actually seeking an answer.

"Yes, milady," the elf warrior dutifully responded.

"Now they remain only because they seek some ancient elven relics in Neverwinter Wood, but what they find, day after day, are my minions, risen from the ash and eager to kill." She paused and looked across the small field to a group of Ashmadai standing beside a trio of different zombies, not ash-colored, but darker hued. Two of the three carried garish wounds, as if their corpses had been fed upon, and indeed they had. "That is the genius of His Omnipotence, is it not? Other armies diminish with death, but his grows with every fallen enemy."

Dahlia's eyes fixed on the third of those corpses, one who had died from a single crushing blow to the side of his head. She had done that, defeating the man in single combat, and it had been a good kill against a worthy opponent. In times past, she would have savored that victory, but looking upon the corpse brought a bitter taste to her mouth.

"Go to Neverwinter Town in the morning," Sylora instructed her. "I wish to know how many reside there now, and how many of the Netherese stalk her streets."

Fists clenched at his sides, Herzgo Alegni looked down upon the town of Neverwinter, focusing his gaze and his anger on that beautiful winged structure that centered the rebuilding.

The Herzgo Alegni Bridge, it had been called, for just a few days. For several years after that, like everything else in Neverwinter, it had been called nothing more than part of the disaster, for there had been no one around to take note of it.

But its name was the Winged Wyvern Bridge once more. None of the new settlers had heard of that decade-old proclamation of Lord Hugo Babris.

Hugo Babris—dead like everyone else who had been in or around the city of Neverwinter on that terrible day, save those Shadovar nobles, like Alegni, who had shadowalked back to Shade Enclave.

And one other, the man who stood beside Alegni even then, and who had informed him—with a bit too much glee in his voice, Alegni thought—of the reversion of the bridge's name.

"You are certain of this?" Alegni asked.

"It was one of the tasks you put upon me to prepare for your arrival," answered Barrabus the Gray. "When have I ever failed you?"

That sarcastic response had the tiefling turning hateful eyes at his subordinate.

"We will not be welcomed in there," Barrabus went on.

"Then perhaps we should not ask their permission before entering," Alegni said with a sneer, and turned back to the distant town and the bridge he had so coveted.

Barrabus didn't even wait until the tiefling had turned before offering a shrug in response, but he did add to it, "These are not enemies to be dismissed too easily, these men and women we will face in Neverwinter, nor are they any friends of the necromancers who pull forth undead from the ruins. These are seasoned fighters and spellcasters who have stubbornly held that patch of ground against a legion of zombies crawling up right into their midst."

"My Shadovar kill those creatures with impunity. And most of the monsters had been raised from Neverwinter, and had long departed, before the first of these new settlers ever arrived, according to your first report."

"True enough, but I caution you to take them seriously, lest we find ourselves fighting to the death for this camp they insist on calling Neverwinter, and even then with so many enemies waiting for us in the forest."

Herzgo Alegni continued to stare at the patch of black rock that had once been a thriving city, and rubbed his weary face. The tiefling—always an outsider, even among the Netherese—had faced severe discipline after the cataclysm, with some Shadovar blaming him personally for not foreseeing the Thayan threat and dealing with the minions of Szass Tam before they could inflict such damage. Few Netherese had been killed in the cataclysm, since most were rarely in the actual city of Neverwinter, but out in the forest pursuing the ancient treasure they so craved.

For the last decade, the expedition had continued, but Herzgo Alegni had not been sent back to lead it. But with the ground trembling yet again and the minions of Szass Tam gaining a clear upper hand—and an unstoppable position should they ever complete their Dread Ring—Alegni had asked for and had been granted a chance for redemption. He had returned just a month earlier, replacing the current commander, with orders to continue the hunt for fallen Xinlenal Enclave and to beat back the Thayan intrusion at all costs.

Xinlenal—a Netherese enclave, a city built on a floating moun-tain—was the first of the legendary Netherese enclaves. It had tried to flee the Fall, but made it only to the edge of the Empire of Netheril's elven frontier. There it came crashing down, as had all the other enclaves save prescient Shade when Karsus stole the power of a goddess and magic itself failed. Thus far, only Sakkors had been rediscovered, once more floated, and eventually settled. The other great enclaves eventually wore away under the blasting sands of the phaerimm's unnatural desert, but Xinlenal had fallen somewhere in what would eventually come to be known as Neverwinter Wood—or so the Twelve Princes believed. And as the Twelve Princes believed, the Empire of Netheril believed.

Of course, Alegni's first act upon regaining command of the recovery of Xinlenal was to summon his principal scout and assassin back to his side, something that had not pleased Barrabus the Gray at all. The assassin had been living in relative luxury in Calimport, putting his skills to work for Netherese agents who sought to rule the street trade there. And best of all, he had seen little of Herzgo Alegni in that time.

It was clear to the tiefling that the one thing most intolerable to Barrabus the Gray was servitude. He could exist in a hierarchy, and had never seemed desirous of the responsibilities of command, but Alegni knew the assassin had acted as an independent assassin, serving the needs of the pashas of Calimport or other interests in return for agreed-upon rewards. That had all changed with Alegni, though, and the dominance the tiefling and the other Netherese nobles had exacted over Barrabus was wrought of magic compul-sion and nothing more.

In the mind of Barrabus the Gray, he was a slave. He was rarely beaten or tormented with their debilitating magic, the demands on him had never been excessive, and he was able to live a very good life by anyone's standards in Memnon or Calimport, or wherever he chose. But the coercion remained, and Alegni knew it gnawed at him.

Herzgo Alegni turned to face Barrabus and said, "You suggest we leave the city alone for now?"

"They are enemies of our enemies," Barrabus replied. "But they are friends of Waterdeep, and so no friends of ours."

Alegni continued to nod. "Then let them and the Thayans kill each other. Spend little time in the city—just enough to inform me of any significant changes."

"And the bridge?"

"They can call it whatever they choose," Alegni decided, though he couldn't help but wince and betray his true feelings as he spoke the words. Alegni had to be careful, and had to find a way to regain his standing in the empire, and with fewer resources and much more to lose.

"Little time in the city," Barrabus repeated back to the tiefling. "Little enough to return to the south in the interim?"

"There is a war raging here and you think to leave?" Alegni answered angrily, just the response he knew Barrabus the Gray had feared. "To Neverwinter Wood with you. I will not assign you to any company at present, but I expect you to be productive in battling my enemies." He handed Barrabus a pouch, and from the sound of it as it was shuffled, it seemed to be full of small metallic vials. "Shy from the undead wretches and aim your blades at these fools who call themselves Ashmadai. And when they are dead, sprinkle this consecrated water upon them to deny the Dread Ring its food, and new minions."

"You call the Ashmadai fools because they pay allegiance to a devil?" Barrabus said with a grin obviously designed to let Alegni know that he was indeed snidely referring to one line of the tiefling's heritage.

"Be gone, Barrabus," Alegni said. "Every tenday, I will know the news from Neverwinter Town from your lips, and as you come in to report, so too shall you offer me your tribute in the form of Ashmadai brands. Do not disappoint me, or you will find yourself serving among the shock troops in the ranks of one of my lesser commanders."

"Over there! Heretic!"

"Kill him!"

The three Ashmadai charged ahead, brandishing their spear-staffs.

"He went into the woods!" one yelled.

Indeed he had, into the woods and up a tree with such grace and speed that the vertical turn had hardly slowed him. Sitting on a branch, Barrabus the Gray watched their approach with amusement. He could certainly understand why Alegni hated these cultists so, even were they not the mortal enemies of the Netherese. They seemed like animals—nay, worse than animals, for they threw aside their reason and logic in a purely savage lust to please Asmodeus.

The idiots worshiped a devil-god.

Barrabus shook his head at the stupidity of it all, his gaze lowering to follow the three frantic forms as they entered the copse, crashing through the brush with abandon. He hopped to his feet on the branch, slipped off his cloak, and circled around the trunk, disappearing into the tangle of leaves and branches.

"He's in the tree!" one of the Ashmadai yelled a few moments later. The woman stood pointing, and even began hopping in her glee that they had apparently cornered their intended prey.

"No, he's not," Barrabus answered from behind the trio.

The woman stopped hopping. All three spun.

"But his cloak might be," Barrabus answered.

He stood with his left hand resting on the hilt of a sword strapped to his hip, his right hand hooked by his thumb into his belt, halfway between the magical buckle and another blade, an elaborate and magical main-gauche he had been given as a gift by a powerful street family upon his return to Calimport nearly a decade before.

"You wished to speak with me, I presume," he said, teasing them, and after only a brief, astonished pause, the three cultists howled and charged.

Barrabus crossed his arms in front of him, his right hand pausing for only an instant to activate the magical buckle, and even as he continued the movement across to reach his sword, he flicked that blade forward.

The female Ashmadai, in the middle, gave a halting gurgle and broke off the charge, staggering backward with the knife deep in her throat.

The other two charged on, the one to Barrabus's left thrusting his weapon like a spear, the other swinging his red-hued scepter as a club, both either not caring or not even realizing that their ranks had been thinned.

Barrabus's main-gauche came free of its sheath and crossed back under his right arm, slower to draw the longer blade, to the left in time to slap against the Ashmadai's thrusting spear, hooking the weapon between its central blade and the cunningly upturned hilt. Even as he drew forth his long sword, Barrabus ducked under the first swing of the club and rotated his left wrist, turning his main-gauche under and around the presented spear. The sword came back to the right to block the second club swing, up high then the third down lower, and all the while, he kept that left hand rotating, forcing the Ashmadai to keep adjusting his grip to prevent having the spear taken from his grasp.

Finally the Ashmadai disengaged the spear, but only by throwing it out wide to the side, and in that split second of opening, his sword still expertly picking off every furious swing by the other opponent, Barrabus rushed ahead and poked the spearman hard in the shoulder as he tried to duck away. The cultist yelped, but quickly regained his balance and re-oriented his weapon, though having staggered a few steps back.

Barrabus seemed not to notice him, his two weapons working in concert against a single enemy. He fought purely defensively, letting the Ashmadai's rage play out, letting him make the one mistake that would allow Barrabus to hook his scepter with the main-gauche and clear the way for a killing sword strike.

The spearman recognized the tactic, and yelled out a warning as he launched his spear at Barrabus. From only a few feet away it seemed a sure strike, and would have been against almost any warrior in Faerûn.

But Barrabus the Gray wasn't just any warrior.

It appeared as if he never even looked at the spearman, but his left hand retreated perfectly and he snapped his hand at just the right moment for his main-gauche to catch and redirect the missile, turning it out in front of him. And at the same time, the suddenly twisting Barrabus brought his sword over and down, behind the missile, and drove it out in front of him, throwing the spear forward.

It was an awkward launch, of course, and had little chance of hurting the Ashmadai with the scepter, but it caught him by surprise, and a moment of weakness against Barrabus the Gray was a moment too long. The man threw his arms up, his club up, batting the missile away, then howled and reversed, trying to slam down against the incoming enemy.

But the assassin's main-gauche caught the descending club and turned it down and across to Barrabus's right as he dropped his right foot back and pulled his right arm and the sword back to clear the way. Before the Ashmadai had even managed to stop the descent, Barrabus's sword darted forth over his trapped weapon. The zealot tried to block with his hand, but it wouldn't have mattered anyway, and he could only grimace as the thrusting sword drove into his chest.

He threw himself backward, staggering as blood began to stain his leather tunic. At first, he seemed relieved, as if thinking he had avoided a serious hit.

But Barrabus knew from the pumping blood that his fine sword had nicked the man's heart, and he paid that one no more heed, turning instead to the unarmed Ashmadai, who stopped his charge abruptly when faced with those deadly blades.

"They're both dead," Barrabus assured him, "though neither likely knows it yet."

The Ashmadai looked to his female companion, who still stood, gasping for breath and trying to grasp the knife hilt, trying to find the courage to pull the blade free.

"She'll feel the poison soon," Barrabus explained. "Better for her to just drive the blade in deeper and finish it quickly."

Over to the side, the bleeding man called out, "Kill him!" but though the cry started strong, his words got crushed in a grimace of pain. As the remaining fighter looked at him, the warrior sank down to his knees, his right hand squeezing at the mortal wound in his chest, his left hand still stubbornly holding his scepter.

"Is he speaking to me or to you?" Barrabus teased.

He chuckled at the absurdity of it all as the remaining Ashmadai, perhaps not as devoted to his devil-god as he thought, turned and fled.

"I'm right behind you!" Barrabus yelled, though he made no move to follow. He turned to the kneeling man, who had bent over and had his hand on the ground as well, needing its support to keep from tumbling down.

A tinge of regret coursed through Barrabus as he walked past the dying man to the woman, who fell back from him, stumbling against a tree, the knife still in her throat.

"If I took you back as a captive, the Netherese would torture you in unspeakable ways before they killed you," he said as he pulled the knife out and drove his sword through her heart in the same movement.

She grimaced and tensed, fighting the inevitable for just a moment before falling limp, and Barrabus retracted his sword and let her slide to the ground. He stepped back to the kneeling man and ended his struggle with a single blow to the head.

With a profound sigh, Barrabus sheathed his main-gauche and pulled forth a pair of the vials from the pouch Alegni had given him. They were made of some translucent metal he didn't recognize, allowing him to view the black, smoky liquid contained within. With his foot, he rolled the male Ashmadai over, popped the stopper on one vial and poured its magical contents onto the dead man's forehead.

He stepped back and turned away as the despoiling magic did its work, the dark gray pall spreading from the man's forehead to all of his face, and continuing to spread, like a mold, it seemed, to cover all of his body.

Angry, Barrabus spun back, hooked his sword under the collar of the man's tunic, and tore the garment off the corpse. He didn't savor the work of slicing off the patch of skin that held the Ashmadai brand, but he did it anyway, then he did the same to the woman, despoiling her with the second vial and taking her brand.

He headed back toward the nearest Netherese encampment, to be rid of the trophies. And with every step, Barrabus considered the insanity of this macabre form of soldier swapping. Had he not despoiled the bodies, the Thayans would have fed them to the growing Dread Ring, to add to its strength and to animate the dead into zombie warriors they could send once more after the Netherese. The living Ashmadai apparently considered that to be the greatest gift they could offer.

But since Barrabus had infused the corpses with the stuff of shadow, their fate would be the same, save for their masters. The Netherese would collect the bodies and send them to some arcane laboratory somewhere in conquered Sembia, where they would be fully infused with the very stuff of the Shadowfell and rise as shadow zombies, creatures of the night that would be turned against their former allies.

"Ridiculous," Barrabus the Gray whispered to the uncaring wood.

CHAPTER 12

CRIES FROM THE DISTANT PAST

MELNIK BRAWNANVIL HOOKED HIS PICKAXE ON A STUBBORN jag of stone and twisted and yanked with all his strength. "Come on, ye piece o' goblin snot," he growled, putting everything into it. He could see the shining silvery metal behind it and wanted to get at that vein.

"Bah, but goblin snot'd've busted yer pick by now," said another miner, Quentin Stonebreaker, working the other side of the tunnel.

Melnik grunted and pressed on.

"Here now, did ye bring me me lunch?" Quentin asked, but Melnik noted that he was looking down the tunnel and not at him, so he just continued with his work. Finally, the offending stone broke free.

Melnik didn't celebrate, though, confused as to who his partner down the tunnel—not up the tunnel, toward the more inhabited regions of the mines beneath Kelvin's Cairn in Icewind Dale, but down the tunnel—could be speaking to. They worked the end of the mine, and there were no other dwarves farther down the tunnel.

"Well, what do ye say, then—?" Quentin asked, or started to. He cut off his words with a gasp and stumbled backward.

And when Melnik came away from the wall to look down the curving corridor, he too sucked in his breath.

Dwarves approached toward them, but like no dwarves the pair had ever before seen.

"They ain't livin'! Run!" Melnik yelled, but he couldn't bring himself to follow his own advice, and neither could his partner.

Help us, he heard in his mind. *Help us, kin o' Delzoun.*

"Did ye hear that?" Quentin asked, even as he started backing away.

"I heared somethin'!"

With a shriek, Quentin turned and ran away.

The ghosts, several of them, came very near to Melnik, and he felt every hair on his shaggy body stand up with fright. But he held his ground, and even put his hands on his hips, spreading his legs wide in a solid stance.

"What do ye want, now?" he demanded.

Kin of Delzoun . . . Melnik heard in his head, along with a jumble of words: *beast awakened . . . lava flowing . . . Gauntlgrym besieged . . .*

They might as well have said nothing other than that one word, Gauntlgrym, for Melnik, like every dwarf of Delzoun heritage, knew that name. Staggering, stumbling with his feet and his words, the dwarf backed away. The ghosts followed, filling his head with pleas for help, though of course he had no idea what to do.

"Stokely Silverstream!" Melnik called, though of course he was a long, long way from the inhabited reaches of the complex.

The ghosts seemed more than willing to follow him, though. Indeed, when he turned and started to run, he kept glancing back to make sure he wasn't too greatly outdistancing them, only to find that they were pacing him with ease.

The realization that he couldn't escape them if he wanted to unnerved Melnik more than a little, but the ghosts had spoken the name of the ancient homeland, and Stokely Silverstream needed to hear it, too.

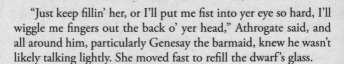

"Just keep fillin' her, or I'll put me fist into yer eye so hard, I'll wiggle me fingers out the back o' yer head," Athrogate said, and all around him, particularly Genesay the barmaid, knew he wasn't likely talking lightly. She moved fast to refill the dwarf's glass.

"Here now, don't you go talking such to Genesay," a man sitting next to Athrogate said.

"It's all the fine, Murley," the bartender said, and with every word, she kept her focus on Athrogate, who sat there simmering with rage.

The dwarf took a long and deep draw, draining his flagon again, and he looked at Genesay and pointed to the mug, then slowly turned to regard the man at his side.

"Ye wouldn't be flappin' yer jaw at me, now, would ye?" he asked.

"Show some manners to Genesay," Murley insisted as he stood up and squared his shoulders to the dwarf.

"Or?"

"Or I'll . . ." Murley began, but he trailed off as a couple of his friends moved up to flank him, both grabbing him by an arm.

"Let it go, Mur," one said.

"Aye, don't you be playing with this one," said the other. "Mighty friends he's got. Black-skinned friends."

That took a bit of bluster from Murley, and Athrogate realized that everyone in the tavern was looking at them then.

"What've me friends got to do with anything?" the dwarf asked. "Ye think I'd be needin' help in putting the three o' ye to the ground?"

"Good dwarf, your mug is full," Genesay said.

Athrogate turned to regard her, grinning at her attempt to distract him and deflect the conversation.

"Aye, so it is," he said, and he picked it up and swung his arm, launching the ale at Murley and his two friends.

"Now fill it again," he told Genesay.

Murley snarled and pulled free of one of his friends, who fell back as the ale washed over him. He took a step toward Athrogate, but the dwarf just smiled and glanced at the man's belt, at the curved sword he had strapped to one hip. It seemed a pitiful weapon indeed against the mighty twin morningstars Athrogate kept strapped across his back.

"Ye might get it out," Athrogate teased. "Ye might even stick me once afore yer head makes a fine poppin' sound."

"Aye, don't fight him, Murley!" one woman called from the other side of the tavern. "His weapons are full of magic you cannot match."

"Oh, but you're a tough one, dwarf," Murley taunted. "You hide behind the damned drow elves and you hide behind the magic in your weapons. Oh, but I'd love to catch you without either, and teach you some manners."

"Murley!" Genesay scolded, for she had seen the same play before, and knew the pirate Murley walked dangerous ground.

"Bwahaha," Athrogate laughed, but not with his typically boisterous exclamation. It was just a sad, soft sound. He turned to his mug, which was still empty. "Fill it!" he barked at Genesay.

"Dwarf!" Murley shouted at him.

"Ah, but ye'll get yer chance to shut me mouth," Athrogate promised.

The moment Genesay put the filled mug in front of him, he scooped it up and quaffed it in one gulp, then hopped from his barstool and faced Murley and his two companions.

"Ye think I'm hiding from ye, do ye?" Athrogate said. He grabbed the buckle of his harness and flicked it open, and with a shrug let the vest and his morningstars fall to the ground behind him. "Well, here now, boy, ye got yer wish."

He took a step forward and staggered, having drained more than a dozen mugs that night.

Murley broke free of his companions and rushed forward, and before the dwarf could catch his balance, the man unloaded a heavy right cross into Athrogate's face.

"Bwahaha!" Athrogate howled in response.

He ignored the left hook and right jab that followed, lowered his shoulder, and charged at Murley.

The man spun to the side and almost got away, but Athrogate caught him by the wrist. The dwarf couldn't stop his forward momentum, though, having overbalanced, and he continued ahead, falling to the floor and dragging Murley along behind him. Murley didn't lose his footing, though, and although Athrogate's strong grip must have felt as if it was crushing his left wrist, the man moved over the prostrate dwarf.

Up on his right elbow, twisted back to the left and with his left hand holding fast to Murley's wrist, Athrogate had no defense against the man's right arm—no defense other than his hard head.

He took a hit and pulled Murley's wrist closer, took another hit, and when Murley tugged back, he let the pirate retreat to the full extent of both their arms.

But then Athrogate yanked the man back with frightening strength, and as Murley fell into him, the dwarf's whole body snapped up, driving Athrogate's forehead right into Murley's face. Murley groaned as his nose exploded under the impact, but he kept his wits enough to dive over the dwarf.

And so did his friends, the three of them burying Athrogate where he lay.

All around the bar, onlookers cheered the three pirates on, for many had felt the bite of Athrogate's heavy fists over the last few years, and some had felt the bite of Athrogate's teeth, as well.

And indeed, it looked as though the dwarf was finally getting his due, with three strong men atop him, pinning him and pounding on him.

Athrogate curled and twisted, finally getting his feet under him, and the crowd quieted. Somehow, impossibly, the dwarf stood up, taking the three brawlers with him. He began to thrash even more wildly then, keeping them off balance and denying them any real footing. Athrogate set himself squarely and bulled ahead, driving the three men in front of him.

"Bwahaha!" the dwarf roared.

A group of patrons at a round table began to scream and dodged aside as the dwarf and his cargo barreled in, splintering wood, sliding chairs aside, and dropping mugs. Metal and glass crashed to the floor along with the dwarf and his three passengers.

Athrogate came up swinging, a left hook that slammed one of the brawlers in the ribs and lifted him off his feet. The man landed two strides back and stared at the strong dwarf in disbelief, then crossed his arms over his broken chest, curled up, and fell over.

Athrogate wasn't watching. He towered over the second of the fighters as the man made it to his knees, and from on high, the dwarf twice snapped his forehead down into the man's uplifted face. The man would have crumpled on the spot, but Athrogate had him firmly by the front of his vest, and with a great heave, the dwarf brought him up to his feet and even higher. Athrogate clenched tighter with his right hand but let go with his left, snapping his hand down over the man's crotch and heaving again, bringing the thug up horizontally over his head.

The third man got up with the help of a chair and without wasting a moment, slammed that chair across Athrogate's back with enough force to send splintering wood flying every which way.

Athrogate staggered forward but managed to turn as he did, to see the pirate advancing, a chair leg held as a club. The dwarf threw his helpless passenger at his friend, but the third rowdy proved nimble, and ducked. He didn't even wince as his friend went crashing down into yet another table full of mugs and plates.

With a roar, the man continued on, launching a series of vicious swings as he bore into the dwarf. Athrogate got his arm up to block—and how that stung!—and continued forward as well, wanting to get inside the weight of that swing. He drove his shoulder into the man's waist, grappling with the swinging club arm with one hand and locking his adversary in place with the other.

But the man managed to wriggle free enough to change from a swing to a straight downward stroke, repeatedly jamming the butt end of the table leg against the top of the dwarf's head.

So Athrogate stopped even trying to block and brought his second arm around the man as well. He stood up straight, lifting the man from the floor, and he squeezed with all his might.

The man kept pumping his arm, and blood soon caked the dwarf's black hair. But the blows grew weaker. The man was off balance, and Athrogate growled and crushed him tighter and tighter, stealing his breath and twisting his spine.

Athrogate began to whip him back and forth and his victim yelled out for help. The dwarf bit him on the stomach, shaking his head like a guard dog might, and the pirate howled out in pain.

Athrogate never saw the next strike coming and didn't even know that it was from one of his own morningstars. All he knew was a sudden explosion of pain, a sudden sensation of weakness as he went over sideways, dragging his bitten victim with him to the floor. Then several others were on him, punching him and kicking him, blocking out the light while all the folk in the room around him shouted and screamed.

"Kill him dead!" cried some.

"Let the poor fellow go!" yelled others.

Then he was up to his feet again, though he knew not how. It took him a few moments to note, through swollen eyes, a tiefling holding him by one arm and a dwarf holding him by the other.

"Ye go sleep it off!" the dwarf yelled in his ear. "Ye don't come back here unless ye're in a better mood!"

Athrogate wanted to argue, and wanted to call for the return of his weapons, but he saw the door approaching—at least, that's what it seemed like, and it took him a few heartbeats to realize that he was approaching the door, and swiftly. He crashed through and went tumbling out into the street.

Stubbornly, he climbed back to his feet and staggered around to regard the posse that stood on the tavern's porch, staring at him.

"And know that ye're paying for the door and the tables, and all that's broken and all that's spilled, Athrogate!" the dwarf yelled at him.

Athrogate brought a hand up to wipe the blood from his lips. "Get me me 'stars," he said. He looked down at his shoulder, bloody and torn from one of those very weapons. "I dropped 'em out o' good manners."

"Get 'em," the dwarf, who was one of the proprietors of the establishment, told the group behind him.

A couple disappeared into the tavern, but only to come back and report that the morningstars and their harness were nowhere to be found.

Thoroughly dejected, dazed, busted, and broken, Athrogate wandered down the streets of Luskan. That hadn't been his first fight, of course, not even his first one that tenday, nor was it the first time he'd ended up face down in the street. Always he took comfort in knowing that he'd given out better than he had taken, but without the glassteel morningstars that had served him so well for all those decades, he found little comfort indeed. And he was hurt worse than any of the other times.

He thought to get back to his own bed, but he wasn't even sure where he was. He looked around, confused, his brain not connecting with his vision or his footsteps. He kept staggering for some time before finally stumbling into an alleyway, where he slumped against a wall and slid to the ground.

"Oh, but we'll get us some fine coin for these beauties," one dirty pirate said to the other, alone in the hold of their docked ship. He held up the harness, holding one of Athrogate's morningstars, the second weapon in his other hand. "What good luck for the dwarf to be so noble as to drop them, eh?"

"Eh!" his friend agreed. "I'm thinking we might be buying us our own boat. I'd like to be a captain."

"What? Yerself the captain? Was myself that took the things!"

"And myself that whacked the dwarf good with one in the fight," the other protested. "Bah, but let's sell them first and see the coin, and see what we might be buying two boats!"

The first started to nod and laugh at that grand proposition. "What good luck!" he said again.

"You really think so?" came a third voice, from the bottom of the ladder, and both men looked that way. And both men blanched, turning as pale as the stranger was dark.

"W-we found 'em," the second stuttered.

"Indeed, and here's your finder's fee," the drow said.

He flipped a copper piece onto the floor between them.

Help us!

"Eh?" Athrogate replied, not sure what he'd just heard, or if he'd "heard" anything at all.

He opened a swollen eye, just a slit at first, then wider when he saw the dwarf before him—and wider still when he came to realize it wasn't the proprietor of the tavern he'd busted up, but one of the dwarf ghosts he had met a decade before in a place he longed to forget.

"Ack! But what'd'ye want?" Athrogate cried, digging his heels in and pressing back so forcefully that his back began to creep up the wall.

He'd lived for more than four centuries, and never had anyone ever accused Athrogate of being afraid. He'd battled drow and dragons, giants and hordes of goblins. He'd fought with Drizzt and Bruenor against the dracolich at Spirit Soaring, and he'd fought against Drizzt before that. Faerûn had never known a finer example of a fearless warrior than the battle-toughened, spit-flying Athrogate.

But he was afraid. All the color drained from his face, and every word came forth through chattering teeth and a lump in his throat so pronounced it might have been one of his lost morningstars.

"What'd'ye want o' me?" he asked, sweat pouring over his bruised brow. "Didn't mean to do it, I tell ye! Didn't mean it . . . never would've wrecked Gauntl—oh, by Moradin's angry arse!"

Help us . . . he heard in his head.

The beast awakens . . .

Blood of Delzoun . . .

They crowded around him, a swarm of ghostly dwarves, reaching for him, begging him, and Athrogate tried to squeeze himself right into the wall, so terrified was he. The voices in his head did not relent, but grew in volume and insistence until Athrogate threw up his arms, yelled, and stumbled out of the alleyway, running along the street, running to escape the ghosts of Gauntlgrym, running from his terrible memories of the great forge and what he'd done.

He stumbled and staggered his way across the city, so many sets of eyes fixing on him and no doubt thinking he'd lost his mind. And maybe he had, the dwarf thought. Maybe the guilt of the last ten years had finally broken him, putting ghosts before his delusional eyes, their words in his head. He finally reached the inn where he rented a room.

A fine inn it was, too, the best in Luskan, and the room had a wide view overlooking the harbor and an exit all its own from the second story balcony. Athrogate rushed up the wooden exterior stairway, so fast that he stumbled and banged his knees. He finally got to the balcony and pulled up short.

There stood Jarlaxle, staring at him with an expression caught somewhere between amusement and disappointment.

The drow held Athrogate's weapon harness, the morningstars still in place.

"I thought you might be wanting this," Jarlaxle said, holding it forth.

Athrogate moved to take it, but paused, seeing a blood stain on one of the straps. He looked at Jarlaxle.

"They didn't feel their finder's fee was adequate," the drow explained with a casual shrug. "I had to convince them."

As Athrogate took the harness, Jarlaxle directed his gaze out to the harbor, where some commotion had broken out on one of the moored ships, which was sitting very low in the water indeed. As he looked on, Athrogate realized that the ship seemed to be sinking, despite the frantic efforts of her scrambling crew.

He looked back at Jarlaxle, who tipped his wide-brimmed, plumed hat in an exaggerated fashion—and Athrogate recalled Jarlaxle's portable holes. What might one of those do, the dwarf wondered as he looked back at the harbor, if dropped in the hold of a ship?

"Ye didn't," the dwarf muttered.

"They are convinced," Jarlaxle replied.

Help us . . . Athrogate heard in his head, and the welcomed distraction of his companion's antics were lost in a rush.

The beast awakens.

Save us!

The dwarf began to pant and look all around.

"What is it?" Jarlaxle asked.

"They're here, I tell ye," Athrogate replied, and he ran to the rail and looked down. His eyes widened and he turned and nearly knocked Jarlaxle over as he charged for his room's door. "The ghosts o' Gauntlgrym! The beast's awake and they're blamin' meself!"

Athrogate slammed the door behind him and Jarlaxle didn't move to follow. He waited and watched.

And he felt . . . a cold sensation, like a short burst of frigid, glacial wind, wash over him. Confused, for he couldn't see any ghosts—and he had certainly seen them in Gauntlgrym—the drow reached into one of his many magical belt pouches and brought forth something he had not worn often since soon after the Spellplague, his magical eyepatch. With a hesitant sigh, he lifted it to his face and tied it on, keeping both eyes closed for a bit, before finally daring to open them.

He used to wear the eyepatch all the time. Many years before, it had protected him from unwanted magical scrying, and had shown him things, extra-dimensional things, that had proven quite helpful in some desperate situations. But in the seventy-seven years since the Spellplague had raged across Faerûn, the eyepatch's other-worldly vision had proven confusing, to say the least.

He turned to the door just in time to see a ghostly dwarf form slipping through it, and predictably, Athrogate started yelling again.

Jarlaxle went to the door and cracked it open, glancing in just to confirm that the ghosts weren't hurting his desperate friend.

They weren't. They were pleading with him. For some reason, the ghosts of Gauntlgrym had come forth onto the World Above.

The drow mercenary blew a heavy sigh, just as hesitant and filled with even more reluctance and dread. He'd spent considerable time researching the disaster of his journey with the Thayan sorceress, and had spent considerable coin as well, determined to pay them back for that awful deception. Jarlaxle didn't much like being played for a fool, and while he was not the most compassionate of persons, the carnage that had been wrought on Neverwinter had offended him greatly.

But he'd let it go in the end, even though he'd garnered some good information, and even though he knew Athrogate wanted nothing more than to rectify the great wrong he'd enacted in pulling that lever. Jarlaxle had let it go because the thought of going back to that dark, and surely utterly destroyed place hadn't set well with him at all, and because he wasn't even sure how he might ever find

Gauntlgrym again. The cataclysm had collapsed the one tunnel he knew of, and his scouts had not found a way around it.

But the ghosts had come forth, claiming, so said Athrogate, that the beast had awakened once more, and indeed, tremors had begun to shake the Sword Coast North.

Perhaps the primordial would take aim at Luskan, a city still at least marginally profitable to Jarlaxle's Bregan D'aerthe.

A third sigh left the mercenary's lips. It was time to go home, and he never looked forward to that.

CHAPTER
13

CHAMPIONS

BARRABUS WATCHED THE UNFOLDING BATTLE WITH GREAT interest, his first view of the elf woman who was champion of the Ashmadai. He knew the champion's opponent, a relatively competent warrior by the name of Arklin—but anyone who hadn't seen Arklin fight before would hardly have called him competent. It seemed as if he was swinging his sword under water, so sluggish were its movements in comparison to the spinning flail of the elf. She hit Arklin repeatedly on the shoulders and arms, every blow painful, but none lethal.

She was toying with him.

Barrabus watched intently, trying to measure the rhythm of her movements. He didn't like how his fighting style, sword and main-gauche, matched up against her twin weapons and their longer reach. He'd successfully faced off against notable two-handed fighters before, but swords, scimitars, and axes were not the same as those exotic spinning sticks. The angles of attack of more conventional weapons were more predictable, and a solid metal blade was not nearly as able to escape a well-executed block as her weapons.

He winced as the elf finally moved in for the inevitable kill. As Arklin lunged ahead with an awkward thrust, she spun her left-hand weapon around the stabbing blade, yanked it out wide, and moved forward inside it. Her right-hand weapon spun up behind her head, coming forward, but to Barrabus's surprise and Arklin's doom, the elf somehow reconnected those tethered poles into a single staff as they came around. As the pole leveled with Arklin's head, the elf warrior tucked her hand tight against her shoulder and drove forward with her weight behind the strike. The end of her four-foot staff caught Arklin right under the chin and the warrior elf continued forward, driving the doomed Netherese back and to the ground. She ran right over him and yanked hard again with her left hand as she did, taking the sword from the gasping Arklin's hand and throwing it far aside.

She fell into a forward roll. Barrabus again had to nod in admiration when she came up, spinning to rush right back at the fallen Netherese. She held not two weapons, not a staff and a flail, but a single eight-foot pole.

Clutching his throat and trying futilely to roll away, Arklin presented an easy target and the elf planted the end of that pole just above the top of Arklin's collarbone and vaulted up into the air, her weight pressing the pole into the squirming, shrieking Shadovar.

A blast of crackling lightning blurred Barrabus's vision as it shocked Arklin's prostrate form. When the elf lightly touched down to her feet on the far side of the fallen warrior, she skipped away, paying his still form no more heed.

Barrabus had seen her, so he had an advantage, he told himself as he started through the forest to intercept her.

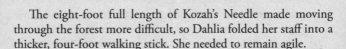

The eight-foot full length of Kozah's Needle made moving through the forest more difficult, so Dahlia folded her staff into a thicker, four-foot walking stick. She needed to remain agile.

He was out there.

The bodies of Ashmadai warriors proved it. Certainly their Netherese opponents had many capable fighters, but the recent kills, so clean, so precise, spoke of the mysterious man who had stepped from the shadows to rain death upon the Ashmadai. The ferocious warrior cultists of Asmodeus, who proclaimed their greatest hope to be dying—even to be raised as undead warriors—for the cause, spoke of the Netherese assassin with a noticeable tremor.

And all of that, of course, had only prompted Dahlia to go out there in hopes of encountering this shade herself.

She let her instincts take over. She didn't try to pick out any particular movement, sound, or smell, but let the whole of the environment guide her.

He was close, perhaps stalking her.

Even before he had become something other than strictly human, Barrabus could slip from shadow to concealment to shadow with the very best of Faerûn's rogues. He needed no elven boots to keep his soft footfalls from the ears of a clumsy human, but with their added benefits, not a creature in the world could hear his approach.

He'd moved with all speed once he spotted the Thayan champion, that striking elf woman with her distinctive weapon. He slowed his pace only as he'd neared the spot, and had lost sight of her only once or twice in that rush. He had to be careful, had to keep obstacles—trees, at least—between himself and the woman.

He didn't want to fight her straight up, not with the stakes so high, and was confident that such would not be the case. Barrabus couldn't see her at the moment, with his back against twin birch trees, but she was there, he knew it, on the narrow path that wound under the oaks.

Poisoned dagger in hand, Barrabus the Gray didn't hesitate. He rolled around the trees and leaped for the spot—and skidded to an abrupt halt.

She was gone!

Concerned, he scanned wildly. Only the brief glimpse, hardly registering, of a spot on the soft ground revealed to him the truth, and just in the nick of time. He fell aside as the elf warrior came down out of the tree—the indentation betraying the point where she'd planted her staff and used it to leap straight up to branches that should have been beyond her reach.

The warrior landed, but Barrabus kept rolling. He heard the hum of air behind him as she swept her deadly staff his way.

He came up in a pivot and launched his dagger—an awkward throw that had no real chance of getting through the defenses of a warrior as capable as she, but one that slowed her advance just enough for Barrabus to draw his sword and main-gauche.

She held her tri-staff horizontally in front of her, rotating her hands just enough to send the two-foot lengths at either end spinning vertically out to either side of her.

Barrabus couldn't help but be drawn to the elf, the cut of her blouse and skirt, the impish smile on her delicate face, the thick braid of red and black hair running down the right side of her head and over the front of her shoulder to lead the eye enticingly to the low **V** of her partially untied blouse. He was as disciplined a warrior as any, but even he had to fight against the distraction, had to remind himself that even the cut of her clothes was strategic.

She circled slowly to the right, and Barrabus moved to his right as well, keeping square with her.

"I knew you were out here," she said.

"I knew *you* were out here," he replied.

"It had to come down to this, of course," she said.

He didn't answer—he hardly heard her. He knew he was at a disadvantage, given the unusual nature of her weapons.

Dahlia kept up her end of the conversation on her own. "It is said among my people that 'the Gray' is a formidable warrior."

He didn't answer, but she continued circling. He had tuned out her distractions—all of them.

Dahlia came forward, punching out with her right hand then her left then turning the tri-staff vertically before her, its ends spinning furiously. She let go with her left hand and let it loop completely around her right before catching it again, now reversing her right grip and pulling her right arm in while punching out again with her left, sending the left-most section sweeping out at her opponent.

He blocked with the main-gauche, trying to hook that end staff, but Dahlia was smart enough to recognize her own failed attack, and quick enough to retract the weapon. She threw her right arm straight back and let go of the shaft, launching the staff behind her, but caught it by the end piece in both hands held closely together, shifting her feet as she did, turning her hips so that she could quickly reverse the momentum with a snapping, whiplike swing. And a simple strategic call to the staff broke the middle section as well, so that as it came forward, it was four equal lengths, separated by the cords.

It rolled out before her, not quite a whip, not quite a staff, the end snap aimed perfectly for the Gray's head.

He fell straight back, narrowly avoiding the surprising move, and the end pole cracked against a tree, releasing a lightning charge that ripped a large piece of bark from the trunk.

Barrabus could hardly believe the power generated in the whipping motion of the strange weapon, to say nothing of the added magical devastation wrought by the lightning.

He hadn't tried any counter to the elf's first routines, preferring to let her play them out in the hope that he would gain some insight into the angles and speed of her attacks, but suddenly, as he threw himself back in a desperate and barely-successful attempt to get out of her reach, he realized his folly.

She was too quick and too precise, and he realized he would figure out the truth of her movements right before she smashed in his skull. There was no learning curve to be found.

His backward rush ended up against a smaller tree and he rebounded off it with fury, coming forward as the elf grabbed up her staff by the central poles. He thought she'd somehow reconnect them, matching his sword and dagger with that tri-staff she wielded so adroitly.

It took him a heartbeat to realize that she did the opposite, breaking the staff into a pair of flails.

The angle of Barrabus's intended attack, straightforward and inside the reach of the tri-staff end-poles, was all wrong!

He dived for the ground, a headlong roll, as the flails swatted in at him from left and right, and came up with a strong presentation of his right foot forward, lengthening the reach of his thrusting sword.

The elf dodged desperately, bringing one weapon in at the last instant to smack against the side of the sword as she faded back and to Barrabus's left.

He pursued. A second stab, a third. He blocked a sweeping strike with his main-gauche and traded parries, sword and flail.

Barrabus rolled his hands in a sudden fury, circles sweeping over and in before him as he pressed forward in a rush. Instead of keeping one foot back, as was typical for his weapons, he had his feet moving side by side, his shoulders squared, daring the elf to find an opening and strike through the blur of spinning metal in front of him.

Indeed she tried, and he had to constantly change the speed of his rotations to block the myriad angles presented by the similarly spinning flails—and worse, on more than one of those blocks, the elf's weapon presented an electric shock, some quite powerful, one nearly ripping the sword from his hand.

But he held on, and he used that unfortunate sting to make it seem as if he couldn't, teasingly interrupting his circular flow.

On came the elf—just as Barrabus reversed his momentum and stabbed straight ahead.

He had her awkwardly dodging, and he pressed all the harder, stabbing and slashing with fury, keeping her on her heels, betting that one of his blades would find her flesh before his momentum played out and his weariness from the flurry allowed her an advantage.

Just when he thought he had her she threw herself backward in a perfect tuck and roll and retreated around the trunk of a thick oak.

Barrabus faked a move to the other side to intercept, and instead followed her directly. He smiled, thinking the Thayan had finally guessed wrong.

He didn't catch her as he pursued her around the tree!

Had she hesitated, Dahlia would have surely felt the Gray's sword stabbing her in the back, and a lesser warrior would have fallen right there.

But Dahlia sprinted forward instead of trying to turn and block. She reconstructed her staff in two quick strides and planted it, leaping up its length, inverting up above it and hooking her legs over a branch, tugging her weapon up behind her and just ahead of her pursuing enemy.

She gained her footing and rushed along the branches, leaping and sprinting in perfect balance, even jumping out to a second tree. She tried to spot the Gray, but he was gone—simply vanished.

She ran out to the end of a branch and jumped down to some brush, converting her weapon once more into a tri-staff and lashing out with wide-sweeping strokes even as she touched down in case he was waiting for her.

Dahlia silently cursed herself for allowing the break in the fighting. She was on her opponent's terms once again, and he knew she was ready for him. She had no idea where he'd run off to.

She knew she was in trouble—she'd heard that this assassin had caught and killed many Ashmadai who never saw it coming. She had to keep moving, and had to keep up her assault on any potential hiding spot she passed by.

If she could only locate him . . . if she could only get face to face with him again!

She spotted movement ahead, off to the side. Even knowing how unlikely it was to be the Gray, she went that way and had to work hard to suppress her relief when she came upon an Ashmadai patrol.

"Dahlia!" two of the nine said together, and the whole contingent came to rapt attention.

"The Gray is about," she told them. "Be alert."

"Stay with us!" one said, the desperation in her voice betraying the female tiefling's desire to avoid the Gray.

Dahlia looked around the quiet forest, nodding.

From the shelter of a pine tree, Barrabus the Gray watched that exchange.

He was no less relieved than Dahlia that their encounter had ended.

He would have to get her by surprise, he thought.

Or he would have to stay away from her.

CHAPTER 14

THE TIME TO ACT

COMING HOME TO MENZOBERRANZAN AFTER YEARS ON THE surface always surprised Jarlaxle, for though the World Above had changed dramatically in the past seven decades, the City of Spiders seemed locked in time—a better time, as far as Jarlaxle was concerned. The Spellplague had caused a bit of an uproar there, much like the War of the Spider Queen and the Time of Troubles before it, but when the lightning bolts and fireballs had settled, when the screaming of wizards and priests made insane by the shattering of the Weave and the fall of gods had died away, Menzoberranzan remained the same.

House Baenre, Jarlaxle's birthplace and blood family, still reigned as First House, and it was there the drow mercenary ventured, to meet with the Archmage of Menzoberranzan, his oldest brother, Gromph.

Jarlaxle lifted his hand to knock on Gromph's door, but before he even managed that, he heard, "I've been expecting you," and the door magically swung open.

"Your scouts are efficient," Jarlaxle said, stepping into the room. Gromph sat off to the side and across the way, peering through a magical lens at a parchment unrolled on one of his desks.

"No scouts," the archmage said without looking up. "We have felt the tremors trembling in the west. You fear that your profitable city of Luskan will be the target of the wakening primordial this time, no doubt."

"Rumors speak of an ash field outside of the last line of devastation."

Gromph looked up at him with impatience. "Such a field would have been the obvious result of the eruption."

"Not from the eruption," the mercenary clarified. "A field of magical ash."

"Ah yes, the Dread Ring of this Sylora Salm creature, then," said Gromph. He shook his head and gave a wicked little laugh. "A wretched thing."

"Even by drow standards."

That remark caught Gromph off guard. He tilted his head and it took him a long while to manage a smile at the observation.

"An efficient way to raise an army, though," Jarlaxle added.

Gromph shook his head again and turned back to his work, an opened spellbook into which he had been transcribing a newly learned spell.

"The reawakening of the beast could prove costly to Bregan D'aerthe," Jarlaxle admitted. "And as such, I would pay well to keep the primordial in its hole."

Gromph looked up, and Jarlaxle felt as if his older brother was looking right through him—a sensation Jarlaxle Baenre hadn't often felt in his long life.

"You're angry," the archmage said. "You wish to repay the Thayan for making you one of her lackeys. You speak of profit, Jarlaxle, but your desires serve your pride."

"You're a better mage than philosopher, Brother."

"I told you how to entrap the primordial, years ago."

"The bowls, yes," Jarlaxle replied. "And the lever. But I am no wizard."

"Nor are you a Delzoun dwarf," Gromph said with a chuckle. "Yet there are few in the world more adept with magical implements than you. These bowls should pose little challenge to one of your skill."

Jarlaxle stared at him doubtfully, and it took the wizard some time to catch on.

"Ah," Gromph said at long last. "You have no desire to return to Gauntlgrym, yourself."

Jarlaxle half-shrugged, but otherwise didn't respond.

"Doesn't Bregan D'aerthe have a few soldiers to spare?"

Jarlaxle continued to stare at his brother.

"I see," said Gromph. "So you do not wish to risk your own assets in this endeavor. As I said, it is a matter of pride, not expense."

Jarlaxle could only smile. Gromph, among all drow, was not one Jarlaxle thought it wise to try to deceive. "Both, perhaps," he admitted.

"Good, now that we've taken care of that bit of nonsense, what do you wish of me? Surely you do not believe I will go to this Gauntlgrym place and do battle on your behalf against a primordial." His smirk reinforced his remark. "Do you expect I've managed to survive these centuries because I'm foolish enough to allow any amount of gold to tempt me into battle against such a creature?"

"You indicated that the creature need not be faced directly."

"You would need a primordial of water to do it for you, or a god, if you could find one available."

Jarlaxle bowed, conceding the point. "I wish only to put the primordial back in its hole—back to sleep, if you will, as it was before that Thayan witch and her vampire lackey coerced Athrogate into releasing it."

"As it was before? You do realize, I hope, that even before your smelly little companion pulled the lever and freed the water elementals, thus freeing the primordial, the magic was waning. The fall of the Hosttower of the Arcane cannot be undone by any magic known in this day."

"I understand," Jarlaxle replied. "But I would accept even that weakened prison if it would delay the beast's release long enough to bleed the rest of what I can from Luskan."

"Really? Or long enough to spite the Thayan witch by denying her her Dread Ring."

"We'll call that an added benefit."

Gromph laughed—not a wicked chuckle, but an actual burst of laughter, and that was something rarely heard in Menzoberranzan.

"I told you how to do it," the archmage said. "Ten bowls, no less, and their slaves re-gathered. When that is done, seal them with the lever."

"I don't know where to place them," Jarlaxle admitted.

"But you have them?"

"I do."

"I'm not going with you, nor do I have the minions to spare to accompany you on your journey. I value them more than you value the fodder of your mercenary army. By Lolth, have that wretched psionic creature of yours carry this out. He walks through stone as easily as you move through water."

"Kimmuriel is unavailable," Jarlaxle explained.

Gromph looked at him curiously, and soon enough a grin widened on the archmage's face. "You haven't told them, have you?" he asked. "None of them."

"Bregan D'aerthe is rarely in Luskan anymore," Jarlaxle replied. "With the coming of the Spellplague, there are so many other—"

"None of them!" Gromph roared, seeming quite pleased with himself, and he snickered all the more.

Jarlaxle could only sigh and take it, for the wise old mage had of course guessed the truth of it. Jarlaxle had not told Kimmuriel or any of his lieutenants of Bregan D'aerthe, had told no one other than Gromph himself, what had transpired in Gauntlgrym.

"Ah, your pride, Jarlaxle," the archmage scolded, and he kept laughing but then stopped abruptly and added, "But I'm still not going to Gauntlgrym, nor do I have any soldiers to lend to you."

Jarlaxle didn't respond, but didn't turn to leave, even though Gromph lowered his eyes to the glass and parchment and resumed his work. Only after many heartbeats did the archmage look up again. "What is it?"

Jarlaxle reached into a pouch and produced the skull gem.

"You brought that idiot back here?" asked an annoyed Gromph, who recognized the phylactery of Arklem Greeth. Gromph had interviewed the insane lich at great lengths over the course of many months back when Jarlaxle had first come to him to try to garner information about the freed primordial and the diminishing magic of the Hosttower.

"The primordial awakens," Jarlaxle said, and he seemed back in control then, back on balance after Gromph's biting observations. "I'll not have it. Speak to Greeth again, I pray you—and yes, I will *pay* you, too. I would know the best way to find Gauntlgrym again, and of how to proceed once I do."

"I told you how to proceed."

"I need details, Gromph," Jarlaxle insisted. "Where to place the bowls, for instance?"

"If those places weren't forever sealed with magma after the first rage of the primordial," Gromph replied. "And I know not where to place them, in any case, nor will Greeth. You can only hope that Gauntlgrym itself shows you the way, if and when you find it once more."

Jarlaxle shrugged. "And when you're finished, I would have you expel Arklem Greeth from his phylactery, into a . . . separate place, that I might have control of the skull gem once more."

"No."

"No?"

"The magic of that gem is the only thing containing the lich."

"Surely there are other phylacteries."

"None that will hold him unless they're properly enchanted, and how that might be accomplished, I do not know. When you bring me such a container, Jarlaxle, and I am convinced that it will hold him, I will place the spirit of Arklem Greeth within it. Until then, he remains in the skull gem. I hardly endeared him to me in those months of interrogation, and I'll not have a powerful lich seeking me out. I have played such a game before, and it was not a pleasant experience."

"My efforts against the primordial will be more difficult without the gem," Jarlaxle explained. "Undead, the ghosts of Gauntlgrym, are thick about the place."

"Then you have a problem," said Gromph.

Jarlaxle stared at the indomitable wizard for a few heartbeats, then tossed him the skull gem that he could begin a new round of interrogation.

"A tenday," Gromph said. "And bring your gold."

Jarlaxle knew better than to ask that he take less time, so he bowed and took his leave.

Gromph smiled as he watched the mercenary depart. He placed the skull gem off to the side of his desk and went back to his scribing.

Only for a moment, though. He sensed something curious about the gem. He stared at it for a few moments then went to his bookcase to find the spellbook containing the proper incantations.

That very night, Gromph had Jarlaxle back before him.

"You have recently encountered a spirit of Gauntlgrym," the archmage said to the surprised mercenary.

"In Luskan," Jarlaxle confirmed. "Several sought out my associate, the dwarf Athrogate, begging his help in saving what remains of their homeland."

Gromph Baenre held up the skull gem. "Your phylactery captured one of them."

Jarlaxle's eyes widened.

"Or perhaps it was Greeth reaching forth to grab a ghost to sate his loneliness."

"Then Greeth is free?" an alarmed Jarlaxle asked, but Gromph's grin dismissed that disturbing possibility before he even answered.

"He's still in there, but so is the dwarf. Good fortune smiles upon you . . . as always."

"Help us! Help us!" Gromph recited in a very old dialect of Dwarvish. *"Seat a king in the throne of Gauntlgrym and harness the beast, we beg!"*

"What does that mean?"

The archmage shrugged. "I can only relate to you that which the dwarf ghost told me. Many questions did I ask of him, and to each, a different variation of that same response."

"Can the dwarf lead me back to Gauntlgrym?" Jarlaxle asked.

"Even now, that spirit is being consumed by Arklem Greeth," Gromph explained. "He's feeding on it, as you or I might devour a rothé steak. Arklem Greeth will never let it go, and I do not intend to go in there and fight him for the sake of a dwarf.

"You have the magical bowls," Gromph went on. "You have the phials of pure water. You have been to Gauntlgrym."

"Will it work? Does enough residual magic of the Hosttower remain?"

Gromph shrugged and was quite amused that he didn't know the answer to that particular question. "How lucky does my dear brother feel?"

———※———

Dahlia rushed across the field and through the trees lining the most active section of the expanding Dread Ring. She took care to avoid the black necromantic ash itself, for though her brooch would protect her from its life-draining powers, she always felt as if her mere presence in a Dread Ring gave Szass Tam and his principal agents, including the hated Sylora, some power over her.

Or maybe just insight into her, and either way, Dahlia was not pleased by the possibilities.

She caught up to Sylora standing on the edge of the ring, where its leeching powers touched some of the volcanic rock. Following Sylora's gaze, she noted a semi-translucent gray hand reaching out of the stone, clenching and unclenching as if the Dread Ring was causing the ghost great distress.

"Not a zombie," Dahlia remarked. "Is this a sign that the Dread Ring is strengthening? Can it bring forth wights and wraiths, specters and ghosts?"

"This one was a ghost before it arrived here, and the Dread Ring caught it and held it," Sylora explained. "There are others, too: ghosts, traveling in a pack, on a mission." She looked directly at Dahlia and added, "*Dwarf* ghosts."

"From Gauntlgrym," Dahlia reasoned.

"Yes, apparently some of that complex survived the primordial's awakening. Close your eyes and open your mind, and you will hear them."

Dahlia did as asked, and almost immediately felt the words *Help us!* form in her mind.

"They wish to be freed of the ring," she reasoned, but Sylora shook her head.

Again Dahlia focused on the telepathic keen of the dwarf spirits. *Help us,* she heard again. *The beast awakens. Help us!*

Dahlia's eyes popped open wide and she gawked at Sylora. "They come out of Gauntlgrym with a warning of the reawakening primordial?"

"So it would appear," Sylora replied. "And if they came here, then it is likely they've traveled to other places as well. Who will heed their call, I wonder?"

"None," Dahlia was quick to respond. "And could any even find Gauntlgrym again should they care to try?"

"I know of one, perhaps two, who could," Sylora replied.

Dahlia mulled that over for a few moments before nodding in agreement. "Some ghosts might have found their way to Luskan's undercity. The Hosttower's tendrils lead there."

"And what are we going to do about this?"

The leading manner of Sylora's question left no doubt in Dahlia's mind as to the Thayan woman's intentions.

"When the primordial awakens once again, its devastation will solidify our work, will create enough carnage to complete the Dread Ring, and that, in turn, will assure our victory over the Netherese. I'll not have that prevented, or even delayed."

"You wish me to go to Luskan to confront Jarlaxle and Athrogate?"

"Do you need to ask?"

"Do not underestimate those two," Dahlia warned. "They are formidable on their own, and Jarlaxle is not without powerful friends."

"Take a dozen Ashmadai—a score if you think it necessary," Sylora replied. "And Dor'crae."

"The lich would help."

"Valindra stays with me. She has almost fully regained her wits, but her power has not yet returned. She is not expendable."

That last line hit Dahlia like a bolt of lightning. "But I am?"

Sylora laughed at her and turned her attention back to the dwarf ghost in the lava rock. Its face had appeared, a desperate grimace, and quite pleasing to the Thayan.

"And so is Dor'crae?" Dahlia pressed, only because she spotted the vampire not so far away and knew he'd heard the last exchange.

"Dor'crae is nimble enough to escape, should that be necessary," Sylora answered without missing a beat.

She always seemed one step ahead of Dahlia. The elf knew it was her own weakness, her own inability to recover from the humiliation of her failure at Gauntlgrym, that put her behind. Ever since she'd returned from that place, Dahlia had walked a less steady path. Where once she'd been aggressive, she had become . . . reactive. And creatures like Sylora preyed on that indecisiveness.

"Find them and learn if they're returning to Gauntlgrym," Sylora ordered.

"I doubt they're even in Luskan. It's been a decade—"

"Learn!" Sylora snapped at her. "If they are there, if they are returning to Gauntlgrym, then stop them. If not, then learn if any others intend to take up the call of the dwarf ghosts. I should not have to explain this to you."

"You don't," Dahlia replied, quietly but steadily. "I understand what must be done."

"Have you yet met this champion of Shade Enclave who haunts Neverwinter Wood?"

"I have. He's human, but with something of the shade about him."

"And you fought him?"

Dahlia nodded, and an impatient Sylora motioned for her to elaborate.

"He ran away," Dahlia lied. "He's better at hiding than he is at fighting, though he's fine with the blade as well. I suspect his kills have come by surprise, mostly."

Sylora seemed a bit confused at that moment, glancing back over her shoulder into Neverwinter Wood.

"I'll not likely find him again anytime soon," Dahlia said. She didn't want Sylora to reconsider her priorities, rather fancying the opportunity to be gone from that creature's side for some time at least, and also seeking no second encounter with the Gray.

"Magic will flush him, then," Sylora said, and Dahlia did well to suppress her sigh of relief.

"To Luskan with you, in all haste," the Thayan sorceress went on. "Find your old companions and ensure that neither they nor anyone else slows the fury of our fiery pet."

Dahlia nodded and turned away.

"Do not fail me in this," Sylora said after her, her tone making clear the dire consequences of failure.

Guenhwyvar's ears flattened and a low growl escaped the panther. She went into a crouch, her hind paws tamping down as if she anticipated springing away.

Drizzt nodded when he noted the pose, a confirmation of the same sensation that had just washed over him, like an otherworldly chill that had the hair on his neck and arms standing up. He sensed that something was about, and that perhaps it was from the Shadowfell or at least Shade Enclave, but that was all he could guess.

He moved slowly, not wanting to provoke an attack from some being or force he couldn't see. Hands on his scimitar hilts, he circled behind Guenhwyvar, and holding all confidence that she would intercept any attack from the front or sides, the drow focused his attention the other way.

He felt more at ease then, his senses telling him that whatever had passed nearby had moved off. He started to relax, just a bit.

Bruenor's scream abruptly ended that respite.

Drizzt sprinted to the shallow cave serving as their encampment, Guenhwyvar close behind. By the time the drow reached the entrance, his scimitars were in hand, and he came up fast, ready to rush in and fight beside his friend.

But Bruenor wasn't fighting. Far from it. He had his back up against the rear wall of the cave, his open hands out before him as if in surrender. He was breathing shallowly, gasping almost, and his face was locked somewhere between fear and. . . .

And what? Drizzt wondered.

"Bruenor?" he whispered, for though he too could sense something in there, as he had outside, some chill and otherworldly presence, he saw nothing that could so terrify the dwarf.

Bruenor didn't seem to even register his presence.

"Bruenor?" he asked again, more loudly.

"They want me help," the dwarf explained. "And I can'no' know what help they're wanting!"

"They?"

"Don't ye see 'em, elf?" Bruenor asked.

Drizzt squinted and peered more closely into the dimly lit cave.

"Ghosts," Bruenor whispered. "Dwarf ghosts. Askin' me to help."

"Help with what?"

"I'm a bearded gnome if I know." Bruenor's voice trailed off as he finished that thought, a confused look coming over him.

Then his eyes widened so much Drizzt thought they would pop out of their sockets.

"Elf," Bruenor muttered as if he had to force the sound past a huge lump in his throat. "Elf," he said again, and Drizzt noticed that he was leaning more heavily on the stone wall then, and recognized that if the wall hadn't been there, Bruenor would have likely fallen over. Beside Drizzt, Guenhwyvar growled and crouched again, clearly agitated.

Bruenor gasped for breath. Drizzt drew his blades and waded in, moving across the floor in practiced steps, each leaving him more than ready to strike hard if need be. Bruenor was mouthing something then, but he couldn't hear until he came right up near his friend.

"Gauntlgrym," Bruenor whispered.

Drizzt's eyes widened, as well. "What?"

"Ghosts," Bruenor sputtered. "Gauntlgrym's ghosts. Asking for me help. Talking of a beast waking up once more."

Drizzt looked all around. He felt the chill, surely, but he saw and heard nothing. "Ask them where," he told Bruenor. "Perhaps they can guide us."

But Bruenor began shaking his head, and he even stood up straight once more, and it wasn't until Drizzt saw that motion that he came to realize that the sensation had passed, that the ghosts were gone.

"Gauntlgrym's ghosts," Bruenor said, his voice still very shaky.

"Did they tell you that? Or are you guessing?"

"They told me, elf. It's real."

Those words struck Drizzt curiously, particularly coming from Bruenor, who had led him on a merry chase for Gauntlgrym for decades. But as he thought about it, he understood Bruenor's surprise, for even when one believes strongly in something, the actual confirmation comes most often as a shock.

Bruenor looked away for a moment, staring off into the distance, then blinked his eyes as if some revelation had just come over him. "The beast, elf," he said.

"What beast?"

"It's wakin' up . . . *again.*"

The emphasis on that last word was purposeful, Drizzt knew, but he still didn't quite get where Bruenor might be going.

"And when it woke up last time, Neverwinter went away," Bruenor clarified.

"The volcano?" Drizzt asked, and Bruenor kept nodding as if it was all coming clear to him.

"Aye, that's it. That's the beast."

"They told you that?"

"No," Bruenor readily admitted. "But that's it."

"You can't know that."

But Bruenor kept nodding. "Ye feel the earth moving beneath yer feet," he said. "Ye seen the mountain growin'. It's waking up. The beast. The beast o' Gauntlgrym." He looked Drizzt directly in the eye and nodded. "And they're askin' for me help, elf, and so they're to get it, or I'm a bearded gnome!"

He nodded with even more determination then rushed for his pack, fumbling with his maps. "And now we're knowing the general area o' the place! It's real, elf! Gauntlgrym is real!"

"So we're going to go there?" Drizzt asked, and Bruenor looked at him as if the answer was so obvious that Drizzt must have lost his mind to even ask.

"And stop a volcano?" Drizzt explained.

Bruenor's jaw hung open and he stopped fumbling with his maps.

After all, how did one stop a volcano?

CHAPTER 15

ALL ROADS LEAD TO LUSKAN

WITH A PILE OF SMALL, SMOOTH STONES BESIDE HIM, BRUENOR went to work. One by one, he pulled the parchment maps from his pack, gently unrolling them and placing them on the mossy ground, securing each corner with a stone.

He tried to categorize them by region first, searching for the ones that seemed to place Gauntlgrym nearest the volcano that had erupted. The dwarf leaned back, kneeling, scratched his head repeatedly, and kept thinking about those ghosts that had come to him, pleading for his help.

Gauntlgrym. It was real. It still existed.

Anyone looking at Bruenor Battlehammer at that moment would have thought him a hundred and fifty years younger, a feisty young dwarf eager for adventure. The years didn't bend his strong shoulders, and rarely had Bruenor's eyes sparkled as they did just then, full of promise and hope.

And indeed, someone was watching him. Someone with coal black skin. Someone lithe and swift, and deadly. And it was not Drizzt.

Bruenor thought he'd suddenly been blinded. Everything just went black. He yelped and fell back, rolling down to his hip and lifting one arm defensively in front of him while fumbling around on the ground with his other hand, trying to find his axe.

A small *pop* sounded beside him and a sharp jolt stung his arm. Then another and another, a series of tiny explosions disorienting him, biting at him.

"Elf!" he yelled out, hoping Drizzt was near, and despite the discomfort, he continued furiously searching for his weapon.

At last he grabbed it, and only then, the popping sounds continuing, did he also notice the sound of parchment rustling.

"Elf!" he yelled again, and realizing his error in falling backward, the dwarf scrambled the other way.

He came out of the strange globe of impenetrable darkness in short order, crawling, stumbling onto the mossy patch where he'd placed the maps.

They were gone.

The horrified dwarf looked to the forest and the rustling brush. He scrambled up to his feet and flung himself forward in pursuit, but as soon as he caught a glimpse of the thief, his heart sank and his legs slowed. It was a dark elf, and one he couldn't hope to catch.

"Elf!" he screamed at the top of his lungs, and he took up the chase anyway, trying at least to keep in sight of the fleeing drow. "Call yer damned cat, elf!" Bruenor yelled. "Call yer cat!"

He continued the chase over a ridge and down into a tree-filled dell, and he kept on running right up the far ridge, though he had lost all sight of the thief. Over that ridge, the underbrush was light, the field of view clear, but the thief was nowhere to be seen.

Bruenor skidded to a stop, hopping about, craning his stocky neck, but with the growing realization that he had lost his treasured maps. Gasping for breath, he ran back the way he'd come, veering to the right, the southeast, hoping against hope that he could make that ridge and catch sight of the thief once more.

He didn't.

Bruenor howled for Drizzt again, repeatedly, as he ran to the western ridge then back to the north and to the east, and finally to the west once more.

Some time later, Bruenor caught a sign of movement to one side of his camp. He took up his axe, hoping the thief had returned, but the dark form showed herself more clearly. Guenhwyvar bounded up to him, her ears flattened, her lips curled back.

"Find him, cat!" Bruenor implored her. "A damned drow elf stole me maps!"

Guenhwyvar's ears came up and she turned her head left and right, taking in the wider view.

"Go! Go!" the dwarf yelled at her, and with a roar that reverberated all around them, Guenhwyvar leaped away, straight to the west.

Moments later, with Bruenor nodding enthusiastically at the departing panther, Drizzt rushed up beside him, scimitars in hand.

"An elf took me maps!" Bruenor cried at him. "Drow elf!"

"Where did he run?"

The dwarf glanced all around, but threw his axe down, sticking it into the ground, and helplessly lifted his empty, trembling hands.

"Which way?" Drizzt prompted.

Bruenor waved his hands and head in despair.

"Where were you when he struck?" Drizzt asked, and for a moment, the flustered dwarf even seemed to be confused about that.

Finally, Bruenor collected himself enough to lead Drizzt back to the mossy patch. The darkness enchantment was gone by then, revealing the pile of stones, a few of them scattered about on the moss. But no maps were to be seen, nor the pack Bruenor had used to carry them.

"He put a damned darkness globe over me," Bruenor grumbled, stamping his foot in outrage. "Blinded me and hit me with . . ."

Drizzt leaned in, prompting the dwarf to explain in detail, but all Bruenor could offer was, "Bees."

"Bees?"

"Felt like bees," Bruenor tried to explain. "Bitin' at me, stingin' me. Something . . ." He shook his hairy head and held forth one arm, and indeed, between his heavy bracer and short sleeve, his bare skin showed many small welts. "Kept me back while he swooped through, taking me maps."

"You're sure it was a drow?"

"I seen him when I came out o' the darkness," Bruenor asserted.

"Where?"

Bruenor led him to the spot and pointed to the ridge leading back to the dell, and Drizzt dropped to his knees, examining the shrubs and the dirt. An expert tracker, Drizzt easily found the trail—surprisingly easily, given Bruenor's description of the robber as a dark elf. He followed that trail into the dell, and there it got far more confusing, for any tracks or bent fronds had been muddled by the tumultuous traffic the low ground had seen, a dwarf running back and forth.

Finally, though, Drizzt did rediscover the trail, and found it to lead out to the northwest. He and Bruenor ascended the ridge there, peering out.

"The road is that way," Drizzt remarked.

"Road?"

"The road to Port Llast."

Bruenor turned his eyes to the west more directly. "Cat went that way. She might've found him."

Off they went, Drizzt easily following the trail—again, too easily. They had barely gone a hundred yards when they heard a growl up ahead.

"Damned good cat!" Bruenor yelped and charged on, expecting to find Guenhwyvar standing atop the thief.

They did find Guenhwyvar, standing in a small lea, her fur all rumpled, teeth bared, growling angrily.

"Well?" the dwarf called out. "Where in the Nine Hells . . . ?"

Drizzt put a hand on the dwarf's shoulder to silence him. "The ground," he said softly, walking past the dwarf toward the cat.

"Eh?"

Bruenor soon understood.

Guenhwyvar was standing in the grass, but the ground beneath the grass was not dark like soil, but white. The cat's muscles flexed and she leaned to the side, trying to pull up her paw, but alas, she was fully stuck in place.

"Like fly glue," Drizzt remarked, coming to the edge of the strange, magical patch. "Guen?"

The panther growled unhappily in reply.

"He sticked her to the ground?" Bruenor asked, coming up to Drizzt's side. "He catched yer cat?"

Drizzt had no answer, other than a concerned sigh. He took out the onyx figurine and bade the cat to be gone. She couldn't pace, as she usually did when she was slipping from her corporeal form into the gray mist that ushered her to her home on the Astral Plane, but she did diminish to nothingness soon after, leaving Drizzt and Bruenor standing in the lea.

"He got me maps, elf," the dejected dwarf remarked.

"We'll find him," Drizzt promised.

He didn't tell his friend that the path the drow thief had left was too clear to miss, that it had to have been purposely left, but he decided not to. They were being led for a reason, and Drizzt was fairly confident of where they were being led and who was leading them.

The drow flipped the satchel off his shoulder, dropping it on the table between himself and Jarlaxle.

"I think I got them all," he said.

"Ye're not sure?" Athrogate asked from the side of the room. "We're talkin' important work here, and ye *think* ye got 'em?"

Jarlaxle flashed a disarming smile at the dwarf then turned back to Valas Hune, one of his most experienced scouts. "I'm sure you liberated the important ones."

"Bruenor was laying them out on the ground," Valas answered. "All of those are in there, and what the dwarf had not yet removed from the satchel. Perhaps he has other maps hidden elsewhere. I cannot be certain—"

"Ain't ye a scout?"

"Forgive my friend," Jarlaxle remarked. "This mission has special importance to him."

"Since he is the one who freed the primordial, you mean?" Valas said, offering a sly look at Athrogate.

His words caught the dwarf by surprise, for who knew of that journey to Gauntlgrym those years before? But then again, Jarlaxle didn't seem the least bit surprised. Athrogate fixed a suspicious, you-told-them glare on Jarlaxle.

"There is little that escapes the notice of Valas Hune, my friend," Jarlaxle explained to Athrogate. "Rest assured that he is among a very few who know of the disturbing events in Gauntlgrym."

"Then why didn't he make sure he got all the damned maps?"

"King Bruenor is not alone," Valas Hune reminded. "I have little desire to try to explain my presence lurking about the camp to Drizzt Do'Urden."

"He is a reasonable fellow," Jarlaxle said.

"More than a few dead drow wouldn't agree with that assessment," Valas replied. "Besides, my friend, you know little of Drizzt of late. I have explored his exploits and talked to those who have traveled beside him, and 'reasonable' is not a word I often hear."

Jarlaxle's eyebrows betrayed a bit of surprise at that, but he quickly dismissed the look. "You could get to know him better, should you decide to accompany us to Gauntlgrym," he reminded the scout.

Valas was shaking his head before Jarlaxle ever finished the thought. "A primordial?" he said. "Perhaps we can instead travel to a different plane to do battle with a true god, though I doubt we'd notice the difference in the few heartbeats of life we would have left."

"I have no intention of doing battle with the primordial."

"I'd be more concerned with *its* intentions, were I you. Which I am not, thankfully." He motioned to the satchel. "There, you have your maps, as you asked."

"And you have your gold, well-earned," Jarlaxle replied, tossing him a small bag.

"There's more," said Valas Hune. "For no extra cost," he added, seeing Jarlaxle's suspicious look.

"They're on your trail?"

"If not, then Drizzt is not nearly the tracker you claim him to be."

"And?"

"There is much stirring in the south. The Netherese all but wage war with the Thayans in Neverwinter Wood."

"Yes, yes, over the Dread Ring."

"And more than that, the folk of the land grow alert to the awakening of the primordial, if that is what is indeed happening."

"Folks should be scared!" Athrogate said. "Ground's shakin'!"

"Some welcome it," Valas Hune replied.

"And some want to stop it," said Jarlaxle. "And those who would welcome it will no doubt try to stop those who mean to stop it."

"There is always that possibility," said the scout. "And to that point, a band entered Luskan only hours before me. They came into the city in small groups, but my contacts at the gate assure me that they were of singular purpose and origin. They wore the clothes of ordinary merchants, but my contacts are quite perceptive, and more than one of these newcomers, I'm told, hid an identical burn scar—a brand—under a collar, cloak, or whatnot."

"Ashmadai," Jarlaxle remarked.

"No small number," Valas confirmed. "And there was a particular surface elf woman among them, stylish and alluring, and carrying a metal walking stick."

Jarlaxle nodded, his expression showing that Valas need not continue. It made sense, of course, that the Thayans would send an expedition their way—as far as they knew, Luskan was the entrance to Gauntlgrym, and the likely starting point of any who would try to prevent the catastrophe that was no doubt well on its way.

"You have scouts in the city, monitoring them?" Jarlaxle asked.

"Some."

"The usual crew?"

Valas nodded. "And they know to report directly to you, through our friend at the Cutlass."

"Ye sound like ye're leavin'," Athrogate remarked.

"I am summoned to the Underdark, good dwarf. There are more troubles in the world than those before you."

Athrogate started to protest, but Jarlaxle stopped him short with an upraised hand. The simple truth of the matter was that Bregan D'aerthe and Kimmuriel had lessened their presence in Luskan greatly in the last few years, and with good reason. With the fall of Neverwinter, Luskan had become far less profitable for the band, and indeed, while Jarlaxle had a vested personal interest in the endeavor, mostly out of spite against that witch Sylora Salm and her treachery, it was personal, not professional. A large part of the reason Jarlaxle had elevated Kimmuriel to a position nearly equal to his own was to allow them both to keep such things separate. Thus, Jarlaxle had hired Valas Hune and Gromph with his own funds, and had asked for no support from Kimmuriel and Bregan

D'aerthe. The primordial, the Dread Ring, the skirmish between Thay and Netheril . . . none of that was of financial importance to Bregan D'aerthe, and Bregan D'aerthe remained, first and foremost, a for-profit enterprise.

Jarlaxle tossed Valas Hune another small bag of gold, which obviously caught the scout off guard. He looked at Jarlaxle with undisguised curiosity.

"For the extra information," Jarlaxle explained. "And please do buy Kimmuriel the finest brandy, as repayment for him sparing his finest scout and thief."

" 'His'?" Valas Hune said with a sly grin.

"For the time being," Jarlaxle replied. "When I return to the Underdark and the matter of this new endeavor, I will reclaim that which is mine. Including the services of Valas Hune."

The scout grinned and bowed. "I look forward to such a day, my friend," he said, then was simply gone.

"Ye think it's her?" Athrogate asked Jarlaxle.

"It would not surprise me, but of course I intend to find out," Jarlaxle promised.

"Makes no sense, elf," the dwarf replied. "Why would Dahlia walk into Luskan like that?"

"It's been a decade."

"To be sure, but who'd forget that one, even after ten years? She comes walkin' into the city in that hat and with that staff o' hers? How would we not know?"

"Why would she think we're even still in the city?" Jarlaxle countered. "And truly, why would she care?"

"Wouldn't we be the ones yer friend was speaking of? Ye know, them what's wantin' to put the primordial back in its cage?"

"Perhaps," Jarlaxle said with a shrug, but he was already thinking along other lines. He had kept some tabs on Dahlia in the years since the eruption. He knew that she had been in Neverwinter Wood, serving Sylora and the creation of the Dread Ring, and harrying the Netherese. And he knew, simply from their encounter in Gauntlgrym, that such a station would not well suit the fiery and independent elf warrior. And there was the matter of her betrayal by Sylora in Gauntlgrym.

Dahlia could easily enough have entered Luskan in disguise, of course. In fact, for her, just wearing ordinary clothing could be considered a substantial disguise. But if Dahlia had come to the city so brazenly, was it because she feared nothing Jarlaxle could throw against her?

Or was it because she wanted Jarlaxle to find her?

The drow nodded, trying to play out all the many possibilities, and reminding himself that two other important visitors would soon enough enter the city.

"Where're ye goin'?" Athrogate asked as Jarlaxle started for the door.

"To speak with Valas Hune's contacts. And for yourself, the Cutlass. Send my love to Shivanni Gardpeck. Let her know of potential visitors."

"Which?" Athrogate asked. "The cultists or Drizzt and Bruenor?"

Jarlaxle paused, mulled over the dwarf's words, and replied, "Yes."

"There are many people here," said Devand, the commander of the Ashmadai squad that traveled to Luskan with Dahlia.

"It is a city."

"I thought it would be more like Port Llast. Is Luskan not a pirate outpost?"

"Luskan is far more than that," Dahlia replied. "At least it used to be."

And indeed the city was noticeably diminished since last she'd been there. The streets were filthy, and vacant houses, some partially burned, seemed to be squeezing out the habitable dwellings. More shops were closed than open, and more than one pair of cold, ill-intentioned eyes tracked them from the shadows of alleys and vacant lots.

Dahlia turned her attention back to the cultists. "A drow and a dwarf," she said. "We seek a drow and a dwarf. There are few dark elves in Luskan, certainly, and rest assured that any you find will know of the one we seek. Divide into small groups—three or four in each—and go out to the taverns and inns. There are many in Luskan, or there were, and those that remain should be easily found. Watch and listen. We will have a better understanding of the city in short order.

"And you," she said, aiming the remark directly at Devand, "gather your three best warriors. We will venture to the undercity, the place Valindra once called home. There lie the tendrils of the fallen Hosttower of the Arcane that first guided me to Gauntlgrym and the primordial, and there, too, lie the tunnels that will take us back to that place, should we need to give chase to our enemies."

"We should have brought Valindra," Devand remarked, but Dahlia shook her head.

"Sylora refused that request," she said. "And I'm glad she did. The lich is not yet controllable, or even predictable."

Devand gave a slight bow, lowering his eyes appropriately and letting the conversation go at that.

The Ashmadai leader chose their companions well and the skilled fighters didn't slow Dahlia as she eagerly descended through Illusk and back to the bowels of Luskan. The Ashmadai scepters also contained a bit of magic in them that allowed them to glow like a low torch, and Devand's was even more powerfully enchanted, illuminating as fully as a powerful lantern. Between that and their brooches, they found little trouble with the numerous ghouls and other undead things of that haunted land. They came upon the former chambers of Valindra in short order.

The place was exactly as Dahlia remembered, though more dusty. Otherwise, everything was the same: the furniture and old tomes, the various twisted and decorated candelabra. . . .

Everything except that the other skull gem, Arklem Greeth's phylactery, was gone.

Dahlia mused over that for a bit, wondering if it was a sign that the powerful lich had at last escaped his imprisonment. Or perhaps Jarlaxle had departed the city, taking Greeth's prison with him. He wouldn't leave a treasure like that behind, after all.

The elf did well to hide her disappointed sigh. She'd desperately hoped that Jarlaxle was still in Luskan.

"The tendrils!" she heard Devand call from outside the chamber, and she moved out to find him and the other Ashmadai inspecting the ceilings, following the green roots of the fallen Hosttower.

"The tendrils!" Devand announced again when she arrived, and she nodded.

"Down there," she said, pointing to a tunnel that ran off to the southeast. "That is the route to Gauntlgrym. You two," she said, pointing alternately to Devand and one other, "follow that trail and see if it remains open."

"How far?" Devand asked.

"As far as you can. You remember the way back to the city?"

"Of course."

"Then go. As far as you may, for the rest of the day and night. Search for signs of recent passage all along the way—a discarded waterskin or the soot of a torch, footprints . . . anything."

With a bow, the pair rushed off.

Dahlia and the others returned to Luskan and the appointed rendezvous with the rest of the team, a shabby inn in the south end of the city, not far from Illusk. The smaller groups returned one by one, reporting on the progress of identifying the various inns and taverns scattered about the city. They were learning the ground, as ordered, but none reported any sign of dark elves as yet.

Dahlia took the news stoically, assuring them all that it was just a beginning, and a solid foundation for their designs. "Learn the city," she bade them, "its ways and its denizens. Enlist the trust of some locals. You have coin. Let it flow freely to purchase drinks in exchange for information."

Again, the elf secretly prayed that Jarlaxle had not left Luskan.

She was a bit less composed when Devand returned before the next dawn with news that the way to Gauntlgrym was no more.

"The tunnels have collapsed and are impassable," he assured her.

"Take half the team with you after you've rested," Dahlia commanded. "Search every tunnel to its end."

"It's a maze down there," Devand protested, "and it's filled with ghouls."

"Every tunnel," Dahlia reiterated, her tone leaving no room for debate. "This was the way to Gauntlgrym. If it is sealed from Luskan, then we can return to Sylora with our assurances that, from here at least, none will inhibit the awakening."

Devand argued no more and departed to get some rest, leaving Dahlia alone in her small room at the inn. She paced about, moving to the one dirty window, and peered out over the City of Sails.

"Where are you, Jarlaxle?" she whispered.

CHAPTER 16

A DROW AND A DWARF

"Ye knowed it was him all along," Bruenor concluded when it became obvious that Drizzt intended to follow the thief's trail all the way to the City of Sails.

"I knew it was a drow who raided our camp," Drizzt said.

"I told ye that."

Drizzt nodded. "And I knew he wanted us to follow him. The trail he left was far too obvious."

"He was in a hurry," Bruenor argued, but Drizzt shook his head. "Got to be him, then," the dwarf muttered, and when Drizzt didn't reply, he added, "Wantin' us to follow him, eh?" He glanced over at Drizzt, who nodded.

"He won't be wantin' that when I find the rat," Bruenor declared, and shook his fist in the air.

Drizzt just smiled and turned his thoughts away as Bruenor launched into a typical tirade, promising all sorts of pain upon the thief for stealing his treasured maps.

And Drizzt was certain the thief was Jarlaxle, or someone working for him. Jarlaxle, above all others, knew of Bruenor's passion for Gauntlgrym, and whoever had raided the camp had come specifically for those maps, had waited until the exact moment when they were most vulnerable.

But why? Why would Jarlaxle reach out to them in such a manner?

Drizzt considered the mountains towering over them to the north, and expected that they would make Luskan the next day, probably before the midday meal.

They camped that night by the side of the road, their rest undisturbed until very early in the morning, when the ground began to tremble and shake.

"The way is blocked," a voice said from the side, and Dahlia spun, surprised indeed.

"Jarlaxle," she mouthed, though she couldn't really see the drow in the shadows of an alley.

"Your scouts tell you truthfully. The way to Gauntlgrym is no more, from crumbling Luskan at least."

Dahlia moved slowly, trying to gain a view of the dark elf. It was indeed Jarlaxle's voice—melodic and harmonious, as would be expected of an elf, particularly a cultured dark elf—but the truth of it was that Dahlia only guessed it was he. She hadn't heard Jarlaxle's voice in a decade, and even then. . . .

"I know you," the voice said. "I know your heart. I trust you will find a proper use for this when the opportunity presents itself."

"What do you mean?" the elf asked, and when no reply came forth, even after she asked again, Dahlia rushed down the alley to the spot where she estimated the drow had been standing.

On an empty, overturned cask she found a cloth, and on the cloth, a small box, and in the small box, a glass ring.

She closed the box and wrapped it in the cloth before stuffing it into a pouch, and all the while, she glanced up and down the alley, surveyed the roofline, searching for some clue, any clue.

"Jarlaxle?" she whispered again, but it occurred to Dahlia then just how ridiculous her hopes truly were, just how much she had allowed herself to fantasize about something so very unlikely.

She rushed out of the alley and down the garbage-strewn street toward the inn and her room, thinking then that her encounter had more likely been with an agent of Sylora.

For the Thayan sorceress would ever test her, and never trust her, and woe to Dahlia if ever Sylora found her loyalty to be less than absolute.

No matter how many times they approached Luskan from that direction, Drizzt and Bruenor always paused on the same hill south of the city's southern gate to take in the view of the harbor. Though other ports like Waterdeep and Calimport had far larger docks, longer wharves, and always had more ships in port, nowhere was there to be found such a diversity of sailing vessels as in the so-called City of Sails. They might have been the dregs of the Sword Coast—pirates, smugglers, and only the most daring merchants—ruffians who outfitted their vessels ad-hoc, with sails of stitched clothing and maybe a catapult that had been designed for a castle's tower strapped onto the aft deck for good measure.

Coastrunners bobbed against the shallower docks, with rows of oars standing skyward. Single-mast schooners and square-sailed caravels dominated the second tier of docks, with many more open-moored farther out, and a trio of three-mast vessels, large and wide, were moored near the outermost docks.

The City of Sails indeed—though Drizzt couldn't help but note that though those ships were in port, there were fewer in all than he remembered.

"Our friend better be here," Bruenor grumbled, stealing the moment. "And better have me maps. Every one, and don't ye think I'll not know if even one's missin'!"

"We'll know soon enough," Drizzt promised.

"We'll know *now,*" Bruenor growled in reply.

"Jarlaxle, tomorrow," Drizzt promised, and started down the road toward the city. "The hour is late. Let us find an inn for the night and shake off the dirt of the road."

Bruenor started to argue, but stopped short and shot Drizzt a glance and a grin. "The Cutlass?" the dwarf said, almost reverently, for what a grand history those two, particularly Drizzt, had with that establishment.

It was in the Cutlass where Drizzt and Wulfgar had first met Captain Deudermont of *Sea Sprite,* one of the most legendary vessels ever to sail out of Luskan. The Cutlass was where a broken Wulfgar had gone when, returned from the Abyss, he found himself mired in the mud of self-pity and strong drink. Delly Curtie, for a while Wulfgar's wife—and thus, Bruenor's daughter-in-law—had been a barmaid there, working for the jovial and well-informed. . . .

"Arumn Gardpeck," Bruenor said, recalling the tavernkeeper's name.

"A good man with a fine tavern," Drizzt agreed. "Aye, when the wealthy came to Luskan in the years before the pirates took hold, they stayed in the far fancier inns higher on the hills, but they would have found better lodging in Arumn Gardpeck's beds."

"Not to doubt," said Bruenor. "And who was that skinny one, with the rat face? The one what stole me boy's hammer?"

Drizzt could easily picture that miscreant sitting on a stool at Arumn's bar. He was always there, always talking, and he had an unusual name, Drizzt remembered, a silly one.

But the drow couldn't quite recall it, so he just shook his head.

"Arumn's kin still got the place, or so I hear," Bruenor recalled. "What was that girl's name, then? Shibanni?"

Drizzt nodded. "Shivanni Gardpeck. Claims to be Arumn's great-great-great grandniece, I believe."

"Think it's true?"

Drizzt shrugged. All that mattered to him was that the Cutlass remained. Shivanni may or may not have been Arumn Gardpeck's descendent, but if she wasn't, she had to have come from a similar bloodline, and if she was, then fat Arumn would be glad to know it, and to know her.

The pair crossed through the open gate, many eyes turning their way. There were only a scant few guards manning the walls and none visible on the towers. They might have been soldiers of one or another of the High Captains who ruled Luskan, but looked more like thugs serving themselves first—a ragtag band of knaves bound by no uniform, no code, and no notion of the common good of Luskan.

The city gates were always open. If Luskan began discriminating about who they let in, they would probably find the city deserted in short order. Even the scurvy dogs who wandered in through the gates paled under the glow of angelic halos compared to the rats who crawled off the ships that put into port there.

" 'Ere now, a dwarf an' a drow," one man said to the pair as they passed under the gate.

"Be ye more impressed by yer eyes, or by yer sharp mind that sorted such a sight?" Bruenor shot back.

"Not a usual pairing, is all," the man said with a chuckle.

"Give him that much, Bruenor," Drizzt said so only the dwarf could hear.

"And what is the news in Luskan, good sir?" Drizzt asked the man.

"Same news as any day," the guard replied, and he seemed in good spirits. He stood and stretched, his back making cracking sounds with the effort, and took a step toward the pair. "Too many bodies cloggin' the waterways, and too many rats blocking the streets."

"And pray tell, what captain do you serve?" asked the drow.

The man looked wounded, and put his hand over his heart. "Why, dark skin," he replied, "I'm livin' to serve the City o' Sails, and nothin' more!"

Bruenor shot Drizzt a sour look, but the drow, far better versed in the ways of the chaotic and wild town, smiled and nodded, for he had expected no other answer.

"And where're ye off to?" the guard asked. "Might I be directin' ye? Ye lookin' for a boat er an inn in particular?"

"No," Bruenor said flatly, aiming it, obviously, at both questions.

But to the dwarf's wide-eyed surprise, Drizzt answered, "Passing through. For tonight, good lodging. For tomorrow, perhaps the road north." He saluted and started away, then said to Bruenor, and not quietly, "Come, Shivanni awaits."

"Ah," the guard said, turning them both back to regard him. "Good ale to be found in Luskan, to be sure. Boatload o' Baldur's Gate pale brew come through just two days ago."

"To be sure," Drizzt answered, and he led Bruenor away.

"When'd ye get a waggin' tongue, elf?"

Drizzt shrugged as if he didn't understand.

"He might've knowed the name."

Again, Drizzt shrugged. "If Jarlaxle wishes to find us, why would we make it difficult for him?"

"And if he ain't lookin' for us?"

"Then we would never have known it was a drow that raided our camp, and would never have found a trail so obvious leading us here."

"Or the trail's a fake. Leadin' us here so we're just thinking it's Jarlaxle." Bruenor nodded repeatedly as he considered his own words, as if he had just had a moment of epiphany.

"In that case, too, I would speak with Jarlaxle, for any so sending us in this direction surely concerns him as well. And a fine ally he will make, in that case."

"Bah!" Bruenor snorted.

"We have no enemies here that I know of," the drow said. "We walked in openly, with nothing to hide and no ill intent."

"Now ye're friends to the High Captains, are ye?"

"Assuming there are any left, I'd kill every one of them if the opportunity presented itself—if they in any way resemble those who defeated Captain Deudermont, decades ago," Drizzt admitted.

"I'm sure they'd be glad to hear that."

"I don't intend to tell them."

"A dwarf an' a drow, just like ye asked," the guard said to the alluring woman who had hired him to watch for that very thing.

The woman, an Ashmadai serving in Dahlia's band, nodded. "This very day?"

"Not an hour past."

"You are certain?"

"A dwarf an' a drow," the guard deadpanned, for how could anyone get something like that wrong?

The woman licked her lips and pulled out a small purse. She turned as she opened it, shielding its contents from the guard's eye, then turned back to toss him two pieces of gold.

"Which way did they go?"

The guard shrugged. "Didn't bother to watch 'em."

The Ashmadai sighed and gave a little growl of frustration. With a disgusted look and a shake of her head, she started away.

"Why would I, when I know right where they're goin'?" the ruffian asked.

The woman spun, hands on hips, glowering at the grinning man. She waited a few heartbeats, but he said nothing. "Well?" she prompted.

"Ye paid me to watch the gate for a dwarf an' a drow. I watched the gate and saw yer dwarf an' drow."

She narrowed her eyes threateningly, but the guard appeared unconcerned.

With another sigh, the woman grabbed up her purse.

"One piece o' gold for the name o' who they're goin' to see," the guard said, grinning all the wider. "Two'll get ye the name o' the place. Three, how to get there."

She tossed two gold coins at his feet. "All of it," she said.

The guard considered the coins, shrugged, and accepted the bargain.

"The skinny one," Bruenor prompted, leaning on the bar, his gray and orange beard lathered with foam.

Shivanni Gardpeck stood opposite him with one hand on her hip and the other tapping at her chin. She was an attractive woman, nearing forty, full-bodied with considerable curves and long dark brown hair that bunched thickly at her shoulders. She didn't remind Drizzt of her distant uncle Arumn in her appearance, but her mannerisms bespoke a family resemblance.

"A long way removed, was Arumn," she mumbled.

"A long time ago," Bruenor agreed. "But the tales came down through yer family?"

"To be sure."

"The tale o' Wulfgar's stolen hammer?"

Shivanni nodded and chewed her bottom lip as if the forgotten name was right there, begging release.

"Ah, by the beards o' gnomes," Bruenor lamented when the woman held up her hands in defeat. He lifted his flagon and drained it, belched for good measure, and nodded to Drizzt that he was ready to go to their room.

Halfway up the stairs, the pair were stopped by Shivanni's call. "I'll remember it, don't you doubt!" she said.

"Rat-faced man with a hammer that weren't his own," Bruenor called back, a light tone in his voice as if the conversation had brought him back across the decades to a place he far preferred. Indeed, his voice was filled with relief, and he grinned widely and threw up his hands, as if all the world had been made right.

Two hours later, Bruenor was deeply sunk into a chair and snoring loudly. Drizzt contemplated whether or not he should disturb his friend, but he knew that if he let Bruenor sleep, the dwarf would likely awaken him in the middle of the night, grumping about a grumbling belly.

Bruenor stopped his snoring with a grunt and a chortle, and opened one lazy eye to regard the dark-skinned hand touching his shoulder.

"It's time for evenfeast," Drizzt said, quietly but forcefully, for it appeared to him that Bruenor was about to bite his hand.

The dwarf shrugged him away and closed his eyes again, smacking his lips as he settled down deeper into the chair.

Drizzt considered the slight for just a moment, then walked around to the other side of the chair, bent low, and whispered into the dwarf's ear, "Orcs."

Bruenor's eyes opened wide and he hopped from his chair in a great explosion of movement, lifting right into the air before landing in a ready, fighting crouch.

"Where? What?"

"Forks," Drizzt said. "It has been a long time since you've used one."

Bruenor glowered at him.

"Evenfeast?" Drizzt suggested, motioning toward the door.

"Bah, but our talk earlier put some old thoughts in me mind, elf, thoughts what turned to dreams. And ye stole 'em."

"Memories of Wulfgar?"

"Aye, me boy *and* me girl."

Drizzt nodded, knowing full well the comfort such dreams could impart. He offered his friend a sympathetic smile, and bowed in apology. "Had I known, I would have gone for my meal without you."

Bruenor waved that away with one hand and rubbed his grumbling belly with the other. He grabbed up his one-horned helm and plopped it on his head, slung his shield over his shoulder, and took up his axe.

"Don't need no damned fork," he said, showing Drizzt his axe, "and if it is an orc, we'll chop it up to bite-sized pieces, don't ye doubt."

Something struck Drizzt as odd by the time he and Bruenor were only halfway down the stairs to the common room. Shivanni wasn't behind the bar, which was unusual though hardly suspicious, but it was more than that, something he couldn't quite sort out. They continued down and found a small table off to the side of the bar, with Drizzt continuing his scan of the room and its patrons.

"Does something seem wrong to you?" he quietly asked his companion as Bruenor sorted himself out, resting his axe against one chair and carefully resting his shield against the axe, so he could comfortably sit.

The dwarf glanced around, then turned back, clearly perplexed.

Drizzt could only shake his head, but then his discomfort registered more clearly: there were no elderly people in the tavern, and no unshaven and grubby-looking characters who looked like they'd just climbed out of a rum bottle and from the deck of a pirate ship.

There was something too . . . uniform, about the tidy crowd.

"Keep your axe close," Drizzt whispered as a barmaid—one he didn't recognize, though, since he was so rarely in Luskan of late, he didn't know them all—came over.

"Well met," she greeted.

"And to yerself, lass, and what might yer name be?" Bruenor asked.

She smiled and turned her head demurely, but not a hint of a blush came to her cheeks, Drizzt noted. And he noticed, too, in the sweep of her half-turn, that she bore a painful-looking burn scar between her left breast and collar bone.

Drizzt again scanned the room, focusing on one tall man bending across the way, the movement opening a gap between the man's shirt and breeches, and revealing a similar scar. Then he spotted a woman seated at a table directly across the way, and from his angle, he could see the neckline of her dress, and enough under it to note a scar—not a scar, a brand—identical to the barmaid's.

He turned his attention back to Bruenor and the barmaid, to find the dwarf ordering a pot of stew and a bottomless flagon of Baldur's Gate Pale.

"No, hold," Drizzt interrupted.

"Eh? But I'm hungry," Bruenor protested. "Ye waked me up and I'm hungry."

"As am I, but we're late for our meeting," Drizzt insisted as he stood.

Bruenor looked at him as if he'd lost his mind.

"I am confident that Wulfgar will have venison aboard his boat," Drizzt reassured the dwarf, and Bruenor looked at him with blank confusion for just a moment before catching on.

"Ah, so'd be me hope," the dwarf said and rose to his feet.

As did everyone else in the Cutlass.

"Interesting," Drizzt said, his hands resting on his scimitar hilts.

"Be reasonable, drow," said the barmaid. "You have nowhere to run. We wish to speak with you two, privately, and in a place of our choosing. Hand over your weapons, and less of your blood will be spilled."

"Surrender?" Drizzt asked casually, and with a hint of a snicker.

"Look around you. You are sorely outnumbered."

"Yerself ain't met me friend, I see," Bruenor interjected, and he grabbed up his axe and banged it against his shield to set the shield firmly in place on his arm.

The barmaid tossed aside her tray and stepped back, but not quick enough. Drizzt's weapons came out in a flash, Twinkle's blade knifing in to stop at the side of her neck.

"I'm bettin' first blood spilled to be yer own," Bruenor told her.

"It matters not," the woman replied with a strange smile. "You'll not get to Gauntlgrym, whatever my fate. You can abandon that thought peacefully, or we will ensure that fact by killing you. The choice is yours."

Bruenor and Drizzt exchanged glances, and nods.

The drow's scimitar flashed, but away from the woman's neck, tearing the shoulder of her barmaid's dress and dropping the fabric down off her shoulder. She reacted instinctively, grabbing for the material, and just as Drizzt had anticipated. He stepped forward and punched out, smashing Twinkle's pommel into her face, the impact throwing her to the floor.

All around the room, from under tables or cloaks, the others pulled their weapons, mostly curious-looking scepters, half staff, half spear.

Bruenor swept his axe across down low, bringing it under his table, hooking it by the leg, and with a great heave and follow-through, sent the table flying at the opponents standing nearby, driving them back.

"Fight or flee?" he called to Drizzt as he rushed behind his friend to intercept a trio coming in.

He saw his answer in Drizzt's eyes, simmering with eagerness—and in the dark elf's actions. The drow rushed forward over the fallen, squirming barmaid to meet the swings of the next two in line with a series of powerful parries and twisting counters. In the blink of an eye, Drizzt had both men reversing direction, back on their heels and working furiously to keep up with his darting scimitars.

Bruenor lifted his shield arm high, accepting the heavy blow of an Ashmadai's clubbing scepter. He swept his axe across under that upraised arm, but the human woman managed to duck out of reach, and two tiefling warriors to her right rushed in at the apparent opening.

But Bruenor was too seasoned and too crafty to make such an obvious gaffe. His swing was genuine, and he added to its weight and momentum purposely, lifting up on the ball of his leading left foot and spinning a perfectly-timed full pivot to bring his shield right back in alignment with the new attackers. The foaming mug held strong against the stab of a sharpened scepter end, and it took only a slight lift for the dwarf to effectively deflect an overhead club from the other.

He went forward, driving his shield and the tieflings' weapons up and out as he did, barreling right under his uplifting shield. Bruenor launched a second slash with his axe, which brought blood, catching the thigh of the tiefling on the far right, and brought a howl of pain as the half-devil fell back and over, holding his torn leg.

Bruenor ran right over him, kicking him in the face for good measure. As he passed, the dwarf skidded down low, sliding right under a table, and there he turned and stood powerfully, lifting the table with him and throwing it and its many mugs and plates, both full and empty, back in the faces of the remaining two pursuers.

With a violent flurry, Drizzt rushed between his own pair of Ashmadai, a lumbering half-orc and a dark-skinned human who might have been Turmishan. Both fell aside with multiple cuts on their arms and torsos, shielding themselves defensively though the drow looked past them, eagerly wading into the next enemies in line.

Drizzt knew that speed was his ally. He and Bruenor had to keep moving ferociously to prevent an organized line of attack against them, and that was just the way he liked it.

He ran to a table, jumped up on it, jumped off again, blades flashing with every step, cracking against staff and spear, slicing clothing and skin. Howls and screams, cracking wood and breaking glass marked his passing, like a black tornado cutting a swath of absolute destruction. More than once he abruptly stopped and spun, defeating pursuit with a flurry of parries and thrusts.

On one such turn, Drizzt brought both his blades in from opposite directions and at different angles, scissoring the thrusting spear with such force that he tore it from his pursuer's grasp. The woman threw her hands up, expecting an onslaught of scimitars, but Drizzt knew that those behind him were closing fast.

He jumped and set his feet on chairs, one left and one right, then sprang up again, tucking a tight back flip as he wound his way over the pursuer, who barreled right under and past him and inadvertently stabbed his own ally. That fact hadn't even set in,

Drizzt knew, by the time he landed behind the stumbling man, Icingdeath sweeping across to slash the back of the man's legs, just below his buttocks.

How he howled!

Drizzt whirled, slashing long and wildly to keep the others at bay; no less than five of the enemy had formed a semi-circle around him. He set himself low, unwilling to commit and ready to react, forcing them to make the first move.

He managed to glance at Bruenor, to find his friend standing atop the bar, similarly surrounded.

"Die well, elf!" Bruenor called.

"Always as intended!" Drizzt yelled back, not a hint of regret in his voice. But before either could put words to action, another voice rose above the din.

All eyes went to the door, where a most unusual creature had entered the Cutlass, an elf woman dressed in black leather, high boots, and a short, seductively angled skirt, and with a wide hat and a metallic walking stick.

"Who is this?" she demanded.

"Dwarf and a drow!" one man yelled back.

"Not these two!"

"A dwarf and a drow—how many could there be?" another man yelled back at her.

"I can think o' one other pair," Bruenor interjected.

"That would be . . . us," came a voice from the staircase— Jarlaxle's voice—and all eyes turned that way to see a second drow and dwarf on the stairs.

"A drow and a dwarf, a dwarf and a drow, a hunnerd times better'n a fox and a cow! Bwahaha!" Athrogate added with unbridled enthusiasm.

The cultists cast about for guidance, obviously caught way off their guard. "Surrender, then, all of you!" one of them demanded. "You are not to return to the beast!"

"The beast?" Jarlaxle replied. "Oh, but we are—and yes, King Bruenor, he is referring to your coveted Gauntlgrym. I have quite a tale to tell to you."

"When we're done smashin' some fools, he means," Athrogate roared, and he came over the rail in a great leap, morningstars spinning out to the sides. He was fairly high up, and so, though his plummeting charge was a bit of a surprise, the cultists below had time to move aside.

Athrogate landed flat on the top of a table, sending plates and glass flying and flattening the wood straight to the floor, where he landed with a great grunt. Anyone doubting that dwarves could bounce would have had those doubts removed, though, as Athrogate, spitting bits of food, various beverages, and broken ceramic and glass, rebounded right back to his feet. Even more astonishingly, he kept his morningstars somehow spinning at the ends of their respective chains.

"Bwahaha!" he roared, and the Ashmadai backed off in shock. Only for a moment, though, then a pair charged at him furiously.

Both were airborne a heartbeat later, one launched sidelong by the weight of one enchanted morningstar—Athrogate having enacted the magic of that one to coat the head with oil of impact— and the other hooked by the ball and chain around one arm as he tried to block. A twist, a turn, and a throw by the dwarf sent the poor cultist into a flying somersault, at the end of which he, like the dwarf, crashed through a table.

"Bwahaha!"

"Go," Drizzt bade Bruenor.

Those two dwarves had fought side by side before, and to great effect. Without the slightest hesitation, using Athrogate's distraction to his advantage, Bruenor charged across the floor, kicking chairs and tables as he went, sweeping glasses and plates, furniture and utensils with his battle-axe, launching them into any and every nearby Ashmadai, just adding to the confusion.

Athrogate saw him coming and likewise cut a path of devastation, seeming more than happy to get beside King Bruenor again for a good row.

Ashmadai rushed the bottom of the staircase, but Jarlaxle paid them no more heed than to toss the feather from his wide-brimmed hat down at them. That feather quickly transformed into a gigantic, flightless bird. The beast cawed, its huge call befitting its stature, echoing off the tavern's wall. It began beating its small wings furiously, its long, thick neck snapping its powerful beak down at nearby enemies, its heavy legs stomping and cracking the floorboards.

But Jarlaxle wasn't watching. He tossed the feather and forgot about it, knowing that his dependable pet would buy him all the time he needed. His focus was on the front door, on Dahlia, the last to enter. He tried to get a gauge of the elf woman, looked for a hint of disconnect in her movements. He replayed her words and tried to picture again her face as she'd spoken them. Did her expression match her words?

Jarlaxle reminded himself that it didn't matter as he drew out his favorite wand and leveled it Dahlia's way.

The fight was on in full below, with Bruenor and Athrogate battling right below him, and Drizzt weaving into that devastating dance of his across the way, yet Dahlia didn't yet move to react. Perhaps that was because there were still more than a dozen of her minions between her and the enemy, or maybe it was an indication of something else, Jarlaxle dared to hope.

But the choice was hers, not his.

He spoke a command word, releasing the power of the wand. A thick green-colored glob of some unspeakable semi-liquid flew forth from the tip, sailing down the stairs and across the room to slam against Dahlia, who seemed to disappear under the splatter of the goo as it fastened itself to the doorjamb and wall.

A second blast was on the way before the first had even connected, further burying Dahlia, completely covering her so that anyone looking to the door for the first time at that moment would have never known an elf woman had stood there a moment before.

Jarlaxle stared at the blob on the wall, and wondered.

Below him, at the base of the stairs, his giant bird shrieked in protest, and an Ashmadai howled in pain as the bird repaid him for the stab of his scepter.

Jarlaxle's grin disappeared as he turned his attention to Drizzt. He watched the fury of the drow unleashed. Jarlaxle had seen Drizzt in action many times before, but never like that. The ranger's blades dripped with blood, and his swings were not so carefully measured.

As in the battle with the ash zombies in the forest, Drizzt Do'Urden fell into himself, let all of his frustration, fear, and anger curl in on itself. Now he was the pure fighter, the Hunter, and it was a role he had cherished for decades, since the Spellplague, since the unfairness and callous reality of the world had shattered his delusions, and his sense of calm.

Bruenor used the tables as missiles, hooking them with his axe or his foot and throwing them into the faces of nearby enemies. For Athrogate, the furniture was merely a nuisance and nothing more, something to smash and overturn, all for the pure love of destruction.

But for Drizzt, the chairs and tables, the long bar and the railing, were props, and welcomed ones. His dance would have been far less mesmerizing and effective on an empty, flat floor. He charged to the nearest upright table, leaped atop it, then sprang off it so gracefully that not a glass, mug, or platter moved. He touched down, one foot on the back of a chair, the other on the seat, his momentum carrying him forward, driving the chair over backward.

He reversed his weight and the chair moved back upright, bringing the drow backward to avoid the stab of an Ashmadai's weapon.

Then he reversed again, quickly, shifting the chair over backward and walking to the floor with it, leaning back as he went to avoid that same Ashmadai as he retracted his thrust and swung his scepter at Drizzt's head like a club.

It went over the bending drow at the same time his left arm straightened, Twinkle stabbing hard into the man's gut. As Drizzt rushed past, he retracted and sent the scimitar in a quick spin, slashing the bending man's leg and sending him howling and thrashing to the floor.

By that time, Drizzt was atop the next table in line, where he leaped and tucked, landed and kicked, and stabbed out repeatedly, scoring hit after hit on the several enemies who had surrounded him. They stabbed and swung with abandon, but the drow was always one leap, one duck, one leg-tucking hop ahead of them. One by one, they fell away, wounded.

But more rushed in to take their places, as they seemed to have the drow trapped.

Seemed.

But Drizzt saw the oncoming explosion, and as Bruenor and Athrogate roared toward the table, Drizzt rushed to the side and leaped away, a somersault that cleared the gathered Ashmadai. All of them watched Drizzt, trying to turn and catch up to him, when the two dwarves plowed through their ranks, shield and axe and twin morningstars working as extensions of the real weapons, the dwarves themselves.

The table flew and the Ashmadai scattered. The dwarves roared and plowed on, burying all enemies beneath the weight of their charge.

And Drizzt was back to his run and his dance, his feet and hands a blur. He slashed both his blades down to the left, batting aside a thrusting scepter. Then back to the right they went, both reaching out in that arc just enough to stick an Ashmadai woman as she departed, sending her, too, falling aside.

Drizzt skidded to a stop, seeing another potential enemy coming toward him: Jarlaxle's bird. The drow went into a flurry with his blades, more show than effect, and he grinned wickedly as the two Ashmadai in front of him watched that flourish too long to sense the monstrous diatryma coming in at them from behind.

The drow darted away, and the Ashmadai turned to follow. One got pecked on the skull with bone-shattering force, and the other found himself flying in an unintended direction as a three-toed foot slammed him on the hip with tremendous force.

What had been twenty against two, then twenty against four—five with the diatryma—had turned much more even. And with their leader lost in a pile of whatever-that-was, the remaining

Ashmadai suddenly seemed more intent on getting away to fight another day than in continuing along a losing course.

And Jarlaxle's bird chased them right out of the Cutlass and down the street.

"Surrender!" Drizzt demanded of an enemy he cornered opposite the door.

He accentuated his demand with a devastating flurry that knocked her weapon left, right, and up in the blink of an eye. She was obviously overmatched, and easy to kill, should the drow choose that course.

But she was Ashmadai.

She moved as if to drop her weapon, her other hand held open before her—and she attacked instead.

Or tried to.

She leaped forward with a scream and a mighty thrust, but hit nothing but air, overbalancing and hardly even aware of the fact that the drow had side-stepped. The woman stiffened as a scimitar entered her side. It slid up toward her lung then stopped and twisted. Her scepter fell to the floor. She stood up on her toes, teeth clenched, hands grabbing at empty air.

Drizzt pulled his blade back out. The woman turned to regard him, grasping at her torn side. Her mouth moved as if she meant to curse him, but no sound came forth as she sank to one knee then eased herself down to the floor where she curled and clenched.

Drizzt scanned the room, just in time to see Bruenor and Athrogate slam into each other, shoulder to shoulder, as they tried to exit the tavern. They jostled for a moment before Athrogate demurred, shoving the dwarf king out first and quickly following.

Behind them came Jarlaxle, his expression deadly serious as he looked back at Drizzt.

"What?" Drizzt asked of him.

Jarlaxle's eyes shifted just a bit to regard the woman who lay crumpled beside the ranger. He shook his head and sighed, but continued on. He didn't follow the dwarves out of the tavern. Instead, he stood facing the goo planted on the wall just to the side of the door.

"She's suffocating," Drizzt said as he walked over. He had once been the victim of that oozing web, himself, and knew well its deadly effect.

"You would prefer to kill her with your blades, I suppose," Jarlaxle flippantly replied, and Drizzt stared at him hard.

Jarlaxle brought his hands down with a snap, his magical bracers depositing a dagger in each. He looked at Drizzt, again grim-faced, and snapped his wrists again, elongating the daggers into long, narrow-bladed swords. With an uncharacteristic growl, he drove one sword into the goo and through it to hit the wall on the other side. He retracted the sword and studied its blade, still clean save a bit of the greenish substance no bigger than a fingernail.

"No blood," Jarlaxle said, and shrugged at Drizzt. He lined up the blade again, this time more to the center of the mass, a certain hit. And again, he glanced at Drizzt with an eyebrow raised.

The ranger didn't blink.

Jarlaxle sighed and lowered the blade. "Who are you?" he asked, staring at Drizzt.

Drizzt met his accusing glare with an impassive look.

"The Drizzt Do'Urden I know would have called for mercy," Jarlaxle said. He pointed about the room with his sword, to the Ashmadai fallen to the drow's scimitars. "Shall we call a priest?"

"That they will be healed and attack me once more?"

"Who are you?"

"No one who has ever made a difference," Drizzt replied.

The apathy, the self-pity, and mostly the callousness hit Jarlaxle like a wall of foul acid. A sneer erupted on his face and he spun back to the glob on the wall and stabbed hard with his sword, then harder with the second, and back and forth in an outraged flurry, over and over, so that anyone caught behind it was surely dead.

"Impressive," Drizzt said. He flipped his scimitars over in his hands, aligning them perfectly with their sheaths, and slid them away. "And you decry my lack of mercy?"

"Look at them!" an angry Jarlaxle shouted at Drizzt, presenting the bloodless blades before him.

"How did you know?" Drizzt asked.

"I know everything that goes on in Luskan."

"Then ye're knowing where me maps might be," said Bruenor, coming back in through the door.

Jarlaxle acknowledged him with a nod then looked around at the fallen Ashmadai, some of whom were squirming and kneeling, and with more than one watching the trio at the door.

"We have a lot to discuss," the drow mercenary said. "But not here."

"I would know the fate of Shivanni Gardpeck before I leave," Drizzt replied.

"She's safe," Jarlaxle assured him. "And will return soon with a host of soldiers." He paused and eyed Drizzt. "And priests to tend to the wounded."

"She knew there would be such a battle in her tavern this night?" Drizzt asked, looking around at the devastation.

"And with enough payment for her troubles to put things right, I promise," said Jarlaxle.

"Put things right?" Drizzt retorted with a snicker to show how ridiculous he found that notion. He led Jarlaxle's gaze across the room, over the destruction, the carnage, the wounded, and the dead.

The two drow locked stares then, each trying to scrutinize the other, each seemingly trying to make sense out of the nonsensical.

"Can coin unwind time?" Drizzt whispered.

Jarlaxle's gaze became the more judgmental, a look of frustration and disappointment, even anger on his face—one that only heightened as Drizzt remained so stoic and unblinking.

"Damned bird's chasin' 'em right to the docks and into the water!" Athrogate announced then, breaking the moment. The two turned to see the dwarf bobbing up beside Bruenor at the Cutlass's door.

"Come," Jarlaxle bade them all. "We have much to discuss."

He snapped his wrists up instead of down, and his swords became daggers, which he flipped up into the air. They hit the ceiling and stuck fast.

"What about her?" Bruenor asked, motioning to the blob on the wall.

"We shall see," Jarlaxle replied.

With Athrogate leading, the four rushed away, sprinting down the street and turning into an alley. The shouts and calls of guards soon followed them. Jarlaxle flipped a portable hole from his hat and flattened it against the wall at the alley's end.

Athrogate jumped through, and when Bruenor hesitated, the other dwarf reached back from the blackness, grabbed him by the shirt, and yanked him through as well. Drizzt jumped nimbly through after his friend, with Jarlaxle following, and from the other side, he pulled the hole from the wall, leaving it impassable, as it had been before.

So ended the pursuit, but the four kept up a swift, though not desperate pace back to Jarlaxle's apartment.

"Ye give me back me maps!" Bruenor insisted as they came to the door.

Just inside the small but lavishly furnished flat, Jarlaxle reached to a side table and tossed Bruenor his stolen pack.

"All but one are in there," Jarlaxle explained. "Perhaps they will lead to great treasures and mysterious places—adventures for another day."

"All but one?" Bruenor growled.

"All but this one, good dwarf," the drow explained, reaching into a drawer and producing a tightly rolled and tied parchment. "This one, which will lead to that which you most desire. Yes, King Bruenor, I speak of Gauntlgrym. I have been there, and though I cannot retrace my steps since the explosion collapsed the tunnels, I know where Gauntlgrym lies." He brought the map up in front of him. "And this is the way."

Bruenor fumbled for words. He looked to Drizzt, who just returned his shrug with a like movement.

The dwarf king looked back to Jarlaxle, licking his lips, which had gone dry. "I'm not for playin' yer games on this," he warned.

"No game," Jarlaxle replied in all seriousness. "Gauntlgrym."

"Gauntlgrym," Athrogate said from the side, and Bruenor turned to regard him. "I been there. I seen the forge. I seen the throne. I seen the ghosts."

That last proclamation had Bruenor, who had so recently met those very ghosts, sucking in his breath in a futile attempt to steady himself.

Drizzt looked at Bruenor with a look of some satisfaction then, but also an unsettling detachment.

Jarlaxle didn't miss that last part, and he found to his surprise that it bothered him profoundly.

CHAPTER 17

DESPERATE TIME, DESPERATE PLAN

B RUENOR ALMOST DISAPPEARED INTO THE OVERSTUFFED CHAIR, having sunk just a bit deeper with Jarlaxle's every word. The drow explained his plan to retake Gauntlgrym, and if Bruenor had thought it a daunting task in the abstract, it sounded positively horrifying in plain language.

"So the beast didn't let the volcano blow," Bruenor said, his voice barely a whisper. "The beast *is* the volcano?" He looked at Drizzt as he asked that question, remembering their flippant discussions about stopping a volcano.

"A primordial of fire, as old as the gods," Jarlaxle replied.

"And as strong," said Bruenor, but Jarlaxle shook his head.

"But without a god's mind. It is catastrophe, devoid of malice. It is power, without intellect."

"It won't raise an army of fanatical cultists," Drizzt added.

Jarlaxle's expression on that point was less than reassuring.

Bruenor glanced over at the table that held the magical bowls they were to use to summon the water elementals, bowls they hoped would hold the monsters long enough for them to re-open the tendrils of the Hosttower of the Arcane, thus setting the old cage back in place. Bowls they had to place precisely, though they knew not precisely where. . . .

"King Bruenor, it is an adventure!" Jarlaxle said, excited, bouncing from foot to foot. "King Bruenor, this is the way to Gauntlgrym! The real Gauntlgrym! Is that not what you sought when you abdicated the throne of Mithral Hall?"

"Bah!" Bruenor snorted and waved the drow away.

Jarlaxle grinned and tossed a wink at Drizzt. "We may have more options, more allies," he said, taking up his wide-brimmed hat and plopping it on his head. "I will return presently."

And with that, he was gone, leaving the three of them sitting in the apartment.

"Ye needed me maps," Bruenor said to Athrogate.

The black-bearded dwarf shrugged and nodded. "The tunnels we walked to Gauntlgrym collapsed. Can't go back that way."

Bruenor turned a concerned look to Drizzt.

"Those tunnels carried these . . . tendrils, of the Hosttower, to the ancient dwarven city," the drow added.

"Aye, that's how we found the place."

"And if those tendrils are damaged?"

Athrogate blew a heavy sigh, then looked directly at Bruenor, his expression very serious. "If ye ain't for goin', I ain't for blamin' ye. It's all crazy, and sure that we're to die—more sure than anything good, I mean. But for meself, there's no choice to be found." He sucked in his breath and visibly steadied himself in his chair. " 'Twas meself, King Bruenor," Athrogate admitted. "Jarlaxle didn't tell ye that, bein' me friend. But 'twas meself what pulled the lever and shut the tendrils' flow, shut the tendrils' magic, and freed the elementals what were holding the beast in its pit o' lava. It was Athrogate that let the primordial roar. It was Athrogate that wrecked Gauntlgrym, and Athrogate that killed Neverwinter."

Bruenor's eyes opened wide and he turned to Drizzt to find the same incredulous expression on the face of the drow.

"It weren't what I expected," Athrogate went on, lowering his eyes in shame after his open admission. "I thinked meself to be re-firing the forge, and bringing the city back to life."

"That is an incredibly daring move to take when you were not certain," Drizzt remarked.

"Wasn't in me own head," the dwarf muttered. "Or more to the point, there was others in me head beside me! A vampire, for one, and that Thayan witch."

"The one in the Cutlass, who somehow fled from under Jarlaxle's glue?"

"Her boss. The one with the Dread Ring. I was tricked and I was pushed." He paused and blew another sigh. "And I was weak."

Bruenor looked to Drizzt again, who nodded back at him.

"So be it," Bruenor said to Athrogate, his voice firm but in no way accusatory. "Ye can't be changin' what happened, but it might be that we can fix it now."

"I got to try," said Athrogate.

"So do we," Bruenor agreed. "And not just try, but to do it. And know that any who get in me way'll be feelin' the bite o' me axe!"

"Aye, but not afore they feel the thump o' me morningstars!" Athrogate said.

He seemed rejuvenated by Bruenor's cheer. Both dwarves looked at Drizzt, who just offered a wry little grin in response. He didn't have to say it, because both dwarves knew already: Any enemies they encountered would feel the cut of Drizzt's scimitars before either Bruenor's axe or Athrogate's morningstars.

Out on the balcony later on, alone with his thoughts, Bruenor Battlehammer considered what lay before him. He would see Gauntlgrym. His quest would be fulfilled, his vision confirmed, his dream realized. Then what? What road would inspire his steps after that? What would lend strength to his tired old limbs?

Or was this his last road, with the end in sight?

He was mulling that over, coming to accept the likelihood, when he spied a familiar face on the street below.

Shivanni Gardpeck hustled along and was met by Jarlaxle, who seemed to come out of nowhere. They exchanged words Bruenor could not hear, and Jarlaxle gave the woman a fairly hefty purse, as he had promised in the Cutlass earlier.

When Shivanni broke away, heading off into the night, and Jarlaxle turned toward Bruenor, the dwarf noticed more than a bit of concern and puzzlement on the dark elf's face.

Jarlaxle came up the stairs to find Bruenor waiting for him.

"Has our friend crossed the line?" asked the drow.

The question caught Bruenor off guard and he crinkled his nose as he stared back at Jarlaxle.

"Drizzt," the drow clarified, though of course that wasn't what confused Bruenor.

"What line are ye talking about?"

"He fights with more . . . fury than I recall," Jarlaxle said.

"Aye, been that way for a long time now."

"Since the loss of Catti-brie and Regis."

"Are ye blamin' him?"

Jarlaxle shook his head, and looked to the apartment's closed door. "But has he crossed over that line?" he asked again, turning back to Bruenor. "Has he started a fight he shouldn't have started? Has he shown no mercy to one deserving? Has he allowed his rage instead of his conscience to control his blades?"

Bruenor stared at him, still puzzled.

"Your hesitance frightens me," the dark elf said.

"No," Bruenor answered. "But might be that he's come close. Why're ye caring?"

"Curiosity."

The dwarf didn't buy that, of course. "Been other things, too," Bruenor said. "Drizzt ain't one for the towns anymore. When we're settling for the winter, in Port Llast, or in Neverwinter afore she fell, or even with a barbarian tribe, he's not one to stay about—uncomfortable in the company. Maybe now he'd be happy in Neverwinter."

"Because there's always someone, or something, to fight in the ruins," Jarlaxle said.

"Aye."

"He relishes battle."

"Never shied from it. So speak it out, elf. What's on yer mind about this?"

"I told you: curiosity," Jarlaxle replied, and he looked at the apartment door once again.

"Then go ask him yerself, and ye might be gettin' better answers," the dwarf offered.

Jarlaxle shook his head. "I have other business to attend to this night," he said.

The drow mercenary turned, shook his head, and skipped back down the stairs.

Bruenor moved to the railing and watched him go, though the crafty Jarlaxle was quickly out of sight. The dwarf found himself thinking about that conversation for a long while, though, and not so much about why Jarlaxle might have inquired in such a way about Drizzt, but the implications of the dark elf's legitimate concerns.

He could hardly remember the old Drizzt anymore, Bruenor realized, the drow who took battle with a shrug of inevitability and a smile on his face, both in confidence and in the knowledge that he was acting in accord with his heart. He had seen the change in Drizzt. His smile had become something more . . . wicked, less an expression of the acceptance of the necessity of a fight but more a look of pure enjoyment.

And only then did Bruenor realize how many years had passed since he had seen the old Drizzt.

When he entered the subterranean chamber that had once belonged to Arklem Greeth and Valindra, Jarlaxle was not surprised to learn that he was not alone.

Dahlia sat comfortably in a chair, eyeing him.

"You did well with the ring," the drow said with a bow.

"Its nature was revealed to me the moment I put it on."

"Still, be not so humble. Few could use the projected image to such effectiveness. Your minions did not even suspect that it was not really you at the door."

"And you?"

"Had I not known of the ring, I would never have suspected," he replied, holding out his hand.

Dahlia looked at him, at his hand, but didn't move.

"I would like my ring," Jarlaxle said.

"It is empty of its spell now."

"And can be recharged."

"That is my hope," Dahlia replied, still making no move to return the item.

Jarlaxle retracted his hand. "I had confidence that you would use the ring. Your distaste for Sylora Salm remains strong, I see."

"No stronger than hers for me."

"She is jealous of your elf's youth. She will be old and ugly while you remain beautiful."

Dahlia waved that thought away as if it didn't matter, indicating to Jarlaxle that her feud with Sylora was rooted in far deeper things than physical appearance.

"You have decided to abandon her cause all together, then," Jarlaxle reasoned.

"I did not say that."

"You don't wear Szass Tam's brooch."

Dahlia looked down at her blouse, where the brooch had usually been set.

"You may be able to lie your way out of your actions at the Cutlass," Jarlaxle said, "but I doubt this breach of etiquette will be accepted. Szass Tam takes such things seriously. In any case, you'll never convince Sylora to excuse your limited role in the fight at the Cutlass."

The elf woman stared hard at him.

"So you have crossed through a one-way door," Jarlaxle finished. "There is no turning back for you now, Dahlia. You have abandoned Sylora Salm. You have abandoned Szass Tam. You have abandoned Thay."

"I can only hope all three of them think me dead."

Jarlaxle spent a few moments looking Dahlia over, trying to get a read of her intentions. But she was a hard one to decipher. Overlaying her obvious charms was a layer of coldness, a perpetual guard against stray emotions. It occurred to him that she would make a good drow.

"And now where, Lady Dahlia?"

Dahlia looked at him, her eyes dark and serious. "Who is your drow friend?"

"I have many."

"The one in the bar," Dahlia clarified. "I watched the fight. Briefly. He is a true two-handed fighter, even by drow standards."

"Athrogate would take offense at your singling out of the drow."

"The dwarf is a different matter. What he lacks in ability he covers with brute force. There is little grace to his dance, and while he is no doubt dangerous, that drow is far more skilled with his blades than Athrogate is with his morningstars."

"Truly," Jarlaxle agreed. "He could have been among the greatest of weapons masters Menzoberranzan ever knew, as was his father."

"Who is he?"

Jarlaxle looked away, imagining he could see Drizzt in the distance at that very moment. "He is the one who escaped," he said.

"From?"

He looked back at her directly. "From his heritage. His name is Drizzt Do'Urden, and he is welcomed in Waterdeep and Silverymoon alike . . ."

Dahlia stopped him with an upraised hand. "So that is the one they call Drizzt," she said. "I suspected as much."

"He has earned his reputation, I assure you."

"And you are his friend?"

"More than he would admit, perhaps, or at least, more than he might understand."

Dahlia looked at him curiously, and indeed, when he reflected on that look, Jarlaxle, too, found himself a bit surprised.

"Why?" Dahlia asked, a simple question rooted in deep and complex emotions.

"Because he is the one who escaped," Jarlaxle answered.

Dahlia paused, nodding, then asked, "And his dwarf friend?"

"King Bruenor Battlehammer of Mithral Hall, though now he travels under an alias. He abdicated his throne to find that which we have already visited."

"So you mean to use that to trick him to accompany you on your return to Gauntlgrym, for of course, you mean to return."

"Yes . . . no, I mean, and yes to the end. I do not mean to trick them. I mean to tell them. I already have, in fact."

"And they will run into the arms of an awakening primordial?"

"They are possessed of too much honor for their own sakes, I fear," Jarlaxle said with a wry grin. That smile disappeared, though, replaced by a very serious expression as he added, "And you?"

"What of me?"

"You have betrayed Sylora Salm, Szass Tam, and Thay herself."

"Your words, not mine."

"You used the ring to run away. But the Dahlia I know relishes the thrill of the fight."

"The Dahlia you know stays alive because she's careful and smart."

"But perhaps not so much where Sylora is concerned."

"You fancy yourself as perceptive, I expect," she replied.

"You accepted the ring, and you used it. You betrayed Sylora when it most counted. Perhaps the arrival of Dahlia—not the image of Dahlia, but the actual warrior—would have changed the outcome of the fight in the Cutlass. Yet you chose not to finish your mission."

"What do you know of my mission?"

"That you were sent here to see if any would respond to the growing earthquakes," Jarlaxle replied without hesitation. "To learn if I meant to return to Gauntlgrym."

Dahlia grinned.

"Well, now you know," the drow said. "I do, and I am not without allies."

"Should I go tell Sylora as much?"

"I expect she will know soon enough, since some of your Ashmadai minions escaped the tavern."

"You know of the Ashmadai?"

Jarlaxle raised an eyebrow, and the corner of his mouth.

"The tunnels have collapsed," Dahlia said, changing the subject. "There is no way back to Gauntlgrym."

"I know a way," Jarlaxle said.

Dahlia's blue eyes flashed for just a moment before she fully suppressed her intrigue.

"And I will lead you there," the drow said, revealing to her that he had seen her slip.

"You presume much."

"And yet I presume correctly. What gain is there for you to pretend otherwise? In the end, and soon, you will be walking beside me and my friends to the halls of Gauntlgrym."

Dahlia came out of her chair in a hurry, standing strong and taking up her eight-foot staff.

"You already gave me your answer when you used the ring," Jarlaxle said.

Dahlia put on a pensive expression, but she was nodding.

"Why?" Jarlaxle asked. "This is hardly the easiest course for you."

"If the primordial is contained and cannot spew its calamity, Sylora's Dread Ring will fail," Dahlia replied. "She will not gain the upper hand in her battle with the Netherese."

"You are fond of the Netherese?"

Dahlia's eyes flashed again, with obvious, unbridled fury.

"I share your contempt for them," Jarlaxle was quick to add. He eyed Dahlia carefully. "But your contempt for Sylora is no less profound."

"Szass Tam will blame her for the failure of the Dread Ring."

"You would like that."

"It would be among the greatest pleasures of my life."

"So that you could return to Szass Tam in a position of power?"

Again Dahlia's eyes flashed, and Jarlaxle realized he'd missed the mark badly with that line of reasoning. It was true, then, he knew. In using the ring, the out, he had given her, Dahlia had seized the opportunity to free herself of not only Sylora, but the lich lord of Thay himself. Perhaps their wretched fascination with death had offended her sensibilities, or perhaps she'd just come to rightly conclude that those who followed Szass Tam were destined to perpetual subjugation, always to be followers, never leaders.

Those were possibilities Jarlaxle intended to explore.

"We should leave soon for Gauntlgrym," he said. "Before word has reached Sylora. Before she can rally her minions against us."

"And when she does, we will kill them," Dahlia replied. "Perhaps this drow, Drizzt, will show me that his reputation is well-earned."

Jarlaxle smiled at that, not a doubt in his mind.

"We should leave at once," Jarlaxle told the trio when he returned to them soon after. "Some of those who would stop us have fled the city, spreading word far and wide of our intentions, no doubt."

"We're not knowin' enough, by yer own words!" Bruenor argued. "Where to put the durned bowls?"

"We will learn much when we arrive in Gauntlgrym, of that I hold faith," Jarlaxle replied, and he privately recalled the words of Gromph, relayed from the dwarf ghost trapped in Arklem Greeth's phylactery: Seat a king in the throne of Gauntlgrym. "Time will work against us now, my friend," he went on. "There are many who would see the primordial awaken and explode once more, for their own nefarious gains."

"Is Bregan D'aerthe about?" Drizzt asked. "Ready for the road?"

Jarlaxle seemed put on his heels a bit by that, and his lips went tight.

"Just we four?" Drizzt asked.

"Nay, five," Jarlaxle replied, and he turned to the open door and motioned with his hand. In walked Dahlia.

"Ain't she the girl in the goo?" Bruenor asked.

"It was a trick, so that she could flee her foul companions under the guise of death," Jarlaxle explained.

"Companions she brought with her the first time we went there," Athrogate protested. "Was her that bringed us there to free the beast!"

"And ye're thinkin' we're to trust her?" Bruenor argued, hands on hips, nostrils flaring.

"Dahlia was deceived on that long-ago day," Jarlaxle replied. He looked at Athrogate and added, "As were we."

"Bah!" the dwarf snorted. "She took us there, tricked us there, to free the beast!"

"I tried to stop you," Dahlia reminded him.

"So ye're sayin' now."

"I speak the truth and you know it," Dahlia said, turning to regard Drizzt and Bruenor—particularly Drizzt—more directly. "I have an interest no less than your own in securing the primordial once more."

"Rooted in conscience or revenge?" Drizzt asked with a wry grin.

Dahlia stared at him hard.

Bruenor started to argue, but Drizzt put his hand on the dwarf's shoulder to quiet him, then nodded for Dahlia to continue.

"I have paid for my disobedience to my masters—my former masters—every day since," she said. "And I pay doubly, because I see the result of my failure. Once I believed Szass Tam to be . . ."

"Szass what?" Bruenor asked, glancing at Drizzt, who shrugged, equally at a loss.

"The lord and master of the realm of Thay," Dahlia explained, "whose minions control the Dread Ring in Neverwinter Wood, and the ash-covered zombies who roam the region."

Both dwarf and drow nodded, remembering the tall tales of the powerful lich.

"Once I believed Szass Tam to be a prophet," Dahlia went on. "A great man of glorious designs. But when I came to understand the price of those designs, I felt quite the fool."

"Revenge, then," said Drizzt, and his elimination of any element of morality from Dahlia's change of heart had the elf staring at him once again, her lips tight, her eyes narrowed.

"I been callin' ye that for ten years now," Athrogate chimed in. "A fool, I mean."

Dahlia just snorted at him. "The minions of Szass Tam, the zealot Ashmadai and Sylora Salm, and even my old companion Dor'crae—"

"The vampire," Athrogate muttered.

Bruenor looked at him, then at Dahlia, with disgust. "Ye keep fine friends," he said.

"Some would say the same of a dwarf and a drow," Dahlia replied, but when Bruenor's eyes narrowed dangerously at that, she could only hold her hands up, admitting that she was guilty as charged. "They will try to stop you . . . us," she said. "I know them. I know their tactics and their powers. You will find me to be a valuable ally."

"Or a dangerous spy," said Bruenor.

Drizzt glanced from his friend to the elf warrior, but his gaze finally settled upon Jarlaxle. Few understood those conflicting gray areas of morality and pragmatism better than the leader of Bregan D'aerthe, after all. Noting Drizzt's questioning stare, Jarlaxle replied with a slight nod.

"The five of us, then," Drizzt said.

"And straightaway to Gauntlgrym," Jarlaxle agreed.

Hands still on his hips, Bruenor seemed less than convinced. He started to argue, but Drizzt leaned in low and whispered, "Gauntlgrym," reminding the dwarf that he was but days from realizing a goal he had spent decades chasing.

"Aye," Bruenor said. He took up his axe, eyed Dahlia suspiciously for good measure, and motioned for Jarlaxle to lead on.

CHAPTER 18

A DARK ROAD TO A DARKER PLACE

BAH, I LET IT OUT AND I'LL PUT IT BACK!" ATHROGATE grumbled as he roughly collected the plates from their breakfast.

Three days out from Luskan and moving swiftly, Jarlaxle was certain they would arrive at their destination—the cave that would lead them to Gauntlgrym, at least—before the sun set.

The night had been punctuated by occasional tremors, but more ominous still, Mount Hotenow—the mountain's second peak, blown away in the first explosion years before—was once again visible. And it grew by the day, swelling under the mounting pressure of the awakening primordial.

"Are ye to beat yerself up on that every heartbeat o' every day?" Bruenor asked Athrogate, helping break the camp.

Athrogate looked at him with an expression somewhere between wounded and self-loathing.

"What?" Bruenor growled at him.

"Ye're a Delzoun king," Athrogate said. "I know I've spent most o' me life pretending that don't matter nothing to me, and most times it don't . . . beggin' yer pardon."

Bruenor offered a slight tip of his head in forgiveness.

"Done a lot o' things I'm not thinking'd be seen as proper for a Delzoun dwarf, Moradin knows," Athrogate went on. "Been a highwayman—err, highway*dwarf,* and some o' me own kin've felt the thump o' me morningstars."

"I'm knowing yer history, Athrogate. What with Adbar and all."

"Aye, and I'm thinking that when me time's done here in this world—if it e'er happens with this damned curse on me head—that Moradin's going to want to be talking to me, and not all he's got to say's to be friendly."

"I ain't a priest," Bruenor reminded him.

"Aye, but ye're a king, a Delzoun king, with royal blood back to Gauntlgrym. I'm thinking that's to mean something. And so ye're the best I got to help me keep me promise. I let the damned thing out, and I'll put it back. I can't be fixin' what I done, but I can be making it hurt the less."

Bruenor considered the tough, black-bearded dwarf for a bit, taking a measure of the sincere pain that shone in Athrogate's eyes—something so unusual for that particular dwarf. The dwarf king nodded and put the plates back on the ground, then stepped over and patted Athrogate on the shoulder.

"Ye hear me good," Bruenor said. "I know yer tale o' Gauntlgrym, and if I weren't believing that ye was tricked to pull that lever, then know that I'd've split yer head wide with me axe already."

"I ain't the best o' dwarfs, but I ain't the worst."

"I know," said Bruenor. "And I know that no Delzoun, not a highwayman, not a thief, not a killer'd be wanting to wreck Gauntlgrym. So ye quit beating yerself up on it. Ye did right in having Jarlaxle get me and Drizzt, and did right in vowing to go back and put the beast away. That's all Moradin can ask of ye, and more'n meself's asking o' ye." He patted Athrogate's strong shoulder again. "But know that I'm glad to have ye with me. Just meself and three elfs and I'm thinking I'd throw meself into a chasm if we found one!"

Athrogate looked at Bruenor for just a moment, then, as the words digested, burst out in a great "Bwahaha!" He patted Bruenor hard on the shoulder, and explained, "Not afore this and not after it, I'm thinking, but know that for this journey, me life's for ye."

Now it was Bruenor's turn to once more put on a puzzled expression.

"For this trip, to Gauntlgrym, to the home of our father's father's father, then ye're me king."

"Yerself follows Jarlaxle."

"I walk *aside* Jarlaxle," Athrogate corrected. "Athrogate follows Athrogate, and none else. Except this time, just this time, when Athrogate follows King Bruenor."

It took Bruenor a while to digest that, but he found himself nodding in appreciation.

"Like ye're other friend o' old," Athrogate went on. "The one what throws himself on anything he can eat and half o' what he can't."

"Pwent," Bruenor said, trying hard to make sure his voice didn't crack, for he hated to admit it, even to himself, but he sorely missed the battlerager.

"Aye, the Pwent!" said Athrogate. "When we fought them crawly things up by Cadderly's place, when we fought the Ghost King, cursed be the name, 'twas the Pwent aside me. Might a king be knowin' a better shield dwarf?"

"No," Bruenor said without the slightest hesitation.

Athrogate nodded and let it go at that, managing a grin as he went back to packing up the camp.

Bruenor, too, went to his chores, feeling a bit lighter in the heart. The conversation with Athrogate had reminded him how sorely he missed Thibbledorf Pwent, and it occurred to the old dwarf king that he might have been kinder to Pwent in all those years of loyal service. How much had he taken the tough and loyal dwarf for granted!

He looked at Athrogate now in that light, and scolded himself for his sentimentality. He wasn't Thibbledorf Pwent, Bruenor told himself. Thibbledorf Pwent would have died for him, would have happily thrown himself in the path of a spear flying for Bruenor's chest. Bruenor remembered the look on Pwent's face when he'd left his friend in Icewind Dale, the abject despair and helplessness at the realization that there had been no way for him to continue beside his king.

Athrogate would never, could never, wear such an expression. The dwarf was sincere enough in his expression of regret for the events at Gauntlgrym, and likely meant every word in his pledge of fealty to Bruenor—for that one mission. But he was no Thibbledorf Pwent. And if it came to that moment of crisis, that ultimate sacrifice, could Bruenor trust Athrogate to give his life for the cause? Or for his king?

Bruenor's thoughts were interrupted by some movement off to the side of the camp, and through the trees, he saw Jarlaxle and Dahlia talking and pointing to the south.

"Eh, Athrogate," he said when the other dwarf moved near him. When Athrogate looked his way, Bruenor nodded his chin toward the couple. "That elf there with Jarlaxle."

"Dahlia."

"Ye trust her?"

Athrogate came up beside Bruenor and replied, "Jarlaxle trusts her."

"Ain't what I asked."

Athrogate sighed. "I'd be trustin' her a lot more if she weren't so damned mean with that stick o' hers," he admitted. When Bruenor looked at him curiously, he clarified. "Ah, but don't ye doubt that she's a mean one. That stick o' hers breaks all different ways, into weapons I ain't ne'er seen afore. She's fast, and with both hands. Meself, I can swing me flails pretty good, left and right, but she's more'n that. More akin to yer dark friend, in that her hands work as if they're two different fighters, if ye get me meanin'."

Bruenor's expression grew even more puzzled. He had never noted anything like humility from Athrogate before.

"I fought yer friend, ye know," Athrogate said. "In Luskan."

"Aye. And what're ye sayin'? That this one, this Dahlia, would be beating Drizzt square up?"

Athrogate didn't answer outright, but his expression showed that he believed exactly that, or at least, that he harbored serious doubts about the outcome of such a fight.

"Bah!" Bruenor snorted. "So ye're afraid o' her?"

"Bah!" Athrogate snorted right back. "I ain't afraid o' no one. Just, I'd be thinking Dahlia less a threat if she weren't so damned nasty."

"Good for knowin'," Bruenor said, and he lowered his voice when he noted Jarlaxle and Dahlia fast approaching.

"We are not alone," Jarlaxle announced when he neared. "Others are about, likely seeking the same cave as we."

"Bah, but how'd they be knowin' about it?" Bruenor asked.

"The Ashmadai at least are all over the Crags, I'd bet," Dahlia replied. "Sylora knows the approximate location of Gauntlgrym."

"We're nowhere near the mountain," Bruenor replied, somewhat harshly. "Going in from the far side . . ."

Dahlia's eyes narrowed for a just a moment, and Bruenor recognized that he'd hit on something there, which was confirmed when Dahlia turned to Jarlaxle.

"Sylora suspected I would go after the primordial, now that we know it's awakening," the drow explained. "That is why she sent Dahlia and the others to Luskan—to confirm, and to stop us."

"By now, she knows that failed," Dahlia said. "Szass Tam's minions are possessed of various magical means of communication."

"And she'd think yourself dead," Athrogate reasoned.

"No more," Bruenor replied, and again his voice was thick with suspicion. "If they're here, they're watching us, and they're watching Dahlia."

The elf woman nodded, but didn't appear pleased by that prospect. That only put a smirk on Bruenor's face.

"So ye're a traitor now, and to be punished if they're catching ye," the dwarf reasoned.

"It gives you pleasure to say that?" Dahlia asked.

"Or ye're a double-traitor," Bruenor said. "And maked us think ye'd maked them think yerself was killed to death in the fight."

"No," Jarlaxle said before Dahlia could.

"No?" Bruenor echoed. He dropped the pack he was holding and drew his axe from off his back, slapping it across his open palm.

"Ye don't want to be doin' that," Athrogate warned, his voice more filled with concern than any threat.

"Listen to your hairy friend, dwarf," Dahlia said, and she sent her walking stick in an easy swing, which brought it across her open palm so that she was holding it similarly to Bruenor with his axe.

Bruenor did relax at that, mostly because a dark form slipped silently out from around a tree behind Dahlia.

"Lady, ye can't help but expect a bit o' suspicion, now can ye?" Bruenor replied, and smiled disarmingly. "Ye come to us for a fight, and now we're to think yerself on our side?"

"Had I joined the fight in the Cutlass, your mission would have ended there, good dwarf," the elf warrior replied. "And you can tell that to your drow friend who is standing behind me."

Behind Dahlia, Drizzt stood up straight, and in front of her, Bruenor's face twisted up at her bravado.

"Telled ye," Athrogate muttered at Bruenor's side.

It occurred to Bruenor then just how young this elf female was. He hadn't really thought of that before, since everything had been such a jolt and a rush from the moment he and Drizzt had entered Luskan. But she showed it. She stood before a dwarf king, and with a legendary drow warrior behind her, and not a hint of worry showed on her face.

Only someone quite young could feel so . . . immortal.

She had never experienced loss, was Bruenor's initial thought, and couldn't comprehend its possibility.

He studied her more carefully for a few moments, though, and saw through the calm confidence just enough to realize that he was probably way off the mark with that last thought. More likely, Dahlia had experienced loss, great loss, and didn't care if that was again a possibility. Perhaps her bravado even invited it.

Bruenor glanced at Athrogate, thinking the other dwarf's warning about Dahlia quite prescient at that moment.

She was dangerous.

"If you're all so anxious for a fight, you'll find one soon enough," Jarlaxle remarked, obviously trying to break the tension.

Despite her outward confidence, Dahlia wondered if she'd played her hand correctly. She stared at the dwarf a few moments longer, trying to rid herself of the nagging notion that the crusty old warrior saw right through her.

She dismissed that concern out of hand. Dahlia had no time for that.

She turned to find Drizzt leaning easily against a tree, his weapons sheathed, his forearms resting on them with his hands crossed in front of him.

"Do you share your friend's concern?" she asked.

"The thought has occurred to me."

"And has it found root?"

Drizzt looked past her to Bruenor before offering a smile and answering, simply, "No."

Dahlia's stare grew intense, and Drizzt matched it. Once again, as it had just been with Bruenor, it seemed to her as if one of her companions was trying to see right through her. But she had her footing back—thanks to Drizzt's last answer. She eased her walking staff down beside her and leaned on it, but didn't relent with her stare, didn't blink, didn't allow the legendary warrior, Drizzt, any sense that he'd gained the upper hand.

But neither did Drizzt blink.

"We should be on our way," Jarlaxle said from the side, and he pointedly walked between the two, breaking their line of vision.

"Did you notice our adversaries?" Jarlaxle asked Drizzt.

"Coming from the south," the ranger replied. "I noted several groups."

"Focused?"

"Searching," Drizzt replied. "I doubt they know our exact location, and I'm certain they're oblivious to the caves we sighted to the east."

"But are those the right caves?" Jarlaxle asked. "Once we enter, we can expect our enemies to seal us off."

A long and uncomfortable silence followed.

"We move quickly," Dahlia said at length, and unexpectedly, for all thought that Drizzt, who had been extensively scouting the area, would make the call.

"Bah, but yer friends're trying to flush us, and ye're leaping from the grass afore their huntin' dogs," Bruenor argued.

But Dahlia was shaking her head with every word. "They're not trying to flush us. They know for certain that we're here," she explained, turning back to Drizzt. "You said there were several groups."

Drizzt nodded.

"Sylora Salm is in a desperate struggle with the Netherese in Neverwinter Wood," Dahlia explained. "She has few Ashmadai to spare. If she's sent more than a handful to the Crags, then she's confident we're here."

"She wants us to lead her to the cave," Bruenor grumbled.

"She would rather none of us even reach the cave," Dahlia replied without turning back to him. "All she desires is that no one interfere with the primordial."

"Would she not wish to aid in aiming the beast's outburst?" Drizzt asked. "To ensure the catastrophe she craves."

"There is malevolence in the primordial," Dahlia replied. "It is not an entirely indifferent force, and not entirely unthinking."

"There is some debate about that," Jarlaxle replied, but again, Dahlia shook her head.

"How precise was its first attack? The easy and nearest target . . ." she reasoned. "Had it blown to either the west or the east, few would have been killed. No, it sensed the life in Neverwinter, and buried it."

"There's life in Neverwinter again," Bruenor said.

"That would be a victory for Sylora," Dahlia answered, finally turning to regard the dwarf. "But not her preferred outcome."

"Luskan," Jarlaxle reasoned.

"The primordial has had a decade to test its prison," Dahlia said, "to recognize the magic that held it, to feel the residual power of the Hosttower, to perhaps send minions along the tendrils to better locate the city."

"So Sylora believes that the beast will facilitate her goals without her aid," Drizzt interjected, and when Dahlia and the others turned to regard him, he added, "The longer we delay, the more we play to her strength."

Dahlia couldn't suppress her grin, glad for the support—support that conveyed a measure of trust not only in her reasoning, but in her sincerity.

"Our best choice is to be aggressive," Dahlia said, nodding.

So, too, did Drizzt nod, and so it was decided.

Dahlia sprinted down the side of a ravine, leaping from stone to stone. The ground was uneven and she realized she was moving dangerously fast—but he was beating her. And Dahlia didn't like to lose. Particularly not with Ashmadai zealots down below in the small canyon, with battle waiting to be joined.

She and Drizzt had come over the high ridge after doubling back to flank the Ashmadai pursuit, their goal to sweep down on the distracted cultists from on high. To the northeast, the dwarves and Jarlaxle had dug in, and Drizzt and Dahlia had barely crested the canyon side when the shouts of the approaching devil-worshipers echoed off the stones.

Without hesitation, the pair had leaped away, but Drizzt had quickly outpaced Dahlia, sprinting ahead with amazing grace—grace Dahlia believed she could match—and even more amazing speed. His feet seemed a blur, fast-stepping forward, leaping from side to side, picking a path that Dahlia might follow, but certainly not at that pace.

So she had taken a steeper route, but still Drizzt moved ahead of her. She simply couldn't believe it.

A silver streak flashed out of the brush down below and to the side. Not only was the drow running at an incredible pace, he was shooting that fabulous bow of his as he went.

Dahlia put her head down and ran on, concentrating on merely finding a solid place to put her feet as she quick-stepped through one particularly uneven stretch. She would get down there right beside him, if not ahead of him, she told herself.

Then Dahlia realized that she no longer had any choice in the matter, that she had let her pride cloud her judgment. She realized to her horror that she couldn't slow down if she wanted to, that if she didn't simply keep throwing one foot out in front of the other, she would stumble and skid down the rest of the slope on her face.

She crashed through some brush and tried desperately to grab on, but the plant came free in the loose soil and Dahlia continued on her barreling way. And that way led to a sudden drop, she realized, as she neared a stony channel some ten feet deep or more, and a like distance wide.

Dahlia didn't even think as she came to the edge. Purely on instinct, she ducked her head and thrust her long staff down below. She kicked off as she planted the end and somehow managed to secure her grip enough on the top end of that staff to cartwheel over and across the channel. With perfect muscle control, Dahlia came right over and back to her feet on the other side of the channel, and managed to wipe the shocked look off her face almost immediately when she noted Drizzt down below, scimitars drawn, staring at her in disbelief.

Dahlia winked at him to reinforce the notion that the gymnastics had been a part of her plan from the beginning, and as she pulled the staff up behind her, she broke it fast into her flails and ended her cartwheel with a spinning move that had her new weapons immediately into the flow.

Much to the chagrin of an Ashmadai cultist, who appeared seemingly out of nowhere to charge in at her.

From a wider opening to the north, Drizzt was surprised to see Dahlia cartwheeling over the narrow chasm, gracefully inverted and coming to her feet with easy and complete balance. Aside from the dramatic and effective move, which was remarkable enough, Drizzt was shocked to see that the elf warrior had so nearly paced him on his descent—his movements were magically enhanced by the anklets he wore, after all.

He watched her go spinning above and past, heard the sound of battle engaged right after, and wanted to scramble up the side of the channel to join her, or at least to witness her fighting.

But the drow had his own problems pressing in on him, with more than a dozen enemies trying to flank him left and right, and he set his focus accordingly. He rushed for the narrower channel, speeding ahead of the Ashmadai and the stones they threw at him. He spun and backed farther in as he entered, the bottleneck of the narrow ravine forcing his pursuers to stumble, practically falling over each other to get at the drow.

It was one against three instead of one against a dozen, and those three found themselves hindered by the vertical stone walls, which reduced the warriors on each end of the line to more straightforward thrusting attacks rather than wide swings.

Drizzt backed quickly, and when the three took the bait and lunged forward, he reversed his movements and darted in, his scimitars sweeping out wide and down, behind the thrusting spears. With hardly a twist, Drizzt deflected those spears inward, nearly crossing them before the Ashmadai in the middle.

The drow disengaged his blades immediately, and in the jumble of his three enemies, he struck hard and fast, rushing forward and stabbing left, right, and center. The Ashmadai tried to cover, tried to retreat, tried to keep some semblance of coordinated defense. But Drizzt was too quick for them, his blades avoiding their parries with ease, scimitar tips poking and stabbing.

The three backed into the next Ashmadai in line and their tangle only worsened.

Relentlessly, Drizzt drove on.

One Ashmadai managed a coordinated throw at the drow, the spear flying in for Drizzt's chest. Before Drizzt could move to block, something landed beside him, distracting him and costing him his defense.

A flail flashed before him, cleanly picking off the spear, and the drow was relieved indeed to find Dahlia standing beside him.

She noted his relief with a wink, and side by side, they pressed forward, whirling blades and spinning flails.

Their enemies knew Dahlia, and some called out her name, and their voices were filled with fear. Ashmadai poured back out of the narrow ravine and into the wider clearing.

"Retreat?" Drizzt asked Dahlia, for that seemed the obvious course. With their enemies stumbling and disoriented, they could run out the other end of the ravine, run toward their companions, who neared the cave openings.

But Dahlia's smile showed a different intent.

That grin! So full of life, and full of fight, reveling in the challenge, wholly unafraid. When was the last time Drizzt Do'Urden had seen such a grin? When was the last time Drizzt Do'Urden had worn such a grin?

His thoughts flashed back to a lair in Icewind Dale, when he had accompanied a young Wulfgar against a tribe of verbeeg.

The sensible move was retreat, but for some reason he didn't quite comprehend, Drizzt dismissed that out of hand and rushed out beside Dahlia into the wider clearing, where they could be flanked, surrounded even, by their enemies' superior numbers.

They didn't fight side by side, really, nor did they move back to back. There seemed no organization at all to Drizzt and Dahlia's dance. The drow let Dahlia lead the way, and merely reacted to her every turn and leap.

She charged ahead, and he cut across her wake to protect her flank. She cut in front of him, and he went out behind her the opposite way then stopped fast and reversed his course so that when Dahlia stopped her movement, he came out beyond her, extending their line of devastation far to the side.

And both of them kept their weapons working fast through every step, blades and flail spinning and reaching out to cut, to sting, to drive back their enemies. The Ashmadai shouted at each other constantly, trying to coordinate some defense against the duo, but before anything could begin to form, Drizzt and Dahlia moved in some unexpected manner or direction, so that the whole of the fight, both sides, seemed nothing more than a series of impromptu reactions.

He crept along the branch, as silent as a hunting cat. He saw his prey below him, oblivious to his presence. Barrabus the Gray was shocked to discover that his daring plan had seemingly worked.

He knew that the Thayan champion, the dangerous Dahlia, had gone out to the north, with her many Ashmadai, and knew that Sylora's eyes had turned that way, too, toward the rising mountain. Barrabus wondered if he might get past the wards and guards, if he might get nearer to this ultimate enemy.

If he could be rid of Sylora Salm, perhaps Alegni would allow him to leave forsaken Neverwinter and return to his work in the comforts of a true city.

He moved out farther on the branch, over the impromptu encampment set below. Sylora was barely a dozen feet in front of and below him, with her back to him as she bent forward, staring into the stump of a large tree.

Barrabus figured he could crouch and spring, and reach her from there, but his curiosity got the better of him and he crept out just a bit farther until he could see over Sylora's shoulder into the top of the stump, which was filled with water.

And images moved about in the impromptu font—a scrying bowl.

Barrabus couldn't resist. He inched out and moved his head low to the side of the branch, peering intently.

He noted the movements of a fight in that pool of clairvoyance, tiny figures weaving and striking. He recognized some of the combatants as Ashmadai, and their movements showed them to be uncharacteristically on the defensive, not nearly as aggressive as Barrabus had come to expect of the fanatics. Then he saw one of their opponents and he understood their hesitance, though the image otherwise added to his confusion. The spinning flail, the acrobatic movements—it had to be Dahlia.

But why would Dahlia be fighting against Ashmadai?

Perhaps it wasn't her. Perhaps there were more warriors like her, Barrabus wondered, and that thought didn't sit well with him. One Dahlia was more than enough for him.

He didn't understand.

The flails spun together in front of her and seemed to fuse together, and what had been two separate weapons comprised of two separate lengths suddenly became a single long staff.

Yes, it was Dahlia, Barrabus knew then without doubt. He watched her stop abruptly before a trio of Ashmadai, who lurched back. She planted the tip of her staff and leaped up high, but instead of going forward into her enemies, she went backward.

And another, apparently her ally, charged into the void.

He saw black skin—and a pair of scimitars spinning in devastating precision.

Barrabus the Gray froze on the branch—to attempt anything other than that would have had him simply falling out of the tree. He couldn't draw breath in that surreal moment, and the world around him seemed to simply stop.

All thoughts of Sylora flew from him—even more so when he heard the newest foe, another elf female, but undead, announcing her presence with the thump of a thunderbolt.

Barrabus didn't want to go up against the sorceress Sylora in a fair fight, and the thought of facing Valindra Shadowmantle was even less appealing.

He held his breath, but couldn't help himself. He looked back to the scrying pool, but it had gone mercifully blank.

The trance broken, a very shaken Barrabus the Gray slithered back to the tree and disappeared into the forest.

Drizzt darted out to the right, cutting in front of Dahlia. He fell into a roll, underneath her spinning flail, and his sudden appearance between the elf and her opponent had the tiefling Ashmadai distracted just enough for Dahlia to crack him on the side of the jaw and send him tumbling away.

Drizzt came back to his feet right in front of a pair of fanatics, his blades going to work parrying and deflecting their furious onslaught. In a matter of a couple of heartbeats he had them both on the defensive. His blades came faster and faster, soon moving from counters to initiating strikes.

He worked around them as well, to gain a look at his fighting companion, and he was caught by surprise to see that Dahlia was no longer wielding a flail, and neither was she carrying the staff. She had something he could only describe as a tri-staff, with a longer center piece and two smaller poles spinning furiously to either side. For just a moment, Drizzt considered the strange weapon she carried, which could be put into so many combinations seemingly at will.

Of course, he had no time to really contemplate the unique staff just then, particularly as a third Ashmadai joined the pair he was already fighting. He had to keep moving, as did Dahlia. They couldn't afford to get caught and surrounded.

Drizzt backed toward Dahlia, moving fast.

"Over," he heard behind him, and he reflexively worked his scimitars in for low strikes, forcing the attention of the trio downward. Drizzt was not surprised when Dahlia vaulted over him—planting one foot on his set back and leaping out again, soaring past—but his opponents surely were, as their expressions showed.

Dahlia came down on them, kicking one in the face, then a second, and bringing her staff—no longer a tri-staff, but a single long pole—in fast behind her, sliding it through her grasp just enough to jab out with it like a spear, right into the throat of the third opponent. She cut away fast, planted the end of her weapon, and vaulted again.

And so it went for a time, with Drizzt down low, sprinting all around, and Dahlia working vertically above him, leap after great leap.

But even with that new twist, their initial momentum was beginning to fail, the Ashmadai drawing together into better defensive groups. Drizzt and Dahlia couldn't win—they'd known that from the beginning, and it was time to create an exit for themselves.

The needed distraction appeared on the ridge high above them a moment later. As always, the dependable Guenhwyvar entered the fray right on time. With a roar that shook the stones and had every eye turned her way, the great panther leaped out far and high, flying down upon the most concentrated group of Ashmadai.

As they scattered, screaming and diving, Drizzt and Dahlia retreated back through the narrow ravine and out the other end, scrambling over stones toward the cave opening where Bruenor and the others waited.

"Friend of yours?" Dahlia asked with a nod back at the cat, and a wicked smile.

Drizzt smiled back, even wider when he heard the wild tumult behind them.

He let Dahlia get ahead of him and he trusted her to keep the way clear as he watched for pursuit. When they at last neared the rocky vale immediately preceding the caves, Drizzt called upon his enchanted anklets and sprinted to catch up to her.

They crossed a small battlefield, several Ashmadai down, a couple moaning. One off to the side hung inverted from a tree, calling for help, held fast by the legs by whatever that was that shot from Jarlaxle's magical wand.

Dahlia veered for the victim and Drizzt winced, thinking she would surely crack open the trapped Ashmadai's skull. To his surprise and relief, she merely patted the trapped woman on the side of the face as she skipped past her with a laugh.

Just past the battlefield, they scrambled over a rocky mound, revealing a small vale below dotted with several cave entrances.

"Here!" Bruenor called from one, and Drizzt and Dahlia moved to join him.

"Your panther," Dahlia said, glancing back.

"Guenhwyvar has already returned to the Astral Plane, awaiting my next call," Drizzt assured her.

She nodded, and skipped into the dark cave, but Drizzt paused to watch her, pleased by her concern for the great cat.

They, even Bruenor, had to belly-crawl to get out of the first chamber of the cave, but they moved with all speed, with sounds of pursuit echoing behind them. They came out of that low channel into a smaller, but higher-ceilinged space, in which Athrogate and Jarlaxle waited. As Dahlia came out, she tapped her staff, in the form of a four-foot walking stick, and a blue-white light glowed from its top end.

"This is the way?" Drizzt asked.

"I hope," said Jarlaxle. "We checked the caves as quickly as we could and this was the only one that seemed promising."

"But there could be other caves in the area that we haven't yet discovered?" an uneasy Drizzt asked.

Jarlaxle shrugged. "Luck has always been on your side, my friend. It's the only reason I asked you along on this journey."

Dahlia reacted with alarm to that, until she glanced at Drizzt to see him smiling.

The five companions moved through a maze of tunnels and crawlspaces, even splashing through a shallow underground stream for a bit. They hit many dead ends, but many more tunnels broke off into multiple passageways, and they had nothing to guide them but their instincts. Dahlia appeared completely bewildered, but few could navigate dark tunnels better than dwarves, and among those few were the dark elves.

Soon enough, they heard sounds far behind them in the tunnels, and knew that the Ashmadai had continued the pursuit into the Underdark.

At one point, the five came into a long, fairly straight tunnel, which Athrogate rightly identified as a lava tube. It traveled in the correct direction, and at a gentle downward slope, so they eagerly rambled along it. Eventually, though, a cold mist wafted past them, and Dahlia sucked in her breath and turned her head, watching it depart up the tunnel behind them.

"What d'ye know?" Bruenor asked, catching her concern.

"Deathly cold," Drizzt said.

"Was it?" Jarlaxle asked the elf warrior.

Dahlia nodded. "Dor'crae," she said.

"The vampire," Athrogate explained, and Bruenor snorted and shook his head in disgust.

"He will bring them to us," Dahlia said, and they all suspected then how the Ashmadai had come to know so much about their location.

"Perhaps he's returning from Gauntlgrym," Drizzt interjected. "If so, this is indeed the correct path."

With that hopeful thought in mind, they pressed on with all speed, and for a long way, hours of walking, the lava tube continued with the same agreeable slope. But then they came to an abrupt end, where the tunnel turned downward sharply, a near vertical descent into seemingly bottomless darkness. There was no way around that hole, and they had seen no side tunnels throughout the last hours of their march.

"Let us hope your luck holds," Jarlaxle remarked to Drizzt, and from an obviously magical pouch, the drow mercenary produced a long length of fine cord. He tossed one end to Drizzt and the other to Athrogate, ordering the dwarf to brace it well.

Without hesitation, Drizzt tied it off around his waist and went over the lip, quickly disappearing from sight. As he neared the end of that length, Drizzt called up, "It levels off to a sharp, but traversable slope."

A moment later, there came a flash and a sharp retort.

"Drizzt?" Jarlaxle called.

"I've set a second rope," Drizzt called from the darkness. "Move!"

"No going back," Jarlaxle said to Bruenor, apparently deferring to the dwarf.

"Then that's the way," Bruenor decided, and he was next to the rope.

When he reached the bottom, where Drizzt had been, Bruenor found the second line, drilled deep into the angled ceiling across the way, set firmly into the stone by one of Taulmaril's enchanted arrows.

The tunnel continued, sometimes a drop, sometimes a gentle slope, and the five managed it fairly well. They were near the end of their endurance, but dared not stop and set camp, and yet, there seemed no end in sight.

But then they went down a small shaft and under a low archway where the tunnel turned sharply and showed them the glow of Underdark lichen. A few moments later, they came out onto a high ledge on a great cavern. Giant stalagmites stood quietly around a still pond, and both Drizzt and Bruenor blinked in disbelief, first at the worked tops of those mounds—guard towers—then at the great castle wall across the way.

Bruenor Battlehammer swallowed hard and glanced at the other dwarf.

"Aye, King Bruenor," Athrogate said with a wide grin. "I was hoping this cavern survived the explosion, that ye might see the front gate.

"There's yer Gauntlgrym."

CHAPTER 19

THROUGH THE EYES OF AN ANCIENT KING

"IT WAS DUMB LUCK," DOR'CRAE INSISTED. "THERE WERE TEN caves they might have—"

"These are dark elves in the Underdark, fool," Sylora interrupted. "They likely ruled out most of the other caves simply by sniffing the air currents."

Dor'crae shrugged and tried to respond, but Sylora growled at him, warning him to silence.

"I'll not have them binding the primordial," the Thayan sorceress insisted. "Its awakening will seal the fate of the Netherese along the Sword Coast North, and it will complete the Dread Ring and ensure my victory."

"Yes, my lady," Dor'crae said with a bow. "But they are a formidable force. The traitor Dahlia strikes fear into even hearty Ashmadai, and this dark elf, Drizzt, is a legend across the North. But we are talking about a primordial here, a grounded god-being. Could Elminster himself, even in his prime, calm such a beast?"

"It was trapped once to serve Gauntlgrym, a prison that lasted millennia."

"A prison keyed by the Hosttower of the Arcane, which is no more."

"But which exudes residual magic," Sylora warned him. "Trust that if there is a way to rebuild the prison, the clever Jarlaxle has discerned it. They are a threat."

"The Ashmadai pursue them," Dor'crae promised her. "And from my recent visit to Gauntlgrym, I can assure you that the primordial has populated its sleeping place with worthy guards, mighty creatures from the Plane of Fire that have answered its incoherent call. A small army of red-skinned lizard men roam the halls."

"Salamanders . . ." Sylora mused. "Then you have time to get back there and join in the battle."

The look of dread on Dor'crae's face as she spoke brought a smile to the sorceress's lips. The vampire had been hesitant from the beginning, and he still harbored fears that Dahlia wanted to move that tenth diamond chip, the one that represented him, from her right ear to her left.

"I can take no chances on this," Sylora went on a moment later. "Awakening the primordial into another act of devastation is our penultimate goal here. Unfortunately, the ultimate goal presses, as the Netherese continue to fight me for Neverwinter Wood, though I still struggle with why, and I dare not leave here. So I send you, in respect and confidence."

Dor'crae's expression told her that he knew the hollowness of her compliments, but he bowed anyway and said, "I am humbled, my lady."

"You will take Valindra with you," Sylora said as Dor'crae straightened, and the vampire's eyes widened with surprise and trepidation. "She's far more lucent now," Sylora assured him. "And know this, Valindra Shadowmantle hates Jarlaxle most of all, and has no love for this other drow, either, whom she blames in no small part for the loss of Arklem Greeth."

"She is unpredictable, her power often minimally contained," Dor'crae warned. "She might have a fit, manifested magically, that would facilitate exactly that which you fear most."

Sylora narrowed her eyes at the vampire, warning him that she didn't like having her judgment so boldly questioned. She let it go at that, though, for there was a measure of possibility in Dor'crae's fears. Indeed, as she thought about her decision in that moment, it occurred to Sylora that the vampire might be right, that Valindra was too much the "unexpected bounce of the bones," as the old Thayan saying went.

Sylora tried to fathom a way to back out of her command that he take Valindra, thinking she might posit that she only suggested

Valindra to test Dor'crae's understanding of the situation. But when such a remark fell flat even in her thoughts, she decided against it. Which left the stubborn leader, who would never admit she was wrong, only one option.

"Valindra will expedite your return to the caverns. And once there, she can move as swiftly as you through the tunnels."

"Unless she wanders off," Dor'crae dared mutter, and Sylora flashed him an angry glare.

"You will guide her," Sylora told him in no uncertain terms. "And when you have caught up to our enemies, point her at the two drow, remind her of who they are and what they did to her precious Hosttower and Arklem Greeth. Then watch in awe as the mighty lich brings old Gauntlgrym itself down on the heads of our enemies."

"Yes, my lady," Dor'crae replied with another bow, though his tone seemed less than satisfied.

"And consider," Sylora tossed out at him, just for the pleasure of it, "if Valindra can lead the assault against our enemies, then you might not have to do battle with Dahlia, though I know how dearly you wish to challenge her."

The biting sarcasm, the bald expression of Dor'crae's fear, wiped away any response from the vampire. His shoulders slumped, his entire form seemed to deflate.

He knew Sylora was right.

———————

As with the cavern outside, the circular entry room had survived the cataclysm nearly intact. The throne still sat there, a silent testament to that which had come before, like a guardian of the past holding to its post.

The whole of the place had Drizzt staring wide-eyed and his jaw hanging slack, as it had done to Jarlaxle and Athrogate—and even Dahlia—when first they had passed through the audience chamber. Worse off than the drow, Bruenor nearly fell over, so overwhelmed was he.

Drizzt regained his composure by considering his friend—his beloved companion of so many decades who stood in the entry hall of the place that had been the focus of his life for more than half a century. Tears rimmed Bruenor's eyes, and his breath came in uneven gasps, as if he kept forgetting to breathe, then had to force the air in and out.

"Elf," he whispered. "Do ye see it, elf?"

"In all its glory, my friend," Drizzt replied. He started to say something more, but Bruenor began drifting away from him, as if pulled by some unseen force.

The dwarf walked across the room, not looking left or right, his eyes fixated on his goal, as if it, the throne, was calling out to him. He stepped up to the small dais, the other four hustling to catch up

"Don't ye do it!" Athrogate started to warn him, but Jarlaxle hushed the dwarf.

Bruenor tentatively reached out to touch the arm of the fabulous throne.

He retracted his hand immediately and leaped back, eyes wide. He hopped in circles, eyes darting to and fro, hands out wide as if he were uncertain whether to flee or fight.

The others rushed over, and Bruenor visibly relaxed then turned back to the throne.

"What happened?" Athrogate asked.

Bruenor pointed to the throne. "No regular chair."

"Ye're tellin' me?" Athrogate, who had been thrown across the room by the power of that throne, replied.

Bruenor looked at him with a furrowed brow.

"Aye, she's quite the fabulous work," Athrogate agreed after a glance at Jarlaxle.

"More than that," a breathless Bruenor said.

"Imbued with magic," Dahlia reasoned.

"Thick with magic," Jarlaxle assured her.

"Thick with *memory,*" Bruenor corrected.

Drizzt moved up beside Bruenor and slowly reached out toward the chair.

"Don't ye do that," Bruenor warned. "Not yerself and not him, most of all," he added, indicating Jarlaxle. "Not any o' ye. Just meself."

Looking to Jarlaxle, who nodded, Drizzt demanded of his fellow Menzoberranyr, "What do you know?"

"Know?" Jarlaxle replied. "I know what I hoped. This place is full of ghosts, full of magic, and full of memory. My hope was that a Delzoun king—our friend Bruenor here—might find a way to tap into those memories." He was looking at Bruenor by the time he finished, and Drizzt and the others, too, regarded the dwarf king.

Bruenor steadied himself. "Let's see, then," he declared.

He took a deep breath and boldly strode forward up onto the dais to stand before the throne. Hands on hips, he stared at it for a long while then nodded, turned, and plopped down on the chair, pointedly grabbing the arms as he did.

Athrogate gasped and ducked his head.

But Bruenor wasn't rejected by the ancient throne. He stared back at his four friends for just a few heartbeats . . . then they were gone. Their forms shivered and wavered then dissipated into nothingness.

The dwarf was not alone. The room around him teemed with his kin and echoed with the whispers of a thousand conversations.

Bruenor steeled himself and did not panic. It was the magic of the throne, he told himself. He had not been taken from his friends, nor they from him, but his mind was looking backward across the centuries, back to the time of Gauntlgrym.

Before him stood a group of elves, most in the type of robes one would expect a wizard to wear, and beside them stood important-looking dwarves—clan leaders, obviously, given their regalia and posture.

Bruenor had to consciously force himself to breathe when he noted one wearing the foaming mug crest of Clan Battlehammer emblazoned on his breastplate. Gandalug! Was it Gandalug, the First and Ninth King of Mithral Hall? Could it be?

Certainly the dwarf resembled the founder of Mithral Hall, but more likely, it was Gandalug's father, or his father's father. Gandalug, after all, had never mentioned Gauntlgrym in the short time Bruenor had known him, after his escape from the drow time prison, and Gauntlgrym was too much older than Mithral Hall, by Bruenor's understanding, for that to be Gandalug Battlehammer.

Bruenor knew then, though, that the symbol on the dwarf's breastplate, the foaming mug crest, was not a coincidence. It was indeed the forefather of Mithral Hall standing before him, standing before the king of Gauntlgrym. A sense of community, of timelessness, and of being a part of something greater washed over Bruenor, flooding him with warmth and serenity.

Bruenor forced himself to get past that tantalizing distraction and focus on the moment at hand. He came to know then that he was seeing through the eyes of the king of Gauntlgrym, as if his own consciousness had crossed the seas of time to be afforded a seat at a time long past. He worked hard to clear his mind, then, to let himself simply absorb what he saw and leave the interpretation of it for later on.

His other senses joined in, and soon he was hearing more clearly the conversations around him.

They were talking about the Hosttower of the Arcane. The elf visitors were from the Hosttower. They were talking about the tendrils of magic and trapping a primordial to fire the furnaces of Gauntlgrym.

Bruenor could hardly believe the scene unfolding before him. The elves were concerned that their gift to the dwarves would be stolen by their dark-skinned relatives, the drow, to wreak devastation on all of Faerûn. The dwarves argued strenuously. One pointed out that they had discussed all of that before the Delzoun Clan had helped build the Hosttower in the distant village.

Village . . . not city.

Bruenor could feel the tension of his host, the dwarf king who sat on the throne of Gauntlgrym. He could feel the king's muscles clenching as surely as if they were his own, and indeed, he wondered if his friends were looking upon his own corporeal form in that distant future place, to see him grabbing the arms of the throne and squirming in growing anger.

An elf woman stepped forward—she reminded Bruenor very much of Lady Alustriel of Silverymoon. She spoke in a dialect Bruenor couldn't easily understand, an ancient Dwarvish broken by her Elvish accent, but he figured out that she was promising the king that her people would abide by their agreement.

"Boot ye moost know ourne terrors on the beast bayin' freyed," she warbled. *"Und te drow pushing fires to the Aboove."*

"Ain't no drow fer to be in me kingdom," the dwarf replied flatly.

"Ain't be yer choosin'," she agreed.

"Ain't to be!"

Bruenor's head spun as they continued their discussion. It was the most critical moment of the Delzoun Clan, he realized. It was the critical moment of their bargain with the wizards, when the Hosttower of the Arcane had repaid them with the power to fashion the legendary weapons and armor of old. That bargain had given the Delzoun clan supremacy among their kin in the North, and had spawned the kingdoms that had survived to Bruenor's day.

He was privy to, looked in upon, the greatest moment in his clan's history, perhaps the greatest moment in the history of Faerûn's dwarves.

"Ye'll have yer fires," the regal elf finished, and bowed.

The room blurred again, the images wavering like the rising air off hot stone on a blistering sunny day.

For a moment, Drizzt and the others began taking shape again before him, but the dwarf rejected that. Not now! He couldn't return to them yet. There was too much yet to learn.

"Bruenor!" he heard Drizzt say, but the dwarf king let the drow's voice slide past him, let it fall away to nothingness as he retreated across the centuries.

That image faded and another replaced it. He wasn't in the audience chamber any longer. He saw a pair of elves holding hands and standing in front of an opened alcove in a wall. Within lay a bowl of water, not so different from those Jarlaxle had brought with them. The water in that bowl rotated as the elves chanted, calling it forth. It swirled into a mist, and that mist grew into a living form, somewhat humanoid in shape.

It stood tiny within the alcove at first. The water in the bowl was not the whole of the beast, but merely a conduit to bring it forth. And so it grew, soon filling the small alcove, and seemed as if it would burst out of that hole like a great breaking wave.

Something caught it and pulled it from inside the wall, and Bruenor watched as the elemental elongated upward and was swept up a chimney within the alcove hole. He understood then that a tendril from the Hosttower was at the top of that chimney, that the elemental had been swept into place as a living bar for the primordial's cage.

And so it went, from spot to spot, the elves setting the magic bowls in place.

Bruenor lost track of time as the corridors of Gauntlgrym rolled past him. He saw, in his mind, through the eyes of Gauntlgrym's king—whose name he still did not know—the great and legendary Forge of Gauntlgrym, and the image was tangible, as if he were actually there.

The whole of the complex became familiar to him, as if his Delzoun blood was imparting the memories from that unknown king unto him. He understood the role the dwarves had played in creating the Hosttower of the Arcane, and the responding gift the elves had given to Gauntlgrym.

He saw the forge room, the legendary Forge of Gauntlgrym, and he was inspired.

And he saw the primordial, freed of the great depths and trapped in the fire chamber beneath the forge, and he was afraid.

That was no orc king, no giant, no dragon even. It was an earth-bound godhead, a literal force of nature that could alter the shape of continents.

What could he do against that?

He witnessed the flood of water as the tendrils of the Hosttower were first activated, bringing nourishment and ocean power to the trapped elementals. He saw and heard the great rush of living water rumble into the critical chamber, dive over the rim, and spin powerfully around the shaft above the primordial forevermore—or so they all hoped.

He saw the Forge of Gauntlgrym light for the first time with primordial power, its glow reflecting on the awe-stricken faces of dwarf and elf alike, and he knew that he was at the moment of the greatest glory his people had ever known.

Then he was back in the audience chamber, a thousand dwarves hoisting foamy mugs high in celebration. Tears streaked the king's face, and Bruenor knew not if they were his or those of his host.

The sound dulled, the image blurred, the forms wavered and lost all color. Then the sound around him was replaced by the din of battle, and the dwarves of old were ghosts, and nothing more.

And he was Bruenor Battlehammer again, just Bruenor, sitting on a throne in the middle of a circular room while his four companions fought for their lives against a swarm of tall, slender humanoid creatures, standing as men and holding spears and tridents as men might, but with fire flaring and bursting angrily around their feet—no, not feet, but tails. They were as men only from the waist up. The rest of them slithered across the rough stone like snakes. Long spikes of black bone bristled from their backs, and twisted antlers grew from their heads.

A vague old memory came to Bruenor then. He knew them— had heard tell of them. Elemental-kin. Salamanders.

Bruenor's eyes opened wide, and with a roar he leaped from the throne, setting his shield and pulling forth his axe as he went. To those around him who turned at his yell, friend and foe alike, the dwarf seemed to swell with power and strength, his muscles thickening, his eyes flaring with an inner fire.

He charged into the nearest group of salamanders with abandon, great sweeps of his axe throwing them aside. A trident stabbed at him from the left, but his shield arm was quicker, rushing across to intercept and deflect the blow up high, and as Bruenor followed through, his axe swept across with tremendous power.

The creature fell apart, cut in half at the waist.

As if the gods of the dwarves themselves had settled into King Bruenor, he roared on, cutting a swath of devastation. And he called allies to his side—not Drizzt and the others, but the ghosts of Gauntlgrym.

"By Clangeddin's hard arse," Athrogate muttered from back near the throne.

The dwarf fought to keep the snake-men away from Jarlaxle, as the drow mercenary concentrated on Drizzt and Dahlia, looking for openings as they weaved, leaped, and spun back and forth past each other. Whenever he found such an opening, the agile dark elf flung a dagger through it, almost unerringly striking one of the creatures.

The four of them fought well together—much like three of them had back at Spirit Soaring those many years before—yet King Bruenor alone was cutting a wider swath of devastation through the massing salamanders.

Drizzt had begun to swing toward his friend as soon as Bruenor had entered the fray. Dahlia, playing off his every move, followed, but Drizzt had quickly changed his mind. Watching Bruenor at that moment, he held back and focused instead on holding his ground.

The tide of battle turned quickly as more and more dwarf ghosts filtered into the chamber. On the far side of the room, the salamanders tried to surround Bruenor, and seemed to be doing just that. Drizzt cried out for his friend, and second-guessed his earlier decision not to help him. He thought Bruenor doomed, and believed it was his own hesitance that had guaranteed that.

But Bruenor faced his enemies with wild eyes and a wicked grin. He lifted his foot, stomped it down hard, and an explosion of lightning flashed out in a circle around him, throwing salamanders through the air like dry leaves in a strong gale.

"What in the Nine Hells?" Athrogate asked.

"Drizzt?" a clearly befuddled Jarlaxle inquired.

Beside Drizzt, Dahlia, whose own weapon could loose such bursts of lightning, gasped in disbelief.

And Drizzt Do'Urden could only shake his head.

High in the shadows of the great room, another set of eyes watched the battle unfolding with great hope that the primordial's minions would do his work for him. Perhaps he, Dor'crae, could fly right back out of the chamber and back to the caves to tell Valindra and the Ashmadai to turn back for Neverwinter Wood.

He dearly hoped that would be the case.

But then Dor'crae stared with increasing disbelief at the spectacle of the godly-empowered Bruenor Battlehammer, and he watched the tide of battle quickly turn. He looked back at the throne and was afraid. Events seemed to be moving past him, first with Valindra and the powerful gift Sylora had given her, then the sight of the mighty dwarf. . . .

He glanced back toward the cavern beyond Gauntlgrym, the approach the Ashmadai and Valindra would soon take, and he considered Sylora's words of warning, and the power she had entrusted to the lich. The thought of trusting Valindra, and more than that, of trusting the power she had been given, made Dor'crae want to flee back to Thay and take his chances with Szass Tam.

He turned back to the battle, hoping against all reason that the minions of the primordial would somehow find a way to put an end to the threat to his mistress's plans.

That blast of godlike power proved the end of the assault, with the salamanders rushing for any exit they could find as fast as they could find them, leaving fiery trails in their wakes.

Bruenor chased one group, leaping high and fully thirty feet across the stones to land in their midst, his axe chopping them down viciously, one after another. The dwarf seemed to get stabbed several times in that mad rush, each drawing a cry of pain from Drizzt, who rushed to join him.

And Bruenor seemed not to notice any of the strikes.

By the time the four others arrived by his side, the dwarf king stood amidst half a dozen slain creatures. The rest of the beasts had fled the room, and the dwarf ghosts had given chase.

Bruenor blinked repeatedly as he considered his friends.

"What did you do?" Jarlaxle asked.

Bruenor could only shrug.

Drizzt studied his friend more closely, even pulling aside Bruenor's collar, but he could find no wound.

"How did you do that?" Dahlia asked. "Stomping your foot as if you were a god of lightning?"

Bruenor shrugged and shook his head. He seemed quite perplexed for a few moments, but then just shook his head again and let it all go, turning to Jarlaxle instead.

"I know where to put yer bowls," he said to Jarlaxle.

"How could you know?"

Bruenor considered that for a short while. How indeed?

"Gauntlgrym told me," he said with a grin.

CHAPTER 20

POWERS OLDER, POWERS DEEPER

THE ASHMADAI CAME INTO THE CIRCULAR CHAMBER WITH tentative steps, though the echoes of battle had long since faded. Valindra Shadowmantle led the way, flanked by two score of Sylora's best warriors. The lich focused almost immediately on the throne, and she drifted that way, floating, not walking, while her minions spread out to examine the corpses scattered about the floor.

She stopped in front of the throne, sensing its great magic. Valindra had spent her life studying the Art, as a wizard in the famed Hosttower of the Arcane. Before the Spellplague, and before she had fallen into death then undeath at the hand of Arklem Greeth, Valindra had been a wizard of great power, impeccable scholarship, and considerable renown.

As a lich, Valindra had survived the Spellplague, though it had surely harmed her mind. But at long last, she was returning to her senses, and gathering her newfound powers in the unfamiliar energies of post-Spellplague arcana.

Its powers having transcended even the dramatic changes that had been visited upon Faerûn, the throne knocked her back to that time before. The magic in it was ancient, and reverberated within Valindra, taking her to a place of familiar comfort she had not known in decades.

She "cooed" and "ahh'd" before the throne, her emaciated, pale hands reaching out but never quite touching the powerful artifact. Lost in her thoughts and memories, in the better times she had known as a living wizard, Valindra failed even to notice when a pair of her Ashmadai commanders came up beside her.

"Lady Valindra," one, a large male tiefling, said.

When she didn't respond, he repeated the words much more loudly.

Valindra started and turned on him, her ghostly eyes flickering with threatening red flames.

"The dead are of the Plane of Fire, we believe," the tiefling explained. "Minions of the primordial?"

Valindra's perplexed expression conveyed that she hadn't even really heard the question, let alone digested it.

"Yes," another voice answered, and the two Ashmadai commanders and Valindra turned just as a bat fluttering up behind the throne seemed to fall over itself and take humanoid form.

"Minions of the primordial—worshipers, really," Dor'crae explained. "These salamanders, and large red lizards deeper in the complex, even a small red dragon, have come to the call of the volcano."

"There are more?" the male Ashmadai asked.

"They are many," Dor'crae replied, walking around the dais to join the trio.

"Perhaps they will do our job for us, then," said the Ashmadai. "Perhaps they already have."

Dor'crae laughed at that notion, and waved out his arm, inviting the others to take another look at the result of the battle—a battle he had watched from the shadows of the room's high ceiling.

"I would not . . ." he started to say, but he paused as he noticed that Valindra paid him no heed, that she had turned her attention back to the throne.

"I wouldn't count on the inhabitants of the complex to defeat the likes of Jarlaxle and his mighty dwarf," Dor'crae told the Ashmadai, "or of Dahlia and Drizzt Do'Urden." He glanced at Valindra again, watching as she ascended the dais, still staring at the throne as if in a trance. "They are formidable enough, or were, but now are even more so. I watched them in this very room, and the other dwarf with them, a king of the dwarves it would seem, has somehow been magically . . . enhanced."

The two Ashmadai scrunched up their faces, glanced at each other, then turned back to Dor'crae with obvious confusion.

"Through the power in that very throne," Dor'crae explained, turning to Valindra as he spoke.

The lich didn't seem to hear him.

"There is some ancient magic there that empowered him," Dor'crae warned them all.

"Magic, yes," Valindra cooed, her hand waving over the arm of the throne. Then, suddenly, the lich slapped her hand down and grabbed the throne.

Her eyes went wide and she issued a hiss of protest. It was clear that she was struggling mightily to hold onto the throne, as if it was trying to throw her aside. Stubbornly, the lich growled and fought back, then she turned and sat down on the throne, grasping the arms with both hands.

She growled and snarled, thrashing about, hissing, and sputtering a stream of curses. Her back arched as if some unseen force lifted her free, and she growled again and uttered a curse at some dwarf king and forced herself back down. To the onlookers, the three before the throne and many others about the room, she seemed like a halfling trying to hold back the charge of an umber hulk.

The struggle intensified. Flashes of lightning, blue-white and black, shot from the chair, and Dor'crae and the Ashmadai commanders fell back.

The throne of Gauntlgrym was clearly and violently rejecting Valindra, but the lich would not accept that.

But at last, with a rumble that shook the chamber, and indeed reverberated deep into the complex of Gauntlgrym, the throne expelled her, hurling Valindra through the air. She magically caught herself in mid-descent, and came down gently to her normal stance, floating just a few inches above the floor.

"Valindra?" Dor'crae asked, but the lich didn't hear him.

She swept back in at the throne, hands extended like killing claws. With a wicked hiss, she shot fingers of lightning from her hands. When the bolts merely disappeared into the magical throne, the outraged Valindra summoned instead a pea of fire, which she threw onto the seat.

"Run!" the Ashmadai commander yelled, and the warriors scrambled all over each other to get away from the throne.

Valindra's fireball engulfed the throne, the dais, and a good portion of the floor around it. The angry flames reached right up to the lich herself, who seemed not to care. None of the Ashmadai were caught in the blast, though one found his weathercloak aflame and had to roll about frantically on the floor to douse it.

When the flames and smoke cleared, there sat the throne, unbothered, unmarred, impervious.

Valindra shrieked and hissed and charged it, again throwing bolts of lightning into it as she rushed in, then clawed at it and punched it.

"She is powerful, no doubt," the Ashmadai leader whispered as he walked up beside Dor'crae. "But I fear her presence here."

"Sylora Salm decided that she should come," Dor'crae reminded him. "That is not without reason, and it is not your place to question."

"Of course," the man said, lowering his gaze.

Dor'crae glared at him a bit longer, making sure he knew his place. They couldn't afford such intemperate and mutinous whispers, not with powerful enemies just ahead. Truthfully, though, when Dor'crae looked back at the throne and the thrashing, insane Valindra, he found it hard to disagree with the zealot's words.

They couldn't begin to control the lich, and he knew without a doubt that if she saw a target for a fireball and the entire squad of Ashmadai happened to be in the blast area, she wouldn't even care.

The tremor grumbled through the stone floor, giving all five a bit of a shake. It seemed nothing too much to Drizzt, but when he looked at Bruenor, the drow had second thoughts.

"What do you know?" Jarlaxle asked Bruenor before Drizzt could.

"Bah, the beast belched, and nothin' more," said Athrogate, but Bruenor's expression told a different story.

"Weren't the beast," he said, shaking his head. "Our enemies have entered behind us. They fight the ancient ones."

"The ancient ones?" Drizzt and Dahlia asked together, and they looked at each other in surprise.

"The dwarves of Gauntlgrym," Jarlaxle explained.

"The throne," Bruenor corrected. "They struck at the throne.

"To what end?

Bruenor shook his head, his expression revealing confidence that the throne was in no real danger. He glanced all around then, however, and added, "The ghosts're gone."

The others all looked around as well, and sure enough, they saw no ghosts in the wide corridor, though there had been some there only a few moments earlier.

"Gone back to fight for the throne o' Gauntlgrym," Bruenor explained.

"And what now for us?" Drizzt asked.

Jarlaxle seemed as if he was about to answer, but like all the others, he deferred to Bruenor.

"We go on," Bruenor said, and marched ahead, Athrogate hustling to keep beside him.

"He seems very sure of himself," Dahlia remarked to Drizzt and Jarlaxle as the dwarves stomped off. "With every turn and every side passage."

It was true enough, and while Drizzt held faith in his friend—and really, what choice did they have?—he was more than a bit concerned. Near to the audience chamber, the passages had been clear and undamaged—or no more so than Jarlaxle, Athrogate, and Dahlia had remembered them—but soon after the five companions had descended the first long stairwell, they had found more ruin and rubble. Corridors had twisted and cracked apart, and the second stair Bruenor had led them to had proven impassable.

But the dwarf remained undaunted and took them off on an alternate route.

Drizzt didn't know what magic might have been in that throne, but he hoped it truly was a memory of Gauntlgrym, not some deception placed in his mind by their enemies—as had been done to Athrogate.

Jarlaxle moved ahead to watch over the dwarves.

"You fought well in that canyon," Drizzt remarked quietly.

Dahlia arched her eyebrow at him. "I always fight well. It is why I am alive."

"You fight often, then," Drizzt said with a slight smirk.

"When I have to."

"Perhaps you're not as charming as you believe."

"I don't have to be," Dahlia replied without missing a beat. "I fight well."

"The two are not mutually exclusive."

"With yourself as the evidence, I am sure," Dahlia replied.

She pressed on faster, leaving an amused Drizzt in her wake.

"Every tunnel!" the Ashmadai commander cried as the whole of his group shrank back toward the entrance that had brought them into the room. The colorless forms of ghost dwarves flooded into the circular hall from every one of the exits in front of them, forming ranks with all the discipline of a living army.

"Can they touch us? Can they hurt us?" one woman asked, her teeth chattering, for indeed the room became very cold.

"They can tear you apart," Dor'crae assured them.

"Then we fight!" the commander cried, and all around him gave a rousing battle cheer.

All except for Dor'crae, who was thinking that it might be time for him to take the form of a bat and fly away. And except for Valindra, who began to laugh wildly, loudly, and so hysterically that the cheering died away bit by bit, each Ashmadai voice going silent as a new set of eyes fell upon the lich.

"Fight them?" Valindra asked when at last she commanded the attention of all. She began to cackle again, uncontrollably it seemed. She brought forth her emaciated hand, palm up, closed her eyes, and her laughter became a chant.

The Ashmadai circled behind her, ready to run away, having seen the destructive power of her magic.

But no fireball filled the room. Instead, a scepter appeared in her hand. At a cursory glance, it looked much like those carried by the Ashmadai, and that brought more cheers. But as each of them came to view Valindra's scepter more closely, those cheers turned to gasps.

The Ashmadai scepters, their staff-spears, were red in color when first presented, but that hue wore away with time and use, and most held weapons of uneven hue, more pink than red. But not the scepter Valindra held. It was ruby, and not just in color. It seemed to have been carved of one giant gemstone, rich red, its color so fluid and deep that several of the nearby Ashmadai held forth their arms, as if they meant to sink their fingers right into it.

Valindra grasped it powerfully and thrust it horizontally above her head, and its ends flared with a powerful red light.

"Who is your master?" she cried.

Confused, the Ashmadai glanced around at each other, some mouthing "Asmodeus," others quietly and questioningly asking, "Valindra?"

"Who is your master!" Valindra yelled, her voice magically magnified to fill the chamber and echo about the stones, the ends of the scepter flaring again in response to her cry.

"Asmodeus!" the commander yelled back, and the others followed his lead.

"Pray to him!" Valindra ordered.

The fanatics scrambled to form a kneeling circle around the lich, and each looped his right arm over the shoulders of the person to his right, left arms reaching high for the amazing scepter. They began to chant, and their circle began to slowly rotate to the left as they crawled on the hard stone.

From a few steps back, Dor'crae watched it all with blank amazement. He knew that scepter. Szass Tam had kept it back in Thay, knowing well that it was the most treasured artifact of the Ashmadai. Dor'crae had suspected all along that Sylora Salm had brought it west with her, given that almost the entire cult of Ashmadai had come to Neverwinter Wood, and given their complete obedience to her. When Valindra had joined their ranks those years ago, Sylora's power over the lich had only confirmed that suspicion.

Dor'crae could hardly believe that Sylora had given the scepter to Valindra, to that unstable and powerful undead creature.

Dor'crae shook those thoughts away. It was not the time. His warriors were on their knees, and the dwarves fast approached.

"Valindra!" he called to warn her, but she, too, was deep into her chanting and she seemed not to hear.

"Valindra, they come!" the vampire yelled, but again, the lich made no sign that she heard him.

The nearest ghosts took on a reddish hue as they came within the wide glow of the ruby scepter, and Dor'crae noted that they seemed to hesitate there, their faces twitching with discomfort, pain even. Smoke began to pour from the scepter's ends, circling between Valindra and the closest dwarves, swirling across the stone floor, and sinking lower, as if reaching into the rock itself. The stone melted, liquefied, red bubbles forming and popping, releasing acrid yellow smoke into the air.

As one, the ghosts stopped and threw up their hands, shielding their eyes.

Through the floor it came, as if standing up in a shallow pond. The large head appeared first, spiked and crested with rows of jagged red bone. Hooked black horns reached out to either side and curved upward and over, where they narrowed into points facing each other. Wide eyes showed no pupils—pits of fire and nothing more, the eyes of an angry devil. A wide mouth curled back in a perpetual hiss, revealing huge canines and rows of teeth that could tear flesh from bone with ease. Taller it climbed as if scaling a ladder in the molten floor, its glorious, naked body coming forth from the lava with not a scratch or burn, its red, leathery wings spreading wide as they came free of the hole.

The whole of the creature was red, hot like the fires of all Nine Hells, its skin stretched over corded muscles and rows of bone. Black spikes lined its back in a sharp ridge narrowing at the base of its spine, where they gave way to a flashing red tail, barbed in a black tip and dripping lethal venom. The long claws of its hands, too, shone black, like polished obsidian. In its right hand, it held a gigantic mace, obsidian black and with a four-bladed head, each side a cleaver in and of itself. Smoke wafted from that weapon, and an occasional lick of flame appeared along its angry head.

Finally the fiend stepped from the bubbling pool, a huge, clawed foot scraping down upon solid stone, black claws screeching.

The beast wore only a green loincloth set with an iron skull in front, black leathery bracers tied tight around its muscular forearms, and macabre jewelry: a necklace of skulls, human sized but seeming smaller on the eight-foot-tall devil, and more skulls tied around its thrashing tail.

The Ashmadai wailed and prostrated themselves, face down, not daring to look upon the glorious devil.

It was not Asmodeus, of course, for to dare to even try to summon that one would have brought ruin upon them all. But Dor'crae's estimation of Valindra jumped mightily at that terrible, glorious moment, and truly he felt the fool for ever doubting Sylora Salm. With the scepter, Valindra had called deep into the Nine Hells, and she had been heard.

Dor'crae was no student of devil-kin, but like anyone else who had spent time with dark wizards, he knew the primary beings of the lower planes. Valindra had been heard indeed, and she had been granted, for her efforts, the services of a pit fiend, one of the personal servants of the devil god, a duke of the Nine Hells, answerable only to the unspeakable archdevils themselves.

The beast surveyed its ghostly enemies, then half-turned to regard Valindra and the groveling Ashmadai. It reached out with its long arm toward the scepter, clawed fingers grasping for the item.

And again Dor'crae thought it was surely time for him to leave, but the pit fiend didn't take the scepter from Valindra. Instead, it seemed to lend her its powers, to be funneled through the item.

The scepter glowed more brightly, and Dor'crae had to turn his shoulder and throw his elbow up high, bringing his cloak up to shield his face. He, too, was an undead thing. So many times had the vampire dominated unsuspecting humans, the weak willed who would give in to his demands. But he realized in that moment the horror of his former victims.

Despite himself, he was on his knees. He found that he could not look upon the pit fiend any longer, and he buried his face in his hands and bent to kiss the floor. Trembling, helpless, he could only die again right then and there. There was no escape. There was no hope.

"Dor'crae," he heard, more in his thoughts than his ears, as Valindra reached out to him, her voice thin and far, far away.

"Dor'crae, arise," she ordered.

The vampire dared to look up. Valindra still stood as she had, the scepter thrust up above her, its ends emitting wave after wave of energetic red light.

The pit fiend stood before her now, having let go of the artifact, and the scepter itself seemed greatly diminished, as the duke of devils seemed greatly enhanced.

Dor'crae's pain subsided, as did his hopelessness. He dared rise to his knees, then to his feet.

"The primordial's minions will not recognize that we also wish its release," the vampire warned. "And there is the dragon—the red dragon from the depths below . . ."

Valindra smiled at him and shrugged, as all around her the Ashmadai struggled to their feet, and the vampire wondered if Valindra had called to each of them, individually and by name, and somehow all at once.

"Lead on, Beealtimatuche," the lich said.

With the pit fiend thus leading, the procession moved past the writhing mass of prostrated dwarf ghosts, the creatures squirming in agony, and stalked out of the chamber.

The Ashmadai said nothing, but the looks on their faces spoke of awe and wonderment, and elation. But no such feelings washed through Dor'crae. He had known wizards to summon beings of the lower planes—usually minor demons or imps. He had heard of those who had dared bring forth more powerful minions, demons and devils, or elementals.

Those attempts at summoning greater servants had not typically ended well. He looked at the scepter, the source of the power for the summoning, and knew instinctively that the bulk of its stored energy had been spent in bringing forth the devil—a mighty devil that had to be tightly controlled.

Pit fiends were servants only to the archdevils themselves, and now, it seemed, a servant to Valindra Shadowmantle.

But for how long?

CHAPTER 21

THE HERITAGE, THE FATE

D RIZZT LEANED AGAINST THE WALL OF A DEFENSIVE ALCOVE
along the ten-foot-wide corridor. Dahlia stood across the
way, in a similar alcove. They heard the pursuit and knew it to be
elemental minions of the primordial. The drow glanced back the
other way, where the corridor spilled into a square room, its door
too broken to be used to slow the pursuing beasts.

"Hurry," Drizzt whispered, aiming the remark at Bruenor and
the others.

Bruenor had determined that that particular room held the
first installation for one of the magical bowls, one of the magical
connections to the tendrils of the Hosttower.

Drizzt glanced along the corridor, at the many metal placards
evenly spaced along the wall, all decorated with various dwarven
images, and none with an apparent clue as to which might be the
correct choice. Then a noise back down the corridor brought Drizzt
from his thoughts. He glanced across at Dahlia and nodded.

The woman, holding her tri-staff, eagerly grinned back at him.
That grin disappeared almost at once, though, and Dahlia lifted
her hand and worked her fingers through an intricate series of
movements.

Your sword.

Drizzt looked down as his belted scimitar, Icingdeath, and
discerned at once the cause of her concern. At the crease where
the blade's hilt sat on the scabbard, a line of blue light glowed.
Icingdeath always had a bluish tint to it, and often glowed more

powerfully, particularly when facing a creature of fire. The scimitar was one of the ancient frostbrands, after all, a weapon built to battle creatures of fire, a weapon hungry for fire elemental blood.

But Drizzt had never seen it glow while in its scabbard. He grasped the hilt and brought it forth just a bit, and his alcove was bathed in blue light.

He slid it back into the scabbard and took a deep breath, and told himself that it was just because of the nearness of the ultimate of fire creatures, the primordial.

He looked back at Dahlia and lifted his hand to respond, but before he did, he realized something quite amazing and unexpected: Dahlia had spoken to him in the intricate drow hand cant. Drizzt had never met anyone other than a drow who could use that sign language.

How do you know the cant? he flashed back at her.

Dahlia's pretty face screwed up as she tried, unsuccessfully, it seemed, to follow his movements.

Slowly, Drizzt signed, *You speak as a drow.*

Dahlia held her hand out horizontally and waggled it back and forth, indicating that she had only a cursory knowledge of the language. She ended with a self-deprecating grin and shrug.

Drizzt was impressed anyway. Few who were not drow, who were not trained from their earliest days at the Academy, could form even the most rudimentary words in the intricately coded language.

Down in the corridor, a door banged open and Dahlia tightened against the wall, her hands wringing on her magical staff.

Drizzt slid an arrow out of his enchanted quiver and set it to Taulmaril's string. He crouched down on one knee and peeked out into the corridor to see a host of red-skinned salamanders slithering down his way.

"Be quick, dwarf," Jarlaxle said, glancing nervously at the hallway door. "I do believe our enemies are fast upon us."

Bruenor gave a hearty "harrumph" and stood with his hands on his hips, staring at the chamber's side wall. No less than ten metal placards lined that wall, with an equal number across the way.

"Just pull 'em all," Athrogate prodded.

Bruenor shook his head. "Got to be the right one. Rest're trapped and sure to kill ye dead."

Athrogate had neared one of the plates as Bruenor spoke, and was even reaching out for one. He retracted his hand quickly, though, and sucked in his breath, turning to look back at Bruenor.

Bruenor pointed two placards down from where Athrogate stood. "That one."

"Ye for certain?"

"Aye," Bruenor said, and Athrogate moved that way. He hooked his fingers on the plate and pulled, but nothing happened.

Cries erupted out in the hallway.

Athrogate grabbed on harder and tugged with all his considerable strength, but the plate would not budge. He let go with a growl and hopped back, spat in both hands, and moved in again—or started to, until Bruenor intervened. The dwarf king walked up to the placard, reached up with one hand, and began talking in a language that sounded like Dwarvish—so much so that it took Athrogate several moments to realize that he couldn't really understand a word Bruenor was saying.

Bruenor gave a slight tug and the placard, the door to the secret compartment, swung open.

"How in the Nine Hells?" Athrogate complained.

"Tied to the throne's magic?" Jarlaxle wondered aloud. The drow was fast to Bruenor's side, to set the bowl on the base of the deep, narrow compartment. He fumbled with his sack for just a moment before producing a small vial, which he handed to the dwarf.

"To enact the magic of the bowl . . ." the drow began, but Bruenor held up his hand to silence his companion.

He knew how to do it. Somehow, he knew the words. He pulled the stopper from the small vial and poured the magical water into the bowl, then gently began swishing it around and chanting softly.

The water seemed to multiply as it swirled around the shallow bowl, growing in volume and in shape. Its form rose up above the rim of the bowl, like a watery humanoid swelling with power, and for a moment, it seemed outraged at being called from its home plane.

It continued to swell until it was too large to fit in the alcove, growing out of the hole and towering over the dwarf. Jarlaxle walked back, and Athrogate called out a warning to Bruenor and pulled out his morningstars, though how they might do damage to such a creature, he did not know.

But Bruenor remained unbothered. He had brought this creature through the magic of the bowl, and he commanded it. He reached right past the elemental as if it were no more bothersome than a potted plant, and slid the bowl deeper into the alcove. He pointed down the narrow tunnel, willing the elemental to retreat into the darkness, for at the other end of that compartment lay an open tendril of the Hosttower, a place designed to be filled by just such a creature.

The elemental swelled in protest, and thick, armlike appendages reached out to either side, great watery fists ready to pound at Bruenor.

But the dwarf just growled and pointed, compelling the elemental to obey. As soon as it retreated into the hole, Bruenor grabbed for the placard. He paused for a moment to consider the sounds within the alcove, like the breaking waves of a seashore.

He took a deep breath then, revealing his relief that the creature had indeed followed his command, and he closed the placard and turned to find Jarlaxle guarding by the door.

"We must be on our way," the drow called to him, but Bruenor shook his head.

"The second one's in here," the dwarf explained, pointing to the opposite wall.

Out in the hall, the tumult grew.

"Oh, good dwarf, do be quick," Jarlaxle said, and he drew out a pair of slender wands and moved to the wall at the side of the door.

One after another, Taulmaril the Heartseeker let fly, arrows trailing silver lightning as they shot off down the corridor. Crouched on one knee, Drizzt leaned out of the alcove and kept up the barrage as long as he could, dropping salamanders with every shot, sometimes two for one mighty arrow, and once even three.

But the losses only seemed to infuriate the monstrous creatures, and Drizzt knew he couldn't drive them all away. They were fighting for the primordial, for their god. The bodies piled in the corridor, but more salamanders slithered over them. And when the drow cut those down, the enraged creatures behind used a different tactic, pushing the pile in front of them instead of scrambling over it.

The drow grimaced and kept shooting—what else could he do? He drew back Taulmaril's bowstring as far as he could and let fly into the center mass, the lightning-arrows drilling holes into the pile and jolting bodies, occasionally breaking through to sting at the living elemental-kin behind.

The press continued, though, and Drizzt was about to put Taulmaril up and draw his swords when a pair of true lightning bolts shot down the corridor from behind him, startling him, blinding him temporarily, and forcing him back into the alcove. He came to the edge and peered around quickly to see a jumble of body parts, blackened and smoking, salamanders scrambling behind the blasted front ranks to rebuild their moving wall.

Drizzt went back to efficient work again with his deadly bow. Behind him, from the doorway of the room, Jarlaxle put his wands to use once more, angling the twin lightning bolts up high so they would rebound off the ceiling and dive down behind the wall of salamander corpses.

"Glob it!" Drizzt cried, for lack of a better word.

"Clear!" Jarlaxle yelled back, and Drizzt fell into the alcove.

A glob of green paste flew past him to strike the floor right in front of the corpse wall.

But still the salamanders came on, tearing asunder their macabre fortification and rushing over. A flying wall of spears led their charge, skipping and bouncing around the corridor.

"They're close!" Dahlia called from across the wall.

"Follow the line!" Jarlaxle yelled from the doorway, and a double flash, one-two, of lightning rumbled past the pair, the reports shaking the stones.

"Now!" Dahlia shouted as soon as the blasts had shot past, and she leaped out into the corridor, brandishing her tri-staff.

Swords in hand, Drizzt joined her, and just in time to flash Icingdeath out to his right, in front of Dahlia, and deflect a thrown trident.

The monsters pressed in three abreast, stabbing furiously at drow and elf.

Drizzt's scimitars worked in circles in front of him, parrying every thrust—sometimes one, sometimes two, depending on the target of the middle creature. The reach of those long spears and tridents prevented him from going forward behind any parries, though. He didn't want to surrender his position beside Dahlia. Together they formed a mighty defensive wall—and more than merely defensive, Drizzt realized as they fell into a side-by-side rhythm. Dahlia's amazing staff, sometimes whole, sometimes twin bo staves, sometimes a tri-staff, sometimes a pair of flails, afforded her all kinds of varying reaches and counters. Drizzt worked more pointedly on defense, easily picking off the strikes of the salamander directly in front of him, and executing continuous blocks on the one in the middle as well.

"Aye!" Dahlia cried, apparently understanding his intent, and she dropped back one step as Drizzt shot by, sidelong, deflecting spear after spear after trident in rapid succession. Wall to wall, the drow worked, his feet a blur as he sidestepped, his hands a blur as he worked his blades to deflect any and every attack.

He went back and to his left, and heard a *snap* beside him. Yet another incarnation of Dahlia's amazing weapon—four equal lengths of stick, joined end to end in a line so that she used them almost like a whip. And to great effect, as the salamander on Drizzt's far right discovered, the end pole turning over powerfully and perfectly to knock a hole in its forehead.

Even as it fell dead, a spear flew in from the next in line, but Drizzt was there with a clean deflection as Dahlia reeled in her staff. He worked back the other way quickly, leaving no hole in their defense.

"Over!" Dahlia called from behind him, and he instinctively ducked just as the warrior elf pole-vaulted over him, landing lightly on her feet inside the reach of spear and trident. Even as she landed, though, her staff whole and cumbersome in the tight quarters, she yelled, "Over!" again.

Her leap had been a diversion and nothing more. She went up again, vaulting backward. Three spears reached high to chase her, but none caught its mark.

Drizzt went quickly forward, under Dahlia, appearing as if out of nowhere in the midst of the salamanders. His scimitars flashed left, right, and a devastating double stab in the middle, slashing the beasts aside. Then he blocked a thrown spear, and a second and a third, and more creatures charged up with shields as if they meant to bull rush him back toward the room.

"Over! Bow!" Dahlia yelled, and Drizzt didn't quite understand how that might work out. He didn't question her, though, and simply fell back in a roll as Dahlia planted the end of her staff beside him and went up high.

He angled his tumble for the alcove, and sheathed his blades and scooped up Taulmaril as he came around, immediately setting an arrow.

Dahlia had not come down. She remained up high, hand grasping the top end of the planted eight-foot staff, feet kicking out repeatedly, unpredictably, and wildly at her enemies. Even when they managed to get a shield in her path, she merely stomped her foot on it and used it to maintain the high ground.

And Drizzt started shooting under her, his arrows clipping under the upraised shield of one, tearing through the creature's torso, and blasting clean through the shield of the one beside it.

Dahlia let out a cry and kicked hard against a shield, throwing herself backward as spears arced up at her from behind the nearest row of creatures. She came down in a controlled roll beside Drizzt, her eyes wide.

"Just run!" she told him, and before he could ask her why, she scampered away toward the room.

Another arrow flashed away, and another, and Drizzt had to fall into the alcove to avoid a wall of thrown spears. He came right back to shoot some more, though, thinking to cover Dahlia's retreat, but when he popped back out, he saw the ranks of his enemies thinned, salamanders diving aside and pressing against the wall to clear a path.

And Drizzt saw what Dahlia had seen from up high, and the same thought, *just run,* came screaming to mind.

"Two!" Bruenor announced, sliding the second bowl deep into its alcove and shutting the placard after it. From behind the metal door they heard the rush of water as the elemental tapped into the tendrils of the Hosttower. The dwarf nodded in satisfaction, and declared, "Two o' ten!"

"Be quick, and lead on," Jarlaxle bade him, words that hardly seemed necessary given the ruckus in the corridor just beyond the broken door. All three—Bruenor, Jarlaxle, and Athrogate—turned and looked that way, then, to see Dahlia diving into the room in a soaring somersault. She planted her staff just to the side as she rolled farther in, and pushed off, throwing herself out the other way, away from the three onlookers.

"What—?" was all Bruenor managed to say before a great rush of flames poured through the door with a dark form, Drizzt, within them, being carried along by the sheer force of the blast.

The drow landed in a short run as the flames dissipated, and looked to his friends, wisps of smoke rising from his cloak, Taulmaril in one hand, Icingdeath in the other, glowing fiercely.

"Oh, joy," Drizzt deadpanned. "They have a dragon."

Bruenor's eyes went wide, as did his mouth, as did Athrogate's features as well, and both let out a howl and ran off for the back side of the room, Dahlia angling to join them.

Jarlaxle put another lightning bolt into the open doorway for good measure, and wisely launched another magical glob into the opening as well, thinking to slow the pursuit. That sticky substance caught a trio of flying spears as an added benefit.

"Two elementals in place," Jarlaxle assured Drizzt when the pair came together, bringing up the rear of the retreat. "Eight more and we're nearly done!"

Drizzt didn't glance back, focusing instead on Bruenor, who stood in the exit at the far end of the room, ready to slam the heavy door.

"You heard me when I told you they have a dragon," the drow replied, and he shook his head and glanced back.

"Not a large one!" the other drow replied.

Drizzt was still shaking his head as they passed by Bruenor, who slammed the heavy stone door behind them. Nearby stood Athrogate, a heavy iron locking bar in hand, and the two dwarves had the portal quickly secured.

"I seen cooked cow, I seen cooked sow," Athrogate sang, "Now thinking for sure that I'd be seein' cooked drow! But ye don't smell roasted and ye don't look toasted, and it's making me ask meself, 'How, now, drow?' Bwahaha!"

"A fine question, if asked stupidly," Jarlaxle concurred as the troupe started swiftly away.

Drizzt didn't answer. He sprinted out in front of the other four, taking up the point, slinging Taulmaril over his shoulder as he went and drawing out his second scimitar.

"Damned good blade," Bruenor explained to the other three a short while later.

"Icingdeath . . ." Jarlaxle realized, catching on.

"Damned sword kept the flames away?" Athrogate asked.

"Carried it once, as I rode a burning dragon," Bruenor remarked.

"A burnin' dragon?" Athrogate asked, at the same time Jarlaxle fell a stride behind and silently mouthed the exact same three words.

"Aye, cooked it meself."

The drow mercenary could only smile then and shake his head, knowing better than to disbelieve any of the outrageous stories those two old adventurers, Drizzt Do'Urden and Bruenor Battlehammer, might tell.

His grin disappeared as he looked ahead to Drizzt, though, seeing even in the way the drow moved the edge that had come to him. Drizzt had often seemed the carefree fighter, enjoying the battle, and Jarlaxle couldn't deny the charm of that. But whatever remained of that carefree attitude had changed, and not subtly. Perhaps it was barely discernable to one who did not know the truth of Drizzt Do'Urden, but for Jarlaxle in particular, the change glared at him. He excused himself from the dwarves and Dahlia and quick-stepped far ahead to catch up to Drizzt.

"One battle after another," he remarked.

Drizzt nodded and seemed bothered not at all.

"But all worth it because of the good we might accomplish here, yes?" Jarlaxle added.

Drizzt looked at him as if he was insane, and replied, "I have spent half a century in search of this place, for the sake of my friend."

"And you care not that our work here may save a city?"

Drizzt shrugged. "Have you been to Luskan lately?"

Jarlaxle shook that comment off and asked, "Would you have come here if not for Bruenor?"

A flash of anger spiked in Drizzt's eyes, and Jarlaxle didn't wait for an answer. He charged into Drizzt, grabbing him by the front of his leather vest and driving him back up against the wall.

"Damn you to Lolth's webs!" he said. "Don't you dare pretend it doesn't matter to you!"

"Why do you care?" Drizzt growled back at him, and he reached up to pull Jarlaxle's hands aside—but so angry was Jarlaxle that he growled through that attempt and pressed all the harder.

"No one who has ever made a difference?" he asked, his face barely an inch from Drizzt's.

Drizzt stared at him.

"That is what you said, back in the Cutlass. How you described yourself to me. 'No one who has ever made a difference.' " Jarlaxle closed his eyes and finally let go, stepping back. "Do you believe that?" he asked more calmly.

"What do you want from me, son of Baenre?"

"Just the truth—your truth. You believe that you have never made a difference?"

"Perhaps there is no difference to be made," Drizzt replied, and he seemed to be spitting every word.

"None permanent, you mean."

Drizzt considered that for a moment, then nodded his acceptance of the caveat.

"Because they all die anyway?" Jarlaxle went on. "Catti-brie? Regis?"

Drizzt snorted and shook his head, and started off down the corridor, but Jarlaxle caught him by the shoulder and pushed him back against the wall, and so full of anger was Jarlaxle's face that Drizzt's hand went to the hilt of his scimitar.

"Do not ever say that," Jarlaxle said to him, spittle flying with every word.

Drizzt's hands came up inside Jarlaxle's grasp, and as the mercenary began to loosen his grip, Drizzt shoved him back.

"Why do you care?" Drizzt asked.

"Because you were the one who escaped," Jarlaxle replied.

Drizzt looked at him as though he had no idea what Jarlaxle could possibly be talking about.

"Don't you understand?" Jarlaxle went on. "I watched you—we all watched you. Whenever a matron mother, or almost any female of Menzoberranzan was about, we spoke your name with vitriol, promising to avenge Lolth and kill you."

"You've had your chance at that."

Jarlaxle went on as if Drizzt had said nothing. "But whenever they were not around, the name of Drizzt Do'Urden was spoken with jealousy, often reverence. You do not understand, do you? You don't even recognize the difference you've made to so many of us in Menzoberranzan."

"How? Why?"

"Because you were the one who escaped!"

"You are here with me!" Drizzt argued. "Are you bound to the City of Spiders by anything more than your own designs? By Bregan D'aerthe?"

"I'm not talking about the city, you obstinate fool," Jarlaxle replied, his voice lowering.

Again Drizzt looked at him, at a loss.

"The heritage," Jarlaxle explained. His voice lowered still as they heard the approach of the others. "The fate."

CHAPTER 22

PARALLEL PASSAGEWAYS

GREAT COLUMNS LINED THE HALL, EVENLY SPACED IN THREE long rows. Each was, in itself, a work of art, a product of the labors of a hundred dwarf craftsmen. Each column was uniquely decorated, personally touched and carved with great love. Even the centuries of dust that had settled there couldn't hide the majesty of the place. Walking through it, the five companions, particularly Bruenor and Athrogate, could well imagine the gatherings that had once been held there. The awakening of the primordial had caused considerable damage, but much of the glory that had once been Gauntlgrym remained intact. They had passed through dozens of chambers and along many stairways and corridors, with doors that opened into mansions and cellars, workshops and kitchens, dining halls and training rooms. Gauntlgrym had, before the escape of the primordial, been larger than Mithral Hall, Citadel Adbar, and Citadel Felbarr combined—a glorious homeland for Clan Delzoun.

"I lost me count," Bruenor announced when they were nearly halfway through the vast chamber. Hands on hips, he stared at the metal placard on the nearest column and shook his head.

"Twenty-three," Drizzt said, and all eyes turned to the drow. "That is the twenty-third plate in the hall."

He said it with such certainty, and with Drizzt being ever reliable, no one doubted him, but all heads turned back the way they'd come, astonished to realize that they had passed so many of the giant columns. Indeed, the chamber was vast, with a ceiling out of sight in the shadows above.

Bruenor shook his head, looked left and right, then turned and pointed to the center column next in line. "Middle plate, two dozen in," he announced, and he walked up to the plate with all confidence—both in the knowledge he had gained from the magical throne, and in Drizzt's count—and grasped its edge, easily pulling it open and revealing the alcove behind, which was different from the previous six, both shallower and higher. Bruenor stuck his head in and glanced up, and in the distance far above, likely at the apex of the column itself, he saw a familiar green glow.

"Tendril," he remarked triumphantly.

In went the bowl, the seventh of ten, and Jarlaxle moved up and handed him a vial. With the appropriate incantation, Bruenor emptied the magical water into the bowl and watched the swirl as the elemental took shape.

Almost immediately, the tendril's magic grabbed it.

"No others in this hall," Bruenor announced, closing the placard door. "Next one's south."

"Onward, then," said Dahlia, moving past him, but Bruenor was quick to correct her.

"South," he explained. "That's to the left."

Dahlia shrugged helplessly, and the dwarves and Jarlaxle led the way to a door at the side of the room, while Drizzt fell in with Dahlia.

"How can he know?" Dahlia asked.

"The throne, somehow . . ." Drizzt replied.

"Not the layout of the complex," Dahlia clarified. "How can he—how can any of you—know which way is south, and which north?"

Drizzt smiled at her and nodded. He would have answered, if he knew the answer. Creatures of the Underdark just knew such things, felt them innately.

"Perhaps it is the pull of the heavenly bodies above," he offered. "As the sun and moon cross the sky, perhaps their energy is felt even down here."

"I don't feel it," the elf replied with a sour look.

Drizzt grinned wider. "When you are above and wish to determine the direction, how do you do it?"

Dahlia looked at him with a wrinkled brow.

"You look to the sky, or the horizon if it's familiar," said Drizzt. "You know where the sun rises and sets, and so you determine your four points based on that."

"But you can't know that down here."

Drizzt shrugged again. "When you're in the forest on a dark night, is not your hearing more keen?"

"That's different."

"Is it?"

Dahlia started to reply, but stopped, and stopped walking, too. She stared at the drow for a few heartbeats.

"You may find that after a while in the Underdark, you will come to sense direction as easily as you do in the World Above," Drizzt said.

"Who would wish to spend any more time in the Underdark than we have already?"

The snide remark, and the short manner in which Dahlia had delivered it, caught Drizzt by surprise. He thought to tell her about all the beautiful things that could be found in the subterranean world beneath Faerûn. Even Menzoberranzan—which Dahlia, as a surface elf, could not likely see as anything but a slave—was a place of dazzling beauty. Drizzt had chosen the surface world as his home, and truly he loved the stars, and even the sunshine, though for years it had pained his sensitive eyes. He found beauty in the forests and the waterways, in the clouds and the rolling fields, and in the grandeur of the mountains. But there was no less beauty to be found below, he knew, though it didn't often occur to him. He had rarely been in the Underdark in the last half-century and perhaps because of that fact, he had come to see it differently. He appreciated its beauty, both dwarf-worked and natural.

He didn't tell any of that to Dahlia, however. She was at a disadvantage there, out of her element and surrounded by four companions who were not out of theirs. She didn't like that, Drizzt realized, and in looking at her as she again walked beside him, he saw a vulnerability in her. She had started the wrong way before being corrected by Bruenor. She didn't know which direction was which. Her perfect armor had revealed a seam, after all.

And in that seam, Drizzt noted a scar, an old and deep wound, a flicker of pain behind the always-intense gleam of her blue eyes, a hesitation in her always-confident stride, a defensive curl of her always-squared shoulders.

His intrigue surprised him. Her appeal at that moment overwhelmed him. Of course he'd marveled at the unusual beauty of the elf, particularly at the allure of her deadly fighting dance.

But something more had presented itself, something endearing, something interesting.

———

"Pull it down! Pull it down!" Stokely Silverstream commanded his dwarves. And the crack team did just that, hauling their ropes from either side and pinning the large red lizard to the floor. Up ahead, more dwarves, aided by the ghosts, battled the salamanders, but the dwarves' victory over their enemy's hidden weapon, a twenty-foot-long, voracious, fearsome fire lizard, had sealed the larger victory.

Stokely himself walked up and dispatched the monster, though it took several heavy blows from his axe to accomplish the task.

By the time he and the rear guard caught up to the others, the fighting had ended. Dead and wounded salamanders littered the wide, steamy tunnel, along with three of Stokely's boys. The two priests accompanying the score of warriors went to work furiously, but one of those dwarves died there in the deep corridor of Gauntlgrym, and one of the other two had to be carried along.

But on the dwarves went, undeterred, following the ghosts and their destiny.

Barely an hour later, still before their midday meal, they heard more noise coming from a side tunnel—a force moving down at them.

Stokely stared ahead uncertainly. Perhaps they could outrun the elemental-kin, but if they tried and ran into more resistance ahead, they'd be trapped.

"Dig in yer heels, me boys," the dwarf leader told his fellows. "More to kill."

Not a dwarf complained, faces set grimly, weapons turning under white knuckles. The few ghosts that had silently led them from Icewind Dale drifted up the tunnel to meet the incoming force, but no sounds of battle echoed down at Stokely's crew.

Just a call, and a cheer: "Mirabar!"

And out they came, two-score and ten, an elite squad of the Shield of Mirabar.

"Well met!" Stokely and others called back, and both sides knew great relief, for both groups had known battle after battle with minions of the primordial for the last several days.

"Stokely Silverstream of Icewind Dale, at yer service!" the leader from the North greeted.

An old graybeard stepped forward from the ranks of Mirabarran dwarves. "Icewind Dale?" he asked. "Be ye Battlehammers, then?"

"Aye, and well met," Stokely replied. "Mithral Hall's our older home, and Gauntlgrym's older still!"

"Torgar Hammerstriker, at yer service, and well met indeed, cousin," said the graybeard. "For two-score years I called Mithral Hall me home. Went in service to King Bruenor, Moradin kiss him, and served King Banak afore Mirabar called me home."

"Ye were there when King Bruenor fell?"

"No bell can sing the tune sad enough," Torgar replied, "and heavy weighed the stones o' his grave. A dark day in Mithral Hall."

Stokely nodded, but said nothing more at that time other than, "A dark day for all dwarf-kin." Perhaps he would discuss the "end" of King Bruenor at length with Torgar later on. Protocol demanded discretion when discussing the death ruse of an abdicating dwarf king, but so many years removed, the whispers would not be out of order.

"Torgar!" came a cry from the side. "By Obould's ugly arse!"

Torgar spotted the shouting dwarf and his face lit up with recognition, and with fired memories of an old war.

"Could that be ye, there?" the Mirabarran leader called back. "Or am I seein' more ghosts than I thinked?"

It was no ghost.

Drizzt rolled ahead and to the right, ignoring the salamander he had just disengaged. He came to his feet, scimitars leading the way into the last pair of beasts, just as he heard a sickly *splat* behind him, then a grunt, and a *thump* as the leading salamander crumbled to the floor.

His parallel blades worked opposite circles, left hand under to the left, right hand under to the right, each wrapping back over spears, and with a powerful exhale, Drizzt threw his weapons and the spears out wide to either side and abruptly stopped his charge, leaning back and leaping up, double-kicking the two salamanders directly in front of him. The drow landed flat on his back, but his muscles moved so perfectly, arcing and snapping straight, that it seemed to any onlookers—and certainly to his two surprised opponents—as if some unknown counterweight had lifted him right back to his feet.

His scimitars struck, left and right, taking the throat from the beast to his right and gashing the shoulder of the other. And still, with help from Icingdeath, Drizzt ignored the blistering heat that radiated from the beasts.

The wounded salamander scrambled to put some ground between itself and the drow, trying to realign its weapon and find some measure of defense.

Before Drizzt could pursue, another form flew past from on high. Dahlia descended from her vault with a flying kick to the side of the monster's head, throwing it to the ground. As she landed, straddling it, the elf woman sent her long staff into a sudden spin then drove it straight down and through the creature. When the metal struck the stone beneath, Kozah's Needle let loose a blast of powerful lightning.

Holding it in one extended hand, her other arm out wide the other way, Dahlia seemed to bask in that energy, that power. She threw her head back, her eyes closed and her mouth wide, an expression of pure ecstasy on her fair face.

Drizzt couldn't tear his eyes from her! If another enemy had crept in and charged at him, he surely would have been cut down!

Dahlia held the pose for a long while, and Drizzt stared at her through it all.

"We have a problem," came a call, Jarlaxle's voice, breaking the trance of both.

"He couldn't summon the elemental?" Drizzt asked.

"The bowl is in place," Jarlaxle replied. "Eight of ten. But the ninth placard is destroyed, as is the alcove behind it."

Drizzt and Dahlia exchanged a concerned glance then followed Jarlaxle from the corridor and through the few small rooms back to the wider hall where Bruenor and Athrogate waited—waited with hands on hips, staring at an impenetrable pile of rubble and a collapsed wall.

"Was here," Bruenor insisted. "Ain't no more."

"What does this mean?" Dahlia asked. "Can we not put the beast back in its hole?"

"Bah, but nine water monsters'll do it then!" Athrogate bellowed. The others looked at him.

"Ain't no choice to it!" he answered with strength and conviction. To the side of him lay two dead salamanders, both swatted down by Athrogate when first they'd entered the room. To put a true exclamation point at the end of his proclamation, the dwarf spat upon the dead creatures then gave a hearty, "Bwahaha!" and thumped King Bruenor on the shoulder.

And to Drizzt's surprise, Bruenor thumped Athrogate right back.

"Come on, then!" King Bruenor declared. "The devil worshipers can't stop us, the fire worshipers can't stop us, and not this primor . . . this prim . . . this volcano beast'll be stoppin' us neither! I got me one more water monster to set and a big lever to pull, and let all the world know that Gauntlgrym's ghosts'll be restin' easy once more!"

And off they went. It did Drizzt's heart good to see his old friend so animated and boisterous and full of fire, and he watched Bruenor for a long while. Gradually, though, his gaze slipped back to Dahlia, who walked quietly at his side. He noticed then three marks in her right ear, just above the single diamond stud set there.

Three missing earrings?

There was a story there, Drizzt knew, and he was surprised once again by the enigmatic woman, and by his own reaction to her, when he realized how much he wanted to hear that tale.

The sound of water rushing over their heads had all the Ashmadai looking up with alarm.

"The magic returns!" Valindra cried. "The Hosttower answers the call of our enemies!"

"What does it mean?" the Ashmadai commander begged.

"It means that you will fail, and your Dread Ring will not sing the praise of Asmodeus," Beealtimatuche the pit fiend growled, and all save Valindra shrank back from the sheer power in the devil's angry voice.

"Nay," Valindra corrected, and she held forth her scepter to silence any further dissent from the fiend. "It means that we must press on with more speed."

"Straight to the Forge," offered the Ashmadai leader, who had been there those years before when Sylora had arrived to bolster the faltering Dahlia.

A huge bat came rushing up the corridor at them then, and flipped over itself in the air right before Valindra and Beealtimatuche, elongating as it came around to assume the human form of Dor'crae once more, his face a mask of concern.

"The water . . ." Valindra warned, but Dor'crae shook his head.

"Our enemies block the way," he explained. "The primordial's minions—not Dahlia's troupe."

"Then they die!" Beealtimatuche roared, and all the zealots cheered.

But Dor'crae was still shaking his head.

"They have a dragon," he explained. "A *red* dragon."

With a stomp of his clawed foot that gouged the floor and shook the walls of the corridor, the pit fiend stormed away, and how the cultists scrambled to get out of his path. And when one was too slow, the devil swatted her aside with his great fiery mace, mulching her shoulder, igniting her leathers and hair, and throwing her into the wall with a sickening crunch of her every bone.

She slumped into an almost formless mass of blood and burning flesh.

And the Ashmadai cheered.

CHAPTER 23

JOSI . . . JOSI PUDDLES

DAHLIA GRIPPED HER TRI-STAFF TIGHTLY, READY TO SPRING OUT and throttle whomever or whatever approached the small room in which she waited with the dwarves.

She relaxed when Drizzt came through the archway.

"Our enemies are close," he warned her. "Ahead of us in every corridor and chamber."

From just outside the room's other door, the one through which the five had entered, Jarlaxle replied, "And they're not far behind, as well."

"We're to be fighting again, then," said Dahlia, and she didn't show a hint of regret or fear at that thought. She nodded to Drizzt, who returned her confident look.

"All the way to the Forge o' Gauntlgrym," Athrogate agreed. "If a hunnerd lizard boys stand in me way, a hunnerd lizard boys'll die! Eh, King Bruenor?" he added, and he turned and slapped Bruenor on the shoulder.

Bruenor, busy inspecting the wall, just grunted.

"We should move on swiftly," Drizzt said. "We'll not want those behind catching us while we're fighting those ahead."

He moved back to the archway, Dahlia right behind him. Jarlaxle entered from across the way and moved to join them, then Athrogate joined as well, after another clap on Bruenor's shoulder.

But Bruenor didn't even grunt in response, one hand lifted to feel the texture of the carved relief on the chamber's stone wall.

"Bruenor," Drizzt called. "We must move."

The dwarf waved his hand at them dismissively, and studied the wall more intently. His mind drifted back across the centuries, to the revelations of the magical throne.

This is the room, he thought. It has to be the room. If I can only find the catch!

Noise from the tunnel they had just descended entered the hall.

"Bruenor," Drizzt said, but more quietly. He rushed over to join the dwarf. "Come," he bade his friend, and he put his hand on Bruenor's strong shoulder. "Our enemies near. We must be gone."

"Aye, be gone," the irritated dwarf grumbled back. He pressed his hand more strongly on the wall, hoping he wasn't about to spring a deadly trap.

Was it possible that the centuries of idleness had ruined the mechanisms? The thought rattled Bruenor. It was Gauntlgrym, after all, the pinnacle of dwarven civilization.

"Dwarves build things to last," he said aloud.

"Build what?"

Finally Bruenor did look up at Drizzt, and he motioned his chin back to the wall and stepped aside. Drizzt moved in quickly. He wasn't exactly sure what he might be looking for. Bruenor had revealed nothing of the reasons for his interest in that particular bas relief, and Gauntlgrym teemed with such carvings.

The drow stared at the carving for a few heartbeats. The others soon came over, pleading with the pair to lead the way out of the small chamber, which was seeming more and more like a trap—or a tomb—than anything else.

Drizzt shook his head, not to answer those complaints, but simply because he saw no anomalies in the relief, not a hint of anything out of place. He closed his eyes, spread both his hands up in front of him, and gently ran his fingers along the wall. The drow opened his eyes and a curious grin came upon him.

"What d'ye know?" Bruenor asked.

Drizzt removed one hand from the wall, then all but one finger of his other hand. He moved the remaining contact up a bit, then slowly slid it back to its original place, and his smile grew with confidence.

Bruenor lifted his hand and Drizzt moved his own aside.

The dwarf closed his eyes and felt for the spot. "Clever dwarf," he whispered, referring to the craftsman who had constructed that particular mechanism.

There was no seam. There was no mark of color or shape. In that one spot, at one point no bigger than the tip of a stubby dwarf finger, the wall was not made of stone, but of metal.

Bruenor turned his finger to get his nail against the spot, and pushed hard.

"Lead," he announced.

"It's a cover plate," said Drizzt.

"Aye, one to be melted." They both turned to Jarlaxle, who always seemed to have all the answers.

"Melted?" Drizzt asked, skeptical. "We could build a fire and heat some makeshift poker, but we've not the time to bring something to that temperature."

"What's behind it?" asked Dahlia.

"Our escape, if I'm readin' their faces right," Athrogate said.

Bruenor looked at the wall, and at Drizzt, who seemed just as perplexed as to how they might get through it. Back in the hall, more sounds echoed, their enemies obviously nearing the chamber.

"Mark it," Drizzt instructed. He stepped away, and as he did, he revealed his plan as he slid Taulmaril from his shoulder.

Bruenor glanced around, and patted his pockets and his pack, trying to figure out how he might do that. He produced one of his maps and tore a piece from its corner, plopping it into his mouth. He rushed back to the spot in front of the wall and gently felt the surface again, chewing all the while. When he had the spot, he spat the wet parchment into his hand, pressed it into place, and stepped aside.

Drizzt already had an arrow fitted to the bowstring. He drew level and took careful and steady aim.

He fired, and a flash of lightning illuminated the room. The enchanted missile hit the mark. It melted the paper first then drilled right through the lead cover and right into the catch behind, ruining it forever. Both drow and dwarf knew it to be a risk, for in doing that, had Drizzt also forever sealed the secret door?

They heard rocks sliding somewhere behind the wall, though whether that was a promising sign or a portent of doom, they couldn't be sure.

But then the stone groaned before them as the counterweights took hold in some unseen mechanism. The hatch fell in slightly, revealing the outline of a dwarf-sized doorway. Dust slipped from all edges and a musty smell, an old smell, filled their nostrils. With a great groan of protest, the secret door slid aside, disappearing into the right-hand wall.

"How did you know?" Dahlia asked, breathless.

"Damn smart throne, eh?" Athrogate said with a giggle.

"Onward, and quickly," Jarlaxle bade them.

Drizzt started for the opening, but Bruenor held out a strong arm and kept the drow at bay.

The dwarf king led the way into the deeper, long-unused corridor, a tunnel that became a steep staircase only a few feet inside.

Last in was Athrogate, who shoved the heavy stone door back in place behind them.

Down they went, Bruenor making a swift pace on the treacherous stone stair. He didn't think of the danger of falling. He knew what was coming.

The stairs spilled out into a narrow corridor, and the narrow corridor spilled out into a wider chamber, lit in orange: the Forge of Gauntlgrym.

Bruenor skidded to a stop, eyes wide, mouth agape. "Ye see it, elf?" he managed to whisper.

"I see it, Bruenor," Drizzt replied in hushed and reverent tones.

One did not have to be a Delzoun dwarf to understand the solemn significance of the place, and the majesty of it. As if being pulled by unseen forces, Bruenor drifted toward the large central forge, and the dwarf seemed to grow with every stride, as ancient magic and ancient strength swelled his corporeal form.

He came to a stop right in front of the open forge, staring into the blazing fires, which were fully alive since the primordial had first been released. His face fast reddened under that heat, but he didn't mind.

He stood there for a long, long while.

"Bruenor?" Drizzt dared ask after many heartbeats. "Bruenor, we must be quick."

If the dwarf even heard him, he didn't show it.

Drizzt moved around to gain Bruenor's stare, but he couldn't. The dwarf stood with his eyes closed. And when he opened them after a bit, he still felt far away and hardly noticed Drizzt and the others at all.

He lifted his axe and stepped toward the open forge.

"Bruenor?"

He pulled off his shield and laid it on the small ledge in front of the fires, then laid the axe upon it.

"Bruenor?"

Not even using an implement, the dwarf grabbed the iron-bound edge of the shield and slid it into the open forge, chanting in a language he knew none of the others would understand, a language Bruenor didn't even understand himself.

"Bruenor!"

They must all have expected the shield, fashioned mostly of wood, to burst into flames, but it didn't.

Bruenor kept up his chant for a short while then reached in and grasped the edge of the shield once more.

"Bruenor!" Drizzt went for him, perhaps thinking to push him aside. But the drow might as well have tried to move the forge itself. He hit Bruenor's arm hard, his whole weight behind the charge, but didn't move the dwarf's arm at all. Bruenor hardly even noticed the collision. He just pulled out his shield, and on it, his many-notched axe.

He didn't cool them in water, but just picked them up, sliding the shield into place and hoisting the axe. Then he stepped back and turned to the others, shaking his head, coming out of his trance.

"How are your arms not blistering to the bone?" Dahlia asked. "How is it the skin didn't slough off your fingers like parchment?"

"Huh?" the dwarf replied. "What're ye talking about?"

"The shield," said Jarlaxle, and Athrogate began to giggle.

"Huh?" Bruenor asked again and he turned the shield to get a look.

The wood remained exactly as it had been, though perhaps a bit darker, burnished by the fires. The banding, though, once black iron, shone silver in hue, and showed not a dent, though it had been marked by many before. And most magnificent of all was the foaming mug set in the middle. It, too, shone silver, and the foam seemed almost real, white in hue and brilliant in design.

"The axe," Jarlaxle added, and all had noticed that, for how could one miss the changes that had come over the weapon? The head gleamed silver, a sparkle running along its vicious edge. It still showed the notches of its many battles—no doubt, the dwarf gods would have thought it an insult to Bruenor to remove those badges of honor—but there was a strength about it that was visible to all, an inner power, glowing as if begging release.

"What have you done?" Jarlaxle asked.

Bruenor just muttered, "Talked to them what was," and banged his axe against his shield.

A noise from the far end of the hall turned them all that way. Drizzt slid Taulmaril off his shoulder as Athrogate then Bruenor came up to flank him. Jarlaxle shrank back a few steps, drawing out a pair of wands.

"Here they come," remarked Dahlia, standing right behind Drizzt. She used her staff to nudge him aside, and stepped up between him and Athrogate.

Drizzt looked over at Bruenor, who wore a curious expression. With only a cursory glance back at the drow, the dwarf put his axe in his shield hand and brought that shield arm out in front of him. Staring at the shield's backing, he grew even more curious and he brought his free hand forward, as if reaching right inside the shield.

How all their eyes widened when Bruenor retracted that arm, for he held a flagon, a great foamy head spilling over its side. He looked back at the shield, eyes widening once more. He handed the flagon to Drizzt then reached in again and produced a second one.

"Here now, one for meself?" Athrogate demanded.

Drizzt handed the first to the dwarf, and turned back just in time to get the second from Bruenor, who already produced the third and gave it to Drizzt as the second went to Dahlia. The fourth he gave to Jarlaxle, and Bruenor took up the fifth and final mug.

"Now there's a shield worth wearin'!" said Athrogate.

"We got us some good gods," Bruenor remarked, and Athrogate grinned.

"What is it?" Dahlia asked.

"Gutbuster, I'm hopin'!" said Athrogate.

The two drow and the elf looked to each other and at the drinks uncertainly, but Bruenor and Athrogate didn't hesitate, lifting their flagons in toast then taking great swallows.

And both seemed to swell with power. Athrogate brought forth his empty metal flagon and crushed it in his hand, then threw it aside and took up his morningstars.

"By Moradin's bum and Clangeddin's beard, who'd ever be seein' such a sight?" he recited. "A party o' five with weapons in hand and ready to take up the fight. But me gods are all posin' and scratching and shakin' and got to be questionin' theirself, to think a royal would be sharin' their spoils with the likes o' two drows and an elf!"

"Bwahaha!" It was Bruenor howling, not Athrogate.

"Drink it, ye fools!" Athrogate told the elves. "And feel the power o' the dwarf gods flowing through yer limbs!"

Drizzt went first, taking a deep, deep gulp, and he looked to the others and nodded, then finished his drink and tossed the flagon aside.

Bruenor blinked. The room seemed clearer to him suddenly, more focused and crisp, and when he hefted his axe and shield, they seemed lighter in his hands.

"Some kind of potion," Jarlaxle remarked. "What a remarkable shield."

"Behold the Forge o' Gauntlgrym," said Bruenor. "Old magic. Good magic."

"Dwarf magic," said Athrogate.

More noise in the corridor across the way brought them back to the moment at hand.

"They have a dragon," Drizzt reminded them. "We should spread out."

"Stay by me side, elf," Bruenor remarked as the others shifted out to either flank.

"No, we should send Bruenor straightaway to the lever," said Jarlaxle.

"Aye," said Athrogate, "and I be knowin' the way."

Just as he took a step toward the small side door on the wall to the side of the main forge, however, a tumult the other way stopped him, and he, and the others, saw the dragon leap from the tunnel.

Or at least, that's what it appeared to be, momentarily, until they realized that it was only the dragon's head, tossed out of the tunnel. It bounced across the floor and rolled, coming to a stop staring at the five through dead eyes.

"Lolth preserve us," Jarlaxle breathed.

Out of the tunnel came the fiend, slamming his fiery mace on one wall with a thunderous report. He leaped forward and skidded to a stop, arms out wide, chest puffed up, tail flicking eagerly behind him and head thrown back with a devilish roar.

"Well," Bruenor said, "at least the dragon's dead."

Out of the tunnel behind the fiend came the Ashmadai forces, led by a quartet of hellish legionnaires, devil warriors likely summoned by the pit fiend. The Ashmadai rushed out behind, running wide to either flank. If that display wasn't enough to unnerve the five companions, the last to make an appearance surely was.

Valindra Shadowmantle seemed a long way from the confused creature Jarlaxle had known those last decades. Holding high a shining scepter, she floated out of the tunnel, grinning hatefully, her eyes twinkling for revenge.

"Die well," Dahlia remarked.

"Josi Puddles," Drizzt whispered to Bruenor.

"Eh?"

"The rat-faced man in the Cutlass of old."

"Ah . . ." said Bruenor, and he looked at Drizzt curiously. "Ye're tellin' me now?"

Drizzt shrugged. "I wouldn't want to die with a faded memory nagging at my thoughts. I thought the same of you."

Bruenor started to respond, but just shrugged and turned back to the approach of doom itself.

"Athrogate and Bruenor, go," Jarlaxle said quietly from the back. "Slowly, and now."

Athrogate slid behind Drizzt to get to Bruenor, and tried to pull him along. But the dwarf king wouldn't budge. "I ain't for leavin' me friend."

"A thousand friends of a thousand friends will die if we don't finish this," Drizzt said. "Go."

"Elf . . ." Bruenor replied, grabbing Drizzt's forearm.

Drizzt looked at his oldest and dearest friend and nodded solemnly. "Go," he bade.

And a burst of fire exploded from the mouths of all the forges in the room, potent lines of flame leaping across the room to scorch the walls.

"The beast!" Dahlia cried. "It knows of our plan!"

The room began to shake violently, the floor bucking and buckling, dust and debris raining from the ceiling.

"Go! Go!" Drizzt shouted at Bruenor, and before the dwarf king could argue, Athrogate tugged him so hard his feet came right off the floor.

The pit fiend roared and directed his left flank to charge behind the main forge and cut off the dwarves. Then the devil staggered backward, then again, hit by a pair of lightning bolts from Jarlaxle's wands, and again a third time, even more profoundly, as Taulmaril's arrow slammed into his chest.

But Beealtimatuche only grinned wider then vanished, disappearing in the blink of a drow's eye, only to reappear right in front of one of the two dark elves, his four-bladed mace up high, spitting fire as it descended on the helpless figure.

Sprinting the other way at that moment, trying to block for Bruenor and Athrogate, Drizzt didn't see the mighty blow, but in the small doorway ahead and to his right, Athrogate did, and cried out, "Jarlaxle!" with such emotion and pain that it seemed to Drizzt as if the tough dwarf had just lost his best friend.

Drizzt glanced back to see a dark form rolling out to the side of the demon, then bursting into flames, and he caught his breath and had to steady himself.

For all his life and in all the world, nothing had seemed more eternal yet reliably unreliable to Drizzt than that strange and strangely endearing fellow drow.

And there stood the pit fiend, triumphant, straddling the still and flaming form and staring hatefully and eagerly for its next victim.

CHAPTER 24

OLD KINGS AND ANCIENT GODS

BRUENOR SALUTED DRIZZT AND RUSHED THROUGH THE FIRST of a series of doors down the small tunnel, Athrogate right behind him.

Drizzt didn't see it, and had to just trust in his friend. His glance back at Jarlaxle, his shock at seeing the drow's demise, had cost him precious seconds, and he sprinted to catch up to Dahlia, who was already furiously working her tri-staff to hold back the rush of Ashmadai. He drew out his onyx figurine as he went and called for Guenhwyvar, but he didn't keep the cat at his side as she appeared, instead ordering her to bring chaos to the ranks of their enemies.

Off Guenhwyvar leaped, and in came Drizzt, hard. Afraid for his dwarf friend and surprisingly outraged at the loss of his other . . . friend, the drow charged into the nearest Ashmadai warrior with his scimitars spinning. He hit the cultist's scepter four times before the Ashmadai man, an ugly half-orc, even knew what hit him. Batting the scepter left and right, not even bothering to work it out to one side or the other, Drizzt had the overmatched warrior confused and off balance. He struck again with a fifth parry, batting the scepter to the right, then hit it with an unexpected uppercut, lifting it away. Even as it cleared the Ashmadai's torso, Twinkle, in Drizzt's left hand, slashed across, slicing open the half-orc's belly. As the Ashmadai lurched forward, the same blade struck a backhand against the half-orc's temple, sending him tumbling to the side.

Up came Icingdeath in a powerful horizontal presentation as Drizzt stepped ahead to meet the next enemy in line. But before he could strike through the opening with his left-hand blade, he had to launch Twinkle out wide to parry a thrusting staff-spear.

Drizzt missed the opening, but Dahlia didn't. Under his upraised blade came her staff, a single long pole once more, to stab into the Ashmadai's chest. When it hit, it threw forth a burst of lightning, launching their opponent through the air and backward. He flew several feet, and several feet high, but he never came back to the floor. A long-bladed sword drove through his chest, impaling him in mid air.

The legion devil easily held the dead Ashmadai aloft with just that one sword arm, and let him hang there for a few heartbeats, arms and legs out wide, lifeblood pouring from the wound. Looking around its macabre human shield, the devil grinned at the drow and the elf, even laughed a bit. Then it jerked its great sword powerfully back and forth and the dead cultist fell to the floor at the devil's feet in two pieces.

Drizzt presented Twinkle horizontally in front of him, left arm out straight, his right hand tucked at the side of his face, Icingdeath atop the left-hand blade. He stood in a crouch, right foot dropped back and holding most of his weight. Beside him, Dahlia broke her staff again into three parts, pointed one end toward the fiend, and set the pole hanging from that end into a lazy, measured swing.

The great devil's three hellish companions stepped out beside it.

"You should have kept the cat with you," Dahlia whispered.

Drizzt shook his head. "We have to fade back to protect the tunnel."

But they were already too late. The pit fiend appeared there, sliding through another dimensional gate to the entrance to the tunnel. With a mocking laugh, it went in pursuit of the dwarves.

Drizzt turned to give chase, but the lesser devils could also teleport, and two of them did, blocking his way so that the four devils surrounded them. In unison, the fiends began banging their black-bladed swords against their iron shields.

Dahlia glanced at Drizzt, and the hopelessness washed from the drow in the wake of an impish, mischievous, exuberant grin.

"You know they're devils, right?" the drow asked her.

"We know what they are, but they have no idea who we are," Dahlia replied.

She exploded into motion, leaping at the nearest fiend, her front pole spinning wildly. Up came the devil's shield to block that spin, but it was merely a distraction. Dahlia prodded ahead with the center piece of her tri-staff as if it were a spear, clipping the devil's cheek as it frantically dodged back.

The elf had the staff presented more conventionally in front of her in the blink of an eye, both ends spinning, and she worked her hands up and down expertly to block the second devil's thrust. The second creature reached far enough ahead to allow the spinning pole to painfully crack against its forearm.

As Dahlia went forward, Drizzt rolled behind her, back to back, his scimitars working in a blur, sweeping side-to-side strokes that picked off the thrusting sword of the legion devil rushing in pursuit. He hit that blade several times in rapid succession, then launched his own attack from on high, forcing the devil to lift its shield to block, once then again. Before the devil could bring its sword back in for a countering stab, Drizzt rushed under that upraised arm as if he meant to run right past the fiend.

The devil turned and so did Drizzt, cutting back the other way, inside the devil's reach. Up went Twinkle, taking the devil's sword arm with it, and as Drizzt stepped back under that uplifted arm to rejoin Dahlia, a backhand from Icingdeath sank deep into the hellspawn's flesh. The frostbrand drank hot devil blood, and the fiend howled in agony.

Drizzt faded fast to the side as a second legion devil came in swift pursuit, and so intent was the creature that it didn't comprehend the "switch" executed by the two elves. Drizzt stepped in to spin his blades against the rush of the two pursuing Dahlia, and Dahlia confidently turned her back on them, trusting fully in Drizzt as she focused on the third. Her flail worked in a blur, over and around, angle after angle, that got them around the blocking shield. The fiend tried to counter with a sudden and overreaching slash, but Dahlia easily slipped out of reach, then came right in behind the cut. Her right-hand flail spun over to connect solidly with a blocking shield, and Dahlia released a powerful jolt of energy at that, shocking the legion devil. Because of that, the hellspawn could not realign its shield in time, nor bring its sword back to fend her off. That gave two-handed Dahlia a clear strike with her left flail.

The metal pole cracked hard against the devil's skull, staggering it backward, off balance and dazed—not a proper defense against the likes of merciless Dahlia.

In short order, the elves had gained the upper hand, but that brought no thought of victory to Drizzt. Ashmadai swarmed around them, and the pit fiend must have been close on Bruenor's heels.

Purely by luck, Drizzt noted Valindra, her eyes and smile wide, reaching toward him and throwing . . . a flaming pea?

Sweat dripping, heat stinging their eyes, Bruenor and Athrogate came through the last door, gaining the ledge around the primordial's pit. Athrogate turned fast to close the door behind them, as he had done to all the various portals. Only a Delzoun dwarf reciting the proper rhyme could get through, after all.

Or so he believed.

Even as he swung the last mithral door closed, Athrogate saw the one behind it burst in, flying from its hinge and tumbling into the corridor, bent and scarred by the mace of the pit fiend. Beealtimatuche stared at him and laughed.

Athrogate slammed the door.

"Across the way, o'er the bridge!" he shouted at Bruenor, trying to hustle the king along.

But Bruenor heard the commotion in the tunnel behind them, and he stopped and turned.

The mithral door went flying from its hinge, up sidelong and spinning in the air right over the ledge of the deep fire pit.

Onto the ledge stepped Beealtimatuche.

"Go! Get ye gone!" Athrogate yelled at Bruenor as he shoved the dwarf toward the small bridge spanning the pit, then rushed back the other way, morningstars spinning, to battle the devil.

Bruenor stumbled a few steps, but stopped fast and turned. His vision blurred, his muscles swelled, and memories of a long-ago time filled his thoughts. He heard the voices of long-dead kings inside him. He felt the strength of the dwarf gods inside him.

As if in a dream, Bruenor watched the scene unfold before him, Athrogate striking with fearless fury, his morningstars flashing in against the blocking forearm of the pit fiend. And the devil winced, but nothing more, and wasn't lurching or off balance as Athrogate's second weapon crashed in, connecting with the devil's mace.

Hooked and tugged, the morningstar was torn from the dwarf's grip and thrown back to clatter to the floor near the door.

Still boring in, undaunted, Athrogate took up his remaining weapon in both hands and set it in a great and mighty spin, up high.

Then Athrogate, seasoned by centuries of battle—Athrogate, possessed of the strength of a giant—Athrogate, as tough a dwarf as ever lived, was simply slapped aside like a child, sent skipping and spinning across the floor, right to the edge of the pit and rolling over. He came around, in control, to his great credit, and managed to hook his free hand on the ledge, holding his place.

"Run, ye fool!" he yelled at Bruenor. "Bah, but get to the lever, or all's lost!" he finished with one last act of stubborn defiance, grunting and throwing his shoulder over the ledge to gain the leverage he needed to launch his remaining weapon at the pit fiend, which stalked in at Bruenor.

The morningstar connected but Beealtimatuche didn't flinch, and the movement cost Athrogate his balance.

He gave a yell at Bruenor, telling the dwarf to "Run!" once more, but his voice grew more distant as he fell away.

But Bruenor didn't hear him, and wasn't running anyway. It wasn't just Bruenor in the body of the dwarf king then. Within his mortal coil loomed the kings of old, the blood of Delzoun. Within him loomed the ancient gods of the dwarves—Moradin, Clangeddin, Dumathoin—demanding of him that he champion their most hallowed hall.

Bruenor wasn't running. He wasn't scared.

He swelled with a titan's strength, from the potion his enchanted shield had given him, from the infusion of the throne of the kings, from the glory of Gauntlgrym itself. Anyone looking at him wouldn't even have thought him a dwarf, so swollen was he with power. And even that larger form could hardly contain the might within, muscles knotting and bulging.

He banged his axe against his shield and waded in for battle.

The drow spun and threw himself over Dahlia, taking them both to the ground the instant before Valindra's mighty fireball exploded in the air just above them. Even with that feat of acrobatics, both would have surely been consumed had Drizzt not been holding Icingdeath in his right hand. The frostbrand glowed an angry blue, and its magic fended off the flames to such an extent that Drizzt and Dahlia felt only minimal discomfort.

He rolled off her, terrified that the three surviving legion devils would simply fall over them where they lay. But the three fiends did not advance, obviously caught by surprise by the fireball as well. While the flames did no harm to the hellspawn, the surprise of the blast gave Drizzt and Dahlia the time they needed to get back into a defensive position.

Drizzt went right back to work on the two devils he had taken from Dahlia, his blades working in defensive circles as he tried to separate the pair. He had found an advantage in that the one Dahlia had earlier struck showed itself to be nearly blind in one eye. As he wedged the fiends apart, he worked his scimitars independently, right hand parrying the sword of one, left hand working on the wounded devil.

Still looking for his opening, still patient, though he knew the Ashmadai were again pressing in, he heard a *crack* and the report of lightning behind him. Dahlia had finished the third.

The drow stepped his left foot forward, snapping off a strike that hit the devil's shield hard. Drizzt rolled behind the jolt, daring to turn a complete circuit that brought him out fast and far to his left. As he'd hoped, the devil couldn't see the move well enough to retract, and the drow came around with both blades working fast and hard against the hellspawn's frantically-parrying sword.

Drizzt could have beaten those parries, if that was his plan, but he instead spun back the other way, reversing his movement. He finished as he came around with two heavy sidelong chops at the devil, one of which slipped past the shield just enough to score a wicked hit across the fiend's upper arm.

And Drizzt disengaged there, completely and without another thought, turning his full attention to the remaining fiend, who was, predictably, coming at him hard.

The one he'd hit tried to come at him hard, too.

Tried to, but the flying form of Dahlia double-kicked the devil in the face, throwing it backward.

"The lich!" Dahlia cried as she nimbly landed. "And now we die."

Drizzt just growled and fought on, determined to at least kill the fiend before the inevitable killing blow overwhelmed him.

But then another cry rent the hot air of Gauntlgrym's hallowed forge, a shout full of passion and determination, a yell Drizzt Do'Urden had heard many times in his life, and surprised as he was, never had it sounded as sweet as it did just then.

"Me king!"

And into the hall they came, scores of dwarves: Icewind Dale Battlehammers, the Shield of Mirabar, and scores of Gauntlgrym's ghosts.

Like towering trees toppled into each other, like two mountains falling over to fill a valley, the dwarf king and the pit fiend threw themselves together. Each swung a weapon, mace and axe, but those seemed secondary to the sheer power of their bodies colliding. They grappled and twisted. Beealtimatuche's tail flipped up over his shoulder to sting the dwarf in the cheek, but if Bruenor even felt it, he didn't show it.

Instead, the dwarf twisted the fiend hard to the right and drove on harder, down and forward. Just as Beealtimatuche broke the grapple and leaped back, so did Bruenor. Tucking in his left shoulder, he plowed ahead with his shield in a sudden and brutal charge. He collided into the turning devil and sent Beealtimatuche flying backward, almost off the ledge.

Almost, but the fiend spread his leathery wings and came right back in, half leaping, half flying, descending upon Bruenor with a tremendous downward chop of his fiery mace.

Even with his shield in place to block, Bruenor should have been crushed by that blow. His arm should have shattered under the sheer weight of the mighty devil.

But he wasn't, and it didn't, and his countering sweep of his axe had Beealtimatuche twisting frantically to avoid being gutted.

On came the dwarf, taking another heavy hit against his indomitable shield, and slashing again and again as he continued to plow forward.

Beealtimatuche slammed him again, but the shield would not yield, and so the devil backed further, took up his weapon in both hands and met the swinging axe with the mighty mace. Sparks and fire exploded from the powerfully enchanted weapons, and Bruenor slipped his shield to his back and took up his axe in both hands to drive on again. The two combatants matched blows, weapon to weapon, to see which would lose his grip first. Like a bell of doom, the many-notched axe and the fiery mace rang out, devil-crafted against god-forged.

Roaring with rage, screaming for the beast to flee the hallowed halls, Bruenor swung mightily again . . . and missed.

And he was overbalanced, the devil holding his swing. Bruenor's right foot stepped past to the left, where he planted it powerfully and threw himself back the other way, spinning a reverse turn, throwing his shield up high off his shoulder and onto his arm once more. As he caught the heavy hit from the mace—a stunning, arm-numbing blow—the dwarf kept turning, his right arm going out wide, axe at the very end of his reach to sweep across as he came around.

He felt it connect with devil's flesh, goring a deep wound on Beealtimatuche's hip and bringing forth a howl from the pit fiend.

Who was gone, then—simply vanished.

Bruenor threw himself forward, twisting to throw his shield arm behind him, and not an instant too soon. Beealtimatuche had "blinked" behind him. He managed to only partially block the mace as it clipped the edge of his shield, and it caught him down across the back, throwing him forward and face down to the stone.

But up he hopped, whirling to defeat the pursuit with another powerful swipe.

His lifeblood dripped behind him, but so too was Beealtimatuche's leg red with blood.

To Valindra Shadowmantle, the moment of her freedom was at hand. When she had finished Drizzt and the troublesome Dahlia, and ended the threat to Sylora, her own place among those who served Szass Tam would be secured.

The drow and Dahlia still battled furiously by the side of the main forge, not quite at the side tunnel. But they couldn't avoid her magic forever, and Valindra was a lich. She had forever to kill them, if need be.

Her eyes glowed with satisfaction. She heard the commotion as the newly-arrived dwarves and their ghostly kin met her Ashmadai legions, but she didn't care. All she wanted was to be rid of one elf, and one last drow.

When six hundred pounds of furious panther slammed into her, knocking her back, the gathering energies of her spell were taken from her. Guenhwyvar flew aside and landed in a turn, claws screeching on the stone floor. Valindra, barely hurt, began casting again, and as Guenhwyvar managed to turn at last and come at her, waves of anti-magic hit the panther. Her strides seemed to slow, as if she were running in water. Then, despite herself and her loyalty to Drizzt, she felt the compulsion to return to her Astral home. She was unable to ignore the lich's persuasion, the powerful dispelling of the magic that kept Guenhwyvar at Drizzt's side. And so she became a gray mist, and with a plaintive wail toward Drizzt to alert him to her failure, the panther dissipated.

Valindra turned back to the task at hand, but too late, for then behind her came a distraction she could not ignore, another force charging into the fray. Salamanders entered through the same tunnel that had brought Valindra and Beealtimatuche and their minions into the Forge. Many were running, some riding large red lizards, and all closed fast on Valindra.

The lich turned and hissed at them, then issued the spell she had planned for the elves. And how the creatures of the fire god, children of fire, recoiled and shriveled and died before the waves of killing ice in Valindra's cone of cold.

The lich hissed at them, screamed at them in outrage for stealing her moment of glory. Lightning erupted from her fingertips, blasting into the ranks of those trying to enter the room, rebounding with killing force back up the tunnel.

She hissed again and waved her arms and a great ice storm formed above the corridor entryway, raining sleet and pelting ice down upon any who dared come through.

Valindra spun back to line up a new killing strike at the hated elves. Her red eyes flared with inner fire as she began her casting. But then she was screaming incoherently, caught in a pillar of unexplained light—bright, burning light.

She thrashed and tried to fight through it to launch her spell, but to no avail. Smoke began to rise from her rotted flesh, and much of it began to roll up under the brilliant glow.

The chamber began to shake and roll. The forges vomited angry fires once more as the primordial reacted to the assault on its minions, and all the room began to quake with such force that most were thrown from their feet.

Not Valindra, though, who floated above the tumult.

But the light did not relent, biting at her, burning her, half-blinding her. She managed a half turn and at last spotted her assailant, and despite the sting, her eyes did widen indeed.

And he tipped his wide-brimmed hat and leveled his wand, and a second beam engulfed Valindra.

And she began to smoke, her skin to curl.

With a shriek that seemed to stop all other chaos in the room, Valindra flailed wildly and out of sheer terror managed to spit forth a spell, one that turned her into the form of a wraith. Her wail continued to echo throughout the chamber, but the lich slipped through a crack in the floor and was gone, her wraith form sliding through cracks in the stones and rushing far from the scene, never to return.

After all, Valindra was a lich. She had forever to kill them, if need be. Drizzt, Dahlia . . . and Jarlaxle would wait.

He tried not to let the sudden chaos in the hall distract him, thrown as it was into wild and heated battle between three distinct forces, each hating the other two. He tried to ignore the room itself, which had become an army of its own, it seemed, with rolling floor and shaking walls, rocks tumbling dangerously from the ceiling and forges spewing forth fire that could melt flesh from bones, and char the bones to ash for good measure.

Drizzt had to put all of that in its proper perspective, with so formidable a foe as a legion devil facing him.

The fighting beyond him was of no interest. And the room he used to his advantage. So swift, so agile, Drizzt accepted the rolling floor rather than try to fight against it. When the floor pitched left, left was the way he went. He rode it, his feet moving back and forth, sideways and sidelong, whichever way was necessary to keep him in perfect balance and speed him along. And if the fight called for him to go opposite the pitch of the floor, he used the roll of stone to grant him lift as he pitched back the other way in a leap or somersault.

His devilish opponent, no stranger to wild battle, did well to hold its footing in the shaking and trembling, but as Drizzt fell into the rhythms of the primordial's angry gyrations, the legion devil could not keep up.

The drow began not only to react perfectly to the quake, but to anticipate its next movement. Confident that he was quick enough to correct if his guess proved wrong, Drizzt worked his scimitars up high in front of his face, rolling his wrists over each other to create a circle of angled downward slashes. As the fiend brought its shield to block, the drow just angled to the side a bit more, keeping the devil on its heels, forcing it to use both shield and sword defensively.

Further to his left Drizzt turned, bending the fiend, turning the fiend, and when the floor rolled under their feet, left to right, Drizzt used the momentum to step back fast to the right, then used the cresting wave of stone beneath his feet to launch himself. Flipping back to the left, even as the fiend, caught in the flow and expecting the reversal, the drow was fast turning the other way.

Right over the sweeping blade went Drizzt, landing in perfect balance on shaky ground, and with the devil's side exposed, shield and sword back the other way. He struck deeply, but only once—it was Icingdeath that bit into the creature of fire. It only had to bite once.

Drizzt held his pose for several heartbeats, the devil immobilized by agony on the end of his blade, hot blood bubbling from the wound. The drow gave a few slight twists and tugs to tear at the fiend's organs, then he yanked the blade out.

The legion devil crumbled to the floor and sizzled away into black smoke and a mist of boiling blood.

Drizzt spun away to help Dahlia, but stopped short and watched in admiration as the elf spun and struck, her advance coming in a series of turns, and through every one and from every angle came a whirling strike from a flail, some spouting lightning, others just smashing with crushing force. The legion devil couldn't match her speed and precision.

She hit it again and again, and by the time she played out her spinning charge, that devil, too, crumbled to the floor.

She looked at Drizzt, and the two exchanged smiles and nods.

"Me king?" Drizzt heard behind him, and he spun, shaking his head in disbelief. He looked to the small tunnel before turning to the dwarf, and so by the time he did regard his old friend, that dwarf had already picked up on the cue and started away at full, rambling speed.

Drizzt and Dahlia started to follow, but hadn't gone two steps before a host of Ashmadai descended upon them.

More to kill.

His shield clipped the mace, stealing some of its strength, but still it came across with enough force to take Bruenor's one-horned helmet from his head, and to gash his scalp in the process.

But the dwarf got the better of that particular trade, his mighty axe crashing against the pit fiend's ribs, opening a garish wound.

They came together, titans wrestling once more, head-butting, biting, and thrashing.

But the fiend had more weapons. Its tail, as if acting of its own volition, whipped about and banged repeatedly against the back of Bruenor's armor, seeking a seam. Its bony, ridged arms ground in painfully against the dwarf, tearing the skin of his arms. And its mouth, so wide, so full of long teeth . . .

Bruenor looked up and into its open mouth and up farther to those wild eyes, as the fiend bit down at him. Instead of dodging, though, the dwarf responded with his own charge, his powerful legs driving him upward, his forehead snapping forward to meet the grasping jaws.

Blood poured over his face—his own blood, Bruenor realized, but he knew, too, that he had put a solid smack into the face of his enemy.

Arms wrapped around the devil, the dwarf handed his axe to his shield hand. Then he brought his free hand back into his chest and pushed up, over the devil's chest and under the stunned creature's chin. Bruenor drove on with all his might. The old kings and ancient gods within him drove on with all their might.

He threw Beealtimatuche away. Half blinded by the gush of his own blood, Bruenor could barely make out the staggering devil, or the smaller form that rushed in suddenly at the fiend's side, leaping upon the beast with abandon. But he did hear a comforting call, a declaration of friendship he had known for so many decades. . . .

"Me king!"

Bruenor staggered backward and shook his head, wiping the blood from his eyes. It was Thibbledorf Pwent!

Of course it was Pwent.

It didn't occur to Bruenor at that moment how odd it was that the battlerager should suddenly appear. Indeed, to him the better question seemed to be, how could Pwent not be there, when Bruenor most needed him, when Gauntlgrym herself most needed him?

And so it made perfect sense to Bruenor, watching the thrashing Pwent tearing at the devil's skin, head spike buried deeply, fist spikes, knee spikes, toe spikes stabbing and jabbing and kicking, ridged armor thrashing lines of red skin wide open.

Bruenor took up his axe, and for a moment it seemed as if he wouldn't even be needed to finish the job.

But Beealtimatuche was a pit fiend, a duke of the Nine Hells, a devil of extraordinary power.

Pwent jerked when a poisoned tail barb popped into the back of his head. He stopped thrashing and Beealtimatuche pushed him away, the devil hissing and roaring as the long helmet spike slid out of his torso. Pwent stood staring at him, obviously working hard just to hold his balance.

A backhand from the devil launched the battlerager flying away, to slam hard into the wall beside the blasted door.

Bruenor watched Thibbledorf Pwent slump to the floor.

And with rage climbing atop everything else churning within the dwarf king—the history of Gauntlgrym, the glory of the gods of Dwarfhome, the essence of what it was to be a dwarf, a Delzoun dwarf, a Battlehammer dwarf—Bruenor charged in once more.

His fury heightened with every swing. He took brutal hits from the fiery mace, but he shrugged them off and unleashed his rage through the blade of his mighty axe. The chamber reverberated with the sound of weapons clashing—not with other weapons or with shields, but with flesh. They traded blows, each staggering after every hit, neither giving ground.

Across came Beealtimatuche's mace, but Bruenor brought his shield up and he ducked away, back and to his right, the mace clipping the shield, but not enough to send him flying—just enough to add to his spin and send him leaping.

Up high soared King Bruenor as he came around, both hands again taking up his axe, lifting it up above his head. And he came down from on high, his whole body snapping in one great moment of complete exertion, muscles screaming in protest, senses jarred.

Right between the turned-in horns went Bruenor's descending axe, the power of Gauntlgrym's forge, the power of the old kings and ancient gods, reaching through King Bruenor and through that blade.

With a terrible *crunch,* the blade split Beealtimatuche's skull, driving down, halving the devil's face. And driving down more as Bruenor descended, crushing the devil down to its knees.

Head lolling uncontrollably, the pit fiend still tried to stand.

But Bruenor's rage was not sated, and he threw down his axe and shield and fell over the fiend, one hand grabbing its throat, the other slapping in against its crotch. As Bruenor stood his full height, up into the air went Beealtimatuche. And though he seemed merely a dwarf again—the power of the throne and the potion, the kings and the gods, no more—still he stood tall and still he pressed Beealtimatuche straight up over his head to arm's length.

Bruenor stalked to the ledge. He looked down into the fire pit of the primordial and witnessed the beast, like a fiery eye staring back at him.

He threw the devil into the pit.

Then Bruenor fell to his knees, his strength leaving him, his lifeblood pouring from a dozen wicked wounds. He went to his chest, flat on the ground, his head hanging over the edge to watch the descent of the devil.

He noted instead a dwarf's form, on a ledge some thirty feet down, broken awkwardly but not dead, and reaching one hand up toward him plaintively, even calling out his name.

But it was a distant call to the dying Bruenor. Far distant.

"The bridge! The lever!"

Thibbledorf Pwent felt the poison coursing through his veins. Wicked poison. Worse than spoilt Gutbuster, he lamented.

He had seen Bruenor's victory and Bruenor's fall, and for a moment, he thought he had to be satisfied in that, that he and his king had died gloriously. What more might a shield dwarf ever want? What greater honor for a battlerager?

But then a reminder, a distant cry.

"The bridge! The lever!"

Pwent saw Bruenor pull himself to his feet. He saw his king begin to crawl. To crawl!

Toward the bridge went Bruenor, one stubborn foot at a time.

But he couldn't make it. He fell over. He tried to get back to his elbows, tried to crawl again, and when he couldn't, he made to slither like a snake.

But he went nowhere.

And so it was Thibbledorf Pwent who had to call upon the greater powers of his heritage at that moment, who had to reach beyond his old and broken body. The battlerager pulled himself to his feet and staggered across the way. He nearly overbalanced and went right past Bruenor to pitch from the ledge.

But he caught himself, and caught up his king under the arms, hoisting him as much as he could and dragging Bruenor on toward that one small bridge that spanned the primordial's hellish chasm.

All Drizzt wanted to do was get through that tunnel to the side of his dwarf friend. He was glad that Pwent had gone through, but it gave him little comfort as the tremors mounted. The pit fiend had gone through as well, and Bruenor had obviously not gotten to the lever.

Drizzt tried to fight his way to that entrance, but there always seemed an enemy in his path. His scimitars worked furiously in an overhand roll, overwhelming the nearest Ashmadai, but as that one fell aside, another was quick to the attack.

With a growl of frustration, Drizzt maneuvered to set that one up for the kill, as well.

Dahlia rushed up beside him—flew past him, actually, vaulting with her long staff. She landed and brought the staff forward, turning it to drive the Ashmadai to the side.

"Go!" she yelled to Drizzt.

He didn't want to leave her, but Bruenor needed him. He sprinted into the tunnel and swung around to fend off any pursuit.

But there was only Dahlia, her back to him, blocking the way.

Drizzt rushed into the chamber. Debris lay all around the ledge—black rocks, some fast-cooling lava, a pair of morningstars, and so much blood. Before him lay the pit and its orange glow. The beast roiled, spitting rocks up above the ledge, some arcing back down into the pit, some bouncing onto the floor, smoking. Hardly looking to the side, the drow, mesmerized by the spectacle of the raging primordial, rushed to the ledge, fearing the worst.

He looked down into the very eye of chaos. Lines of fire erupted from the lava, reaching high. Rocks bubbled and spat forth, lifting up toward him. He had looked upon dragons, but the primordial, he knew, was something more.

Some movement broke him from his trance.

"Bruenor!" he started to yell, but it was not Bruenor. It was Athrogate, on a ledge, badly wounded and trying to cover as the rocks and fire spat up about him. Stubbornly, the dwarf managed to point up and to Drizzt's right. Following that, Drizzt caught sight of his friends, both Bruenor and Pwent, crawling along the far side of a narrow arching bridge that spanned the divide.

He took a step that way—almost a step—then he saw the primordial leap up at him.

Drizzt flung himself aside as a column of lava leaped from the pit, rushing up through the room to disappear through the hole in the ceiling high above.

"Bruenor!" he screamed, blocking his ears against the roar of the beast.

He fell and covered his head with his hands as rocks and bits of hot lava rained across the ledge. It seemed to go on forever and ever, but in truth it was only a matter of heartbeats before the column dropped back down. Had Icingdeath not been in his hand, the dark elf would likely have been burned to cinders.

Drizzt scrambled to his feet, calling for the dwarf. The bridge was gone, blasted apart by the force of the eruption—but there were Bruenor and Pwent, across the way, holding each other and crawling together for an archway.

Doing his best to keep Icingdeath in his right hand, Drizzt pulled a cord from his pack, nimbly tying one end into a knot while still holding the frostbrand. He drew out an arrow, poked its head through that knot, and chanced sheathing Icingdeath to take up Taulmaril.

A flutter behind him alerted him at the last second and he dived aside into a roll, dropping his bow and drawing forth his blades as he came around. The danger had passed—for him—and he realized then that he had narrowly avoiding being knocked from the ledge by the attacker, a giant bat. The creature had clawed him as it passed, and Drizzt reached up to his temple to feel the hot wetness of blood.

Still confused, the drow watched the creature fly across the pit, and on the other side, right before the archway, it flopped over weirdly in mid-air and landed, no longer a bat but a man, staring back at Drizzt.

Cursing himself for his hesitance, Drizzt sheathed his blades and leaped back for his bow. He took up the arrow and knocked the rope aside, setting the missile and letting fly.

But the vampire was quicker, slipping under the archway, and the arrow hit nothing but stones, exploding in a shower of sparks.

"No, Bruenor, no," Drizzt mouthed, grabbing up the rope, pulling forth another arrow and taking aim. He let fly high above the archway, the arrow driving hard into the wall, burrowing the rope deeply into the solid stone.

More commotion came from behind Drizzt, and he turned just in time to see Dahlia speeding his way.

"Dor'crae!" she yelled, and she dropped her staff to the floor as she charged right past Drizzt, yanking the rope from his hand and swinging across the open lava pit. She leaped off and landed in a run, disappearing under the archway.

Frantically, cursing with every movement, Drizzt fumbled for another length of rope. He glanced back as yet another figure entered the chamber, and how his eyes widened when he saw that it was Jarlaxle.

"How?" he asked.

The drow mercenary replied with a grin and brought his hand up to his mouth to flash the same ring he had given to Dahlia before the fight in the Cutlass.

"Get me across!" Drizzt yelled at him, not having the time to sort it out.

The room shook then, so violently that it threw Drizzt from his feet. Jarlaxle, though, managed to stay standing, and even collected a pair of morningstars lying on the floor. He held them up, his face a mask of puzzlement and horror.

"Athrogate?" Drizzt explained, and as if on cue, they heard the dwarf cry out from the pit below.

Jarlaxle tucked the morningstars into a magical bag as he sprinted to the ledge and looked down.

"Bruenor is across the way!" Drizzt yelled at him. "The lever!"

Jarlaxle turned to face him, the mercenary's face twisted in pain.

"You cannot!" Drizzt cried.

"My friend, I must, as you must go to your Bruenor," Jarlaxle replied with a shrug. He put his hand over his House Baenre emblem then, and with a tip of his cap to Drizzt, he hopped off the ledge.

Drizzt growled at the frustration, at the insanity of it all, and went back to his rope, knotting the end.

And the primordial roared, a column of lava once again leaping up from the pit, rushing skyward to the ceiling and beyond.

"Jarlaxle," Drizzt wailed repeatedly, shaking his head, but he didn't cover his ears against the roar of the volcano. Instead he kept working at the rope.

Dahlia rushed under the archway just in time to see Thibbledorf Pwent, his throat torn, tumble to the stone beside Bruenor. Gasping, the dwarf reached up, his hands clawing the air as he tried futilely and pitifully to grasp the vampire.

Dor'crae turned to face Dahlia, his face bright with Pwent's blood.

"You wretched beast," she said.

"You can leave this place and be redeemed," Dor'crae replied. "What have you gained, my love?"

He finished abruptly as Dahlia leaped across the small room at him, all punches and kicks.

But just punches and kicks, for she had left Kozah's Needle behind. As fine a fighter as Dahlia was, even unarmed, the supernaturally strong vampire had no trouble pinning her arms and spinning her around, slamming her into the wall.

"At last, I feast," Dor'crae promised.

But then he froze in place, only his eyes widening.

"Does it hurt?" Dahlia asked him, poking her finger, tipped with the wooden spike from her ring, harder at his chest. "Tell me it hurts."

Dor'crae's head went back and he began shaking, and smoke began wafting from his skin.

Dahlia's wooden stake stabbed at his heart again.

"Ah . . . me king," she heard from the floor behind her, a voice gurgling with thick liquid, and she glanced back to see a bloody, strangely armored dwarf somehow rolling himself over to one elbow, his other arm coming across to grab at Bruenor Battlehammer.

Somehow, impossibly, Pwent got his knees under him and heaved Bruenor upward, then fell forward with him, right beside the lever. Like a loving father, Pwent lifted Bruenor's hand, cupping it with his own, and set it against the angled pole.

"Me king," Pwent said again, and it seemed the end of his strength. His head dropped down and he lay there very still.

"Me friend," Bruenor answered, and with just a glance at Dahlia, the dwarf king summoned his strength and pulled.

Dor'crae was babbling for mercy the entire time, pleading with Dahlia to let him live, promising her that he would make everything all right for her with Sylora.

"You think I will let you fly away, when I am surely doomed?" Dahlia said, face to face, letting him see the absence of mercy in her freezing blue eyes. As if in response to her, perhaps, but surely to the reversed lever, the primordial roared again and the room lurched.

Dahlia tried to drive the wooden stake in harder, but the tremor stole her balance and the desperate Dor'crae managed to slip aside. Sorely wounded, the vampire wanted nothing more to do with Dahlia. Once more, he took the form of a bat.

———

The splattering lava and bouncing black stones had Drizzt shielding himself and ducking away, and thinking that they had failed, that the volcano had again fully erupted. To his great relief, though, the lava column again dropped back down below the rim, and the drow was fast to the ledge, bow in hand.

Without the protection of Icingdeath, the heat proved too intense, but he couldn't help but look down, though he feared what he might see.

The lava had climbed far up the pit, and was barely twenty feet below the rim, waves of heat assaulting the drow. And it was up above the ledge where Athrogate had lain, and there was, of course, no sign of Jarlaxle, who had descended almost as the lava had rushed back up.

For the second time that day, Drizzt had to shake off the loss of Jarlaxle, for not even Icingdeath could have protected him from that rush of lava.

His next arrow flew, setting a second rope near where the first had been—before the lava had rushed up to burn it to nothingness. Without even testing the rope, without even a thought that the lava might leap up at him, the anxious drow sprang from the ledge and swung away, landing easily across the way.

Even as he caught his balance, he had to duck aside once more, as that same giant bat flew out from under the archway. Its flight was noticeably unsteady, as if it were gravely wounded, and Drizzt dropped his bow off his shoulder, thinking to shoot it from the sky.

He needn't have bothered, though. As soon as the bat crossed the lip of the pit, it seemed as if all the water of the Sea of Swords had come charging in to battle the fire primordial. It poured from the hole in the ceiling like a giant waterfall, and through that thunderous, translucent veil, Drizzt could still see the bat. Obviously, its flight was as much magical as physical—it resisted the downpour.

But that didn't much help the creature. The bat became a man again, and the vampire looked back at Drizzt, though whether he could actually see the drow, Drizzt couldn't know. He reached out plaintively, hanging there in the curtain of water, his face a mask of agony.

Then he blew apart, like so many black flakes, and was washed down with the waterfall.

It stopped as abruptly as it had started, but Drizzt knew the primordial's trap was back in place, knew that they had won, for below the rim, he could see the water, not like a pond or puddle, but spinning furiously along the sides of the pit.

Down below, the primordial responded, the ground shaking violently, the lava column trying to rise, the room filling with steam. The water did not relent, though, and the beast sank back, far below, and the room went quiet, a stillness that seemed more complete than it had been for many years.

Drizzt wasn't watching, though. As soon as he regained his balance, the drow sprinted under the arch.

Dahlia sat against the far wall, exhausted and sweating, but she nodded to Drizzt that she was all right. He wasn't looking at her, anyway. He couldn't with the other sight before him.

Thibbledorf Pwent had met his end. He lay on his back, blood on his throat, his eyes open wide, his chest not lifting with breath. There was a serenity to him, Drizzt recognized. The battlerager had died in a manner befitting his life, in service to his king.

And there lay that king, Drizzt's dearest friend, half on his side, half face down, one arm extended with his fingers still gripping the lever.

Drizzt fell beside him and gently turned him over, and the drow was shocked to find that Bruenor Battlehammer was still alive.

"I found it, elf," he said with that smile that had brought Drizzt joy for most of his life. "I found me answers. I found me peace."

Drizzt wanted to comfort him, wanted to assure him that the priests would be right in and that everything would be all right. But he knew beyond doubt that it was over, that the wounds were too much for an old dwarf.

"Rest easy, my dearest friend," he mouthed, not sure that any sound came out.

But the look of comfort on Bruenor's face, the slightest of nods, the slightest of contented smiles, told Drizzt that his departing friend had indeed heard him, and that it was indeed all right.

EPILOGUE

DRIZZT STOOD AT THE EDGE OF THE PIT, LOOKING DOWN AT the swirl of the water and the elementals. Every now and then, he could make out a watery face in the unending swirl around the pit, and far, far below, he could see the primordial, like an angry eye of liquid staring back up at him.

"It is as it was when first we found it," Dahlia said to him, walking up beside him and draping her arm casually around his lower back. "We did it. Bruenor did it."

Drizzt continued to scan the opposite wall, trying to make out through the water the ledge where Athrogate had been, where Jarlaxle had gone, but alas, there was nothing. Of course there was nothing. What could have survived the breath of the primordial?

It surprised the drow how badly it all hurt. Not just Bruenor, but the loss of Pwent, and not just that, but the loss of Jarlaxle, and even of Athrogate! He'd hardly seen either Jarlaxle or Athrogate over the years, but somehow, just knowing they were there, in Luskan, never far from reach, had brought him some comfort.

And they were gone, and so was Thibbledorf Pwent, and Bruenor Battlehammer himself—and though his dear friend had died as he would have chosen, not only having found Gauntlgrym, but saving it from total destruction, the profound pain launched Drizzt back to another time and another place, when he had watched Catti-brie and Regis melt through Mithral Hall's solid wall on the back of a spiritual unicorn, gone to Mielikki's rest.

He had never thought he could feel such pain again.

He was wrong.

Across the way, some dwarves stumbled into the room. Stokely Silverstream and Torgar Hammerstriker spotted Drizzt and Dahlia and began calling out as more of their brethren entered the chamber.

Dahlia let her hand slip from Drizzt's back, coming to his side where she grasped his hand.

"Shoot an arrow and let us be gone from here," she whispered.

In a dark, dark place, Jarlaxle Baenre opened his eyes and dared bring forth a bit of light. He could hear the rush of water, and knew what it meant. And he heard Athrogate stirring beside him.

He saw his elemental, the last of the ten, the one that had not been set in place, still standing guard at the entrance of the portable hole he had used to pull himself and Athrogate away from the primordial. That creature of the Elemental Plane of Water seemed diminished, no doubt from holding back the fires of destruction, and Jarlaxle sensed that it was agitated as well, eager and frustrated all at once.

"I release you," the drow said, and just that easily the elemental leaped out of the hole and into the sidelong swirl of the enchanted water.

The drow slipped a ring onto a finger, adjusted his eyepatch, and left his body in a spell of clairvoyance, seeking answers—which he found as soon as his vision lifted out of the pit. He saw Drizzt and Dahlia, and the dwarves across the way, and still forms lying under the archway.

Jarlaxle turned to Athrogate, who lay broken, his skin blistered, one leg shattered beneath his prone form.

"It's time to go," Jarlaxle whispered to him, and the drow produced another ring, a teleportation device that would send them home.

"I ain't to make it," Athrogate whispered back, barely able to draw breath.

Jarlaxle smiled at him. "My priests will find us in Luskan. They will tend you, my friend. Now is not your time to die. Your kind has lost enough today."

He began to enact his magic, but Athrogate grabbed him roughly by the arm, commanding his attention.

"Ye could've left me!" he snarled.

Jarlaxle just nodded and smiled, and started to chant once more, but again, Athrogate interrupted.

"Wait," the dwarf begged. "Is it done? Did King Bruenor win the day?"

Jarlaxle smiled warmly, a hint of a tear in his crimson eyes. "Long live the king," he assured his bearded friend. "Long live King Bruenor."

They buried Bruenor Battlehammer, Eighth King of Mithral Hall, under rocks beside the cairn of Thibbledorf Pwent. They buried him with his one-horned helm, with his enchanted shield, and his mighty, many-notched axe—for what dwarf other than Bruenor Battlehammer would deserve such weapons?

There had been talk of bringing Bruenor home to Mithral Hall for burial—Stokely had even suggested Kelvin's Cairn in Icewind Dale as an appropriate resting place. But Gauntlgrym, the most hallowed and ancient of Delzoun halls, somehow seemed more fitting.

So they buried their heroes, and there were many that fateful day, and they took their tour of what remained of ancient Gauntlgrym. Outside the main wall, in the vast cavern with the pond, they said their farewells. Both Stokely and Torgar offered Drizzt a home, Icewind Dale or Mirabar.

But he refused them, without even giving any real thought to their offers. Neither place was for him, he knew, nor was Mithral Hall.

Nor was anywhere, it seemed.

When he at last exited the tunnels east of the mountains, Guenhwyvar beside him, Drizzt Do'Urden turned to stare to the north, toward Icewind Dale, the place that had been his truest home, the place where he had known his truest friends.

And he was alone.

"Where's your road lead, drow?" Dahlia said, walking up beside him.

Guenhwyvar favored her with a low purr.

"Where is yours?" he asked in return.

"Oh, I mean to finish this with Sylora Salm, don't you doubt that," the elf warrior promised without the slightest hesitation. "To Neverwinter Wood, for me. I will tell the witch to her face that her Dread Ring has failed, that her beast is trapped once more. I will tell her that, right before I kill her."

Drizzt considered the declaration for a few moments then corrected, "Before *we* kill her."

Dahlia stared at him with a grin that told that was exactly what she wanted to hear.

Drizzt looked her over, head to toe, and he realized only then that she had moved the last diamond stud out of her right ear and set it in her left.

There was a story there. There were many stories in the memories and the heart of that most curious elf.

He wanted to hear them all.

Bruenor Battlehammer pulled himself up to his elbows, opened his eyes, and shook his head to clear his jumbled thoughts.

He only became more confused, though, when he noted his surroundings: a springtime forest, and not the dark halls of Gauntlgrym.

"Eh?" he muttered as he hopped to his feet with energy and youth he hadn't known in centuries.

"Pwent?" he called. "Drizzt?"

"Well met," said a voice behind him, and he spun to see Regis standing there, looking in the prime of health and life, with a grin from ear to ear.

"Rumblebelly . . . ?" Bruenor managed to gasp.

He stuttered as he tried to continue, when from out of a door in a small house behind Regis stepped another. Bruenor's jaw fell limp and he didn't even try to speak. His eyes welled with tears, for there stood his boy, Wulfgar, a young man once more, tall and strong.

"You mentioned Pwent," Regis said. "Were you with him when you fell?"

Those last words hit the dwarf like a thrown stone, for indeed, he had fallen, indeed, he was dead. And so were the two before him, in a place that so confused him—even more, for surely it was not the Halls of Moradin.

"Thibbledorf Pwent is with Moradin now," Bruenor said, more to himself than to the others. "Got to be. But why ain't meself?"

He hardly noticed the growing sound of music behind him, but when he looked up, he saw Wulfgar looking past him, an enchanted expression on his face. Regis, too, stared over Bruenor's shoulder. The halfling motioned with his chin and Bruenor glanced around.

His gaze went across a small and still pond, to the trees across the way.

And there she danced, his beloved daughter, dressed in a layered white gown of many folds and pretty lace, and with a black cape trailing her every twist and turn.

"By the gods," the dwarf muttered, so completely overwhelmed.

For the first time in his long life, and his long life was no more, Bruenor Battlehammer fell to his knees, was literally knocked from his feet by overwhelming emotion. He put his face in his hands and he began to sob.

And they were tears of joy, tears of just rewards.

In search of an end to the Era of Upheaval . . .
From the Avatar Crisis to the Spellplague,
divine drama has shaped Faerûn.
Now it's time for the heroes to decide.

THE SUNDERING

Six novels, six authors . . .
an epic odyssey through the Forgotten Realms®
begins Summer 2013

THE COMPANIONS R. A. Salvatore August 2013	**THE REAVER** Richard Lee Byers February 2014
THE GODBORN Paul S. Kemp October 2013	**THE SENTINEL** Troy Denning April 2014
THE ADVERSARY Erin M. Evans December 2013	**THE HERALD** Ed Greenwood June 2014

THE SUNDERING story continues in-store with D&D Encounters™.
Play through D&D® adventures penned by
R.A. Salvatore and Ed Greenwood.

DungeonsandDragons.com

All trademarks are property of Wizards of the Coast LLC.
©2013 Wizards.